A DIFFERENT KIND OF GAME

He had settled comfortably in the chair. A contained man, unruffled and smooth. A handsome man, at ease with his body and presence, confident of his physical impression. A determined man whose clear eyes watched her with patience. He was prepared to wait her out. *Take your time,* his whole pose said. *We have all day, if you want to do it that way.*

"I would like you to bring up that dress that you spoke of, Dante," she said. "I will put it on and leave."

"You are to rest, and I could not permit you to walk away on your own even if you were well."

"I will go to the house and ask for help. It will be better this way."

"No." He folded his arms across his chest.

He watched her. Too much and too long. It became a compelling examination. She grew uncomfortable in a strangely exciting way, and embarrassingly aware of that frightening something that shimmered around him like a subtle force.

"I think that we will pass the time with a game," he said.

"What kind of game?"

"You do not have to look so suspicious. Not that kind. Although having you in my bed, but in a condition that prevents me from trying to breach your defenses, is enough to make me weep."

the
SINNER

Madeline Hunter

BANTAM BOOKS

THE SINNER

A Dell Book

PUBLISHING HISTORY

Bantam mass market edition published January 2004
Dell mass market reissue / September 2007

Published by
Bantam Dell
A Division of Random House, Inc.
New York, New York

This is a work of fiction. Names, characters, places, and incidents either are
the product of the author's imagination or are used fictitiously. Any
resemblance to actual persons, living or dead, events, or locales is entirely
coincidental.

Library of Congress Catalog Card Number: 2004573347

Dell is a registered trademark of Random House, Inc., and the colophon is a
trademark of Random House, Inc.

ISBN 978-0-553-59021-0

Printed in the United States of America

www.bantamdell.com

OPM 10 9 8 7 6 5 4 3 2 1

*This book is dedicated to my sister Frances,
who was my first friend and playmate, and who
started me on the path of a writer by being
both audience and collaborator for the
make-believe stories of my childhood.*

the
SINNER

chapter I

Utter ruin provokes soul-searching in even the least reflective of men.

Dante Duclairc was contemplating that unwelcome discovery when he heard the horse outside. He opened the cottage door to find one very annoyed physician standing in the moonlight at the threshold.

Morgan Wheeler peered severely over the top edge of his spectacles. "This had better be *very* serious, Duclairc. Your brother's land steward pulled me out of bed."

"It *is* very serious, and I am sorry that your sleep was interrupted."

"No one said you had come down to Laclere Park. Why haven't you called on me?"

"Only the steward knows I am here, so you must swear to keep this visit a secret. I should have sent for a surgeon, but you are the only medical man in the region I could trust to be discreet."

Morgan sighed heavily and stepped into the humble abode. "Why did you send for me?"

"There is a woman upstairs who needs your attention."

Morgan set down his bag and removed his frock coat. "She is alone here?"

"Except for me."

"Why does this woman require me?"

"The lady has been shot."

Morgan had been rolling up a sleeve. He stopped, arm outstretched and fingers engaged. "You have a lady visitor who has been shot?"

"Grazed, actually."

"Where was she shot? Excuse me, *grazed*?"

"In this cottage. Accidentally. We were playing a little game and—"

"I meant, where is the wound?"

"In the rear nether region of her trunk."

"Excuse me? Are you saying that you shot your lover in the buttock?"

"Yes. Come upstairs and—"

"One moment, my good friend. My dull life has feasted off the excitement of yours for years, but this is too much. You have secretly brought a woman, a *lady*, to a rustic cottage on your brother the viscount's estate, where you engaged in some orgiastic rite that resulted in her being shot in the buttock. Do I have the essential facts correct?"

"Her arm is hurt and she hit her head too."

"Not like you, Duclairc, getting rough like that. You surprise and disappoint me."

"I assure you that this was an accident. A little game gone awry."

"How? What? My imagination fails me. I try to picture it but . . . If I am going to debase myself by doing a surgeon's work, the price of my skill and silence is an explanation."

"As it happens, that is precisely what I can afford. Please come up now. The steward had some laudanum and we dosed her up so she is still out, and it would be best if you did this quickly."

"Details, Duclairc. I shall expect details."

As Dante led Wheeler up the stairs, he considered that details were exactly what his friend would never get. No one would. The woman awaiting Wheeler's attention had come to this cottage through bizarre circumstances. Dante knew in his gut that speaking of them to anyone would only cause him untimely trouble.

What had she been doing out there, dressed like a man and brandishing a pistol, on a night when the countryside was alive with a mob burning farming machines and a posse on the chase? Dante had taken his own gun to the highest hill of Laclere Park, in a nostalgic effort to protect the estate on his last night in England. When he had been surprised by a trespasser he had returned fire, only to discover to his horror that he had not shot a radical but a woman.

As it happened, not just any woman.

Dante paused outside the bedchamber. "If you ever reveal what has occurred here, or that she was with me, she will be ruined."

"Discretion is a physician's second name. I never failed you in the past, did I?"

Wheeler became all business as soon as they passed into the chamber. He walked to the bed, took the patient's pulse, and felt her cheek. Ever so gently, he turned her head toward him.

He froze.

"Oh, my God."

"Exactly."

"Oh—my—God."

"Now you know why discretion is essential."

"It is Fleur Monley, Duclairc. *Fleur Monley*."

"So it is."

Wheeler collected his wits. Shaking his head, he proceeded to examine his patient. "*Fleur Monley*. Even I, who have seen women of highest repute faint at your smile, am thoroughly impressed. No one ever got Miss Monley to the altar let alone into bed, let alone playing games that get women shot in the buttocks. The closest was when your brother Laclere almost got engaged to her. . . ." The implications of *that* had Wheeler wide-eyed again. "He will probably kill you if he finds out."

"Another reason for discretion."

"Of course, of course. I promised silence and am bound by it, but it will be hell to honor my word. I will burst." He stripped away the bedclothes to reveal Fleur demurely dressed in one of Dante's nightshirts. "Charming, Duclairc, but why did you bother? She is drugged, I am a physician, and you are her lover."

He had bothered because he could hardly present her in those farm-boy rags, and because it did not seem dignified to leave her naked despite her unconsciousness and the ribald story he was feeding Wheeler. No matter what a man's reasons for stripping off her clothes, even a scoundrel did not leave the Fleur Monleys of the world naked for someone to see.

Morgan touched her bare leg. "She is damp. Did you bathe her?"

"She felt warm, and I thought that I should." It was one more bold-faced lie. Upon removing the rags he had discovered a very dirty body and had washed off the worst of it.

"Of course. Next time, do not give laudanum if the patient has a head wound."

"It wasn't much, and we dosed her some time ago when she began to moan as she came to. I am concerned that it may wear off, so you should get busy."

Morgan was not to be rushed. He touched all around her scalp. "It does not seem too serious. Fell, did she? Went out? She will have a bad lump. She will have to rest quietly for a few days."

"Surely she can be moved."

"Best not. You will have to make some excuse if anyone is expecting her return. She should stay here at least two or three days, in bed. *Resting*. It will give this arm time to repair too. Bad sprain. I can only guess how *that* happened. Some exotic position for coitus that country boys like me never get to learn, no doubt. Hindu?"

Wheeler's grin invited explication. Dante ignored him. Fleur Monley was going to create problems. He could not keep her here for several days, because he had no intention of being here himself. In approximately ten hours he planned to meet a fishing boat on the coast that would spirit him over to France.

"Help me to turn her so I can see about this gunshot. Gently now."

Together they turned Fleur on her stomach. Morgan pulled up the nightshirt. Dante turned to leave.

"No you don't. She was only nicked but you were right, it needs to be sewn. Get over here and hold her. The laudanum made her sleep but she is not unconscious. If she wakens while I am at it, I want someone backing me up."

Dante truly did not want to stay. In his thirty-two years he had seen more women nude than he could count. He had long ago learned to release or suppress his sexual reactions at will, much like a canal lock controls water. Still, seeing Fleur like this was making him uncomfortable.

She was injured and needed care and he lied about being lovers only to protect her from the posse out there looking for blood. Having her in this bed, naked from the waist down and her face pressed in his pillow, appeared a desecration of sorts. All the same, he was annoyingly aware that stripping her and washing her and seeing her body had raised the lock's water level more than he would like.

That surprised him, because he had grown fairly jaded about such things. Furthermore, her reputation and condition made sexual reactions either ridiculous or despicable.

Then again, her very presence here indicated that the world may have gotten that business about her unblemished virtue very wrong. The woman Fleur Monley was supposed to be would never run through the countryside in boy's clothes on a night when the radical rabble were out committing crimes.

What the hell had she been doing out there? For that matter, where the hell had she come from? The last he heard, she was visiting France.

He sat beside her on the bed and carefully placed his palms on her back. Behind him Morgan prepared the needle, sloshed something over Fleur's bottom, and went to work.

She gritted her teeth and held in the tears. She wanted to scream. If she did, however, these men would know that she was awake. That would be too humiliating to bear, and possibly very dangerous.

Where was she? The bed seemed clean but she could

smell earth and damp and she doubted that she had made it to Laclere Park. That man who shot her must have given her up. She was probably in a farmer's cottage, being tended before they carted her off to gaol.

Better that than Gregory, she supposed. Unless he learned about it and bribed them to get her back. In that case she would be right where she started.

The man holding her had not spoken much. She wished that he faced away. She would not have to swallow the pain so much if he were not looking at her. He was definitely doing that. She could feel his attention on her, despite his brief responses to the other's comments about horses and boxers.

A hand moved from her back to her head. She barely caught the cry of surprise that jumped to her throat. Fingertips gently brushed her hair back from the pillow and lightly stroked her head. She held her breath, cheek crushed against the down, and prayed that he had not seen her jaw clench or heard her shocked intake of breath.

That caressing hand should repel her. It implied dangerous interest and she was horribly defenseless. Instead, she found the light touch comforting and sympathetic and not at all insinuating. Who was this man who bothered to reassure an unconscious woman?

"I don't remember her being so thin," the voice near her rump mused. A painful skewer by the needle accompanied the comment. She tasted blood as she bit down. "I can see her ribs plainly. Normally people gain weight on the Continent, not lose it. I have to say that even so she has a nice, um, how did you so elegantly put it, rear nether region."

He spoke as if he knew her! If so, the night's risks had probably achieved nothing but more danger.

"Just sew," the man beside her muttered. "Aren't leeches

supposed to be above noticing such things? Rather like artists?"

"I am a physician, a man of culture and learning, not a leech. If you think artists grow immune either, you are doubly a fool. All the same, I accept your correction. Although, coming from *you* . . ."

"I do not like my lady friends discussed by other men, that is all."

Her ears were half-smothered in the pillow, but that voice sounded familiar. Why would he be claiming she was his lady friend? A dreadful possibility opened. Could this be the man she had heard speaking with Gregory last night?

"Considering how quickly you tire of your mistresses, I have always thought your reticence in talking about them a little priggish and ungenerous," the physician said. "Although it has never been the ladies who interested me but the strategies for winning and loving them. You could save yourself a lot of curious questions by writing a treatise as I suggested years ago."

"Maybe I will do that. I will have plenty of time in France, and it may pay my keep for a few years."

The rhythm of the needle stopped. "France? My good man, you are not! Has it come to that?"

"Afraid so."

"How bad?"

"Very bad. They are on my trail."

"Surely your brother—"

"I have been to that well far too often, and I will not go again. Once settled in France I will write and explain to him."

"Now I am distraught. You have ruined my humor completely."

"Well, finish up here, come downstairs, and I will tell you all, but it is such an old and tired story that I am sure you have heard it often before."

Efficient hands bound a bandage to her hip. More gentle ones slid the nightshirt down and carefully tucked bedclothes up around her shoulders.

They left. She exhaled the strain of keeping her composure and stillness. Her rump hurt badly now, even worse than when she had first woken in shock to that sewing needle. Still, the pain both existed and didn't, like something floating in part of her mind while the other parts daydreamed and slept. She did not know how long she drifted around the edges of consciousness.

She wondered if only the physician had recognized her or whether the other man had as well. He spoke in the cultured manner that said he moved in the sort of circles where she could have met him at some point over the years.

She clung to the hope that he was not anyone who had anything to do with Gregory, and certainly not the man who had spent last night bargaining for her like she was some four-hoofed animal.

A door below closed on mumbled farewells. Boot steps sounded on the stairs. Someone entered the chamber. She closed her eyes but she felt the warmth of the candle near her face.

"He is gone. Let us see if we can make you more comfortable now, Miss Monley."

She heard his voice plainly this time. Jolting up on her good arm, she twisted in shock.

And looked right into the resplendent brown eyes of the most charming wastrel in England.

chapter 2

The women of English society could bicker and argue with the best of them, but on one point they had always been in total agreement.

Dante Duclairc was a beautiful man.

That was the word they used. Beautiful. His luminous eyes, thick, lustrous brown hair, perfect face, and devilish smile had mesmerized any female he chose to conquer since he turned seventeen. Fleur knew three ladies who had committed adultery only once in their lives. With him.

The years had added some hardness to his countenance, but they had not dulled the heart-skipping effect that his attention provoked.

Even in her, and he wasn't even trying.

His expression bore curiosity and wry amusement. He smiled with warm familiarity, instantly bridging time back to that period ten years ago when his brother Vergil, the Viscount Laclere, had courted her. And yet underneath his cool, refined composure there shimmered a dangerous, exciting energy. With Dante it was always there.

Right now it frightened her speechless.

Somehow she knew without asking that they were alone. There was no female servant in this cottage, which meant that Dante had probably undressed her and put her in bed. What he had seen while the physician tended her had been the least of it.

"You are uncommonly brave," he said. "Wheeler never suspected that you were awake." His tone implied that he had known the exact moment when she had come to. He had caressed her head aware that she would feel him do it.

"It was my hope to avoid giving explanations to strangers."

"Since I am hardly that, you should not mind giving one to me. Let us get you comfortable first."

Her reaction to the Dante Duclaircs of the world had always been to run away, but she could not do that now. She suffered his lean strength hovering over her bed, propping pillows and arranging to her comfort. When he began to ease her onto her side, she stopped his hands with a freezing gesture and managed it on her own.

That left her looking up at him and him looking down at her. He had removed his coat and collar, and his shirt gaped open above his waistcoat. As an unmarried woman, she never saw men this relaxed in their dress.

Her vulnerability hit her with force. She said a quick prayer of thanks that of all the libertines in England, she had been fortunate enough to fall into this one's hands.

After all, they had come close to being related. That should count for something. She hoped.

He crossed his arms and regarded her. For a man with a reputation for being good-natured, his scrutiny appeared more critical than one would expect. She tucked the bed-clothes around her neck.

"This is a remarkably singular occurrence, Miss Monley. Finding you, of all women, in my bed."

He wasn't going to make this easy.

She eased back against a pillow and winced when her bottom stung from the pressure. "I trust that you did not hit your target."

"Of course I did. Be glad I did not aim for your head, which is where you almost got me."

"Only because you veered to the right. I did not aim anywhere near you and was just trying to scare you off."

"Why? I expect you to explain what you were doing with a gun, in those clothes, running around this county."

"I would rather not."

"Then you leave me no choice but to assume that you are part of the mob burning machines and fields. Their leader? I hope so. There is a considerable bounty on that head, and, as it happens, I could use the money."

Yes, he probably could, if he was fleeing to France. Gregory would probably pay handsomely to get her back too. Best not to let him know about that.

"Is your brother at Laclere Park?" she asked.

"He and Bianca have been spending a few months in Naples, where she is performing. My sister Penelope traveled with them. Since Charlotte and I prefer London, there are only servants at the house here."

Despair stomped out the small flame of hope that she had been carefully stoking for two months.

Dante's tall form towered over the bed. "Is that why you are here? You came looking for Vergil?" One finger gently slid under her chin. He tilted her head until he could see her face. "Are you in some trouble, Fleur?"

She could not answer. That last bit of hope had been very fragile, but it had sustained her. With its destruction all her strength simply disappeared. All was lost now. Her freedom, the Grand Project, her dream of having her life mean something—If Gregory entered the chamber right now she would agree to whatever he wanted.

Dante gazed down at her. He owned the most beautiful, clear eyes, and the concern in them surprised her. She had never seen him look serious before. He was the sort of man whom one assumed did not care about much at all.

He had called her Fleur, which he really shouldn't do, and was touching her, which he definitely shouldn't do, but she *was* in his bed, wearing his nightshirt. There was nothing insinuating about his behavior, in truth, and the breach in formalities comforted her. She was relieved to be able to respond in kind. "I am very tired, Dante. My head is still swimming. Perhaps in the morning I will feel up to explaining."

His hand fell away. "Of course, Fleur. My apologies for pushing you."

She fell asleep almost immediately. The laudanum must still be making her drowsy. Dante walked around the bed to get the candle.

He held the light closer to her face. As a girl Fleur had been the epitome of fashionable beauty with her dark hair and ivory skin and bowed red mouth. She possessed a willowy grace and demure demeanor too, along with a significant fortune. All of that had made her one of the most prized girls on the marriage mart. When it looked as though his perfect brother Vergil was going to win her, it had seemed evidence that the world indeed functioned like a well-designed clock.

Then Vergil had married an American opera singer and Fleur had disappeared onto the Continent for two years. Upon her return she had been a changed woman. She withdrew from society and shunned balls. She grew indifferent to her beauty and dressed unfashionably. Charity work, not pleasures and diversions, absorbed her interest and income.

The mumble that she had lost her looks was untrue. Dante thought her still extraordinarily lovely.

She was in trouble and frightened. Frightened enough to walk cross-country during the night to seek refuge with his brother.

Foolish of him to think that she would confide in him instead. Just as well that she had not. She would be trouble enough without entangling him in whatever misadventure had involved her.

He left the door open and went down to the sitting room to contemplate providing for her protection after he left tomorrow. While he did so he cleaned both of their pistols. No sooner was he finished than he heard the sounds of horses and dogs that said the posse was approaching.

Tucking the pistols away in a cabinet, he strode to the door and waited on its threshold.

Ten horsemen thundered into the little clearing and reined in their animals. Pearson, the steward, flew off his mount and ran to Dante.

"Had to bring them. They stopped at the big house

and demanded entry. Said the dogs had a scent of one of them on the big hill, heading this way." He lowered his voice and tipped his head closely. "They demanded to check every damn cottage, especially the vacant ones. I insisted on coming to keep an eye on them and to reassure the tenants."

"Good man. Try to stay when they leave. I need your help."

Sir Thomas Jameson, the county justice of the peace, heaved his considerable bulk off his horse and paced forward. "Who is that there?" His beefy face jutted toward the door's shadow as he tried to see in the moonlight.

"It is Mr. Duclairc, the viscount's brother," Pearson said.

"Duclairc? Didn't know you had come down. What are you doing here?"

"I am visiting the family seat. What are *you* doing here?"

"Damn question to ask. Someone's got to protect the property and uphold the law while the likes of you waste your time in gaming hells and brothels. Now step aside. We are searching for one of them seen coming this way."

"I have been here all evening, so I can assure you that one of whatever you hunt is not in here."

"Still, got to check. Last month the men of the county decided it was how we would do it, no exceptions."

"I must insist upon one."

"I said step aside, or we might get suspicious about why you refuse."

"My good man, politics bore me and everyone knows it. I would not know the difference between a radical and a radish."

Another man left the horses and joined Jameson. "Humor him, Duclairc, so that we can all do our duty and get home to bed."

Upon hearing the sardonic voice, Dante immediately lost his sense of humor. "You are a long way from London, Siddel."

"As are you. An odd coincidence to meet you here so soon after our last encounter."

Dante's blood flowed hotter at the reference. Their last encounter had been at a card table two weeks before and, he was almost positive, Siddel had cheated. "Laclere Park is Duclairc property, Siddel. You are the one with no ties to Sussex."

"I was in the county visiting a friend and decided to join the fun. A rare treat, hunting man instead of fox."

Icy currents of ill will flowed between them. Jameson did not seem to notice. "Can't wait all night, Duclairc. Step aside."

There was nothing to do but try and contain the damage. He backed into the cottage. "Surely two of you will be enough. I am not prepared to host a county assembly."

Jameson nodded. He and Siddel stepped inside.

The search did not take long, since the cottage held only a sitting room and kitchen down below. Jameson conducted some ridiculous poking into chests.

Dante lounged in his chair but kept one eye on Siddel's dark hair and thickening form. He had been a sportsman in his youth, a regular Corinthian, but excess and drink had taken its toll and turned him soft.

It was hard to believe that the man had a shrewd head for investments, as was reported, and counted great financiers and wealthy aristocrats among his associates. The style in which he lived confirmed those rumors, however. His despoiling cynicism proved, to Dante's mind, that the belief that virtue and success went together was nonsense.

Jameson plodded to the stairs.

Dante wished that he could spare Fleur this, but he saw no way out. "Gentlemen, I must warn you that there is someone up there sleeping. Not him whom you seek, but a lady."

Siddel grinned. "I doff my hat to you, Duclairc. Even as the bailiffs sniff for your trail, you dally for your pleasure. That is true style."

"Thank you."

"Still, while we are all gentlemen and your word should be sufficient, it would probably be best if we verify your description of the person above." Siddel headed for the stairs with unseemly anticipation.

Jameson had turned to come down and he flushed furiously when Siddel blocked his path. "Yes, of course. Needs to be done. Damn embarrassing though," he muttered as Siddel shooed him up.

"She is sleeping," Dante called after them. "I trust that you will do nothing to disturb her. She is very tired."

Siddel laughed. Jameson stumbled.

Dante listened to their boot steps on the boards above his head. He heard them pace over to the bed. He heard Jameson exclaim in shock.

Both men beat a retreat to the sitting room.

Jameson gaped at him. "It is . . . it is . . ."

"I doff my hat again," Siddel said dryly. "What brought her here?"

"My charm, I assume."

"I meant, what conveyance. There is no carriage outside."

"I hired one and fetched her when I heard she was back in the country. My last indulgence."

Siddel's lids lowered. "Most definitely that."

The threat was unmistakable. Dante recognized the tension pouring off Siddel, because he had provoked it often enough before. The man twisted with suppressed fury, just like a husband who had been cuckolded.

Jameson was so flustered one might have thought *he* had been caught with a saint in his bed. "Very good, very good. Done here. All finished. Out we go. The soul of discretion, that we are, eh, Siddel? Our lips are sealed. Good night to you, and give the viscount my regards. . . ."

His words rambled out the door after him. Siddel did not follow immediately. He turned on Dante from the threshold, limned in moonlight.

"You will regret touching her," he snarled.

This more blatant threat piqued Dante's annoyance. "I did not realize that you had an affection for her, Siddel. If I had but known . . . Well, it actually would not have made any difference at all. You will see to Jameson's silence, I trust?"

Siddel muttered a curse and swung out of the cottage.

Horses began pouring down the lane. Pearson eased in through the garden door as the sounds receded.

"Where is my sister Charlotte?" Dante asked.

"She is visiting Brighton with the St. Johns."

"First go to the house and find some women's clothes. See what Charl or Penelope have left there. Then I need you to ride to Brighton immediately and tell Charlotte that I need her here at once. Get St. John to come too. Tell him it is important."

The steward ducked out to claim his mount. Dante gazed up toward the chamber where Fleur slept.

If he had any sense, he would take Pearson's horse and ride himself. To the coast. The disgrace waiting if he did not would be worse than anything he had ever visited on his family. However, he could not go until he handed Fleur over to someone he trusted to protect her.

She was in trouble, of that he was sure. In the morning he would make her tell him about it. It would give him something to think about while he languished in prison.

Fleur opened her eyes to the whitewashed walls of the cottage and the sun streaming through simple curtains.

Last night's despair tried to submerge her again. She forced it down. Actually, if one looked at it a certain way, her situation was quite humorous. She had come looking for help from the one man she trusted, but he was gone, living his life as he should be. Instead of the viscount, the paragon, the rock of authority, she had found the brother, the rake, the wastrel. She needed the protection of a man who could intimidate judges and lords. Instead, she had been shot in the bottom by one who could not pay his tailor.

She struggled to sit. Movement sharply reminded her of her infirmities. She managed to get to her feet and inch around to take care of necessary business. She was contemplating how to get back into bed when Dante appeared at the doorway.

"You should have called me."

"I can do it. Please go away."

Strong arms braced under her shoulders and knees. He swung, lifted, and lowered. A sheet billowed down to cover her.

"Where are my clothes?"

"You mean the rags that you were wearing while armed men tried to hunt you down? The ones that led me to think that I was shooting a man? I burned them."

"What am I supposed to wear?"

"If you have grown fond of trousers, you can have a pair of mine. Or you can use the dress that the steward secreted out of Laclere House."

"Does the steward know why you wanted it?"

"I am sure we are both glad that he knows it is not for me."

Fluttering panic beat in her chest. "Did he see me?"

"He knows you are here. Several people do, I am afraid." He pulled the chair over and sat, propping his boot on the bed's edge.

"We had visitors last night. Jameson—the justice of the peace—and his men. They were searching the whole estate. I could not keep your presence a secret. I assumed that you would not want them to know how you really got here, so I let them think that you were my guest."

"Your guest? That is putting it very finely. Surely they did not believe you."

"Well, Fleur, they did not want to, but the evidence was rather damning. Their shock almost brought this roof down when they found you in this bed."

"Are you saying that they saw me? In this bed? Men whom I do not know witnessed this?"

"I regret to say that they did."

"How could you permit such a thing?"

"A better question is how could I have stopped it." He fixed her with his brown eyes. "Did I err, Fleur? Should I have told the truth instead?"

"Of course not." She said it too quickly. "Only, the idea that people would think that we . . . Who saw me?"

"Just Sir Thomas Jameson and Hugh Siddel."

"Siddel! He knows? Oh, dear Lord." That promised to be very humiliating. Her mind began filling with the potential complications Mr. Siddel's discovery could create.

"Forgive my impertinence, but do you have some relationship with him? He acted as if our love affair directly insulted him."

"When I came out as a girl, Siddel briefly courted me, but that was years ago."

He did not seem to notice that she had not answered his question. "My instincts on this are well honed by experience, Fleur. He was in a fury at the evidence that we were lovers. I half-expected him to call me out. As it happens, right now a duel is the least of the trouble the man can cause me." Suddenly his attention focused on her face. "Which is why you need to explain things now. I find myself involved in a situation not of my making or understanding. I must insist on knowing why you acted as if you were running for your life last night."

He had settled comfortably in the chair. A contained man, unruffled and smooth. A handsome man, at ease with his body and presence, confident of his physical impression.

A determined man, whose clear eyes watched her with patience. He was prepared to wait her out. *Take your time,* his whole pose said. *We have all day, if you want to do it that way.*

"I would like you to bring up the dress that you spoke of, Dante. I will put it on and leave."

"You are to rest, and I could not permit you to walk away on your own even if you were well."

"I will go to the house and ask for help. It will be better this way."

"No." He folded his arms over his chest.

The temptation to tell him, and pretend that there was some hope that he would know what to do, almost defeated her.

He watched her. Too much and too long. It became a compelling examination. She grew uncomfortable in a strangely exciting way and embarrassingly aware of that frightening something that shimmered around him like a subtle force.

"I think that we will pass the time with a game," he said.

"What kind of game?"

"You do not have to look so suspicious. Not that kind. Although having you in my bed, but in a condition that prevents me from trying to breach your defenses, is enough to make me weep."

"I doubt that you will weep when you are so clearly laughing. At me. Now, what kind of game?"

"The rules are simple. I ask you a question and you answer it honestly. Then I ask you another one and you answer that. And so on until I run out of questions."

"It does not sound like a fun game at all. At the least I think we should take turns. You ask a question, then I ask one of you. And so on."

"Sounds almost too sporting. I think that I should be

allowed to press my advantage in some manner, since you are indisposed and cannot be seduced."

"Stop teasing me like a clumsy lothario. Everyone knows that you are much smoother when you are really after a woman."

That caught him off guard. "Does everyone know that, indeed?"

"Yes. Everyone," she said, pleased that she had tipped the balance in this game, whatever it really was.

"Are you saying that a few of my lovers have been indiscreet?"

"You have been discussed in retiring rooms for years. I heard all about you when I was a girl. It is a wonder that you continue to be successful, what with every seductive strategy of yours so well documented by personal testimony."

"I find this disconcerting. *I* have never discussed what occurred between myself and any woman."

"As a gentleman, you are prevented from doing so. Women are not so constrained."

"How naughty of you to listen to such things." He smiled devilishly, and she realized that his dismay had been a ruse. He had deliberately led her into a very inappropriate conversation.

And, it appeared, was not going to let her out.

"I do not think that I could seduce you now, no matter how darling you look in my nightshirt, Fleur. I would be expecting you to be fresh and ignorant. Instead, you would be checking items off a list as I progressed."

She swallowed hard. This conversation had gotten too personal all of a sudden.

His head angled. His lids lowered. He regarded her

with a man's warmth. That something shimmered. Right into her.

"I can see it now. I would be caressing up your bare leg and you would remind me I missed the sensitive spot behind a woman's knee that I discovered that night with a certain duchess."

He had definitely crossed the line with that. If she could find her voice she would give him a good scolding.

"Or I would be kissing your back and you would instruct me not to forget the trick involving the hollow at your spine's base, as related by the wife of a prominent M.P."

This had become outrageous, but his shocking descriptions of loveplay cast a spell. She could not take her eyes off him. Her pulse beat so loudly in her ears that she worried he could hear.

He angled forward in the chair until his face was not far from hers. "Perhaps if my performance did not meet expectations, you would demand that I show you how some parts of a woman's body could be even more sensitive after lovemaking than before, as an indiscreet baroness confided I once showed her."

"You are a depraved rogue."

"And you are flushed and ready and I have not even touched you."

He took her hand in the warmth of his. She gaped as he raised it to his mouth and kissed her fingers. Her body gave a physical shriek that scared her out of her wits.

She snatched her hand away. "How *dare* you."

He relaxed back in his chair, bright eyed with dark amusement. "A very small dare, to remind you that I am not a fool. You are safe from me, but only because I choose to make it so. Do not goad me, because if challenged the choice of weapons is mine."

Her heart, her blood, her very breath badly needed to settle. She struggled to keep him from seeing the horrible internal strife that his touch had provoked.

An exciting, mounting euphoria had crashed headlong into a sickening, numbing dread.

She stared down at the hand he had kissed and felt again the warmth of his breath. Her warring reactions left her nauseous.

This had never happened before. The fear had never permitted it. Not when she was a girl, and certainly not since she had put herself on the shelf.

"I have badly frightened you, haven't I?" He reached toward her face, but stopped himself. "I should not have done that. Your virtue is really very safe with me. However, if I am to keep you safe in other ways, I need to know what this is about."

He did deserve an explanation. She had involved him, now that others had seen her here. She had not had time to come up with a good lie, however. She would have to give him the truth. Or at least part of it. She would simply have to skirt any references to the Grand Project.

"Last October I left England to visit some friends in France. I stayed through the new year. I returned two months ago, in February."

"February? No one ever mentioned your return or seeing you in town."

"That is because my stepfather, Gregory Farthingstone, met me at the dock in Dover. I have been imprisoned by him ever since."

chapter 3

I had written that I planned to sail home on the *Sea Dragon* in February. Gregory was waiting in Dover. I was surprised but glad to see him. One can always use help after a long journey," Fleur explained.

"Then he imprisoned you?" Dante tried to keep the incredulity from his tone. The accusation was bizarre enough that one might wonder if the fall had affected her brain.

Gregory Farthingstone was a man known for good sense and moderate living, and a trustee of the Bank of England. It would be easier to believe that Fleur had imprisoned Farthingstone rather than the other way around.

Fleur had been fussing with the sheet, tucking it up around her neck as if his earlier teasing had left her naked. Now she forgot about that as resentment lit her eyes.

"He claimed that he was looking out for me, and protecting me, and ensuring that I got the help I needed. He said that as an old friend of my mother's family, and as her second husband, he was only fulfilling his responsibility. However, his intentions are far less benign than that."

"What intentions would those be?"

"He is trying to claim that I am irrational and incompetent."

"Why would he think that?"

"Because I have been giving my fortune away. That is how he sees my contributions to charities."

Fleur's generosity to schools, hospitals, and reform causes was well known. "Have you risked your own future with your largesse?"

"I have not given away all of it, but enough that Gregory thinks it is irresponsible. However, enough remains for me to live very comfortably. I am of age, and an independent woman. He is not my guardian and has no authority to interfere in my life. He says that he is the closest thing to family, and it is his responsibility to make sure that I receive the guidance and care that I need."

"Where did he bring you after he met you at Dover?"

"To one of his properties, in Essex."

"You walked here all of the way from Essex?"

"We were traveling. Gregory would not say where he was taking me, but I think it was one of those places near the sea where families put their problem relatives. I recognized that we were in Sussex and ran away, hoping I would find Laclere."

Yes, Vergil would be formidable enough to take on Gregory Farthingstone.

"I am not addled," she muttered, looking to her hands and their tense, entwined fingers. "It is not irresponsible to use money to help people. If I spent my fortune on ball gowns and jewels, no one would question it."

She should have done both. If she had bought those gowns and jewels, she would have been safe from suspicion.

It had been her repudiation of society and marriage that had raised the specter of instability.

She kept gazing sightlessly at those twisting fingers. He got the impression that there was more to tell and that she was deciding whether to do so.

She had given him the explanation she owed him. He would not press for more, but he hoped that she would go on.

"There is something else," she finally said. "The night before last we stopped at an inn. As he has since Dover, he locked me in my chamber after supper. He did not realize that part of the wall had been removed to build in a wardrobe. When I opened the door of that wardrobe, I could hear a muffled conversation in Gregory's chamber. Another man was there late at night. They were talking about me, I think."

"Would it not have been obvious if they were?"

"At first I thought that they spoke of a thing, not a person. You see, the man was offering to buy the thing. Only later did I realize that maybe it was me."

Now she *was* sounding a bit strange, like one of those people who thinks everyone plots against them. "Fleur, Farthingstone cannot sell you. If he did, what good would it do the buyer? As you said, you are an independent woman of mature years."

"No, he cannot legally sell me. But then, he cannot legally imprison me, yet he has done so. 'It will be over before she knows what happened, and she will be the happier for it,' the man said. 'If she fights it, then we will put her away.' I do not know what you think, Dante, but that sounds like a forced marriage to me. For my own good, no doubt. To make sure someone has the authority to take care of me."

"Conveniently arranged before more of your fortune is gone."

"I never liked Gregory. I never understood why my mother married him after my father died. He assumes that I should defer to his judgment, but he is not my father, and no blood relation. It would not surprise me to learn that after this marriage he and that man intended to divide up whatever I have."

"Assuming that they discussed you at all. You do not know that." For a woman not addled, she told a bizarre tale. Still, it would not be the first time a woman had been used thus.

A frown puckered while she considered that. "I suppose. At the time . . . it was that which made me decide to run away. Gregory saw to it that I had no money. At his manor and on the road I was closely watched. Getting away would not be easy. But the idea that he might force me into a marriage gave me courage. Imprisonment I might have surrendered to, but not marriage."

"Certainly not. With that, he had definitely gone too far."

"The next evening I climbed out my window, got down the building, and snuck away. I stole those clothes and left my dress as payment. Outside a tavern I traded a ring I had for the gun. Then I ran. We must have been ten miles from here. When you shot me and I fell, I think that I went out as much from exhaustion as from the bump."

With the conclusion of Fleur's tale a peaceful quiet filled the chamber, as if the very telling of it had calmed her fears.

Dante rose and paced to the window. For whatever

reason, she had chosen a different path than most. In a man such eccentricities would be accepted. But a determined Gregory Farthingstone might make a case showing sufficient instability that would convince a judge to take away a woman's independence.

"I ask a favor of you, Dante." She appeared so helpless in that bed. Small and fragile and very alone. "When Laclere gets back, please tell him. Perhaps he will find me to see if things turned out all right."

"Of course, Fleur, but it will not come to that. Whether you understood that conversation or not, he still has no right to confine you. If you went to such risk to get away, we should see that you do not go back."

"Since I have been seen here, Gregory will learn where I am. I have been waiting for the sounds of his carriage."

"If you hear a carriage, do not assume it is Gregory. I sent the steward for my sister Charlotte and Daniel St. John. They are in Brighton and should be here after noon."

Her eyes brightened with something that might be hope. She relaxed into the pillows. "Even last night you thought to do that? It was very kind of you, Dante."

"Nonsense. I do things like that every time I shoot a woman in the bottom. You rest now. I will go down and see about some food for you. You are not to worry."

He reassured her with more conviction than he felt. Charlotte and St. John had better not tarry in leaving Brighton. If Farthingstone learned where she was, this could be a race to the finish.

She slept after breakfast, and Dante paced the lower level while the hours passed and the sun moved.

Most likely her concerns were not founded on anything real. Possibly she had behaved erratically in ways a chance acquaintance would not notice. Maybe Farthingstone just wanted to be sure she rested after her voyage. Undoubtedly she had misconstrued what little she had heard through that wardrobe.

Still, Farthingstone's connection to her through marriage to her mother gave him the semblance of authority. Worse, he could put her away with no one knowing, since it was thought she still traveled the Continent.

Ridiculous, of course. She was in no danger.

He removed both pistols from their cabinet and loaded them.

A little before midday he heard her moving around on the bed. He went up and found her sitting on its edge, trying with her good arm to spread out the dress he had procured.

"I do not want them to find me like this," she said. "I will dress, at least."

"If you wish." He brought over the undergarments that Pearson had found. He lifted her from the bed and set her on her feet.

She realized his intentions. "I can manage."

"I know that you cannot. I will help you."

"You must not."

"Do not let my earlier attempt at wit discomfort you. The repetition of pleasure has dulled my susceptibility. I must deliberately light the candle or there is no flame. I am utterly indifferent. Like a physician or an artist."

"The physician yesterday said they are not indifferent, but I can see how *you* might be. The first naked woman would be exciting but the thousandth would be boring. A bit like too much marzipan."

"Precisely. Except you are not the thousandth. I only recently passed eight hundred."

She turned shocked eyes on him.

"I am joking, Fleur. Now, left arm up."

He assumed the bland countenance of a valet and averted his eyes, but the candle glowed all by itself when the nightshirt dropped to the floor. Indifference hardly described his reaction when he glimpsed her ivory skin and feminine curves and high breasts. She looked away and blushed as he slid the chemise over her shy, trembling nakedness.

Getting the rest of the garments on was a clumsy process, due to their mutual attempts to pretend the other wasn't there.

He roughly made the bed and then lifted her back onto it.

"See. No liberties. It was your lucky day when you got shot by a sated, jaded rake like me."

She laughed. It was a beautiful sound, like the watery notes of a harp.

"My lucky day, Dante, but not yours. Now, I am all arranged, and dressed and fed. I think that you should go to the stables, get a horse, and ride to the coast as you had planned."

He sat in the chair. "I cannot do that, Fleur."

"I will be safe. Someone will be here soon."

"It could be the wrong person. What if someone does not come? Tonight could be like the last, and those marauders might choose to burn this cottage or come in and hide here. I cannot leave you alone."

"You could get someone from the house to stay with me."

"The servants cannot stand against Farthingstone if he arrives looking for you. We will wait for Charl and St. John together. I said that you would be safe, and you will be."

"I am sorry this has happened," she said. "Are the bailiffs really on your trail?"

"Certain creditors sold my notes to a man, Mr. Thompson, who demanded payment. A bad night at cards ruined any chance of negotiating."

"Couldn't you ask Laclere to help you?"

"I could, and he would. It is probably what Thompson hopes for. But I will not. Verg has already been too generous."

He wondered why he spoke so candidly. Maybe dressing her had deepened their familiarity. Maybe taking care of her had.

He experienced a peaceful companionship with her. Probably the survivors of shipwrecks developed friendships quickly too, while they shared a raft and tried not to watch the horizon.

"I would say it was unfortunate that things did not end happily between you and Bianca, except she and Laclere are so obviously right together," she said.

Fleur was referring to the time when she was Vergil's intended, and the plan had been for Bianca to be Dante's. "I was not disappointed about Bianca wanting Vergil. She and I did not suit well, and she is good for him. However, I would lie if I denied that I have on occasion regretted losing her fortune."

She laughed again. "I have smiled more this last hour

than I have in the last year. Odd, that. After all, sooner or later I must face Gregory, and you must get away. If you miss that boat, how will you escape?"

"There are other boats."

"How selfish of me, to be so caught up in my own problem that I did not see sooner how I had made yours worse. Please do not delay for me."

"Until I know that you are safe, I will remain here. Any gentleman would, and despite my circumstances I hope that I am still that."

"You are most definitely that, and much more, dear friend."

Her gratitude touched him. The serenity he remembered in her from years ago had settled on her.

He should probably leave her to her privacy, but the bedchamber was airy and pleasant and her company pleased him. A day of waiting stretched out ahead of them.

He made himself comfortable. "I will tell you how I wasted my life, if you tell me how you have been flourishing in yours."

The harp played again while she laughed.

She had never realized that he could be so kind. She should have guessed. His lovers always spoke well of him. They knew going into the affairs that he was inconstant and that the passion would be brief. If hearts had been broken, and some had, she suspected it was not because he promised more than he gave.

Not all kindness, however. A little ridge of darkness lurked within the charm. She could see it in his eyes sometimes, and hear it in his voice. It could manifest itself unexpectedly, as with his threat to turn her in, or with that toying flirtation this morning. She sensed that it wanted to become something bigger, but he controlled it. Most of the time.

He amused her with stories of daring at the gaming tables and horse races, and of fortunes won and lost. He appeared contrite when he admitted the times he had turned to his brother when he had gotten in too deep.

She already knew the details that he did not add. She knew about the disastrous finances that his brother Vergil had inherited when their older brother, Milton, died. Only *déclassé* ventures in trade had saved the Duclairc family at all. Still, Dante's allowance might have been adequate for a different sort of man. He could have devoted himself to some employment and not just pleasure.

All the same, she envied him. Here was a man who had truly lived for the moment. That doing so had led to ruin was one of those moral tales that one was supposed to nod at approvingly. Instead, she couldn't help resenting it.

Her own story, of charity and good works, should shine in comparison. Instead, it embarrassed her to have so little real joy to describe. In certain essential ways, she was the one who had lived a wasted and barren life.

She might have told him about that. About the loneliness and emptiness. About her plans to find some fulfillment through her Grand Project. She came near to doing so. The ease with which they spoke encouraged confidences. But their few hours of friendship were too short. Sounds on the lane in mid-afternoon heralded their end.

Dante went to the window as commotion filled the clearing outside.

"This should be interesting," he said as he slid on his

frock coat. "It was a dead heat. Both Charl and Farthing-stone have arrived together."

Her peace disappeared in an instant. "I will come down. Please, help me up."

"If you insist on coming, I will carry you." He lifted her into his arms.

She began to object, but it felt very safe and secure to be nestled in his arms. She realized with a start that she had embraced no person since her mother's death, and no man for over ten years.

He bore her down the steps. Their visitors had just entered the sitting room, arguing.

His younger sister, Charlotte, her dark hair a little disheveled and her pert face most distraught, fretted beside the darkly handsome Daniel St. John. Gregory's aging, freckled face turned pink with consternation while he queried them on their sudden arrival.

Dante's boot on the bottom step caught Gregory in mid-bluster and everyone turned in surprise. More horses were arriving outside.

"No need to put her down, Duclairc. You can just carry her out to my coach," Farthingstone ordered.

Dante set Fleur's sore rump carefully down in a chair.

"See here—" Farthingstone began.

"No, *you* see here. Charl, I thank you for coming. Miss Monley is injured, and in need of both care and sanctuary. Whatever else happens, St. John, I ask you to promise that you will not allow Farthingstone to take her away."

St. John made a slight bow in Fleur's direction. "We met many years ago, Miss Monley, here at Laclere Park."

"I remember. Thank you for interrupting your visit to Brighton."

Charlotte hurried over to her. "Fleur, what are you doing here? I thought that you were touring the Continent. You are injured? What has happened?"

"She was grazed by a bullet," Dante said.

"Grazed . . . she was shot? Where?"

"Actually, in the rear nether region."

Charlotte blinked. "In the rear nether . . . you mean that she was shot in the . . . oh, my."

Gregory's face had gone red beneath his white hair. "How she was wounded needs investigation, but one thing is clear. Duclairc kept her here so that he could compromise her."

"Dante, you didn't! Not Fleur *too*! Vergil will have apoplexy."

"His plot is obvious," Farthingstone sneered. His bulbous nose made the expression more comical than disdainful. "However, it will not work, sir. There're men outside wanting to see you, and my stepdaughter is not in her right mind and cannot be held responsible for your dishonorable use of her. I will take care of her now."

"My honor is my business and not Mr. Farthingstone's," Fleur said, ignoring Gregory and speaking to Charlotte and St. John, who were her only hopes. "Your brother has seen to my care and protected me. I beg you to hear him, and to refuse Mr. Farthingstone his demands. He has no legal rights to me. I will not go with him of my own will."

The door stood open. Two large, rough-looking men darkened its threshold.

"Ah, our salon is complete," Dante observed. "Would you be Mr. Thompson's bailiffs?"

"Aye," one mumbled. "You be coming with us nice and easy now, Mr. Duclairc. Don't want no trouble."

"No trouble at all, I promise. Can I ask how you found me?"

"Word came up to London during the night. We rode hard and it will be a long ways back, so let's be going."

"Dante, now what is *this*?" Charlotte cried.

"Destiny, sweet sister."

He turned to St. John. "I leave Miss Monley in your protection. She should not be traveling, and her complaints against Farthingstone are well founded. Promise me that you will at least hear her out."

"She will be safe." St. John glanced meaningfully to the waiting bailiffs. "Allow me to see to this other matter for you, Duclairc."

"No. It is an amount I could never repay."

Fleur knew a thing or two about the fate that Dante faced. "Mr. St. John, Dante has no horse. They will make him walk all the way to London."

"Stop by the stables and get a horse for him," St. John ordered the men. "I will settle it with Laclere."

"Dante," Fleur whispered frantically, reaching toward him.

He bent over her. "St. John will see to you now, Fleur. He is not nearly so strict as he appears. Tell him and Charlotte what you told me."

"It is not that. Those men . . . How much, Dante? How much do you owe?"

He raised her hand to his lips. "An obscenely high amount. Do not even offer. I have never dunned friends, and I would never accept a penny from a woman."

"But it is my fault."

"No, Fleur, it is mine alone."

Assuming the cool elegance for which he was famous, he walked out of the cottage.

chapter 4

Fleur stepped out of Daniel St. John's carriage and accepted the footman's escort to the gaol's front door.

There was one great convenience to being a twenty-nine-year-old woman on the shelf who devoted herself to charity. When you told little lies, people believed you. Mr. St. John and his wife, Diane, thought that today she was attending a meeting to plan a new school for workers' sons.

Fleur knew all about London's gaols. She supported the reformers like Elizabeth Fry who sought to improve their condition. She noted with distaste that Mr. Thompson had arranged for Dante to be put in one of the worst of them. The narrow, crowded street smelled of rotting food and offal, and a din of voices poured out of the old buildings. The crumbling plaster of the gaol, black with age and damp, depressed her spirits.

It would hurt Dante's pride for anyone he knew to see him in such a place. She rehearsed once more the plan that had brought her here.

The gaoler's wife let her in with a display of bowing, indicating that the care Fleur had taken with her appearance had been successful. She had sent to her house for her only fashionable dress, a broad-skirted one in ice-blue muslin. Considering her mission today, she did not want to look too much the dowd.

The woman brought her into the sitting room of the fetid inn that housed debtors while their creditors tried to extract payment. The chamber's few windows let in little light, but she could see the negligible attempts at providing comfort. Considering the squalid environment, the high spirits of the men playing cards and wagering with pieces of straw surprised her.

In the thick of it, joking and laughing, still playing the games that had brought him here, sat Dante Duclairc.

In contrast to the poor appearance of his comrades, Dante looked impeccable. His cravat showed several days' wear and his frock coat needed pressing, but he had shaved and dressed for a day on the town even though he would never leave these walls.

"You've a visitor, Mr. Duclairc. A *lady*," the woman called.

They all looked at her. Dante's smile froze. He threw in his cards and came over.

"Miss Monley, this is surprising." His tone conveyed disapproval. "I will take her out back, Meg."

"For ten pence you can use my chamber if you want," Meg offered with a bawdy grin.

"We will go out back, Meg."

He led her out to a garden. Three pigs grunted in a pen at one end and chickens pecked around the almost-bare ground. A crude bench sat against the far wall.

"You should not be here."

"Do not scold, Dante. I have seen such places before. I brought you something from Charlotte."

"She already sent enough money to pay for meat. Tell her I do not need any more."

"It is not exactly from Charlotte herself." She sat on the bench and extracted a small purse from her reticule. "A lady came to visit your sister once we got back in town last week. She said that you had given her these jewels recently, as a parting gift. Having heard of your circumstances, she does not feel right keeping them."

She opened the little purse and revealed two amethyst earrings.

He gazed at them. "No doubt you think it reckless of me to have used my last guineas in such a way."

"I think that you decided those guineas would not make much difference, and it was important to maintain standards."

"Very open-minded of you, Fleur." He took the purse. "And very good-hearted of the lady. Now you must go. This is no place for you."

She refused to budge. A night of debate and panic had driven her here, and she would see it through. "I also came to visit with you, Dante. It is rude to throw me out."

"My apologies. Of course Saint Fleur would want to bring comfort to the imprisoned. I have not even asked after your health. You are better now? If Charl brought you to town from Laclere Park, I assume that you are healing properly. You look lovely today. That blue brings out the color of your eyes."

The courtesies tripped off his tongue in a slightly

sarcastic voice. The dark ridge had bared itself. Yes, his pride was hurt to be seen here. He clearly wanted her gone.

"I am well healed, thank you. I have been staying with the St. Johns while I recover."

"And Farthingstone?"

"St. John held him off. For now."

His hard expression broke. The man she remembered, the Dante who had been her friend for a day in that cottage, looked down with concern. "What is he up to?"

"He is going to Chancery to ask that all my finances be put under his control, due to my erratic emotional state and my inability to make sound judgments. St. John's solicitor thinks he may succeed. The way that I ran away, and the discovery that I was with you in that cottage will not help my case. Along with control of my finances, he also will request guardianship over me."

He sat beside her. "Damn the man. If it comes to it, maybe you should request someone else get the authority. My brother should be back in a month. He will agree to do it."

"While I would trust Laclere with my life, I do not like the idea of putting those responsibilities on his shoulders, or of being answerable to him. I have been thinking of a different solution."

"If I can help in any way, I am at your command." He rose with solicitous grace. "Now, this is an unhealthy place, and if it is learned that you came, Farthingstone will only have more odd behavior to describe. It was good of you to visit, Fleur. I confess that I have worried about you a bit during my days here. However, you really must leave."

"Please sit, Dante. I want to tell you my solution and hear what you think of it."

He complied with a sigh. She angled away from him so she could watch the chickens and pigs and not his reactions. She was very sure that she would not want to see them.

"Dante, did Laclere ever tell you why he and I never married?"

Stillness instantly occupied the space where he sat.

"Of course not," he finally said. "I assumed it was because of Bianca."

She had known Laclere would never speak of it to Dante, but she had rather hoped he had anyway. It would make this easier.

"It was not because of Bianca. There was never a true courtship between Laclere and me. It was all a pretense. I did not want to marry, and acting as if we were going to wed each other spared me for a year."

"That explains quite a lot. I always thought that Verg treated you badly. Love excuses much, but you and he were all but engaged before Bianca came to England."

"It was a feint from the beginning. I planned never to marry. Ever since I was a girl, I have been very sure of that." She closed her eyes, took a deep breath, and plunged forward. "Except, as our friendship grew, it occurred to me that there might be an alternative. A very special kind of marriage. I offered it to him and he refused."

"What are you saying, Fleur?"

How did one say it outright? She never had to with Laclere. Somehow, he had just known what she meant.

"Fleur, did you offer my brother a white marriage? One without physical intimacy?"

She felt her face burning. "I was not surprised that he refused. I think that my fortune made it tempting, but as viscount he would want a son."

"Why are you telling me this? Are you thinking of marrying?"

"Last night, after meeting with Gregory, I began to contemplate it. A husband would have authority that Gregory could not violate. I am thinking about a marriage such as I offered your brother. Such an understanding would end all of this. I am right, aren't I? Don't you think so?"

Stillness again. Total silence for a long pause.

"What I think is that you had better be very, very careful about the man whom you choose, Fleur."

A resonance in his tone made her face him. He regarded her with a thoughtful, speculative gaze.

"Yes, very careful," she said. "It would have to be someone I trusted. Someone who accepts that I cannot be a true wife to any man. The understanding on that would have to be very firm."

He just watched. She almost lost her courage, but the memory of Gregory's florid face demanding her return from St. John and of the unctuous, patronizing way he had spoken to her, as if she were a stupid child, kept her resolve together.

"It would have to be someone who has a full life already, and interests that the marriage would permit him to pursue freely," she continued. "A man who would accept half of my income and live within its means, and who would agree to permit me to use the rest as I choose.

We would both have separate lives in reality. You might say that we would not really be married at all."

"You are describing a man of undisputed honor, like my brother. A paragon among men. There are few like him."

"I am describing an honorable man, but not a paragon. Maybe I am describing a man who would never accept a penny from a female friend but who might accept an extremely high amount from a wife. A man whose vast experiences mean that the candle does not burn unless he lights it. A man who need not seek pleasure with a wife because he can find it anywhere for a smile. A man like you."

There. It was said.

His expression grew more intensely contemplative. He studied her as if he tried to decide if she was serious.

It seemed an eternity that they sat there with their silence broken by the sounds of city life and yard animals. She prayed that his enigmatic reaction did not hide abhorrence.

She had to look away. "I never thought to make this suggestion to another man, Dante. I know that you must think me unnatural, in ways that make Gregory's accusations pale."

"Not so unnatural, Fleur. However, are you sure that you have not outgrown your girlhood fear?"

"It is not a girlhood fear. My blood turns to ice at the thought of . . . When I heard that man bargaining for me . . . I could not breathe." Her voice sounded frantic to her own ears. Her chest and mind filled with panic as it had that night.

He reached over and lightly stroked her hair. "Calm yourself, pretty flower. If you say it is so, I believe you."

The silence stretched again. She closed her eyes and prayed he would not reject her outright.

"You have mentioned two agreements, regarding intimacy and money, that are out of the ordinary, Fleur. Are there any other unusual terms or specifics that I should hear?"

His willingness to listen gave her hope that the life she knew, the plans she had laid, would not be stolen from her. "The income derives from the trust my father left. I have lands and other funds, however, mostly inherited from my aunt. I want a promise that I can use or dispose of that property and income as I choose, if I want to. I want an agreement that you will not interfere and will sign any documents as become necessary."

His reaction indicated he found these particular terms most unusual, as indeed they were. By law, husbands were supposed to get everything and control any lands. Reserving property to her own discretionary use was almost unheard of, but she desperately needed him to agree to this. She had lived independently too long, and had gone too far on her Grand Project, to be subject to any man on her decisions, especially to a husband who really wouldn't be a husband.

"Even without that independent fortune, my inheritance is significant, Dante. Half the income from the trust is a handsome amount."

"How handsome?"

"Your share would be three thousand, to use as you please. I would continue to maintain my household with my own part."

He laughed. "That is certainly handsome, Fleur. However, look where we are. Where I am. Forgive me, but it is not very sensible for you to make this proposal, with all of these private financial understandings, to a man in gaol for debt. Don't you worry that someday I will be in too deep again and will take all of it?"

"All of our arrangement will be grounded on your honor, Dante. That is sufficient guarantee for me. I do not doubt that you will keep any promises that you make. Even if someday you want all of it, I do not believe that you will take it. I also think that you will never incur debts that would jeopardize what is not yours."

His expression turned enigmatic again. She could not decide if he was flattered or if he tried to hide his opinion that she was a fool.

"You must be thinking it odd that I do not jump at this offer. It is very generous, and solves my present problem very neatly."

"As it solves mine. The mutually beneficial aspect of the solution is the best part of it, I think."

"It is far too optimistic of you after our brief friendship. You do not know me, Fleur."

"I trust you. I know you are honorable. I also enjoy your company, and that is a rare thing for me with a man."

"You can do better."

"I do not think so."

He rose abruptly and paced away, his arms crossed over his chest and a thoughtful scowl on his handsome face. A burst of laughter from inside the gaol reminded her of how peculiar a place this had been for a proposal. But then, the proposal itself was so odd that no place would have really been appropriate.

He returned to stand in front of her. Propping one booted foot beside her on the bench, he bent over his knee and lifted her chin with his dry, warm fingers, forcing her to look into his luminous eyes.

"It is an astonishing idea. Totally unexpected. I am not exactly the marrying kind, Fleur."

"This is not exactly a typical marriage. I will never ask you questions about your lovers, Dante. I know that I will have no right to. There will be no jealous scenes."

"The freedom to have lovers is not what concerns me right now. We speak of a lifetime. Just how separate do you expect us to be? It would raise questions if we are never together."

"We need not be strangers. We can share a house, and entertain mutual friends if it suits us."

"I think that we would have to at first, don't you? It would not do to make people suspicious, especially Farthingstone."

"You can move to my house in Mayfair after the wedding. There is enough room for one more."

His expression went serious, and she knew that he was deciding her future in that moment. His gaze fell to her lips. For an instant that special energy shimmered intensely.

His thumb brushed her mouth. "Will I be allowed to kiss my wife sometimes?"

"Friends do, don't they?"

He touched his mouth gently to hers. The softness and warmth of the kiss caused a bright light to blink through her.

"When do you plan to hold the wedding, Miss Monley? As it happens, my social diary is without commitments at the moment."

It was the money that swayed him. He would have been an idiot not to grab for it.

Dante told himself that many times over the next few days while he contemplated why he had accepted Fleur's offer.

He had agreed because the marriage would rescue him from dire straits, but he confessed that her appeal had touched him in other ways.

She trusted him. It was a novel notion, and a surprisingly compelling one. So it was really about the money, but the flattery of her trust may have nudged him a little.

It was an unusual arrangement, but in many ways ideal. The day-to-day coexistence would not be unpleasant. He would have every freedom he had ever had, but now with the blunt to pay for it properly. He would finally be free of his dependence on his family.

Yes, financially speaking, he had done very well.

The only cloud on the bright horizon, and it was a very small cloud to be sure, was that while Fleur was indifferent to men, he was not indifferent to Fleur.

In that backyard, while the chickens pecked around his boots and he weighed her offer, that part of the agreement had struck him as rather dismal. When he had held her hand in acceptance, it had taken some strength of will not to pull her into a very different kind of kiss from the one she had just permitted.

That should take care of itself, however. Once he was back to his old life, his attraction would pass quickly. It rarely settled in one place for long.

Even though it was all about her money, she had made

it clear that it was not about *all* of her money. Therefore, when the Duclaircs' solicitor, Julian Hampton, arrived at the gaol to discuss the settlement, Dante did not quibble over the three thousand a year that would be his free and clear, even though in a normal marriage he would have much more.

He did not blink when Hampton explained that the land would also be at Fleur's disposal and that Dante would be agreeing to permit her to use it and its income as she chose.

He even remained impassive when Hampton explained that he could leave the gaol. The solicitor had already spoken with Thompson on Fleur's request, and informed the creditor that Dante's bride would be paying the outstanding debt of fifteen thousand pounds in full.

After itemizing Fleur's terms, Hampton moved on to a fuller discussion of the matter.

"As your family's counselor, I advise against this marriage." Hampton spoke in his most formal tone. He had been a friend of the family for years, but signaled with his voice and demeanor when he fully assumed his occupational role.

"The terms are unusual, but not ungenerous. I am unlikely to do better."

"You are promising to agree to financial decisions even if they are unsound. She could squander the entire fortune not in trust, and you would have no authority to prevent it."

"Then we will live on the trust income. However, I think it unlikely that she will squander all the rest."

Hampton rose and paced over to the grimy window of the gaol's tiny bedchamber. This time Dante had paid Meg the ten pence for some privacy. As Hampton gazed out on the scrubby yard, his entire demeanor was that of a tall, dark pillar of professional responsibility. One would never guess that they had played together as boys, when Dante tagged along during Hampton's visits to Vergil.

"The private agreement has no standing in the law, of course. If you conclude she is not acting sensibly, or break it for other reasons, no judge will uphold it. I explained that to her," he said.

"I think she understood that risk already."

"Yes. It will be a matter of your honor. So she said. I would prefer it only be words on paper. Those can be interpreted and argued. If you promise these provisions on your honor, there will be no recourse except acting dishonorably."

Hampton turned, his face impassive, his dark eyes enigmatic beneath his tousled dark hair. One rarely knew what Hampton was thinking. He was a silent foil to others' wit and verbal excess, an observer of the world. Dante knew that many women found Hampton mysterious and romantic, although men were more likely to think him merely proud and reserved.

"I still must advise against it, for other reasons. I have been making inquiries about her."

"I did not ask you to make any inquiries." Dante kept his pique at the presumption under control, but his jaw tightened.

"St. John and I thought it best to find out if Farthingstone's accusations had any basis."

Hampton was also St. John's solicitor, a position acquired through their common friendship with Laclere. They were all part of a circle of friends who for years had fenced together. When young men, they had dubbed themselves the Hampstead Dueling Society, and Dante had been absorbed into the group after he left university.

"How fortunate for me that you and St. John are my guardian angels."

"With Laclere in Italy—"

"To hell with St. John, and *you*."

"We are your friends, Duclairc. Be angry if you want, but hear me out. Miss Monley refused to explain some of the matters I asked about, and I have doubts whether there were any explanations to give in any case."

"You spoke with her during these inquiries?" The image of Fleur being examined by Hampton's precise, probing solicitor's questions angered him further.

"I also spoke with Farthingstone."

"Damn it—"

"Just listen." Hampton traced the edges of the window's rough stone sill as he spoke. "The change in your future bride after she broke with Laclere is well known. However, recently she has gone much further in her largesse. It is no longer a matter of spending her income. She has sold out some funds not in trust and donated the money to a variety of causes. Most are predictable charities. However, last year she sent a goodly sum, at least a thousand, north during the work stoppage in the coal mines. It was used by the colliers and the keelmen to support their families."

"That only means she does not like to see people starve."

"It also means that she has connections to some radical groups, and not those who work through normal channels. Which in turn raises the question of whether she was only running away when you found her or was actually involved in what was happening on the estates that night."

"I do not believe that."

"It also means, at the very least, that Farthingstone will have very powerful men who will not want that flow of financial support to happen again."

This latter point was worth knowing. No doubt some of those powerful men had the ear of the judges in Chancery court.

"The diminishment of her inheritance has been significant the last two years. The death of her mother appears to have something to do with her increased generosity. Farthingstone is in a position to know the details. He calculates that fifty percent of the land is gone. *She sold it*."

No wonder Farthingstone claimed she was addled. No one sold land. They hoarded it and entailed it and coveted it.

"That still leaves a very large fortune."

"There is more. When asked how she decides which property to sell and when, and which causes to support, she claims to have an adviser. She will not name the man, however. Farthingstone thinks there is no adviser, only a fantasy of her imagination."

"He claims she is hearing voices now? Seeing invisible friends? Surely you do not believe—"

"She is currently planning to sell her largest tract of land, a significant estate in Durham. She inherited it from her aunt Ophelia. Did I mention that her aunt was quite an original? It is in the family, it appears." Hampton continued as if the anger pouring toward him was not there.

"It is in my family too. I don't see anyone trying to label my sisters incompetent."

"There was another aunt, also deceased. That one was strange enough that even the eccentric Aunt Ophelia kept her in seclusion." Hampton just kept talking in that damn, flat, factual voice. "Miss Monley would not say to whom she plans to sell the Durham property, and neither I nor St. John can discover the name of the purchaser. We fear that she is about to be the victim of a swindle. Secrecy is often demanded in such cases, and on this transaction she will not disclose anything at all."

"Perhaps that is because she does not think you have the right to demand the details, just as Farthingstone does not."

"No, but you do, no matter what the private terms of this marriage will be. I suggested that she write the facts down, seal the letter, and allow me to bring them to you. She refused. It is, and will be, none of your affair, she said."

Her response did not shock Dante. Hearing it stated so bluntly, however, made forcefully clear what Fleur had meant when she proposed. His anger retreated as he absorbed the implications.

Separate lives, she had said. Not really married. She had meant it.

"Again, I must counsel you not to agree to this marriage," Hampton said. He did not use the solicitor's voice this time, but the friend's.

"I have already agreed to it, Julian."

"She is in no position to claim breach of contract. St. John will pay what is owed Thompson, and Laclere will reimburse him upon his return."

"Fifteen thousand is a large sum even for my brother."

"I am in a position to know that he can afford it. The viscountess's income alone can cover it."

"So now I am to be bailed out by my brother's wife?"

"It is an alternative solution to your current dilemma. As for your acceptance of the proposal, I can take care of that."

Except Dante did not want Hampton to take care of it, any more than he wanted to rely on St. John and then Laclere to pay this debt. He did not want this alternative solution.

He realized he did not want it for the simple reason that he did not want to let Fleur down.

She needed help, had come to him, and he had agreed to her plan. Maybe she was addled, or maybe she was rational as a clock. In either case, he had promised to protect her.

"Much of what you describe is merely the action of a good-hearted woman, who may be a little eccentric or overly generous, Hampton. If she says she has an adviser, I'm sure that she does. If that adviser is taking advantage of her, I will find out and deal with him."

"What if she will not confide in you? The day may come when she demands your signature on documents you know nothing about, or of which you do not approve. That agreement may mean that you one day contribute to a plan to defraud her."

"I will not sign anything that has not been explained to my satisfaction as financially sound. In the hierarchy of honor, my duty to protect her comes first. No matter what our agreement, she will still be my wife and I will take responsibility for her."

"You are determined then? If so, as both your friend

and solicitor I will aid you, even if I think it unwise. Laclere may have my head, but that is a problem for another day."

Dante had to laugh. "When my brother gets back, I will explain that you did your best to save me and that, as always, I am a victim of my own recklessness."

chapter 5

F arthingstone learned of the pending nuptials with surprising speed. Fast enough to convince the archbishop to delay in giving the special license.

Soon enough to request a meeting with the chancellor, Lord Brougham, so he could lay out his claims that Fleur Monley's emotional condition rendered her incapable of entering into a contract of marriage.

Three days after Dante left gaol, Fleur found herself with him and Julian Hampton in the garden of St. John's house, getting the bad news.

"It will not be an official hearing," Hampton explained as they strolled through the plants wakening to the spring. "However, Brougham was sufficiently concerned that he will advise the archbishop to refuse the license until the matter is settled. He is sure that you will agree that it is best not to wed until Chancery can assess Farthingstone's claims."

"I don't agree at all," Fleur said.

"It is not your agreement he assumes, Miss Monley,

but Duclairc's. Brougham is sure that no man would want the world thinking he took advantage of a woman's weak condition."

"I have no *condition,* least of all a weak one."

She was not convinced that Mr. Hampton believed that. He was so enigmatic, one never could tell what his own opinion was. Also, she doubted he had fought Gregory very hard on this. He had not approved of the private settlement and had asked too many impertinent questions about her affairs.

Dante appeared less than distraught by this development. So much that she wondered if he welcomed it. "When will Farthingstone have his meeting?" he asked.

"He is to give his argument in the high chancellor's chambers in a fortnight. Miss Monley will be asked to attend. I will recommend a barrister to accompany her."

Dante gazed at Mr. Hampton very directly. "Will Farthingstone succeed?"

"Possibly. I should tell you that among his other claims, he is using her choice of husband as further evidence that she cannot make sound judgments."

"I expected a husband to solve the problem, not make it worse," Fleur said.

"Farthingstone says no sensible woman would ally herself with Duclairc's reputation. He says no responsible woman would hand a fortune to a man she had to bail out of debtor's prison. Of course, he does not know of the private agreement, but if he did, it would only make things worse."

"So I will be at Chancery's mercy, after all." It vexed her that her life was being meddled with, by all these men who claimed to have her welfare in mind. Now it appeared that her attempts to thwart them had only expedited her doom.

Hampton stopped to finger some buds on a bush. "I am obligated to advise you to await Chancery's decision, of course."

Dante still appeared unconcerned by the entire conversation. "If we triumph at this meeting a fortnight hence, will that end it?"

"Farthingstone will still be able to bring a brief. He may persist in challenging her competence to contract a marriage, which means challenging the marriage itself. Such a case would be long and tedious and very expensive, in the way such things are. Also, if she is married, that compromises his position in all kinds of interesting ways."

"In other words, obeying the Lord High Chancellor benefits us little and leaves Fleur very vulnerable."

"One could say that."

"Thank you, Hampton. I think that Miss Monley and I need to speak privately now."

With a vague smile, Mr. Hampton turned and walked back to the house. Fleur almost stomped her foot in frustration. "I do not think he is very clever at all. He hasn't helped us much."

"He helped enormously."

"I did not hear him tell us anything except to wait."

"He could not give advice to disobey the Lord High Chancellor, but he let me know that we should. The course is clear, Fleur. We have to elope."

Dante had years ago accepted that if he ever married well, it would either be at the point of a sword or after a secret elopement. A decent family would accept him only if their girl's virtue had been compromised or if faced with a *fait accompli*. Therefore, sweeping Fleur away to Scotland seemed the fulfillment of fate.

The next day Fleur moved back to her house, and two mornings later her hired coach stopped in front of the building where Dante leased his chambers.

He settled in, pulled the curtains, and they were off.

"I think that we should not go to Gretna Green," he said. "Any place in Scotland will do. Once we are out of the city I will instruct your coachman to go north toward Newcastle. It will mean another half day's journey, but with Farthingstone bound to head west if he pursues, we can travel at our leisure."

"We will do it however you think best, Dante."

What a submissive, wifely thing to say. A pang of acute reality struck him. Wifely. *Wife*. The intended outcome of this journey suddenly demanded cold-blooded recognition.

No going back now. The sails were unfurled, the anchor was raised, and the winds would take them to the port of matrimony.

The journey was long and tedious. Even with spirited bouts of conversation and relaxed stops for meals, the hours weighed heavily. Dante fought a periodic tendency to lazily contemplate the delightful ways he could be spending the long ride alone with a woman if the woman was any other woman but Fleur Monley.

By the second day he occasionally lost the battle. Erotic images occupied his head.

. . . Peeling off the simple gray dress and petticoats . . . Sucking the pert tips of her round little breasts . . . Holding her soft, naked bottom as she moved up and down on him, while her slender knees straddled his hips and her fingers gripped his shoulders in her frenzy . . .

Sometimes she caught him looking at her during those reveries. She would break into her warm, trusting smile. He forced an expression of protective solicitation in return.

Both nights they stayed at inns and retired to separate chambers. Of course they did. However, with another woman . . .

The second night the inn was all but deserted. He lay restlessly, picturing the woman on the other side of the wall, hearing the sounds as she turned in her sleep. He imagined her body spread on his bed, naked in the moonlight streaming through the window, welcoming his hands and mouth as the night cooled the sweat of their passion.

The unbidden fantasy left him hard and hungry. He dressed and went for a long walk under the starry sky in order to break its spell.

So much for the flame only burning if he lit the candle. It had been insane of him to agree to this. He should direct the coach into Newcastle tomorrow, bid his leave of her, and hop a ship to the Continent.

He paused under an oak and debated that option. It would be a disgraceful breach of trust, but if he explained . . . Explained what? That the jaded rake found himself unexpectedly edgy with lust? That he lacked enough control to see it through and give her the protection that she had sought with this arrangement? That even fifteen thousand pounds and three thousand a year could not buy a little continence from him?

The abstinence forced on him by recent events probably had a lot to do with this hunger. Back in London he would find the necessary diversion. He would also no longer be in constant proximity to her. Even sharing a house, they would barely see each other.

He returned to his chamber convinced that he had matters in proper perspective. The low flame that would not die said otherwise. He threw himself on his bed, annoyingly aware that he had not wanted a woman like this in many years, and that the last time it had led to disaster.

But that had been an evil woman and Fleur was all goodness.

Still, it would be best to get back to London and out of her constant company as quickly as possible.

"On our return journey could we stop at my property in Durham? We passed nearby it yesterday, and it is not far from the mail road." Fleur made the request as the carriage crossed the northeast border into Scotland. "We could stay at the house there, instead of an inn."

"Whatever you would like," Dante said. "Do you intend to ask my permission about such little things now? It will be a senseless pretense, since I will have no authority in the big ones."

His fitful night had left him churlish, and her renewed presence had only made that damn flame burn hotter.

He saw her surprised reaction and regretted his tone. There she innocently sat, dressed in her blue gown, with a lovely silk shawl draping her delicate shoulders. He had turned his frustration on her like he was some randy schoolboy.

He realized that the shawl was probably new. The white kid gloves appeared fresh too. The bonnet with its blue bow near her right temple, bringing out the rosy tint of her cheeks, was more fashionable than her normal millinery.

She had not had time to have a wedding gown made, but in the two days before they left she had done what she could to deck herself in new finery.

It would not be much of a wedding, but it was all that she would ever have. He realized that her request had been the first thing she had said since entering the carriage this morning. He noticed now the worry glistening behind her serene composure.

She was unsettled, as well she might be. He gave up almost nothing in this marriage and gained considerably. She was the one taking all the chances.

He took her hand. "Of course we can stop and remain as long as you like. But today why don't we just cross back and go to Newcastle and stay over at the Versailles? It is one of the finest hotels in England, and contains all of the newest conveniences."

"That sounds like fun."

He held her hand in reassurance until they entered a large village. They pulled to a stop in front of a stone church. It was well before noon, and he sent the coachman off to find the vicar and another witness. While they waited they strolled through a lane of shops and he bought a hothouse rose from a flower girl.

He handed it to Fleur when they returned to the church door. "It will not be the prettiest flower present. You look even more lovely than usual today."

She blushed and looked down, biting her lower lip.

"You can change your mind. I will understand," he said.

"I do not want to change my mind."

Again he experienced that sense of sharpened reality. The immensity of what they were about to do pressed on him.

He took both her hands in his. "Inside we will speak the traditional vows, but I promise you now that I will take care of you and protect you. I will never raise a hand to you and will never knowingly hurt you."

She looked up. Her eyes moistened and her smile trembled. "And I will take care of you, and be a true friend and helpmate, and stand by you through times good and bad, as long as you want me at your side."

He offered his arm. "Ready, then?"

She took a deep breath. "Yes."

They strolled in the churchyard while they waited for the carriage.

"Married," Dante said. "Getting accustomed to the idea will require some time."

"It certainly will."

"Do you want to dine before we go?"

He could be a very considerate man. It was one of his appeals to women, she suspected. Did he show the same thoughtfulness when he made love? It would explain much. Other men who were just as handsome were not as successful.

"I could not eat now. Perhaps when we get to Newcastle."

They meandered down the path of the small garden.

"You probably always thought that if you married you would have a grand wedding at St. Martin's," he said.

"I never dreamt of that. This was perfect."

It *had* been perfect. Just the two of them exchanging vows of friendship in a little stone church on a bright day. The quiet privacy had stirred her emotions.

She glanced to his hands and remembered how he had held her face at the end. Strong, gentle hands. No one else had existed but the two of them for that moment. His dark eyes had been luminous male depths that seemed to look into her heart. She had felt so connected to him, and her soul had filled with the honest affection of his two kisses. One on her forehead, the other on her lips.

She wondered if he kissed his lovers like that. She imagined that second kiss deepening, and those hands moving. The strange, scurrying excitement that she had known in the cottage scampered through her, followed by a poignant regret.

It seemed that her nature would permit vague wonderings. A fantasy posed no danger. Reality would leave her paralyzed.

Just as well. He did not want her like that. This marriage suited him because it left him free. That dark edge had bared itself this morning on the way to the church. No doubt he had been contemplating the potential restrictions on his pleasure if she did not behave as promised.

An alien pain stabbed at the thought of those hands on another woman's face. Soon, she had no doubt. She scolded the silly jealousy away. She had no right to it, and succumbing would only make her ridiculous.

Still, she had experienced something in that church that she had not expected. She had been given a taste of what some other women knew on their wedding day. She had felt a glimmer of the consummate intimacy that the true joining of two hearts and bodies could create.

She suspected that she would lick at the sweet memory of that moment for a very long time.

When they arrived in Newcastle they took a late luncheon in the Versailles's elegant restaurant. While Fleur nibbled her cold beef she kept looking past Dante's shoulder curiously.

"Does that dark-haired man back there know you?" she asked. "He keeps glancing our way."

Dante twisted to see a man his age reading a newspaper while he worked his way through a plate of cakes. "That is Ewan McLean. We were at university together. His estate is north of Berwick."

"Why hasn't he greeted you?"

Dante knew why. "Excuse me, while I go speak with him."

He walked over and took a seat at his friend's table. "Are you giving me the cut, McLean?"

McLean's black eyes twinkled. "Just trying to be discreet, Duclairc. If you came all this way north, I assume that the lady does not want to be recognized."

"Not discreet enough. She noticed you noticing."

McLean's face broke into a roguish smile. "Very lovely. She looks familiar but I cannot place her."

"Fleur Monley."

The smile fell in astonishment. He peered Fleur's way more obviously. "*No.* I'll be damned. You devil. If you are discovered it will be your undoing. I should upbraid you for corrupting an innocent, but instead I am moved to admire your audacity."

"Miss Monley and I have just been married."

McLean displayed genuine shock. "Say that you jest. You have no business getting married, and you damn well know it. We simply are not the type, Duclairc. Not to mention that if you have tied the knot, my visits to London promise to be considerably duller. I had planned one in a week, but if you have been domesticated there is no point in going."

"Your heartfelt congratulations touch me."

"Forgive me. Of course I am delighted for you. She is quite a catch and I only wish for your happiness. You must excuse me if I see this in symbolic terms that do not bode well for me, however. It is one of those watershed moments of history, like the Vandals conquering Rome. An era of pleasure is ending before my eyes."

"Well, compose yourself and come meet her. You are the first to know, by the way."

"You eloped? Stupid question. Of course you did. Even independent women have someone looking out for them that the likes of you and I would have to dodge."

He brought McLean to Fleur and introduced them. The Scot showed more tact in congratulating her.

"You are on your way back to London?" McLean asked, making himself comfortable in a spare chair and sending for his cakes. He pressed one on Fleur.

"We had planned to stay the night here at the Versailles first," Dante explained. "However, they are full, so we will find another hotel."

"I would say that is unlikely. Haven't you noticed how crowded the city is? A huge wedding is to be held tomorrow. The joining of two great coal families. Everyone in the north country has come for it. I doubt that you will find a stable with space to lay your head tonight."

"I suppose that we could push on until we are outside the city," Dante said. "Could you manage that, Fleur? You have been in a carriage for three days and I know that you must be tired."

McLean had been busy feeding his sweet tooth. "I have a better idea. As it happens, I was not invited to this great wedding, having once been discovered in a compromising situation with the bride's sister—" He caught himself and grimaced at Fleur. "My apologies."

"None are necessary, Mr. McLean."

"I assure you that it was only very slightly compromising. More a misunderstanding—"

"Your better idea," Dante said.

"I keep a suite of chambers here. It serves as my home in Newcastle. Why don't I be the one to push off, and the two of you can make use of it? I had planned to depart tomorrow anyway."

Fleur looked amenable to the suggestion. Dante shot McLean a meaningful glare. "Are these chambers similar to the ones that you keep in London?"

"Much more elegant. You will find them acceptable, I think." He belatedly understood the question's true meaning. "Oh. You mean . . ." He glanced at Fleur. "Not at all. For the most part, these are very traditional in their decor. And the library, while small, is almost entirely composed of the predictable classics."

Dante remained skeptical of "for the most part" and "almost entirely." Mclean's London rooms comprised a sexual play yard. And the library . . .

"You will not be embarrassed, Duclairc," McLean mumbled while Fleur was distracted by a server. "Nor will your bride be shocked."

"I would prefer to delay more travel until tomorrow, if we could," Fleur said, her attention returning. "If it would not inconvenience you, Mr. McLean."

"No inconvenience at all. I am joyed to be of assistance." He rose. "I will have the servants prepare for you. All should be ready in a couple of hours. Duclairc, I will let you know when I am next in London. Perhaps you will call on me." He took his leave.

"What a thoughtful man," Fleur said. "He is a good friend?"

"Yes."

"He appeared a little sad when he left. He thinks that you will have to repudiate your bachelor friends now that you have tied the knot, doesn't he?"

"It is often the case."

"He will be relieved to learn that it is not *your* case."

Her indifference to that unaccountably annoyed him.

Of course she would be indifferent. He wanted her to be. He certainly did not want her resentful and demanding. That would turn this white marriage into a farce worthy of the lowest opera house.

He knew why he was reacting like this. The little ceremony in the stone church had moved him in unexpected ways. It had left him both surprisingly happy and oddly melancholy. It had been the deeper part of him, a part he preferred to ignore, that had experienced the latter sentiment.

It stirred in him now again.

"Have you finished?" he asked. "If so, why don't we take a turn and see the old city."

His beautiful wife dabbed the last of McLean's cake from her lovely lips and extended her little feminine hand to him.

The staff of the Versailles were expecting them. When they arrived at dusk they were ushered into McLean's suite.

Dante quickly examined its entirety while Fleur went to remove her bonnet in the bedchamber.

The *only* bedchamber, he discovered.

He stood in the middle of the sitting room and examined the delicate furniture laid out around him. In London, McLean's sitting room was full of soft chaise longues and deep divans. Every seat invited sprawled comfort and provided convenience for seduction.

He would gladly exchange this room for the one in London at the moment. He would find a way to explain the swing hanging from the ceiling if it meant getting a good night's sleep.

"Oh, my, this is amazing," Fleur's distant voice exclaimed.

He followed the sound through the bedchamber and dressing room to a large tiled closet.

"Look." Fleur bent over a large tub shaped like a shoe and turned a handle on the wall above it. "It comes out warm. They must heat it on the roof before sending it down through pipes. What a novelty. I will have to use it."

She left him. He stared at the contraption and pictured a naked Fleur, slick with water, reclining in it.

"Oh, my," he heard her say again.

This time he found her in the bedchamber, holding a candle high and looking up under the drapes. "How very clever."

Dante strolled to the red, satin-covered bed. Luxurious. Huge. He peeked under the canopy to see what fascinated Fleur.

A large mirror hung directly over the bed and under the drapes, suspended on stiff wires.

"Do you think this is another of the hotel's new conveniences?" Fleur asked.

"More likely McLean added this himself."

She moved the candle around. She did not appear very shocked at all. "He is a very inventive man."

"He prides himself on it."

"Look how it reflects the light off this candle and makes it grow. Why, if you lit several you could read all night almost as if it were day. Mr. McLean must be devoted to books to have come up with such a brilliant solution."

"In his own area of investigation, the man is a renowned scholar."

Their gazes met across the glistening expanse of that satin bed. She froze, as if she suddenly realized where they were. Or as if she read in his eyes the images of reflected loveplay romping through his brain.

"Come to the sitting room and have some wine," he said. "McLean arranged for some to be sent up."

She walked around the wonderful bed. In the sitting room she perched herself on a little chair. "It was kind of your friend to do this for us. I am more tired than I had realized. These chambers are perfectly beautiful."

"Perfectly beautiful, perhaps, but not perfectly convenient, despite the piped warm water. There is only one bedchamber."

She glanced a sharp question to a door on the other side of the room.

He shook his head. "A study."

He handed her a silver goblet of wine, realizing belatedly that it bore relief images of satyrs having their ways with nymphs.

She did not notice. She was examining the fragile furniture of the room. "I don't suppose that there is a divan in the study?"

"Afraid not. I will take some blankets and make myself comfortable on the rug out here."

She peered down at her wine. "It is really not necessary for you to sleep on the floor. You could use the bed too."

It took a five count for him to absorb what she had said. "Excuse me?"

A deep flush rose up from her neck. "It is a very big bed, and we are both very tired and face a long journey. It will be a little awkward, I admit, but I expect over the years this situation will occur again. When we visit people, for example."

His body instantly announced that sharing a bed with her would be a mistake. The very idea had him hardening. Sanity demanded that he make do with the rug.

However, the notion of sleeping with her, even chastely, held an unexpected appeal. He could not explain why he wanted that intimacy, but he did. And just maybe . . .

"You are sure? I would not want you frightened or embarrassed."

"You never frighten me. I trust you completely."

So much for "just maybe." He would prefer she did not trust him. There was no reason why she should, and it was damn inconvenient that she did.

"This is very considerate of you. We will get a servant to help you with that bath. I will wait until you are asleep before I retire myself."

"That is very thoughtful."

She rose and disappeared into the bedchamber. When a manservant came to the door, Dante sent for a woman. He paced the sitting room until she arrived and went in to assist Fleur. Soon the sounds of splashing water drifted through the suite. Images of his wife washing her body lapped against his mind, defeating attempts to remain distracted.

He gladly would bathe her himself. And later lift her from the tepid water and dry her with the soft towel and carry her to that satin bed and take her slowly under the diffused light of that big mirror . . .

The water sounds stopped.

The servant emerged, curtsied, and departed.

After some movement, the bedchamber grew silent.

He checked his pocket watch. He would wait a solid half hour. That should do it.

He entered the study and perused McLean's library. Almost entirely the predictable classics, but not completely. He spied his friend's greatest prize, the only known surviving copy of *I Modi*, the series of erotic engravings by the Renaissance artist Raimondi. He flipped through the graphic images of sexual positions.

All of which were out of the question tonight.

Just as well. Changing that part of their arrangement

would alter everything about it, and he certainly did not want that.

The half hour up, he entered the bedchamber. A candle burned on a table beside the bed, and the mirror spread its pale golden light, dimly showing Fleur's hair streaming down over the satin coverlet. She slept on her back. Her thick dark lashes feathered against her cheek.

He went to the dressing room and pulled off his clothes and put on the nightshirt that his recently rehired valet had sensibly packed. Trying not to wake her, he eased onto the bed.

He settled on his back and watched her in the mirror. She looked so peaceful and beautiful. He had never seen her hair down before. It flowed in thick waves over hands that were clasped atop the sheets on her stomach.

Her lashes flickered and her lids rose. They looked at each other in the reflection. A body's width separated them on the bed and they both lay almost rigidly beneath the mirror's moving light.

"I did not mean to wake you."

"I was not sleeping yet." She glanced down the bed. "This is a little strange."

"Yes."

"But not unpleasantly so."

"No, not unpleasantly so."

She looked at him again in the reflection. "Thank you for marrying me."

He had no idea what to say to that.

She closed her eyes. Her clasping hands relaxed and fell to her sides. He sensed her getting drowsy, but she looked up again. Her brow puckered into a thoughtful frown.

"Dante. This mirror. You don't suppose . . . It is a

scandalous thought to have, but could it be that he put it there so that . . ." A blush deepened the rosy glow of her cheeks.

He reached over and patted her hand. "Most likely it was just to help his reading."

Her small hand turned under his. He left his atop it, enjoying the sensation of palm on palm. He reined in the impulse to roll toward her and make the connection one of mouth on mouth and body on body. There was a simple, pure affection in their handholding, and he enjoyed it more than he expected, but his blood wanted more.

"Good night," she muttered sleepily.

"Good night, pretty flower."

chapter 6

$\mathbf{M}$y aunt Ophelia owned this property," Fleur explained while the carriage followed a little lane through rolling Durham farmland. In the distance behind them a slow cart lumbered, carrying a few servants that she had hired at the nearby village.

"Her husband had died in the war, and her sister had disappeared, so she made my mother, her half-sister, her sole heir. It came to me through my mother."

"You have an aunt who disappeared?"

"Aunt Peg was not mentally sound. She was forever childish. Aunt Ophelia had her live in a little house within sight of the main one, with a servant who cared for her. Then one day she wandered off on her own and didn't come back."

She was talking too much, trying to fill the silence. Dante had been very quiet this morning, as if sharing that bed had made him uncomfortable with her. His manner had pulled back from yesterday's easy friendship.

"She was never found?" he said.

"Gregory and the men of the county searched for days, but to no avail. Ten years later her bones were found in a ravine miles away. She must have fallen and perished there."

"Farthingstone was your aunt's friend? Is that how he met your mother?"

"He has property that adjoins this on the north. Aunt Ophelia introduced him to my parents here years ago, and he became an adviser to them on financial matters. After Father died, my mother and I spent most of a summer here and he and she grew closer."

The coach brought them to an impressive stone house surrounded by tall trees. "I rarely visit here, but it should be presentable," she said. "There is a couple who care for it."

She was relieved to see that Mr. and Mrs. Hill had kept it very presentable. Dante strolled through the rooms on the first level.

"A lady's home," he observed, running his fingers across the light patterned cloth on the drawing-room chairs. "Is this a large property?"

"Not so large. The income is not very significant."

She wondered why she said that, since it was not true.

She realized that she did not want him thinking that her decisions about the disposition of this property were addled, the way Gregory claimed. It might sound that way if she had to explain it to him. Once everything was arranged and worked out, however, he would see the soundness of the Grand Project and sign any deed necessary.

When the servants arrived, she sent one up to prepare two chambers. Two chambers, two beds, two lives—that was the future they began this day. The notion made her a little sad.

Last night had surprised her. She had never guessed at the comfort to be had in lying beside a man. It created a special closeness that she had never imagined could exist.

This morning they had lain there after she woke and sensed that he was alert. She had kept her eyes closed, wanting it to last, not moving so that she could drink in the cozy mood for a little longer.

She rather regretted they would not share that again.

After a light meal they made a walking tour of the property. The day was crisp and a lovely breeze moved fluffy clouds across the deep blue sky. She brought him to a hill about a mile from the house, from where one could look out over surrounding land.

She stumbled on the way up. He righted her and gently swept the grass off her skirts. She was very aware of the discreet pressure of his hand through her petticoats. With any other man it would be improper, but he *was* her husband and friend.

He took her hand to help her climb the rest of the way. The renewal of contact warmed her, and she was grateful that he did not let go when they reached the summit. They surveyed the countryside hand in hand, in something like yesterday's partnership.

"That cottage down there is where Aunt Peg lived," she explained, pointing east. "I am giving that building and the surrounding ten acres to a school that will be built here."

She did not know why she impulsively confided this essential part of the Grand Project. She only knew that she felt moved to share it with him.

"I thought that you were selling this property, not giving it away."

"I will be selling some of the rest, to create an endowment for the school."

"The income cannot be so small, if it can support a school."

Now she remembered why she never spoke of this. Explanations had a way of leading to the parts of the project she should not reveal because they would sound somewhat mad.

"The sale of the land will only provide part of the endowment, of course." It was the truth, but she did not like dissembling.

"It is out of the way for a school. I thought the ones you supported were in cities."

"This will be a special one, for colliers' sons."

"How will the boys get here?"

"There is a coal town about three miles north, and we expect some to come from there. Others will live here during the week and go home on Sundays."

He appeared interested. "Can their families afford to permit it? Not only the cost of the school, but the loss of wages if the boys do not work?"

"We hope to convince families of the benefits of educating boys with the talent and willingness to learn. This school will not just teach religion like most places for the lower orders, but practical things like mathematics and science. When the boys are grown they will be able to manage those mines, not just dig inside them. If the families are poor, the school will take the boys for no fees."

"We?"

"The Society of Friends will manage it. Their schools are well respected. They have agreed to my ideas of what should be taught."

He laughed. "I am sure that they will include a large dose of religion all the same. I approve, not that it did much good with me."

She squeezed his hand. "You are hardly the devil in disguise."

He looked directly at her. For a moment she experienced again that startling connection she had known in the church. She grew very conscious of the warmth of his palm and fingers encircling hers.

He looked away. "You do not know the half of it, Fleur. It would be a mistake for you to forget who I am." He pointed to the north. "Is that one of the school's buildings being constructed over there?"

She rose on her toes to see what he referred to. A rock below her shoe made her lose her balance. His arm caught her by the waist to steady her.

"No, that is Gregory's land. He must be having a new cottage built. Our school's property will stop right down here, on the field beyond the hedgerow, where those men are farming. I gave permission for a tenant to use the land and cottage until we begin building."

She came down off her toes. His arm stayed around her. That scurrying excitement fluttered. He inspected the field and appeared unaware that he still held her.

"Tell me where you will put the buildings."

"The main building will replace Aunt Peg's house because there is already a well there. The outbuildings will go there and there." She pointed out the spots and he leaned closer to follow her arm's directions. He did not seem to notice their physical proximity.

She did. It distracted her so much that her voice faltered twice. The excitement kept growing, filling her with an amazing elation. She waited for the freezing fear, dreading its inevitable claim on her.

"Why not move all the buildings closer to the house?" he suggested. "Then you would have plenty of space nearby for a playing field. Boys need to do more than study."

She said something about that being a good idea, but barely heard herself. The fear had not reared yet to kill the physical response now mesmerizing her.

The excitement awoke her senses. The breeze felt so fresh against her flushed skin, and the day looked so vividly clear. Dante's strength, close but still a little removed, called to her. The light weight of his arm around her waist absorbed her attention.

He still appeared blandly oblivious.

A silly euphoria swept her, as if the blood tingling through her limbs had rushed to her head. A foolish smile stretched without her willing it.

She had to stop this. If not, she would embarrass herself and insult him, and he would not even know why it had happened. She did not want him concluding that he had to stay ten feet away from her for the rest of their lives.

She forced herself to step aside, light-headed still. His vague smile made her wonder if he had known what was happening but had been politely ignoring it.

"Come, I'll show you a little drop in the next hill where there is a small waterfall," she said.

The steep decline was more difficult than climbing up. Once again her skirt interfered and she stumbled. This time his hand reached too late. She began rolling.

She could have stopped herself, but her intoxicated senses loved the dizzying spin. It reminded her of when she was a girl and had deliberately climbed hills just so she could descend like this. Over and over she tumbled, laughing with delight at the childish thrill of it, watching grass, sky, and hedge flip past.

She stopped at the bottom of the rise, near the hedge. She could hear the farmers working on the other side in the field. She gazed up at the white mountains of puffy clouds while she caught her breath and savored a glorious lightness of spirit.

A shadow fell over her face. Dante stood beside her, looking down.

"It has been a lifetime since I did that," she said, as she pushed up to sit. "I think that I will include this hill in the school's property so the boys can play on it."

He slipped off his frock coat and sat down. He laid his coat behind her.

"They can roll down the hill and then lie here and find animals in the clouds. My brothers and sisters and I used to do that when we were children." He stretched out and pointed. "See, there is a dog."

She angled her head. "Its nose is wrong. More of a cat."

"No cat has a tail like that."

She fell back on his coat and raised her arm. "That one over there could be a horse if it had three more legs."

"It will be a unicorn soon if the breeze keeps stretching its head."

They played the child's game for a while, arguing and laughing. They lay side by side, placed almost identically to how they had been in the bed last night. Dante's easy manner had returned, and that delighted her. One of the farmers had moved closer to the hedge. She could hear him humming.

"I see a bear in that distant cloud," she said.

"I see a woman."

"It has to be an animal, Dante."

"I see a woman. A very beautiful woman, happy and free."

She turned her head to find him up on his elbow, looking not at the sky but at her.

His expression sent her blood tingling again. The farmer began singing the song he had hummed, his low melody drifting on the breeze.

Dante reached out and stroked the back of his fingers on her cheek. Wonderful sensations shimmered out from his touch. No fear stopped their path.

"A lovely woman, bright-eyed with a child's innocence, laughing in watery melodies."

She couldn't take her eyes off his beautiful face and luminous eyes. A man's eyes, watching her with a man's intensity. Waiting, no doubt, for her signal that he was crossing a line they had sworn not to approach.

She could not give it. She did not want to. The fear had miraculously not come and she wanted him to look at her like that, the way a man looks at a woman. She wanted him to touch her and give physical form to the connection she felt to him.

He rose on his arm and leaned over her, his head above hers, blocking the clouds. Expression serious and eyes fathomless, he watched his hand smooth down and gently encircle her neck. His thumb brushed a line along her jaw and chin before his fingers traced the skin at the top of her dress. Her breath caught at the force of her reaction to his slow, wandering caress. He looked into her eyes with a piercing acknowledgment of what he was doing to her.

"I am going to kiss you, pretty flower. Friends do, don't they?"

She knew it would not be a friend's kiss. The depths of his eyes warned her of that. She felt no fear at all, but only pulsing anticipation. The only thing that froze was time.

It was a wonderful kiss, more beautiful than she had ever imagined when she permitted herself to wonder. Warm and careful and restrained. Deep enough to speak his intentions, however, and long enough to make her body thrill.

He looked down at her while he caressed her hair and face. He knew exactly what she was experiencing, she had no doubt of that. This was Dante Duclairc. It would take more worldliness than she would ever possess to hide it from him.

He brushed kisses on her cheek and neck. Warm breath titillated her ear. He caressed gently across the sash of her gown, and the sensation of his hand on her stomach affected her whole body.

"If I frighten you, you must let me know."

She nodded, but it would not happen. Not here, not now. She just knew that, and the freedom filled her with indescribable happiness. There could be no room for that cold dread when such warm pleasure and affection saturated every inch of her.

More kisses, building in demand, pulled something wild from her depths. Wandering caresses, learning the outline of her body, left her trembling. A power flowed from him, as if his masculinity wanted to overwhelm her.

Astonishing sensations streaked and quavered, awakening yearning desires in the most womanly parts of her. Her awareness narrowed, focusing totally on those feelings and his command of them. Only the low song of the farmer intruded, reminding her that they were not alone.

He heard it too. He paused and glanced to the hedge.

His gaze returned and fell on her lips. With the gentlest strokes of his fingertips he cajoled them apart. He lowered his head and body and claimed her in a more intimate kiss and embrace.

The small invasion shocked her for an instant, and then a whirlwind swept her up. She embraced the man pressed against her chest, filling her arms with him.

Less restraint now. Deep kisses, skillfully seductive. On her mouth. Her ear. Her neck. Trailing to the skin exposed by the scoop of her bodice. Tantalizing her through the cloth of her gown until her breasts strained with a begging ache that left her whimpering.

Maybe he heard. Certainly he understood. His caress rose to cup her breast with an encompassing warmth that sent her spinning. Those fingers began exploring. Craving pleasure and hungry physicality pulsed down her body, building a shocking focus of need.

He rose above her. Her arms had to stretch to hold him and she pulled, wanting him back. She could see in his face and feel in his body that they were together in this passion.

He glanced once more to the hedge behind which the farmer invisibly worked and sang. He listened for a while before turning his inflaming gaze back to her.

His hand slid under her back. "Do not be afraid. I will make sure that you are not embarrassed. But I want to see you. I have been thinking of little else all day."

The bodice of her gown loosened. He slid it down her shoulders, then pushed down her chemise too.

The breeze shocked her naked breasts. The contrasting warmth of his hand comforted and aroused. He watched his caress follow her curves. She had never imagined she could want anything as badly as she hungered for that touch to continue.

It did, in wicked, devastating ways. The low sounds of her crazed desire filled her ears like a staccato rhythm against the deeper pulse of his breath.

He eased onto her, until his length covered half of her and his leg buried in her skirt between her thighs.

His head turned and lowered. Soft brown hair brushed her face. He kissed the fullness of her breast, and then the tip. Excruciating pleasure shot through her. He licked and nipped and drew, making it wonderfully worse. She grasped him tightly, clinging as utter abandon took over. Not thinking or caring about anything but her body's astonishing reactions, she pressed up against his leg, instinctively trying to ease the itching vacancy that was driving her to delirium.

A new tension stretched through him. He moved completely on top of her. "Part your legs, darling." The low instruction penetrated and she obeyed. "More."

He settled between her spread thighs. The many layers of their clothing could not obscure the intimate connection of their bodies. Like a wanton she leveraged to accept the pressure that afforded some relief.

In her daze she felt him stroke low on her leg. Her essence thrilled to it, welcomed it. If he did not cover her she would have torn the interfering petticoats off, so mindless had she grown. He did not need her help. His hand lined up her hose to her bare thigh, raising her skirt and petticoats as it ascended.

Even as her body welcomed that touch and moved into it, something of her essence retreated. A single drop of the old fear plunked into her euphoria, creating ripples of uncomfortable rationality. She cringed against the dreaded intrusion.

He sensed it. He stopped, and again that tension strung through him.

The farmer shouted to someone across the field just then. Dante looked to the sound and briefly closed his eyes, as if he focused his will on something.

He rolled off her and smoothed down her skirt. "You are right. Forgive me for going too far. This is not the place."

Relief drenched her. Then dismayed her. She realized with a jolt that she had counted on this. Even while she lost herself in the wonderful passion, she had assumed that it would never go too far on the grass behind a hedge while a farmer sang and worked nearby.

In seconds he had the gown fastened again. Stretching out on his back, he pulled her to him in an embrace.

The drop of fear had evaporated as quickly as it had come. She rested happily in the circle of his arm while they both once again looked up at the sky. She gazed at the clouds against the vivid blue, thinking it almost a vision of the heaven she was feeling.

Maybe. Maybe . . .

She knew that he intended to make love to her when night fell. All through the afternoon it was in his eyes and attention. During their casual strolls and light discussions that special something in him shimmered relentlessly, leaving her giddy and clumsy and excited.

She had never guessed that mutual attraction could create such a palpable, physical pull. She reveled in it, enjoying every moment of anticipation as much as she had relished the startling pleasure by the hedge.

But then, while they ate dinner on the garden terrace, another drop of the fear splashed onto her euphoria. Then another and another, until a faint drizzle of misgiving began to ruin her happiness.

She stared helplessly at some white flowers turning into ghosts in the dimming light. With all of her will she tried to control the horrible vise wanting to grip her stomach. A tremble of revulsion shook her.

Please, no. Not now.

Dante reached across the small table and took her hand in his. "Is the evening breeze chilling you?"

"No." Nor, for a blessed respite, was the fear. The warmth in his expression reduced the terror to something small and weak. And, maybe, manageable.

He rose and took her hand. "Let us go into the library anyway, so the servants can finish their duties."

She walked within his embracing arm to the library. A dance was beginning in which he would lead and she could only hope that she had the courage to follow.

They sat side by side on a divan, perusing a volume of archaeological engravings. Acute awareness of his closeness obscured any real study of the images. Did he feel it too? Could he also sense the ugly other thing in her, planted like a choking vine in the pit of her being, casting out a tendril now and then to remind her of its power?

It will not overcome me. I will not let it.

The door to the library stood open and they could hear

the servants completing their work. She took comfort in the domestic sounds. They were not alone yet. But they would be soon.

I can do this. I want to.

Silence slowly descended on the house. Skirts swished by the door as the women headed to their chambers in the attic. One of them would wait for her upstairs, to help her undress.

Dante took the large volume from her lap and set it aside. He shifted to face her, embracing her shoulders with his arm.

A kiss. A lovely, sweet kiss. The fear withered under the light of affection, but did not disappear.

Another kiss. Deeper. The stirring of her body almost made the fear insignificant. Almost.

Please, please . . .

He caressed her face. He looked so beautiful in the candle glow. Beautiful and riveting and dangerous.

"I want to sleep with you again tonight, Fleur. Not as friends this time, but as husband and wife. It is not what we agreed to, but I think that we might make a real marriage out of this alliance. I would like to try."

His shimmering force flowed into her, and suddenly nothing mattered except feeling it forever. His luminous eyes captivated her, as if he saw into her soul. Had any woman ever refused him? Something in the depths of his eyes said that no woman had, but that he thought she might. She flattered herself that she saw something else too. Concern, as if her answer mattered.

I can do this.

"I would like to try too."

"That makes me very happy, darling." He stood and

offered his hand. "Go up now. Your woman is waiting. I will follow soon."

Legs wobbling and heart pounding, she climbed the stairs to her bedchamber.

With every step, the choking vine cast out another killing tendril.

The woman helped her out of her clothes. She slipped on a pink nightgown and nervously fingered its thin silk. She'd had it made years ago, before she went on the shelf. Why had she brought this silly, lacy thing on this journey? To play a child's game of bride? Or because she had secretly hoped this night would happen? She pulled on its matching robe so she would not feel too foolish.

Please, please . . .

The woman brushed out her hair and then left her alone in the chamber. Alone, and defenseless against herself.

Like the monstrous enemy it was, the fear grew abruptly with cruel vengeance, wrapping her heart and panicking her soul.

Brutal images flew through her frantic mind. Filmy pictures of agony and blood and despair. No sounds accompanied them. The screams were silent, formed by mouths twisting inaudibly.

She ran to the window and threw it open to get some air. With more resolve than she had ever mustered before, she forced some control over her disquiet. The tiny corner of calm that she claimed instantly filled with anguished disappointment.

He would come soon. He would enter through that door, and all that she could give him was her rejection or her madness.

Better if she had kept more distance. Better to have not tasted a passion that she could never fully share. Better to have never seen what her deficient nature prevented her from experiencing.

Tears streamed down her face. The chill shaking her had nothing to do with the night breeze. The panic had retreated, leaving only the sickening dread that enslaved her body.

The door opened and she glanced over her shoulder. He had removed his coats and collar. His white shirt gleamed as luminously as his eyes. Her heart split into pieces. This fear knew no mercy at all. It permitted her to desire. It just forbade her having what the desire wanted.

She tried to speak but the words would not emerge. He came over to her and she turned back to the open window so he would not see her tears. He caressed her shoulders and arms and bent a kiss to her neck.

The panic surged. Her whole body involuntarily stiffened.

He stopped.

Neither of them moved for what seemed an eternity. She had never known such humiliation before.

She had to say something.

"I cannot do this," she whispered. "I thought that I could. I had hoped . . ."

"You do not have to be afraid. If you were told stories as a girl, they were probably much exaggerated. I am not going to hurt you."

"It is not that."

He stood behind her silently. She did not have to see him to know that the dark edge had emerged. She could not blame him. It had been heartless of her to do this to him.

"I do not understand," he said.

"Nor do I. I wish I were different. Normal. I have never wished it more than at this moment. After this afternoon, I thought maybe I could be. But I realize that behind that hedge I could be free of this because I knew that you would not make love to me there."

He stepped back with a deep sigh.

She found the courage to turn and face him. "Please do not hate me, Dante. I hate myself enough already."

"I do not hate you. If it is how it must be, then I accept it, as I promised I would. You were honest with me."

"Not entirely. This afternoon I lied, without intending to. To both of us. I am very sorry."

He smiled ruefully. "This is probably just as well for your sake, Fleur. I doubt that I would be a good husband in the normal sense. I would only make you unhappy eventually."

Maybe so, but she would have traded that risk for the chance to learn where this friendship might have led.

He walked to the door. It went without saying that they would not share a bed tonight. Or ever again.

He began to leave, but paused. "It would be best to return to London soon. I would like to leave in the morning."

"Of course, Dante."

The door closed behind him. The cursed, triumphant fear released its hold, leaving her empty and spent.

She sank to her knees beside the window and cried out her disappointment in herself.

chapter 7

Gregory Farthingstone walked through the streets of a city just wakening to a day without sun. Barely able to see in the fog, he aimed toward his destination with long strides.

He hated rising before the dawn for these appointments, not to mention having to walk so no one would know where he went.

Actually, he hated this whole business. Hated the worry and the subterfuge. He detested the vague foreboding and the sense that he inched along a precipice. Mostly, however, he resented playing a game in which someone else held all the best cards.

He turned down a little lane, then hurried along the alley between two rows of handsome houses. Entering the garden of one, he strode to the stairs leading down to the back kitchen door.

Like a damn servant. That was how he visited this house.

There was no choice. He hardly wanted to be seen. All

the same, it raised his irritation. He did not need it to be so obviously demeaning.

The cook was up as she always was when he came. She paid him no mind as he hurried through her fief. A scullery maid sat by the hearth, building up the fire. Presumably they had been ordered to ignore him, but anyone with a few shillings could probably loosen their tongues.

Up above, the butler waited for him. As he followed the butler up the stairs, he noted once again the very fine appointments in the home. Its owner had a taste for luxury that far surpassed Farthingstone's own. He preferred a more sober environment himself, as befitted a bank trustee and man of serious disposition. He would not choose to live among all this color and texture even if he could afford them.

A hot resentment beat in his head all the same. He knew very well how these carpets and chairs and paintings were purchased. He knew all about the legacy that had paid for them.

He found his host in his bedchamber, sipping coffee while perusing a newspaper. The man still wore his robe and had not even bothered to don a morning coat yet. Farthingstone did not miss the reminder of who held the good cards.

The valet poured another cup from the silver server, offered it to Farthingstone, then left.

"Well, this is one hell of a mess, Farthingstone," Hugh Siddel said, smacking the newspaper down on the table that held the coffee service.

Farthingstone did not need to examine the paper to understand the reference. He recognized the notice of Fleur's marriage to Dante Duclairc from ten feet away.

"You said it was dealt with," Siddel added.

"It *was*. Brougham clearly instructed them to wait. I never thought they would be so bold—"

"If you had not hesitated that night, not allowed sentiment to interfere—"

"What you proposed was *illegal*."

"And what you intended was not? At least with my plan she would have been permanently controlled."

Farthingstone paced away. His heart fluttered uncomfortably. The last few months had taken a toll he did not care to assess. An agitation of the spirit caused palpitations in his body that were not healthy.

He forced some calm on both and faced Siddel. "Brougham will be angry that they took this step. He will now be amenable to expediting my petition. Once the court declares her unfit, the Church will put the marriage aside."

Siddel snorted in derision. "Duclairc is certain to fight you. By the time it is all settled, he will have let her sell all the property she owns. He is the kind who prefers money to land. Easier to squander." He scowled and combed his dark hair back with his fingers. "Those damn Duclaircs. Her entanglement with Laclere at least made some sense, but this marriage to Dante truly is madness."

Farthingstone did not have a high opinion of Duclairc, but he had less confidence than Siddel that Dante was a fool. Also, Duclairc might have some affection for Fleur. Siddel's own interest in her had always seemed a little unhealthy.

"You will have to be indiscreet if you want things settled quickly," Siddel said. "Let it be known that she has gone strange. You probably should claim that you saw it in her mother too. You will have to get society's opinion behind you. That will make it easier in Chancery."

Farthingstone's heart thudded again. Fleur was one thing, but Hyacinth was another. While he had hardly married for love, he still had some loyalty there.

He glanced over to the newspaper. He did not welcome doing what Siddel suggested, but there was probably no choice now.

It was Fleur's own fault. If she had just listened to reason . . . but, no, she never would, and now she had gone and married that man.

"If I succeed in having the marriage annulled due to her inability to make sound judgments, she will be unable to marry anyone else, of course." He mentioned it offhandedly, but he wanted to be sure the implications had not been missed.

"Of course. Since you hesitated that night, that plan is now out of the question."

"Then we are agreed. I will try and rectify this unfortunate development. I will find a solution to overcome the complication that this marriage creates."

"I certainly hope so, my friend." Siddel rose and headed for his dressing room. "After all, this problem is yours alone, and always has been. I am merely an interested observer who has been trying to help you out of your dilemma."

A week after his marriage was announced in the London papers, Dante entered Gordon's gaming hall. Sidelong glances and a low buzz followed his progress through the smoky, cavernous room.

He aimed toward a group of young men at tables in the northwest corner. Someone had years ago dubbed the fluid group that congregated there the Younger Sons Company. The name referred to the diminished expectations in fortune and marriage caused by most of their birth orders.

This was the first time that he had seen most of them since his aborted run to France. Some heralded his approach with alerting jabs at their comrades. Each step closer brought more eyes on him.

He took a chair at a *vingt-et-un* table where McLean sat with Colin Burchard, the amiable, blond-haired, second son of the Earl of Dincaster.

Three tables away a young man rose to his feet. With exaggerated ceremony he bowed to Dante. Then he brought his fist down on the table in a slow series of thumps.

Another rose and joined him. Then a dozen more. They all pounded their tables in time. Even Colin and McLean got to their feet. Soon Dante found himself the center of a thundering ovation.

The man who had started it raised his glass. "A toast, gentlemen, to honor greatness in our midst. May we all be punished for our debauchery and sin in the manner he has been."

"As you can see, they are as impressed as I was," McLean said after everyone returned to their drink and gambling. "We exult in admiration that you not only escaped ruin but did so by marrying the wealthy and beautiful Fleur Monley. Only the marriage of Burchard's brother, Adrian, to the Duchess of Everdon surpasses this triumph."

"My brother's marriage is a love match," Colin said defensively.

"Of course it is," McLean said. "As is that of Miss Monley to our friend here, I am sure. More reason to celebrate his good fortune. I am delighted to see you back among us, Duclairc, and so soon after your nuptials."

"My wife is not only beautiful but of sweet temperament. She does not expect me to sit in attendance on her for several weeks, as if we have entered a period of mourning."

He did not add that their one week of togetherness had been an exercise in strained, careful politeness, relieved only by the distraction of settling him into Fleur's house. His wife had not appeared surprised or disappointed to see him leave this evening.

"Very open-minded," Colin said.

"Isn't it," McLean drawled. "Although her mother's husband may not see it that way. I daresay he will fill everyone's ears with a different interpretation."

"Farthingstone? Has he been spreading tales?"

"McLean is just being indiscreet, as usual," Colin said.

"What is my wife's stepfather saying?"

"That you have taken advantage of an addled woman, in whom you have no interest beyond her fortune," McLean said. "Don't give me that severe stare, Burchard. If the whole town is hearing it, he should too, so he can deal with the man."

"Farthingstone has shown a tenacious interest in my wife's affairs. However, I expected cynical gossip from him and others."

"He has been telling 'the true story,' as he calls it. Everyone knows that he went to Lord Chancellor Brougham about her condition and that you were told to wait on Chancery before marrying. Everyone knows that Brougham is angry about the elopement. Everyone knows that she bought your way out of a sponging house with fifteen thousand."

"I'm sure that Duclairc is delighted to learn that his marriage is the tattle of every club and drawing room," Colin said. "You have outdone yourself in tactlessness, McLean."

"That is what friends are for."

Dante gestured to the tables surrounding them. "If everyone has heard Farthingstone's claims, this welcome surprises me."

"The decent men assume that you conveniently found happiness with a rich woman. The scoundrels are reassured to know that, faced with an incredible opportunity, you grabbed it just as they would have done."

"Whatever anyone believes, I want to make it very plain that my wife is not addled."

"Of course not. Anyone who knows you has no trouble understanding why a completely sane Miss Monley would marry you. Women are drawn to you like iron to a magnet, and it seems that even angels are not immune. I wish that I knew your secret. The good ones always run away from me."

"You would not know what to do with one of the good ones," Colin said.

Nor do I, Dante thought.

He tried to force his mind away from thoughts about the good woman to whom he found himself abruptly and permanently tied. She had been all grace and sweetness the last week while she rearranged her home to accommodate his intrusion.

She had turned the study over to him. She had given up the large bedchamber adjoining hers that she had used as a private sitting room, and had refurnished it for the new master of the house. Masculine dark furniture and textures now filled that space. During the days workmen still repainted its wood.

One door had not been refinished. The narrow white door that stood between Fleur's dressing room and his.

She did not lock it. He had discovered that two nights ago, after a quiet evening of reading together in the library. They had barely spoken through those hours, but it had been surprisingly pleasant all the same. Maybe that was because looking at those pages permitted them to be together without looking at each other.

Embarrassment still glimmered in her expression whenever their eyes met. He suspected that everything he tried to hide behind a forced good humor was reflected in his own. Reading those books had let them drop their guard a little. Something of the old, relaxed friendship had returned in the companionable silence.

However, a dropped guard could be dangerous. It had stripped him of the indifference that his frustration and anger had constructed that night in Durham after he left her chamber.

Late at night, raw with desire, he had found himself facing that provocative adjoining door.

The easy turn of the handle implied a level of trust that was hardly warranted, considering his intentions. It had been enough to send him back to his bed alone, however, where he had spent the next few hours making love to her in his head in every way imaginable.

McLean broke into his thoughts with a nudge and a point. "It appears that your arrival has piqued the interest of someone outside our notorious circle."

Dante's gaze followed the gesture to where Hugh Siddel stood by the roulette table in the center of the room. He kept glaring in Dante's direction with dark eyes glazed from too much drink.

"It is probably your recent wedding that has provoked him," Colin said.

"Another man with a peculiar interest in my wife's welfare."

"Peculiar only in the persistence of the interest," Colin said.

"What do you mean by that?"

"He was besotted when she came out as a girl. He and I were friends back then, and I have rarely seen a man so enamored. He even stopped drinking while he courted her. He did not take it well when she settled her affection on your brother."

Dante resisted looking Siddel's way again, but he could feel those bright, liquid eyes on him. Colin's memories explained Siddel's anger at finding Fleur in that cottage, at least.

"Hell, here he comes," McLean muttered.

Siddel's shadow edged over their table like a storm cloud. "Duclairc, good to see you again. My congratulations on your marriage. Fleur Monley, no less. Word was that she had decided never to marry."

"It appears word was wrong."

"Our last meeting at Laclere Park revealed that much more was misunderstood about her than that."

He smiled like a man amused with his own clever wit. Colin leveled a warning gaze at him that he blithely ignored.

"The saintliness, for example. The whole world believed it."

"The evidence of her virtue speaks for itself."

"We both know that recent evidence speaks otherwise. Her alliance with you, for example. Hardly the choice of a saint." He cocked his head in mock consideration. "Unless the rumors are correct, and she is too addled to know her own mind. But surely not. That would make you an insufferable scoundrel."

"Which would make me excellent company for you. However, I assure you that her mind is clearer in its judgments than yours has been for years."

"Then we are left with a misunderstanding of her character. The woman we all thought her to be would hardly agree to marry you if she was in her right mind. Did your brother discover the truth about her? Is that why he threw her over? Since we all know that he was never the paragon he pretended to be, I daresay it was more likely that he initiated her before he dropped—"

"One more word and I will kill you." It was out before he realized it, a reflexive response to the insults being flung at Fleur. The brittle coldness of his voice revealed the icy fury that had gripped him. He meant what he had just said. If Siddel uttered one more word about Fleur, he would kill him.

McLean spoke in a lazy drawl. "Siddel, when you are only half-drunk you are sometimes half-amusing, but you are neither tonight. Show a penny's worth of sense and leave before I hand Duclairc the pistol that I have under my coat and let him make good his promise."

Siddel stood his ground. A snarling smile distorted his face. "Did I hear a challenge?"

"You heard a warning," Dante said.

"Ah. Of course. Not a challenge. You don't issue them, do you? You let your brother fight your duels for you."

Something snapped. Resentments and agonies roared out of time past. White heat flared, burning away the ice and obliterating thought. Dante rose and grabbed Siddel's collar. In the next instant, he slammed his fist into that smirking face.

Siddel flew. His whole body catapulted backward onto a hazard table. Dice jumped, glasses overturned, and players cursed with astonishment as he landed like a dead weight, sprawled unconscious amidst the game.

A curious hush spread from the corner to the whole hall. It held for a few moments while heads angled for better views, then everyone calmly returned to their games. The men whose play had been interrupted merely moved to another table.

McLean went over to examine the damage. He ambled back, sat, and lit a cigar. "Out cold. I haven't seen you do that since we were at Oxford. Here I thought that your marriage might make you dull company."

Dante scowled down at his knuckles. "He was almost out cold when he walked over here."

"The hell he was. That was quite a blow. He certainly deserved it, though," Colin said. He looked over at the body. "I think that I'll get some of Gordon's boys to put him in his carriage." Colin went looking for help.

McLean checked his pocket watch. "I must be gone soon too. I have an appointment with Liza, and her performance is almost finished." He smiled slyly. "Just how generous is your wife? Liza has a new red-haired friend who is breathtaking."

Dante pictured McLean's comfortable chambers with their soft, welcoming furniture. He imagined a few hours taking his pleasure with the breathtaking friend. He thought about the warmth and relief promised if he accompanied McLean, and remembered the bed of nails and the damn white door waiting at home if he did not.

"Not that generous. We *are* newly married."

"Of course," McLean said gravely. A twinkle in his eyes indicated that he had not missed the possibilities left open by the second statement.

Colin returned with three husky men. They proceeded to carry Siddel away.

McLean watched with amusement. "None of my business, but it was just Siddel being Siddel."

"I lost my temper. It happens to all of us."

"Rarely to you." He casually tapped out his cigar. "What did he mean? Right before you hit him? That remark about your brother fighting your duels."

"I have no idea."

McLean rose. "I must be gone. I almost hate to keep my appointment. You will probably start a street brawl and I will miss it. You are sure that you will not come along?"

"I'll join some of the others here."

McLean left, and Dante carried his wine over to the dice. As he passed the spot where Siddel had recently lain, he felt again the man's bones beneath his knuckles.

He would like to say that it was the insinuations about Fleur that had provoked it, but they had only primed him. It was the remark about his brother fighting his duels that made his mind go white and had caused his fist to fly.

He had reacted so strongly because Siddel was right. Years ago his brother Vergil had in fact fought a duel that he should have stood to. Only a few people knew about it, and none of them had ever revealed the details of that cold day on the French coast.

Or so he had always thought.

Fleur gazed at the letter she was writing. The words turned into blotches as her sight blurred. She rubbed her eyes and scratched another sentence. She should be in bed, but she had already tried to sleep, with no success.

She paused and looked around her new, crowded sitting room. A yellow damask settee almost blocked her writing desk, and the apple-green chair near the hearth barely fit. She would have to store some of the furniture. This chamber was only half the size of the one she had given to Dante.

She returned to her letter. It dismayed her that she had not been able to concentrate on this missive regarding her Grand Project. These plans had excited her for two years. She had returned from France to complete them, and had escaped from Gregory to pursue them. Tonight, however, she actually resented the role they played in her life.

She found herself thinking what a sad substitute they were for really living. The Grand Project struck her as just another good deed by the uninteresting, virtuous Fleur Monley.

Worse, they had done nothing to distract her from the speculations about Dante that had interfered with her sleep.

He had not returned yet. She had spent the last few hours trying not to wonder where he was. No, that wasn't honest. She really had been trying not to think about whom he was with.

A woman, probably. Maybe not. Most likely. Almost definitely.

Of course he was.

The only surprising part was that he had waited this long. She had expected him to disappear the first night back in London. It had startled her to find him staying in their home for a week. He had done that for her sake, so that people would not talk.

It had been awkward for them both. The new intimacy of sharing this house had only reminded her, and probably him too, of the other intimacy that she had cut short. The last week had taught her that living with him was going to be very difficult.

Especially on nights like this.

Hopefully, with time she wouldn't even care. Eventually she would barely take note of his leaving. Soon, surely, she would not fill with awe when he came down from his chamber, crisply dressed, as dangerously beautiful as a dark angel, that shimmering quality surrounding him like an invisible halo.

Perhaps next time her heart would not fall like a lead weight when she realized that he was finally going out to find his pleasure elsewhere.

She had not been able to move after he had gone. She had just sat there, fighting the sickly hurt, trying to rationalize the disappointment away, knowing that she was reacting stupidly. It was the bargain. What did she expect? Nothing, really. Nothing at all. Only, that did not stop the horrible sensation.

She could probably sleep now. The hours of battling jealousy had exhausted her. Unwarranted, ridiculous jealousy. She scolded herself again. This was the life that her nature had given her. She had better get hold of herself, or it would be one long hell.

As she closed her *secrétaire*, an unwelcome image flashed through her mind. Dante's face, above her, looking down while he caressed her body in the sunlight behind the hedge, lowering to kiss her in that exploring way.

She began to rise but a sound stopped her. Steps were mounting the stairs. It must be Dante, because the rest of the household was asleep.

Through her closed door she listened to his boots as he approached his chamber. Suddenly they stopped. She held her breath and hoped that he would not notice the light leaking from this room.

The boots sounded again, coming toward her.

She wished that she could fly through the wall to her bed, but the door that she planned to have cut between the two rooms had not been constructed yet.

She hurriedly sat down and opened the *secrétaire* again. She hoped he would not conclude that she had been waiting up to see if and when he returned. That would be too humiliating.

The door opened and he looked in. Seeing her, he

entered with the confident ease that always marked his movements.

"I thought someone had left a lamp burning, but you are still awake. It is very late, Fleur. Well past two."

His glance raked her from head to toe. She became acutely conscious of what he saw. The saintly spinster, writing letters in the shadows, wearing an old bed cap and a plain, serviceable, pink cotton robe over her full, high-necked bed gown. A comical, pitiable image. He had probably just left perfume and lace.

"Is it that late? Goodness, I lost sense of the time." She made a display of closing the desk.

She expected him to leave. He didn't. He paced around, taking in the chamber. "It doesn't all fit in here."

"I will be moving some things and rearranging the others."

"I have disrupted your household and habits."

"Change is not the same as disruption."

He examined the porcelain figures set on the mantel. The polite thing would be to ask how he had enjoyed his evening. She could not bring herself to do so. It might sound like the probing query of a jealous woman.

He turned with a thoughtful expression. "I am glad that you do not mind change, because I have decided that you need to change a few other things."

Her heart kept fluttering, as it always did when he was near her. It was one of the discomforting things that she was trying to learn to live with. Tonight, with the silence of the house looming, it was worse than normal. Or maybe it wasn't the silence, but the lights in his eyes and the way the candles emphasized the perfect planes of his face.

"What sort of changes?"

"Farthingstone has been talking. All of it is around town, including his accusations about your judgment. We both knew he might do it, but I hoped he would show some discretion."

"We angered him, I suppose."

"I want you to go out and be seen. Make a presence in society again. Purchase some fashionable clothes and attend some parties. The best argument against him will be you yourself, mingling with the people who matter."

Not "I think that you should" or "it may be best if you did," but "I want you to." Not a suggestion but an instruction. He had left this house a guest, but, by some inexplicable turn, had come back a husband. Even his entrance into this room, *her room*, had happened as if he assumed it was his right to demand her company when he chose.

"I was long ago struck from most social lists."

"Only because you regularly declined engagements. Call on my sister Charlotte and let her know your plan. She will see that the first invitations come. After that it will take care of itself."

"If you think it would help, I suppose I could try." Actually, it might be nice to move in society again. She had only withdrawn in order to avoid the attentions of suitors. Now that she was married, that reason was gone. "If I am going to reestablish myself, I suppose we will need a carriage. A coach for evenings, at least. Maybe a landau—so we would be able to have it open for rides in the park— will be necessary too. Would you see to that part of it?"

"If you like."

"If that is all, Dante, I think that I will retire."

"Not quite all. I saw you returning to the house this morning. Do you often walk out alone?"

"I have become accustomed to it."

"That should end now too. It will appear that you are careless with both your safety and your reputation otherwise and give Farthingstone more fuel for his fire."

She had no intention of obeying this command. Being free of trailing footmen or maids was one of the only benefits of spinsterhood. No one noticed when she walked out, and no one would care.

Dante lifted one of the figures from the mantel. The movement caught her attention.

"Did something happen to your hand? It looks red and sore."

He returned the porcelain to its place and stretched out his fingers. "A small altercation."

"Are you hurt?"

"Not nearly so much as Siddel."

"Siddel?" The news shocked her. She could do without Dante starting brawls with Mr. Siddel, of all men.

He turned his attention fully on her. "Did you know about his affection for you? During your first seasons?"

"He paid addresses to me, like some others."

"Like many others. So you explained in the cottage when I inquired about his interest. But did you know that it was more than that? That the man was in love with you?"

She could not shake the impression that she was being interrogated. Nor could she ignore the signs that the dark ridge had risen to the surface. If they shared a normal marriage she would think him jealous, but that was an absurd notion. Still, there was a definite husband-to-wife quality to this entire conversation.

"If what you say is true, I was not aware of it. I did not welcome the attentions of suitors. If a man was in love with me, I would not have paid enough mind to notice or care."

Something changed in his expression. A sharpening. A darkening. It flickered in his eyes and straightened his mouth.

"I expect that is true. You would not notice or care."

His flat statement made her uncomfortable. "That sounds like blame."

"Not your fault, but it would be hard for a man to take when he realized it. An open dislike is one thing. Indifference is more insulting. I do not think he forgave you that."

"I am very sure that he never thinks about it anymore."

"I wonder." He headed to the door. "I will bid you good night. I will see about the carriages in the next few days for you."

"Thank you."

At the threshold he paused and looked back at her. Again his bright gaze took her in thoroughly, resting a moment on the pink robe. "I think that there are some other changes that I want you to make, Fleur."

More instructions. To her mind, this had not been part of the agreement.

He gestured to her cap and robe. "Do you always dress like my childhood nurse when you retire?"

"My garments are practical, and no one sees me but my maid."

"I may see you now. When we have a late conversation

again, for example. When you order the new wardrobe, have some prettier things made."

"I doubt that we will have more late conversations."

"I expect that we will. I am rarely in the mood to sleep as soon as I return at night, and it appears that you keep late hours too."

If he expected her to entertain him when he came home from his rutting, he had better think again. "I cannot countenance such a frivolous expense."

He walked over to her. With warm, rough fingers under her chin, he angled her face up toward his. She looked into eyes distressingly similar in their penetrating warmth to the ones she had just seen in her memory. Her skipping heart took a huge, trembling leap.

"You can accommodate the expense, and you will do so because I require it of you. It displeases me to see you shrouded like a poor, old woman. I am your husband, Fleur, and your beauty is mine to enjoy, even if the rest of you is not."

His hand fell away and he walked back to the door.

Her reaction to his touch dismayed her, but a prickly irritation rose too. What did he care if she dressed for bed like an old nurse? His lovers would surely display enough feminine beauty to satisfy him.

"Is there anything else? Any more changes?" She threw the questions at his back and heard them crackle with resentment.

"One other. I want you to lock the door between our chambers. A saint should know better than to taunt the devil."

chapter 8

Gregory Farthingstone avoided looking at the man soiling the library chair. It wasn't the man's clothing that besmirched the upholstery. The garments were actually of astonishingly good quality, and the man well turned out. Only his hard expression hinted at his character. For all the fine clothes, there was no mistaking the sort of man this was.

Well, what did he expect? He'd gone looking for a criminal, and now he was facing one in his own home. A very successful criminal, from the looks of things.

The ease with which he had found this man was shocking. A vague query to a pawnbroker who traded in some of society's jewels had led to a moneylender who bled some of society's sons. A request for references there had resulted in this dark-haired man who called himself Smith arriving card in hand as if he were a friend. The note scrawled on the back of the card, the secret word Farthingstone had said should be used, assured that he was received.

"You make an odd offer, Mr. Farthingstone, and not what I expected," the man said. "What you require is not my usual occupation, so to speak. There's them that do this all the time for men of your cut. Why not go buy a runner?"

Farthingstone forced his attention on his guest. It was the eyes he did not like. Slit and sly, they displayed a boldness that was disconcerting, as if they saw something familiar in the man they examined.

"I do not require a runner. I merely want her followed and her actions reported to me. Any unusual actions, that is."

"Well, now, what do you mean by unusual? There's some things that are more usual than some men want to believe, when it comes to women." A smirking smile accompanied the observation.

"I am not seeking evidence of—It goes without saying that you will not discover that she has a lover. I speak of odd behavior. Eccentric activities. If her carelessness endangers her, for example. If she appears to wander the streets aimlessly. I don't know what you may discover, damn it. If I did, I would not need you to do this."

"No need to get angry. Like I said, it is an odd thing you ask, so you can't mind me wanting to understand just what you expect."

The hell of it was, he did not know himself what he expected. He only knew that he needed as much evidence of Fleur's peculiar habits as he could get. He had to go into Chancery well armed. All the stories he had let slip about her erratic behavior might not be enough.

Despite his reassurances to Siddel, things were not looking good. He needed fresh evidence for his case. At the minimum, he needed to get the court to prevent her from disposing of property while the matter was examined. Otherwise, she might convince Duclairc to allow her to go through with her intention to sell her aunt's property in Durham and build that damn school.

The very notion had sweat dampening his brow.

"You are not to let her see you or guess that she is being followed," he said very sharply. "Nor are you to in any way interfere with her."

"I'm never seen if I don't want to be."

"There is something else. She has a husband. They are not together much, but if she is with him, make yourself scarce. He is the worst scoundrel and may be more alert to being watched than she would be."

"What does he look like?"

"He has brown hair, dresses fashionably, and has a face that causes women to make idiotic fools of themselves."

"You speak of him with some emotion. You dislike the man?"

"I hate the man. He is the source of all the trouble. If not for him I would not need your services. If not for him, I would not be—" He caught himself, remembering that he spoke to a stranger, and one without honor at that.

Those sly eyes narrowed. "If he is such a trial to you, why not remove him?"

Farthingstone stared aghast at his visitor. To have such a thing so blandly said in one's library . . . But the shock did not come only from astonishment. It also derived from an instant of horrible epiphany as, in a split second, he saw how removing Duclairc would indeed neatly solve the entire problem.

"You are never again to imply that I require such a thing. When I had the word passed that I needed a man,

I spoke of someone who could move about quietly and invisibly. I do not seek . . . what you suggested."

The man shrugged. He held out his hand. "I'll be taking the first payment now. My reports will go to that printing establishment, as you want, and you can leave notes for me there too. There's not much cause for a lady to do odd things, is the way I see it. Won't be hard to notice if this one steps out of line. I'll let you know if she does."

Farthingstone ignored the open hand and placed the pounds on a table. He strode to the door, to be away from the whole distasteful situation.

"If you change your mind on how to solve your problem, you just let me know," the man said to his back. "Same money for you and less lurking around for me too. A sure thing as well, and your problem is done with quickly."

Fleur perused a letter that had arrived for her in the prior day's post. It had come in response to a letter of her own, the one she had started two nights ago while she waited up for Dante.

She needed to find a way to accommodate the plans she had arranged through this correspondence. She had been back in London over a week and it was time to take care of a few matters. This was definitely one of them.

Her dressing completed, she went down to the breakfast room. Softly lit through northern windows, it was one of her favorite spaces in the house. The new day always appeared fresh and welcoming through those windows, and the proportions of the room formed a perfect cube that instilled a harmonious mood.

Dante was finishing his meal as she entered. She saw he was dressed for riding.

"I am going out to Hampstead," he explained. "I will also begin looking for the carriages and horses as you requested. Do you have any preferences? Some women are very particular about the colors of both coaches and cattle."

"Since your sister will be taking me to order a new wardrobe, I think I will have enough colors to worry me for a long while. Choose as you prefer, Dante."

"Is that how you will be spending the day? At the shops with Charlotte?"

She wished he had not asked, and mentally slapped herself for inviting the question. "We begin tomorrow. Today I must plan a meeting that I will be holding next week regarding the new school." It was the truth, just not the whole truth.

"We are to be invaded by the Friends? I should probably make myself scarce that day too."

Yes, that would be convenient. Instead of saying that, she laughed lightly, as if he had made a humorous allusion to his sin offending their goodness. Maybe he had.

That was not why she would prefer he not be here, however. She was not at all ashamed of him. She simply did not want anything to provoke questions from him about the school. She had already skirted too close to such curiosity in Durham.

She watched him walk away, with other memories of Durham floating around her, making her sad.

She thought about the letter upstairs. She was glad it had come. Picking up the threads of her life would stop this sighing over what she could not have. Besides, it was past time to do what she had returned from France to see through.

· · ·

"Are you going out, madame?"

Fleur pursed her lips at her butler's query. Of course she was going out. She was wearing a hooded cloak, wasn't she? "For an hour or so. No more."

"May I send a man to hire a coach?"

"No, I will walk."

"Very good, madame. I will send for your abigail."

"If I wanted my maid with me, I would have told her already. I will not need any escort or carriage, Williams."

"Of course, madame. It is just that Mr. Duclairc saw you returning alone from your walk several days ago, and expressed a preference that you not lack an escort in the future."

Oh, he had, had he?

Williams appeared resolute. The servants did not know the details of the marriage and would assume that Dante was now master of the house. And of her.

"If Mr. Duclairc learns of my disobedience, he may express his displeasure to me. However, I do not see any reason for him to become aware of it, do you, Williams? On this matter, I think that we can continue as we have for the five years you have been with me, don't you?"

Williams had no answer for that. Contented that she had thwarted the butler's inclination to switch loyalties in a heartbeat, she left the house.

A half hour later she entered the church of St. Martin's-in-the-Fields. A few petitioners dotted the nave, lost in their prayers and oblivious to the world. She pulled the hood forward a bit on her head so it obscured her face and walked to a pew along the shadowed northern side.

A man sat there.

He rose and made room for her to sit beside him, next to the aisle. "It has been a long time since I have seen you," he said. "I trust your visit to France was pleasant."

She noticed the discoloration and swelling on the cheek below his left eye. She hoped that his resentment over that blow would not affect his dealings with her.

"My visit was very enjoyable. However, it has not been so long since you saw me, and we both know it." She had decided it would be futile to pretend Hugh Siddel had not seen her in that cottage bed. "I trust you comprehended that the last time you saw me, I was indisposed."

"Of course you were. There was no other explanation to my mind or anyone else's."

"If everyone had been as chivalrous in their discretion as in their interpretations, my reputation would have been well served. Unfortunately, someone spoke of it, because my presence there became known to my stepfather."

"Ten men rode up to that cottage. It is possible that Jameson confided what we saw to one of the others. It was an unfortunate business all around, and I am sorry you were embarrassed by it."

"Since it all turned out well in the end, I cannot say it was all that unfortunate."

She thought she saw annoyance flex over his face at this allusion to her marriage. It reminded her of that tense conversation with Dante when he claimed Siddel had once been in love with her.

Her mind stretched back to her first season. She remembered dancing with Hugh Siddel a number of times and a few conversations when he came to call. Ladies warned her mother that he drank too much, but there had never been evidence of it. Nor had she noticed any indication that he was in love.

She examined his eyes for any signs that he was a resentful, spurned admirer. None was evident. He was always polite and congenial when they met.

"I offer my heartfelt felicitations on your marriage," he said. "Although I must confide that some of the partners have expressed apprehension. Your marriage was not expected at all, and a husband's involvement was not part of the plan."

"My husband will not be involved."

"You cannot sell now without his approval."

"We have an understanding on the matter. Reassure the investors that the property remains under my total control. My husband will not interfere. Nor can my stepfather, now that I am married. No doubt you have heard his outrageous claims about me. I am told it is all over town."

"I was able to bear witness regarding Farthingstone's accusations myself, and the investors are satisfied on that count. After all, no one is in a better position to testify to your good judgment than I am."

"Now you can explain that there will be no interference from Mr. Duclairc either. We are going forward. However, I must now express my own concerns. When we first met and I agreed to have you find the purchasers for my land, you told me it could be settled in a few months. That was half a year ago. I expected to receive word in France that it was all in place. Instead, my letters to you went unanswered."

"I assure you I answered your letters and provided full details of my progress. Perhaps they missed you as you traveled?"

"Perhaps. Did you agree to this meeting so you could tell me it is finished, then?"

"Not quite. I comprehend your impatience, but the need for secrecy means that approaching investors takes time and discretion. I am confident, however, that—"

"Mr. Siddel, where are we exactly? How close are we to our goal?"

"I require two more partners. There are several likely candidates, and I am deliberating the best way to solicit them."

It was as she suspected. He was not applying himself to this with proper determination. He no doubt had many such affairs to tend to, and he had let this one languish.

"I would like the names of the investors you have already found, Mr. Siddel."

"My dear lady, I have promised them all anonymity until the entire matter is arranged. They do not even know one another's names. Only I do."

"Since my role is integral, I think I should know as well."

"I must refuse. Even one word in the wrong ear would have serious consequences. Which returns us to the reason some of the investors are concerned about your marriage."

His lowered lids and serious tone caught her off guard. "I do not understand."

"Your husband is not a man famous for prudence. Furthermore, these men find it hard to believe that a woman can keep a secret from a husband, or would even want to."

"Then they do not know much about women."

"May I give them your promise that you will not breathe one word of this to Mr. Duclairc? That you will resist confiding in him?"

The request startled her. She had returned from France suspicious and discontented. She had demanded this meeting so she could express her displeasure, and now suddenly she found herself on the defensive. Worse, she sensed that if she did not make this promise, the whole Grand Project would unravel.

She had already concluded that she would not inform Dante of these plans until all was in place. It surprised her, then, that giving this promise was harder than she expected. In reality she felt a little uncomfortable keeping things from Dante. Dodging the truth this morning had made her uneasy. It implied a lack of trust. Furthermore, he *was* her husband.

But, not *really* a husband. Not in the normal sense. This was the other half of their arrangement, wasn't it? He had his life and his lovers, and she did not ask about any of it and was not supposed to mind. In turn, she had her life and her plans, and he was not to question them.

That was how it was supposed to work, at least.

Mr. Siddel awaited her response. Considering that he still wore the marks of Dante's fist on his face, she doubted she could convince him that her husband's reputation for recklessness was exaggerated.

"Mr. Siddel, did you agree to see me today so that you can bring my promise back to the investors?"

"I am afraid so. Without it I expect several to remove themselves. We will be set back by months, and going forward may be impossible."

If the concerns were that extreme she really had no choice. "You have my promise. If my husband should learn of this, it will not be because I told him."

chapter 9

Dante rode up to the old manor house in Hampstead. Plaster gleamed between its half timbers, bright white from a recent application of wash. The grasses growing in its clearing had been recently cut. The Chevalier Corbet, whose fencing academy occupied the premises, maintained the property in a way that communicated a tidy, rural, picturesque effect.

Recognizing the three other horses tied to the front posts, Dante cocked his head and listened for evidence of their owners. The sounds of metal biting metal drifted to him.

When Hampton had sent the note suggesting they meet here for some exercise, he had not mentioned that other members of the Dueling Society would join them.

Inside the house, Dante entered the small room used for dressing. Despite the chill in the building, he removed his coats and shirt. The first time he had come here to take lessons he had been his brother's shadow, a boy still in university awed to be admitted to this fraternity of men of the world. No one had questioned Vergil's right to include him. In many ways, Vergil was the hub of this wheel, and all of the spokes had been added because of him.

Naked from the waist up, he walked the few steps to the large hall that served as the practice chamber. Inside, two pairs of men sparred with military sabres. They were all in his state of undress, a requirement of the chevalier, who insisted that learning to use a sword while wearing pads meant not learning to use one at all. The result was that most of the bodies displayed a few scars.

The worst one marked the side of Julian Hampton, the solicitor. He had gotten that wound during a practice much like this one, while he sparred with a friend who was now dead. They had been here alone; not even the chevalier had been present. It was not until months later that anyone had seen that scar or known it existed.

Dante watched Hampton conduct his deadly dance with Daniel St. John, thinking about that scar and the private practice that had caused it. No one had ever asked Hampton for the details, although the scar hinted at mysteries in a story everyone thought was completely known. No one ever spoke of the man who had inflicted that wound or about the events surrounding him that had involved every person now gathered in this Hampstead house.

Dante doubted he would be thanked when he broke that silence today.

He had not brought his own sabre, so he took one from the wall near the entrance. The sound of its removal from its scabbard stopped the clashing metal behind him.

The aging chevalier hailed him. "*Bon*, I am glad you are here. Take my place. Adrian is exhausting me. This old man can no longer meet such skill for long."

"This young man is incapable of meeting such skill for even a minute," Dante said as he took the chevalier's place. "Try not to kill me, Burchard. We both know this is not my weapon."

"From what I hear, your best weapon now is your fist," Adrian said.

Adrian had no doubt gotten a detailed description of the damage that fist had done at Gordon's. He was Colin Burchard's younger brother and the third son of the Earl of Dincaster. Except that everyone knew he really wasn't the earl's son and was only Colin's half brother. His dark, Mediterranean features and hair had branded him as a bastard from the day he was born. Since his marriage last year to the Duchess of Everdon, Adrian had ceased pretending the facts were other than they were.

Not for the first time, Dante thought about the ways in which temperaments forge friendships. Of the two Burchards, he was more likely to spend time with the elder Colin than with Adrian. He was more comfortable with Colin's carefree manner than with Adrian's darkly mysterious one.

Perhaps that was because he knew that for all of his elegance and good humor, Adrian Burchard was a dangerous man. Dante was not flattering Adrian in requesting to be spared from damage. Adrian had actually killed men with his sabre, most recently in a duel eighteen months ago.

"Colin probably exaggerated the skill of my fist. It was a small scuffle."

"Siddel is still wearing the brand on his face and stares daggers at anyone who asks about it."

"Then I had better practice, in case he intends to send pointed weapons in my direction."

"Since I have the advantage here, let us go shoot later, where you have learned to excel. It will even the score."

Dante was in the process of taking his position when that overture came. He proceeded with his salute.

In that moment, however, he realized that the Dueling Society had arranged this. They already knew the questions he would ask and had designated Adrian Burchard as the person to answer them.

Water splashed in basins as the four men washed and dressed. Dante threw aside his towel and reached for his shirt.

Julian Hampton came over to tie his cravat in the mirror tacked to the rustic wall. He appeared oblivious to the rest of the mirror's reflection. For a handsome man, he displayed no vanity, and no awareness of the way women flirted with him. To Dante's knowledge, Hampton strolled past the gauntlets the ladies kept throwing, apparently oblivious to the way they littered his path.

"Our barrister sent an appeal to Chancery, arguing against Farthingstone's right to be involved in the matter of your wife," he said quietly. "He is rightly raising the whole issue of jurisdiction as well."

"There is no need to whisper. I am sure that everyone here knows what is happening. St. John certainly does."

"Not the specifics of my actions. St. John respects my discretion on your behalf, just as he demands it when I act on his."

Dante looked to where St. John buttoned his waistcoat, and then to where Adrian Burchard loitered by the window. "You all think I seduced her, don't you?"

"It is forgivable. She is very lovely and, if I may say, very interesting."

"I prefer hearing that to what you implied during our conversation in the sponging house."

"You have behaved honorably in marrying her, and that is all that matters to any of us." He picked up his hat and riding whip. "I must return to the city. I will keep you informed of developments."

His departure left Adrian and St. John. The latter did not appear ready to follow Hampton out to the horses.

"St. John, Duclairc and I were planning to go shoot before we rode back. Why don't you join us?" Adrian posed the offer as if it hadn't been planned.

"Perhaps I will do that."

"Splendid," Dante said. He had intended to question all of them. Two would be enough, however.

Dante had not always been good with a pistol. As a young man he had been as indifferent to this weapon as to the sabre. Both had been nothing more than sport to his mind.

Which was why, when the time came when skill mattered, his brother had taken his place in the duel he should have fought.

He fired his fourth shot into the target tacked to the tree deep in the woods behind the chevalier's house. As he reloaded, his companions took their turns.

St. John had perfect aim, and Adrian's had improved over the years. Not as much as Dante's own, however.

After that episode, he had never treated this or fencing as mere sport again. For two years he had practiced relentlessly at both. No one in the Dueling Society had ever commented on his new commitment.

"What did Colin tell you about that altercation with Siddel?" he asked Adrian.

St. John busied himself reloading his pistol, but turned so he was part of the conversation.

"That he was insulting your wife and your marriage."

"I should have called him out, but he was drunk."

"Colin also indicated that your fist actually flew after Siddel made an allusion to Laclere fighting your duels for you."

"Did Colin understand the allusion?"

Adrian set his pistol down. "He did not, nor did he even realize it was that comment that set you off. However, you are wondering if any of us have spoken about that day, aren't you?"

"Someone did."

"It could have only been a metaphor," St. John said.

"He *knew*. It was in his eyes and his sneer. It was no allusion to my brother's support."

"He did not learn it from either of us," Adrian said. "I have spoken of it to no one, not even my brother. Nor has St. John here. It goes without saying that Laclere would never divulge what happened, and I think it safe to say that Hampton holds greater secrets in his head than this. He barely talks at all, let alone gossips."

Dante knew all of this. He had almost hoped that one of them had been indiscreet, however. It would have provided a simple, if infuriating, explanation.

"There were others there that day," St. John said.

No one spoke for a while. They all knew they were broaching a subject that everyone hoped had been put in the past.

"Wellington would never speak of it," Adrian said.

No, the Iron Duke never would, Dante thought. If that duel became known, it would provoke questions that would be damaging to important men.

"Nor would Bianca," St. John said.

Certainly not. It would be easier to imagine Vergil breaking silence than his wife, Bianca.

"Nigel Kenwood has his own reasons for keeping silent," Dante said.

"Well," St. John said. "That leaves the woman."

The woman.

Dante felt his face tighten at the reference. An ugly anger entered his mind.

The woman who had used his conceit and arrogance to her own ends. The siren who kept stepping back, luring him to follow, until she had him wrecked on the rocks of his own lust. The one woman he had wanted too much, mostly because she did not yield.

He had been young and stupid and vain. The cost of victory when she let him catch her had been devastating.

"Does anyone know what became of her?" he asked.

"She remained in France for a few years. I saw her once, from a distance, when Diane and I were staying in Paris six years ago," St. John said. "I heard that she then went to Russia."

"I am sure that she has not been back to Britain," Adrian said. "Wellington all but threatened to hang her with his own rope if she returned. She is not a fool."

No, not a fool. A bitch from hell, but not a fool.

"It is possible she spoke with someone, who in turn traveled here and spoke to Siddel, but I think it unlikely," St. John said. "Not a word of what she knew ever got out. If she wanted to do harm, describing that duel was the least of it."

"I think she understands that breathing one word of any of it could be dangerous for her," Adrian said.

Dante had a memory suddenly of Adrian going into a cottage on the French coast and emerging with a woman some time later. He recalled the hard look on Adrian's face as he followed the beauty into the yard where her partner in crime had just bargained for her freedom.

"There is one other way that Siddel could have known of it," Dante said. "If he was involved in those crimes, she would have had a very good reason to send a letter directly to him, telling him what happened."

"Possibly," St. John said. "There may be no way to know for certain, unfortunately."

Maybe not, but Dante knew he would have to try now. If Siddel had been involved in the events leading to that day, he wanted to know.

He stepped forward and raised his pistol. Hugh Siddel had suddenly been complicating his life in all sorts of ways. With no planning or intention, their lives had become entwined.

Fleur formed part of that knot too. Siddel's interest in her was troubling. Had he been the one to inform Farthingstone that she was in the cottage at Laclere Park? If so, Siddel knew Farthingstone was nearby in the county that night.

"Has either of you seen anything to suggest that Siddel has a friendship with Farthingstone?" he asked.

"I cannot recall ever seeing them in conversation," St. John said. Adrian nodded agreement.

"Whom *do* you see in conversation with Siddel?"

St. John thought about that. "He is often at the Union Club when I go there, no doubt plying his schemes among the men of trade and finance who are members. The only association of his that I noted is one with John Cavanaugh, who is a factotum of sorts to the Broughton family of Grand Alliance fame. They are sometimes head to head in quiet talks."

The Grand Alliance was the cohort of families grown wealthy off the coal of the northern counties. The Broughtons were one of the few aristocratic families to have enriched themselves along with the men of lesser birth.

Dante raised his pistol. He knew Cavanaugh from their days together at university. Perhaps he would use his own membership in the Union Club and renew that acquaintance.

He sighted his aim with careful precision.

chapter 10

Hugh Siddel moved through the knot of buyers as a bay gelding stood on display at Tattersall's. Bids bounced off the timber roof of the open-air shelter as the auction began.

Hugh made his way to a man standing on the edge of the little crowd. The man's dress and demeanor marked him as a gentleman. Carefully styled blond hair showed beneath his hat, and a small, womanish mouth pursed in his long, bland face. When he saw Hugh approach he stepped back a few more feet.

"All is in hand," Hugh said, looking at the gelding and not his companion. "I met with her two days ago. Our plans remain private, and she understands the need for secrecy to continue. She has told her husband nothing, nor will she until all is arranged."

Since all would never be arranged, that was no problem.

"An odd promise from a new bride."

"Isn't it." Hugh had been surprised and delighted by

how easy it had been to extract that promise. It had opened possibilities about all kinds of other deceptions.

"And the delay?"

"She understands that such things take time." The news of Fleur's marriage had badly displeased this particular partner. It would not do to admit Fleur's impatience.

He thought about the meeting at St. Martin's, and how pretty her eyes had looked as they peered out from under the lowered edge of her hood. The poor thing had married Duclairc to avoid scandal. She obviously held no real affection for him.

If Farthingstone had not been such a coward—well, there was no profit in dwelling on that. In the least, however, Farthingstone should have gone to that cottage at once and taken her back. But no, Farthingstone had sent word to London and then waited for the bailiffs, and now look where Fleur was.

He struggled to block out images of Fleur in Duclairc's bed, but they snuck into his head anyway, inciting the livid anger that they always brought. It was infuriating that she was tied to that wastrel forever.

Or until Duclairc died, at least.

"What about Farthingstone?" his companion asked.

"He remains ignorant and useful. He knows nothing of my relationship with her on this matter, nor of mine with you."

"I do not want them reconciling. If they do and she grows impatient, she may turn to him. He can effect in a month what she wants. Thank God she did not go to him to begin with."

"Rest assured that he does not want that land sold either. Farthingstone represents no challenge or danger. He seeks control of her and that land for his own reasons. If he succeeds at Chancery, we are safe. If he doesn't, we go on as we are. She relies on me on this matter, Cavanaugh. I can keep her dangling indefinitely."

"Assuming that Duclairc doesn't get suspicious."

"He also represents no challenge or danger."

Cavanaugh angled his head and caught Siddel's eye. Hugh turned his attention from the bidding when he saw the subtle smirk on the face examining him.

"I would not dismiss the man, Siddel. He and I were at university together. Duclairc was a lot of fun, always in trouble, good humored and devil-may-care."

"It appears nothing has changed."

"Yes, well, the thing is, when it was all over it turned out he had done very well in his studies. He was the best mathematics scholar while I was there."

"So, he can add. Your point is?"

"My point is that he is far from stupid. Also, it appears that when he sets his mind to do something, he accomplishes it."

"So long as he does not turn his mind to interfering with us, what do you care?"

"As it happens, I wonder if he *has* turned his mind to that."

The suggestion startled Hugh. "What makes you say that?"

"He is a member of the Union Club, but rarely comes. I do not think I have seen him there in years. Imagine my surprise, then, to find him sitting down with me last night."

"He is friends with St. John and some others who frequent the club. No doubt he was meeting them and paused to speak with you because of your old acquaintance."

"Possibly. Mostly we spoke of the usual things, politics and horses and whatever. However, toward the end, he cleverly moved me to another topic."

"What topic was that?"

"You."

Hugh forced a bland, bored expression, although this revelation annoyed him. "He lost a large amount to me some weeks ago, and then he and I had an argument last week. If he is curious about me, it is a personal matter, and not related in any way to my business with you."

"I see that you still wear the remnants of that argument on your face. I hope that you are correct. I am out on a limb with you, and we are both now indebted to powerful men. You will receive no more payments if I think that you have lost control of the matter. Furthermore, I will have to consider other solutions if yours falls apart."

"It will not fall apart. She trusts me."

She did not trust him. Fleur admitted that to herself after several days of ruminating on her meeting with Hugh Siddel.

He had distracted her by raising those concerns about her marriage. She should have pressed him for the names of the investors before they parted. If she knew their identities, she could use their reputations to find the rest of the participants herself. It vexed her that they were so close but that Mr. Siddel expected her to simply wait while he did things in his slow, plodding way.

She could not leave it all to him, that was clear. She

needed to learn who had thrown in already and do a little wooing herself. She was not without wealthy associates. Even some of the Friends had invested in such partnerships in the past. . . .

A feminine hand moved in front of her face, turning a colored fashion plate. The gesture jolted her out of a trance of contemplation on the problem.

"Now I know why mothers so enjoy it when their daughters come out," Charlotte said as she pushed an image of a gown in front of Fleur's nose. "Helping someone else buy a whole new wardrobe is almost as wonderful as purchasing it for oneself. This is even better than doing it for a daughter, since I won't have to face the bills of exchange."

Large bills, and getting bigger, Fleur thought. She sat across a table from Charlotte under the expectant eyes of the third modiste whom they had visited, choosing designs for new gowns. The day clothes had been expensive enough, but Madame Tissot had just convinced her to order three evening designs that would prove exorbitant.

She had always loved beautiful clothes, but it had been years since she had indulged in this feminine pastime. She was out of practice in defending her purse against the seduction of the colors and textures.

All of the modistes had smelled her vulnerability. One glance at her simple dress had also informed them of the work to be done. They had shown no mercy.

"That gown is perfect," Charlotte said. She had accepted the mission to relaunch Fleur in society with enthusiasm, and had planned the shopping excursions with meticulous care. "You must choose it."

She studied the plate that Charlotte favored. It showed a

lusciously deep-violet ball gown. Madame Tissot cocked
her tawny-haired head in question. Fleur held the plate up.
Extravagant. Excessive. Gorgeous. "Yes, this one, I think."

"*Bon*, madame. A superb choice. Four ensembles of un-
surpassed loveliness you have chosen. Now, perhaps you
would like to see the plates for garments more intimate?
The most important gowns are the ones worn in privacy
with a husband, *n'est pas?*"

The modiste walked to the shelf, holding the plates.

"I think that I am quite done, thank you."

"Oh, you have to see them," Charlotte whispered.
"Some are quite shocking, but in the most elegant way. I
always ordered one when I had exceeded my allowance. I
would wear it the same night I confessed to Mardenford
that I had overdone it. It made for a very short scold."

Fleur envied the way Charlotte spoke of her late husband, Lord Mardenford. They had been young when they
married, and everyone could tell they were much in love.
After three happy years, however, the young baron succumbed to a fever. Charlotte had grieved intensely and
then gotten on with her life. She always spoke of him
freely as she did now, and one never felt that his memory
was painful to her.

Three perfect years. Three years of consummate love
and unity. Charlotte acted as if they had been enough to
sustain her for a lifetime.

"I am suddenly exhausted and could not face another
stack of plates. As it is, I wonder that I will have the presence of mind to choose fabrics."

The modiste regretfully returned the designs to their
shelf. "Perhaps another day, when you come for your
fittings."

"Perhaps."

Fleur scheduled those fittings, then she and Charlotte walked down to Oxford Street. After an hour at a draper, choosing fabrics, most of the afternoon was spent.

"If you are tired, we should visit that last warehouse another day," Charlotte said. "Let us go to Gunter's for an ice and check our list to see where things stand."

Charlotte's coach took them to Berkeley Square, and her footman went into the confectionery to find a server. Soon two ices arrived at the carriage for their refreshment.

"Diane St. John told me all about the brawl," Charl confided after she had enjoyed a few spoonfuls. "Well, not really a brawl, since Siddel didn't have a chance to land a blow. St. John heard about it at his club and told Diane the next morning. I am proud of my brother for thrashing Siddel after the man cast aspersions on your marriage. Very dashing, I say."

Fleur had not realized that the fight with Mr. Siddel had anything to do with her.

Charlotte handed her empty dish and spoon out to the footman, then pulled out the paper that listed the wardrobe she had decided Fleur needed. Together they ticked off the numerous purchases made the last few days. Gowns and dresses and gloves and wraps and bonnets and petticoats and shoes.

"I think that we overdid it," Fleur said.

"Nonsense. Your restraint was annoying. If self-denial has become ingrained, tell yourself that you do it for my brother. It would reflect on him if you looked unfashionable."

Charlotte stuck her nose to the list again. "Are your

feelings hurt because he has been going out every night?" She asked it very casually.

"You know about that too?"

Charl glanced up with chagrin. And sympathy.

Fleur swallowed her embarrassment. She would have to learn to ignore looks like that. She must never let anyone know that her heart broke every night when Dante walked out the door. The familiar hollowness crept through her, ruining her mood.

"It is very normal, Charlotte. I am sure that Mardenford went out in the evening too."

Charl's expression said it all. That of course Mardenford had done so, but that a man's visit to his club or the theater was one thing, and Dante's long hours on the town were another. That Mardenford's company had changed with marriage, but that Dante's had not. That Dante was undoubtedly up to things that a wife might not be expected to suffer stoically.

Unless she had a special understanding with him, that is.

She wondered if Charlotte had heard some specifics, such as whether her brother had already taken another mistress or lover. She may even know the woman's name.

Fleur hoped she would be spared confidences on that. Casual indulgence with anonymous women would be bearable. An ongoing liaison with a particular woman would be torturous to know about. Just admitting the possibility provoked a desolate sadness.

"That is very understanding of you," Charlotte said through pursed lips. "I had rather hoped—"

"Do not distress yourself on my account."

"Well, he had better be discreet or I will give him a

good scolding. And when Vergil returns, he will do more than that, I daresay."

Vergil. Fleur had been trying not to think about the Viscount Laclere's inevitable return.

"He is expected soon?"

"They will be delayed a week or so. I received a letter yesterday. Penelope took ill, and they will stay in Naples until she is well. Vergil wrote that we are not to worry. It is not serious, but they did not want to risk her on a sea voyage. When they get back, they are in for a wonderful surprise, because Dante asked that I not write and tell them about your wedding."

"Breaking the news in a letter may be the wiser choice."

"You do not expect him to disapprove, do you? Surely not." Charlotte patted her hand. "That is long in the past, and he and you remained good friends. He will be happy that Dante found someone as good as you."

Approval and happiness were not the emotions that Fleur anticipated seeing in Laclere when the time came to face him. He, and he alone, would suspect immediately just how thoroughly the marriage was a fraud.

"Now," Charl said. "Tell me about your jewels so we can decide if you need to buy or hire some more."

chapter II

The meeting to plan the boys' school ended at two o'clock. Fleur escorted her ten guests to the door in order to have a few private words with some of them.

They took their leave with the same blank-eyed graciousness that had marked their behavior since they arrived. Everyone was pretending not to notice that Fleur's dress today contrasted starkly with her normal ensembles.

No one had commented upon the fact that her blush, wide-skirted muslin set her apart from their own practical dark hues. The women had refrained from asking what had brought about this change in her.

That was because they didn't need to. As they filed down to the street, the reason drove up in a handsome open landau. Their critical eyes took in the elegant carriage and the dashing, beautiful man holding the reins.

Fleur read their minds. The unspoken consensus in this circle of society was obvious. Dante Duclairc, the wastrel and libertine, had turned Fleur Monley's head and was in the process of ruining her completely. The implications for her charitable work had coerced them to develop a schedule for building the school. They wanted it done before Dante spent all the money.

Fleur welcomed the new determination on the school. Unfortunately, it had been over a week since her meeting with Mr. Siddel, and she had received no indication that he had yet found the two additional partners. Her mind considered her options while she sent off her guests.

Dante hopped down and greeted the departing Friends and vicars and reform ladies.

"You move in elevated circles in your charitable work, Fleur," he said when they were gone. "I did not know that you counted the famous Mrs. Fry among your conspirators."

"Her judgment is respected, and I have never had reason to regret supporting her causes. She was kind enough to agree to be a trustee of the school."

"The members of Parliament whom she petitions on her reform projects think that she is an eccentric nuisance."

"No more than I am, Dante."

He laughed, and turned her toward the carriage. "What do you think of it? Old Timothy over in the borough got it, along with the matched pair. Brought it in from Hastings two days ago, and it is as fine as he promised. The horses are better than I expected, and two more are coming. They will do for the coach when it is finished too."

The carriage and its brass fittings had been scrubbed and polished until it looked like new. Two strong young chestnuts glistened in front.

A young man, no more than eighteen, held the horses. He had come in the landau with Dante and now surveyed the house with naked curiosity. He had a half-starved look to him. An old brown livery coat hung on his skinny frame. Wisps of straw hair poked out from beneath a shapeless, low-crowned felt hat.

"That is Luke," Dante explained quietly. "He loiters about Timothy's yard, picking up odd hires. He followed me all around town the last few days once he learned that I was buying a carriage. He offered to serve as coachman and groom for a chamber and meals."

"Are you sure he can manage it? He appears almost frail."

"He is stronger than he looks. He worked in the pits up north as a lad. I have decided to try him for a few weeks, while we decide if we want more servants for the equipage. He will look presentable once I clean him up."

Luke noticed her examining him and looked away. He tried to appear as if he did not care what she decided, but his drawn, pinch-featured face and cautious eyes betrayed his desperation.

It touched her that Dante had taken pity on the young man. "He can live in the room atop the carriage house, of course. However, we should pay wages even if he is young and inexperienced."

"More experienced than you would think. He has been dawdling around stables all his life. He has a natural hand with the animals and has handled a pair before. Get in and we'll see how he does. He can drive us."

He called to Luke and then handed her into the carriage.

"Where are we going?" she asked while Luke moved the horses to a slow walk.

"I thought that we'd take a turn in the park first, then go to the city. Hampton wants a meeting, and I sent word that we would visit him in his chambers."

Luke drove through the narrow streets very cautiously.

He took the first corner too broadly and refused to permit the horses more than a funereal pace.

Dante sat beside her, keeping one eye on the new coachman's progress. When they got to the park he instructed Luke to bring the pair to a trot.

The horses took the signal with gusto. An unexpected swerve to the left sent Fleur sliding up against Dante.

He moved his arm around her and calmly gave his new coachman some pointers.

"He has never handled a landau before, has he?" she asked.

"He is doing fairly well. Don't worry. If he loses control, I will take over." He took her hand in reassurance. "I will not let you come to harm. Take the path on the left, Luke, and keep them on it. Watch the right horse. He is the one who tries to break stride."

Getting on the path squashed Fleur closer to Dante. His embrace tightened. It felt very snug and secure in his arm and she did not try to move away. He continued giving Luke instructions.

"Your day has been pleasant?" he asked blandly, as if every curve on the path did not mold them closer together. The proximity, even for safety's sake, had started a silly tingling all through her. He began absently caressing her inner wrist with his thumb, in a slow manner that suggested he was not even aware of his action.

She was. A significant portion of her was aware of nothing else. The slow, velvety strokes mesmerized her.

She struggled to find her voice. "The meeting was most productive. Normally we talk for hours and accomplish little, but today everyone seemed intent on moving forward. If we are going to keep to the schedule that we set for opening the school, I will have to transfer that land to the trustees and also sell some property in the next few months to pay for the building."

"Perhaps you should mention that to Hampton when we see him. He could help."

Up and down, circling, circling—the touch on her wrist sent shivers up her arm, into her body. "I need to decide which land first. I ultimately intend to sell those farms around the school itself, but for now I think the ones in Surrey that my father left me would be easier. What do you think?"

"I am incapable of giving advice, since I was not aware that you hold land in Surrey and know nothing about its quality or income. Unlike most new husbands, I never received an accounting of your property and worth."

"That was an oversight. Things happened so quickly. I apologize. Of course you have a right to know."

"Not really. It is yours to control. One more way in which our union is out of the ordinary, and I assure you that I do not mind." Something in his tone suggested that he did mind, a little.

The wandering caress had her thoroughly flustered now. She was sure her face was flushing. She should extricate her wrist from this tiny assault, but she could barely move. Nor did she really want it to end.

She tried to distract herself. "You will be happy to learn that you were correct about Charlotte's help. Two days ago I accompanied her on a call on Lady Rossmore and she indicated that she would invite us to her ball two weeks hence. Do you think I should accept?"

"Certainly. You will attend looking beautiful and

heavenly and completely unaddled. It will show Farthingstone's claims for the nonsense they are."

She thought about entering a ballroom for the first time in ten years and facing those curious eyes. They would have all heard Gregory's stories. Her stepfather might even be there. Her appearance, her manner, even her conversation would be scrutinized.

She instinctively cowered a little nearer to Dante. He had been occupied with giving Luke directions to the streets, but he turned into the subtle movement and looked down at her.

His face, so close that she could feel his breath on her cheek, blotted out her sense of everything else. His sensual vitality slid around her as if he wrapped them both in one cape.

She swallowed hard, very conscious of his arm surrounding her. And the hard body pressed along her side, snug against the side of her breast. And the light, delicious touch on her wrist.

Gentle amusement sparkled in his eyes, as if he recognized her foolish, feminine reaction. Of course he did. He had seen it often enough in his life.

She saw something else in his long gaze, however. A dangerous, calculating light. Like a casual test of his effect, he had deliberately released his masculine power. She could only look at him, as stunned as a deer mesmerized by a bright torch.

He lifted her hand and gently kissed her inner wrist. It sent a shock through her whole body. "You will attend looking beautiful and I will come with you. You will not face it alone. We are in this together, Fleur."

He kissed her lips, and lingered a long moment. His

power quivered into her through the connection and spread mercilessly, making her tremble. It was all she could do not to go limp.

She stared at him when he finally released her mouth and retreated.

"You do not have to look so horrified. We agreed that I am permitted the occasional chaste kiss." His smoldering eyes revealed that he knew the kiss had not been very chaste, nor her reaction especially horrified. The latter darkly pleased him, for reasons she could not fathom.

His embrace relaxed slightly, like a signal that she could pull away if she chose.

She shifted so they were not pressed to each other. Although every instinct shouted for her to get away, she refused to scoot to the refuge of the landau's far corner like some frightened goose. She didn't really want to. Her womanhood had relished the closeness, and the touch and kiss, even though he cruelly played with her.

"It is unfolding just as I expected," Mr. Hampton said. "No one has any idea what to do, so a hearing on your wife's ability to make sound judgments is indefinitely delayed."

"And Farthingstone?" Dante asked. He stood behind Fleur's chair in Hampton's inner chamber at Lincoln's Inn. The solicitor sat on the other side of the desk, playing with the feather of a quill.

"Your wife's stepfather had such a violent reaction to Brougham's announcement that we feared he would suffer apoplexy."

"Only he didn't. That would strike him dumb, and he

has hardly stopped talking. However, by my question I was asking whether he will give up now."

"I doubt that. I make a handsome living because most men refuse to back down. His intention, I am sure, is to first establish your wife's incapacity to make contracts, and then take that to the Church to request an annulment of the marriage."

"Might he succeed?" Fleur asked.

"Possibly. Eventually. Slowly."

"How slowly?"

"I will explain how things stand. The hearing has been delayed so that the jurisdictional confusion can be untangled. The court needs to decide if Farthingstone has standing at all and whether this should go to the Church at once. Normally, with you married, he wouldn't and it should, but since he is claiming you could not reasonably enter into such a contract—well, you see the wedge he is using. There will be a search for precedents, etcetera, etcetera. Short of your doing something outrageous, something that makes your lack of judgment explicit, I expect everyone will take a good while to deliberate this situation."

"So the argument that the marriage itself is proof of a lack of judgment will not stand?" she asked.

"I doubt that will signify much." Hampton fixed his gaze to her. "It would help if you did nothing to provoke Farthingstone's concerns. We do not want him pestering Chancery to the point that they actually do something just to get rid of the nuisance. You should behave very sensibly."

"Dante thinks that it would help if I reestablish myself in society. Then everyone can see how normal I am."

"That is the very advice I intended to give you today. With Farthingstone spreading tales, you need to be present among those who matter to counter the effect of the rumors. Furthermore, you should curb your gifts to charity. Pull back on the largesse for a while."

"That will not be possible. I am committed to build a school. In fact, I will want your advice regarding the sale of property—"

"Would this be the Durham property that we discussed? Your buyer is ready to move?"

She did not like the sharp look he gave her along with the question. Mr. Hampton had been very suspicious of that sale when they spoke of it while Dante was in gaol. She did not want his curiosity infecting Dante. "I am referring to other property."

"Yet more sales of land? I do not advise it. Not now. If there is another significant disposition of land it will only give Farthingstone dangerous ammunition."

"But the plans for the school are set."

"I cannot stop you, madame, but it is my advice to put it off for a spell." This time the sharp look went past her, to Dante. *She is your wife. You must make sure she listens to reason,* that look said.

"How long a spell?" Dante asked.

"I would think that, barring any surprises, the court will have this thoroughly buried in a year, eighteen months on the outside."

"A year! We hope to have the school almost completed by then."

"The slowness of the courts works in our favor. Of course, there is one way in which matters will be settled at once. If you are blessed with a child, this will end immediately. The issue of your judgment becomes moot then. The Church will never set aside a marriage for such a reason if there are children."

"I expect that is true," Dante said.

"Most definitely."

Dante offered his hand to help her to rise. "Then we must double our prayers for a child, isn't that so, my dear?"

Dante aimed Fleur away from the carriage when they emerged from the building. "Let us take a turn before we ride back. I wish to speak to you and do not want Luke to overhear."

He guided her firmly down Chancery Lane so she could not disagree. She looked as if she would like to.

Her glance darted to where he tucked her arm against his body. Wariness flickered in her eyes as she gave him a sidelong gaze. She was thinking about that kiss. He could just tell.

A mild breeze swam around them. It contained the freshness of spring, and even the smells of the old city could not contaminate it. Its rise and fall fluttered the ribbons on Fleur's bonnet. It was one of her new ones, a pretty little heart-shaped design that sat back on her crown and tied under her chin. The bonnet was part of the new wardrobe that was arriving at the house.

The dress she wore, with its low, broad neckline and full sleeves and skirt, complimented her form in ways her old ensembles never had. Her beauty had bloomed again as she prepared to reenter society. She wore the new garments even in the house, and now wore her hair in a fashionable style. She was enjoying the indulgence more than she would ever admit.

So was he. Sometimes when he returned from his calls he came upon her unexpectedly and she took his breath away. Some detail would mesmerize him—a lock of dark hair skimming her cheek, or the glow of her ivory skin above her bodice. As they chatted he would burn relentlessly, the flame getting larger and hotter until all he wanted to do was pick her up and carry her to bed.

She cast him another sidelong look and his own gaze met hers. During the next five steps of their stroll an entire love affair played out in his head.

In flashing fantasies of startling clarity, he nuzzled and nipped the lovely, flushed ear just visible within the frame of her bonnet. He licked the tight nipples of the breasts pressing against that blush muslin. He lowered the petticoats and skirt and laid her back on a bed so that he could kiss down her naked body and spread her thighs and use his tongue to claim her deepest passion. She resisted none of it in the secret world of his mind. She accepted and joined and begged.

The shout of a passing peddler pulled him out of his reverie. Or perhaps it was the stiffening of Fleur's arm, as if she guessed what he was thinking.

"Hampton's advice is worth heeding. There is nothing else for it, Fleur. You must delay the plans for the school."

"I cannot do that. There is a schedule."

"Explain that the schedule must change because you must not sell any property at this time. The poor will always be with us. Your school will be needed a year later."

"I do not want to change the schedule."

"I must insist that you do."

"You are so confident in Mr. Hampton's judgment?"

"I am confident in my own. His merely agrees with mine."

"Except it is *my* judgment that rules in this matter. You agreed that I would have full control over the management of this part of my inheritance."

He was beginning to hate much of what he had agreed to, and her pointed reference made his mood sharpen. "I am fully aware of the limitations imposed by that settlement, I promise you. However, you sought this marriage for a reason. It is imperative that Farthingstone be given no cause to make a case that will justify an annulment. As to my interfering, I did not bargain away the duty to protect you. Turn your attention to other charities. It is the sale of land that is at issue, not your other contributions."

She pulled her hand free and stepped away from him. Their suddenly stationary bodies formed two obstructing boulders in the flow of the crowd. Passersby jostled and bumped and cursed, but Fleur was oblivious to them.

She faced him with eyes glistening with tears of frustration. "You do not understand at all. This is not like other charities."

"The ultimate goal of them all is the same. So is the satisfaction."

"I never felt *any* satisfaction in the rest of them. I only got involved in such things because I had to do *something* since I wasn't going to have a family. I thought charity work would make me feel my life had some meaning, but it really didn't. Not until I thought of this school."

"Putting food on tables certainly has as much meaning as building a school. There is so much need that you can find many good causes."

"This will be *mine*. It will be something that *I* conceived and saw through. These boys will not be nameless, faceless, deserving souls. I will watch them learn and grow. They will be the only children that I will ever have. Just planning for it makes me feel alive and young instead of old and drab. Can you imagine what it is like to live years with no purpose and then to find one that is exciting and vital?"

"Yes, I can."

"Then you know that the notion of possibly losing it because of a delay—it is unthinkable. I must go forward."

"I must forbid you to do so for now."

Her chin tilted up. "You have no right to forbid."

"I am your husband."

"Not really."

So, there it was, the part of this arrangement that definitely needed clarification. Soon.

"If you send money to radicals, if you use your income to buy an elephant, I will not say a word. However, if your plans threaten the security you sought from me, then I will exercise my rights as your husband. I am doing so now. I say it again. I forbid you to sell any property in the near future, and if that means that the school must be delayed, so be it."

She glared at him. Tears made her rage sparkle.

She turned on her heel and marched back toward the carriage.

As he fell into step alongside, he glanced at her angry, distraught expression. He thought about her long years of being the saintly Fleur Monley who had put herself on the shelf.

The world thought she had answered a special calling.

Such a life was supposed to bring enormous contentment. From what Fleur had just said, it barely sustained her.

She would not allow him to help her into the carriage. She refused to look at him when he joined her.

"I understand that you are disappointed, but there is no choice at this time," he said. "I am sorry, but you must obey me on this."

chapter 12

Fleur cocked her head and examined Luke. He stood in the middle of her morning room. Instead of the second-hand livery that he had worn since he came, a brand-new brown coat and white trousers encased his thin frame. The brim of a high hat shadowed his gray eyes.

Luke moved his arms and looked down his body. "Seems a bit tight."

"You are accustomed to clothes that are too big for you. That is why this coat feels tight in comparison."

Mixed with Luke's skepticism was a heavy dose of awe. Fleur could tell that he had never had a single garment made new for him before. Like most of the people in his world, he lived in the castoffs of others.

"I'll look fine holding the ribbons, won't I? I'm getting better with four-in-hand too. Mr. Duclairc has been helping me learn and says I'm getting expert at it quickly."

He examined his new clothes, half-awkward boy and half-cocky man, alternating between enthusiasm and caution.

Suddenly he looked up and his gaze met hers. Naked gratitude crossed the space to where she sat.

"There is another shirt in that package, and some other things," she said, pointing to a wrapped bundle on the table.

He felt the bundle, frowning. "One shirt is enough. I'll be needing to send my wages north, you see, and could wash the one shirt and then—"

"The cost of the shirts will not come from your wages. All of this is a gift from Mr. Duclairc. You will still have wages to send home."

He pondered that, flushing and frowning. "They say you are an angel, they do. I think they are right."

"You are here through my husband's generosity, not mine."

"If you had objected, he wouldn't have done it. You knew I wasn't really fit for the work."

"You will be fine for the work."

"I hope so, since I wasn't fit for the pits. Kept coughing when I went in, like the dust sucked right into me. Others don't, but I coughed so bad I couldn't catch a breath." He shook his head. "Not a bad life, even if it was dirty and long. Fine thing when a son of a collier ain't fit for the pits."

"Well, you will be fit for this work. Now, no more about my being an angel. The servants are foolish to speak of me that way, and I do not want to hear it from you."

"Not the servants here who say it. It's them in the north that do. The women, mostly. My mother told me about it last summer when I visited, how the money you sent kept food on the table when the men went out and didn't work. An angel had sent them food, she said." He grinned sheepishly. "Imagine my surprise to learn I was in service to one and the same. Could have knocked me over with a breeze when the cook told me your unmarried name."

Fleur had never met anyone connected to the families who received that money. "It helped, then, a little? It makes me very happy to know that."

"No one was eating meat, but no one in their village starved." He patted down his torso, proudly feeling the new coat. "I'll look the blood when I drive Mr. Duclairc tonight, that's for sure. He said he'll be using the coach."

His reference to the night had her heart sinking. If Dante wanted the coach, he must have some very special plans.

It was taking longer to overcome this silly jealousy than she had expected.

"He will be proud to have you at the ribbons," she said as she left. "His friend will be suitably impressed."

"There she is. The third peasant from the right. Hair like flames," McLean said. "Her name is Helen. Came up from Bath two months ago, where she had done some small roles. Liza has taken her under her wing."

McLean's mistress, Liza, had the leading role, but the red-haired Helen almost upstaged her. Her sloe-eyed, milky-skinned, fine-boned beauty shone amidst the anonymous village folk populating the play's last act.

"Two months and no protector?" Dante asked. He sat beside McLean in a box favored for its good view of the women displayed on stage.

"Liza has encouraged her to set high standards and avoid any casual dalliance that may cheapen her. Good advice. She has the potential to be the mistress to a duke."

"If Liza is grooming her to be mistress to a duke, she will try to be very expensive."

McLean laughed. "She will think that your face is as good as two hundred a month. Nor is she ready for dukes yet. With your change in fortune, you can afford her now."

Probably. He had never arranged such a formal affair before. He wondered what Fleur would say if she discovered he was contemplating such a thing.

Nothing. Nothing at all. She assumed that he would take mistresses. She counted on him doing so. If he kissed her again as he had in the carriage three days ago, she might even demand outright that he get on with it.

Not that she hadn't liked that kiss. Which made the whole situation only more hellish.

"What do you think?" McLean asked. "She is well disposed toward meeting you."

"We will see."

"You do not sound very enthusiastic. What more is there to see? She is a jewel."

"I may not care for her character."

"*Character?* You are going to keep her. If she had a good character, she would not let you." He threw up his hands in exasperation. "This must be your wife's influence at work."

"Do not criticize Fleur if you value our friendship."

"What ho! Do I hear anger? Chivalrous protection? An odd reaction regarding a wife whom you spend every night pretending does not exist. It is none of my business, but—"

"You are damn right. It is none of your damn business."

A tense silence throbbed between them. On the stage the play began winding toward its *dénouement*.

"It *is* none of my business," McLean finally said in an oddly gentle tone. "However, if you are here tonight, it is not hard to deduce what the problem is. I can offer no advice, except to say that I have always assumed that decent women, especially maidens of some maturity, require great patience."

"You do not know what you are talking about."

"Of course not. I have never bothered with either decent women or maidens. However, a lady who was both has taken you on as a husband and deserves whatever patience is required."

"I do not need your guidance about women, especially my wife."

"Mere hours ago I would have agreed. Yet you are so sullen and ill-tempered that one might think you are experiencing pangs of guilt. I find myself moved to tell you—and I assure you that the impulse astounds me—to go home to the sweet lady who is waiting for you."

"It is laughable for you to lecture me on marital duty like some bishop."

"Well, this bishop will be sore annoyed if his lover gets angry tonight because his friend insults a certain red-haired beauty. Now, the curtain descends soon. Are you coming? Then shake your insufferable mood. I don't want to have to make excuses for you like you are some raw boy up from the country for the first time."

McLean led the way down the staircase and to the corridor behind the stage. He pushed them through the clutch of men waiting to shower hopeful flattery on the actresses. He entered Liza's dressing room like he owned it, and Dante followed.

They heard the roar when the play ended and then commotion in the corridor. Liza and Helen took their time coming. McLean occupied himself poking around pots of paint.

The door opened and Liza and Helen entered. Both carried several bouquets of flowers bestowed by admirers. Liza dumped hers on a chair and ran to McLean's arms. Helen's slanted eyes examined Dante from behind her colorful blooms.

His own gaze sized her up quickly. Her finely molded face would become either more beautiful or sadly hard as she aged. She exuded an awareness of her beauty, and a cautious reserve about bestowing her charms. She was more refined and inexperienced than Dante had expected.

Liza broke McLean's kiss. "We are being rude, McLean. This is Mr. Duclairc, Helen. The gentleman whom I wanted you to meet."

Dante said the right things and smiled the right smile. Helen looked in his eyes and her caution melted.

That was that. The decisions were all his now.

"We need to dress, gentlemen. Helen's things are here too, McLean, so you cannot stay. Out you both go."

The corridor was emptying of admirers. "You seem more yourself suddenly," McLean said.

Definitely so. However, the Helens of the world were child's play. There was no challenge if you knew that you would not fail. And no illusions about what you won.

He would welcome the clarity of cost and benefit that would mark this arrangement. Some blunt sensuality would be a relief.

"I have a supper waiting in my chambers. Will you join Liza and me?" McLean offered.

"Has Helen ever seen your chambers? I did not think so. Better not, then. She is still capable of being shocked."

"You think so? How like you to perceive the nuances. It is probably why Liza thought you would suit her."

The door opened and Liza emerged. "Helen is still dressing. She will join us shortly."

McLean took her arm. "I think not. Duclairc has other plans. We will dine alone."

They ambled off, and Dante turned to the door. He stared at its panels and pictured the woman behind it. He had rather counted on her being coarse and vulgar. Or at least experienced and calculating.

You should go home to the sweet lady who is waiting for you.

He pictured Fleur in her new sitting room, writing her letters. Not waiting for him at all, but instead relieved that he was not at home. Glad to be free of the hunger that he could barely hide.

If she were completely cold, he could bear it. If she did not tremble when he kissed her, he would cease doing so. But her sensuality was not dead. It was very much alive, just incomplete.

The knowledge of that was slowly driving him mad.

He felt her body beside him in that bed.

He remembered her gasps of pleasure behind the hedge.

He saw her dismay after that last kiss in the carriage.

He pushed the paneled door open.

Liza's maid was just finishing with the fastenings on Helen's pale yellow gown. Helen tossed her flaming hair over a milky shoulder as she turned her head on his entrance.

He gestured the maid aside and finished the fastenings himself. Helen blushed but did not object.

"Liza has left with McLean. I will take you home in my carriage, if that suits you."

She reached for a long blue silk shawl and draped it over her arms. "Thank you."

He escorted her toward the carriage. She had dabbed herself with scent, and its musky, exotic odor wafted toward him like a hot breeze.

Fleur rarely used scent, and when she did it was a light floral one that reminded him of that fresh afternoon in the grass by the hedge.

"You are enjoying London?" he asked.

She responded at length. Her explanation of learning to manage the city's size and complexity filled their walk to where he had told Luke to wait with the new coach.

Luke gaped when he saw the beautiful Helen. He barely hid his discomfort at aiding in his master's infidelity.

Well, the lad had better get used to it. Dante gave Luke directions to Helen's home, then climbed into the closed carriage and sat beside his guest.

"Liza said that your brother is a peer," she said.

"He is a viscount."

"She said that he married an opera singer."

"His wife did not begin performing until after they had been married several years."

She laughed. "But, of course, Mr. Duclairc. It could never happen any other way. It was very generous of him to permit it, however. Very understanding."

"Many think it was insane and scandalous."

"An unusual man, to have permitted it knowing many would think that. Don't you agree?"

"She will be performing in London before Christmas. Perhaps you will be able to hear her."

Helen let the shawl drop down her milky shoulders. "This is a wonderful coach," she said with admiration. "My father had a carriage. No so fine as this, but it could take a pair."

"He does no longer?"

"He and my mother died several years ago."

Hell.

"I shouldn't have said that, should I?" she said.

"I am interested in learning about you."

"Not about things like that. Now you are afraid that I am going to pour out a tale about being left destitute with three little sisters and claim that I really would not have accepted your company except for my dire straits."

"Is that your situation?"

She laughed again. It made her scent fill the carriage. "I was an only child, and left with a modest but livable income. The income gave me the freedom to go on stage, which is what I wanted to do. Rest assured, Mr. Duclairc, you are not taking advantage of me. I know what I am about." Her hand slid up his chest to his neck. She leaned forward until her breasts pressed his arm. "I will show you."

She kissed and caressed him. Not with great art, but it was enough. His arousal quickly traveled a well-worn trail. The pleasure suffused him, as familiar as a boyhood home.

However, like a well-known place that one visits anew

after an absence, he saw both its charms and its worst flaws. Empty. No real intimacy. He had never noticed that before, or never minded, at least. The warmth was only physical and the excitement almost . . . lonely.

He sensed that more than thought it. The raw hunger pounding through him permitted little consciousness. He simply possessed a new awareness.

It wasn't because of what she was, or planned to be. It had been the same with all of them. There had been little emotion in any of it, all these years. That had been a choice. A calm, deliberate choice.

He sensed the vacancy for another reason. He knew what it lacked because he had tasted what it could be. With Fleur. Not just behind the hedge, although that had been glorious. Even riding in the coach, holding her hand. Lying beside her in that bed. Reading a book on the other side of the library. In comparison to those pleasures, this old one seemed almost bleak.

Things were moving quickly and Helen displayed no hesitation. When he instinctively stopped his hands and cooled the kisses, she was surprised.

"We will be on your street soon," he said.

That appeased her. She rested in his embrace, pecking little kisses on his cheek.

"Was Bath your home when you were a girl?"

"A village near it."

"Did you have a lover there?"

"I am not a virgin, if that is what you want to know. You are in for no pleasant surprises."

"Unpleasant surprises, you mean. I do not ravish innocents."

"You don't, do you? That is rather sweet."

"Did your lover offer to marry you?"

"Of course. He thought that he had to."

"Maybe he wanted to get married."

"Well, I didn't."

She kissed him again, aggressively. Her hair feathered his face and her scent saturated his breath, inciting needs too long denied. Her body pressed, offering the oblivion of pleasure.

The carriage stopped in front of an attractive house on a street behind Leicester Square. He guessed that Helen paid a high price to live at this address, but it was money well spent. It let men know that she was a woman to be taken seriously, and a mistress with certain ambitions and expectations.

Luke opened the door and set down the steps. Dante ignored his coachman's stony expression and handed Helen out. He escorted her to the house.

"You do not intend to stay, do you?" she asked, leading him into the reception hall. She had tastefully decorated it with framed engravings and a good table.

"What makes you think that?"

"You gave your coachman no instructions. He can hardly hold the horses out there all night."

She faced him, her beauty enhanced by the glow coming from the brace of candles left lit on the table.

He did not lie to himself. He wanted her. At least part of him did. But the part that didn't truly did not.

"No, I will not be staying."

For an instant she looked very young and vulnerable. Then she drew herself straight and gazed at him boldly. "You think that I am too inexperienced."

"Yes, but that is easily remedied, isn't it? It really has nothing to do with you."

She moved closer and laid a hand on his chest. "I would like to be with you. I will do anything that you want."

"Do you think that my face and my birth make it different? That you can pretend it is other than it is? Ask Liza what it is really about, and what men sometimes want."

"I already know."

He removed her hand from his chest. "You should go back to your village near Bath."

She snatched her hand away. "Has the famous lover become a reformer?"

He turned to the door. "Go back to your village and marry the man to whom you gave your innocence in love, if that was how it was. If you have known that, this can only be sordid."

He was crossing the threshold when he heard her response. "Not with you, I do not think so. If you change your mind, you know where to find me."

Hers was not the door that he wanted left open, but he lacked the strength to slam it shut. His frustration gave him one hell of an argument all the way to the coach.

Luke waited there, wearing a grin of relief. Dante wanted to punch the young coachman in his glistening teeth.

"Home," he snarled, jumping in the coach before his body could have its way and run back.

He closed his eyes and forced his warring reactions into a truce.

He began laughing, at himself.

Damn, but he was becoming a ridiculous figure. Here

he was, leaving a woman who offered him anything he wanted, to return to a woman who could give him nothing at all. His freedom had become an unwelcome burden, and his life a marvelous joke.

In marrying his saint, he had made a bargain with the devil. Tasting paradise had thrust him into hell.

And the worst of it, the absolutely worst part, was that he couldn't wait to see her tomorrow.

chapter 13

The window in Fleur's sitting room faced the back garden. She sat in the dark on its deep ledge, letting the cool breeze tickle her skin and hair while she listened to the music.

The house next door, grander than hers by half, had a garden of its own separated from hers by a brick wall. The barrister who lived there with his young wife was entertaining tonight, and the music came from their drawing room. She could see the open doors from up here and the guests who strolled on the terrace and ventured down into the garden. Bits of laughter and conversation drifted on the breeze.

They sounded so gay. She pictured herself among them, lighthearted and carefree.

Despite the low commotion next door, she heard the carriage rumble down the alley. At the far end of the garden, a coach lamp twinkled along the wall and stopped. Then a brighter light shone through the distant window of the carriage house. Soon the hulking form of the coach obscured the window. The light moved away, toward the stable in the mews.

Luke was back. She pictured him removing his new hat and coat and unharnessing the horses. He would take a long time rubbing them down, making sure he did it perfectly. He would want to be certain that Dante would not find fault.

Dante. Her ears sought the sound of him in the house. She listened to the void and comprehended its meaning. Luke was back, but not his passenger. Dante was spending the night elsewhere. Early tomorrow morning Luke would hitch up the horses again and go fetch him from his lover's bed.

The sickly sensation swelled inside her. She gritted her teeth and forced it down. He had probably done this before. She made it a point to retire long before she expected him back so that she wouldn't know. Tonight the music had distracted her, however, so she did know.

The chamber suddenly felt confining and hot. Her own body did too, as if her skin encased a restless and anxious spirit. The breeze promised the refreshment of more than her body.

She went to her bedchamber for her robe. She would go sit in the garden and enjoy the party from behind the wall. Maybe the music and laughter would soothe her.

He noticed her as soon as she emerged from the house. She looked like an apparition floating in the moonlight as she strolled among the plantings. Not a ghost, however, despite her light garments. More like an angel.

It was not a formal garden that framed her slow, aimless walk. No neat beds such as one might expect of the tidy Fleur Monley. Instead, spring flowers peeked out from under shrubs and blazed amidst carpets of ivy. Only by the wall could one find a little patch of nothing but blooms.

He watched her from the shadows beneath a tree where he sat on a stone bench. As she passed nearby he saw that she was wearing the pink robe. Its pale color caught the moonlight almost as much as the billowing white gown beneath it, making her glow. Her flowing hair made dark streaks against the luminous cloth. The long row of buttons, dark blue as he remembered, formed so many dots from her neck to her breasts.

The musicians next door stopped playing. Fleur halted, as if she required the notes to move.

A waltz began. She looked to the wall and listened. Her body began to sway to the music.

Her arms rose and she swung around, dancing a few steps with an invisible partner. She stopped abruptly and her arms fell to her sides, like she feared someone would see her foolishness.

The music would not release her. Her arms rose again and this time she succumbed. Stepping and swirling, she floated among the plantings, dancing an angel's waltz.

He rose and walked toward her. She saw him and froze in mid-turn. The bed gown kept moving, its billows of drapery sliding around her legs.

He opened his arms, offering to take her ghost partner's place. She hesitated, then took the step that brought them together.

They waltzed in the moonlight. The narrow garden

paths confined them, giving him an excuse to pull her closer. Only thin cloth separated his palm from her warm back. Their bodies grazed each other as they turned and flowed.

She looked so lovely. Her unbound hair flew out in the turns and the gown fluttered around his legs. Her small smile showed in the moonlight, and her joy in the dance spiraled along with their movements.

It both lasted forever and ended too soon. The waltz's conclusion seemed abrupt, a rude interference in the swirling ecstasy. Dancers frozen in time, they faced each other motionlessly, still poised for more.

No music came. Voices in the other garden increased as guests came outdoors to refresh themselves. He felt Fleur's breaths slow as her body calmed from the waltz's exertion.

Awareness of their formal embrace broke through her fading euphoria. She glanced around, suddenly self-conscious. Her hand fell from his arm and she began turning away.

"Thank you. It has been years. I had forgotten how enjoyable dancing could be."

He did not release her other hand. It stopped her short, body half turned away.

"I think that I will retire now," she said.

"No."

"It is very late. I am tired."

"No," he said more firmly. "It is a beautiful night, and I want your company."

"I don't think—"

He touched her lips with his fingers, gently silencing her. He did not want to hear her denials, because they would not make any difference. He could not let her leave. He had known he would not as soon as he saw her enter the garden.

He let his touch linger and caressed her lips, treasuring the sensation of their delicate warmth. The pools of her eyes stared cautiously.

He drew her to him. He shouldn't, but he was beyond really choosing this.

The embrace made her tremble in that subtle, innocent way of hers. Any shreds of conscience disappeared as those little tremors saturated him. He held her feminine warmth tightly, relishing the soft curves under his hands and against his chest.

She reacted. He heard it in her breath and felt it in her body. She also resisted the reaction. Her hands held his shoulders, neither accepting nor denying.

He began to kiss her. With a little gasp she angled her face away.

"It is just a kiss, darling. We agreed it was permitted."

"Like friends. Friends do not kiss when embracing like this."

"Husbands and wives do, and we are married."

"Not truly."

"Truly enough for this."

He kissed her. Lights burst in his head and blood. Somehow he found the restraint not to consume her. Instead, he lured her with small pleasures before finally demanding more intimacy.

Bliss. Holding her, caressing her, pressing her. Tasting, exploring, entering. Sensation layered on sensation. The warmth deepened and spread and engulfed. His body and soul exulted in the pleasure and intimacy.

He wanted more. It could never just be a kiss. Not tonight. His mind filled with images of everything he wanted, most of which he could never have.

But he could have her at least. For a while. In his arms. He could have whatever passion she could know, and whatever closeness she could give.

He kissed more deeply, pulling her arousal higher. Despite her trembling, her body arched toward him. He caressed the swells of her hips and cupped her bottom with his hands and pressed her closer. She turned her head away with a gasp.

"You do not have to be afraid. You are safe with me. I know what you cannot give."

"Then you should not . . ."

"Probably not. But you are beautiful in this night, and I have no defense against that."

His desire demonstrated how little defense he had. Hunger cracked through him like a clap of thunder. He cradled her head, holding it to a fierce, reckless ravishment.

Her objections melted away. She molded into his embrace with shy compliance and slid her arms around his neck. The fast rhythm of her heart beat against his chest, and the lovely sighs of her breath played in his ear.

He broke the kiss and held her to him, bending to kiss the fluttering pulse in her neck. He glanced around the garden, half blind. He should stop, but he couldn't.

The music began again. He took her hand and led her toward the wall, right into the bed of flowers. He shrugged off his coat and laid it out. Lowering to his knees, he tugged gently on her hand, coaxing her to join him.

She resisted, and glanced over her shoulder to the carriage house.

"Luke is asleep by now, and there is that tree outside his window anyway. He could see nothing," he reassured. "Sit here and enjoy the music and night with me."

She gazed down at him and her confusion was palpable. He pulled her to her knees in front of him, a devil tempting a saint.

"You are as safe as behind the hedge in Durham. More so. At least fifteen people laugh and talk on the other side of this brick wall. But if nary a one did, you would still be safe." He moved so that he sat with his back against the wall. "Sit with me."

His position must have reassured her. She crawled over and sat beside him with her legs cushioned in the flowers. "It is their first large party," she said. "He remarried two months ago. A young girl. She is his third wife. His last one died two years ago."

"Was she your friend?"

She nodded. "I knew it was going badly. You can just sense it, when a woman is lying in and things are taking too long. The house was like a tomb for two days. Catherine had been so happy as her time approached, but I was so afraid for her." She turned her head, as if she could see through the wall. "I am glad he waited this long to remarry. I think it means he held some affection for her, don't you?"

"I think so, yes."

It wasn't much reassurance, but she seemed thankful for it. She rested her head on his shoulder. "Luke was grateful to receive the livery today."

"He looked very smart in it, and very proud."

"It is very nice that you are giving him this chance. You can be very kind sometimes."

He turned his body toward hers and slid his hand

into her hair. "Sometimes, Fleur, but not always. Not tonight." He kissed her the way he had wanted to for weeks. Frustration drove him and it turned hungry and hard and then consuming and furious. The passion that was not dead responded until, when he finally released her, she was breathless.

He did not give her time to think or object but lifted her onto his lap so that her back rested against his chest and he could embrace her. "Forgive me, darling, but tonight of all nights I need to hold you."

His arms gave her no choice, but any hesitation she felt melted. He guessed that she found her position safe enough. They were not lying together. He was not on top of her, much as he wanted to be.

The music played behind them. Voices mumbled through the stone. Fleur relaxed. He turned his head so that his mouth rested on her temple and he could inhale her sweetness.

Her palms rested on his arms. They stayed there when his hands moved. He could never just hold her. She had to know that. His subtle caresses did not seem to surprise her. The entrancement of the music and the garden made it a natural thing to do.

He stroked through the cloth of her garments, feeling the soft curves of her sides and hips. "You are beautiful. Even that pink robe appears ethereal and lovely."

She laughed. "It is the moonlight. Even your child-hood nurse would look beautiful in it."

"The light is not that generous." He kissed her shoulder and released his crossing embrace so that his hands could move more freely over her body. She could bolt now if she wanted to.

He felt the slight flexing of her hips that revealed she was aroused. Her bottom pushed against his erection until he pressed against her cleft.

He clenched his teeth and accepted the unintended caress. He returned those of his own with his hands, more purposefully glossing her body through the wrap, stroking her stomach until her shortened breaths told him she was past rejecting this pleasure. With kisses and nips on her ear and neck, he lured her in deeper, so he was not the only one going mad.

His contained desire possessed a savage edge. The press of her hips maddened him. Half blind, he peered down at the obstructing dark buttons. Deliberately, ruthlessly, he caressed up her body until his hands cupped her breasts. Before she could object, he gently fondled their fullness and stroked their nipples with his thumbs.

She both accepted the pleasure and fought it. The little battle caused her body to move. She pressed her hips against him harder to relieve the sensations. Her breaths shortened and little sounds of desire floated on them to his nearby ear.

He listened and caressed until he knew pleasure had defeated any resistance. Continuing to arouse her with one hand, he began unfastening the buttons with the other.

She stiffened when she realized what he was doing. Her hand covered his, as if to stop him.

He ignored the gesture. "You will let me, darling. If you truly did not want me to, you would have left by now."

She whispered something, but his hunger did not let him hear it. He parted the robe and made quick work of the bed gown's ribbons. He spread the halves of both garments until her breasts were exposed. He watched his fingers follow the lovely outlines her curves made.

The sight of her body, the warm connection of skin on skin, almost turned his desire cruel and dangerous. He leashed the primitive impulse to possess, but granted it one small liberty. Not waiting for signs of assent, he pulled the garments down her shoulders and arms until she was naked from neck to waist. At least this part of her would be his this night.

The exposure frightened her, but also aroused her more. The cautious notes on her cries barely sounded among those of a woman approaching abandon. Using his hands, he deliberately seduced her closer to that, to prove to them both that it was in his power to do so.

He stroked her breasts slowly, making circular patterns with his fingertips, teasing close to the tips. Their fullness swelled as her passion rose and rose. Her hips squirmed, rubbing him erotically.

When he finally moved his fingers toward her nipples, her body arched, begging for it. Her relief when he finally touched her did not last long. He palmed the tips very lightly, tantalizing her. The intensity of the pleasure soon had her crazed and biting back whimpers of frustration.

Her cries and movements made the urge to take her rise in his blood. Only focusing on her reactions and finding ways to increase her pleasure kept him in control. The impulse grew, however, dark and determined and convinced she wanted it. An emotion deep in his soul checked him. He could never betray her trust that way, nor risk hurting her.

That kept him from laying her down even though his body roared for him to. Even though her cries and movements said she was as ready as any woman he had ever had. Instead, he caressed down her body with one hand, to at least give her release from the mounting insanity.

She did not comprehend his intention at first, but her body knew. As he slid the bed gown up her legs, revealing their slender beauty, her legs parted and her knees bent, as if her womanhood welcomed what her mind did not understand. The movement made the garments' billows slide down to her hips.

He pulled them up more, so he could see the top of her raised thighs and the dark patch of hair and the way she waited for what she insisted she did not want and could not have.

He caressed the soft flesh of her inner thigh and watched her hips subtly rise in invitation. Erotic images flashed in his head, of kissing where his hand lay, then higher. Of teasing the soft flesh hidden amidst those dark curls with his tongue until she moaned with pleas for completion.

The sight of her, the rocking of her hips, the intense fantasy, her cry of pleasure and surprise when he touched her—they all created a chaotic and relentless spike of need. When he slid his finger deep within the cleft obscured by those curls, his hunger peaked and split apart as release flooded him.

While the little cataclysm blinded him, Fleur rolled away and scrambled onto her hands and knees. She faced him during a moment of frozen silence that echoed with spent passion and shattered arousal. He doubted that his climax had shocked her back to her senses, since she was too inexperienced to understand what had happened. Probably the intimate touch had frightened her. She watched him like a cornered animal might eye a hunter.

He reached for her. "Come back, Fleur."

She scooted away and rose up on her knees. Fingers fumbling, she covered herself and fussed with the buttons on the robe. "I do not understand you. You have no need of me for this."

"If I had no need of you, we would not be here tonight." He leaned his head against the wall and watched her fix her garments. Her confusion filled the air and colored her accusatory words. "Also, I think you understand me very well. It is yourself you do not understand."

She got to her feet. "I understand myself, Dante. You are the one who forgets the truth." She turned away. "I should have heeded your warning when you said you would not be kind tonight."

He jumped up and grabbed her arm and swung her around to face him. "You found me unkind, Fleur? If I had decided to take you, do you think those voices in the next garden would have stopped me? I'm not even sure *you* would have stopped me."

"I would have had no choice but to try."

"It did not sound that way to me. Do not pretend that you did not enjoy it."

She pulled her arm free and walked away. "Do not do this again, Dante. It does neither of us any good, even if at first I enjoy it."

Fleur sat at the window of her chamber again, unable to sleep. The party next door was ending, and muffled farewells came from the street in front of the houses.

Down below in the garden, Dante still sat among the flowers. What was he doing there? Perhaps he had fallen asleep.

Memories of being down there with him would not leave her head. Sweet memories, of the beauty of the night and music, and the intimacy of his embrace. Heady memories of pleasure owning her for a while, as it had behind the hedge in Durham.

Dreadful ones, assaulting her when he touched her in that scandalous way. The shock of the intense sensation had shattered her stupor. She had sensed the dangerous energy rising in him like an uncontrollable force. Awareness of her vulnerability had split through the mindless fog he had created in her head. Opening her eyes, she had seen her legs bent and spread and his hand reaching around her and . . .

And blood. She had seen red covering her thighs. That image had been in her head, but it looked so vivid and real. A chill had slid through her. It had numbed her so much that the pleasure instantly disappeared.

Only when she claimed the sanctuary of this chamber had she begun warming again. Returning to life. With resurrection had come the same horrible disappointment she had experienced in Durham. Disgust with her inadequacy still permeated her.

Dante still had not moved. He just sat there, one leg bent and knee raised, with his head angled back against the wall, as if he looked to the sky above her.

It *had* been unkind of him. He did not need her in that way, least of all tonight when he had surely been with a lover earlier. It had been cruel to remind her of what she could not be, could not have. Was he incapable of restraining himself when he was with a woman? Even her? Had she been so reckless as to tie herself to a man with boundless, indiscriminate appetites?

If so, they could not even be friends. That saddened her so much she almost could not accept it with composure. For a while tonight it had been much as it had on their wedding journey. Their embrace and pleasure had been as harmless as that behind the hedge.

Until her trust had been destroyed by that touch, and the image of blood, and the dangerous power he exploited.

It is yourself you do not understand. Maybe not completely, but she understood enough. She had known that all her life.

She could not have passion. She could not have a husband or children. She could not have what most women took for granted.

It now appeared that she could not even have the pretense of some kind of a marriage. She could not have a friendship and closeness unthreatened by sensual expectations.

She had been stupid and naive to think it could be different with Dante Duclairc, of all men.

Dante still had not moved, but she did. She forced herself away from the window and tried to shut the sad longing out of her heart.

She looked at her *secrétaire* as she passed it. A letter lay there, written but not posted. It was to Hugh Siddel. She had delayed in sending it for reasons she did not even understand, reasons having to do with Dante.

The letter would go out in the morning.

She would not pretend anymore that her life had changed and that she should accommodate this husband.

After all, they were not really married.

Nor would they ever be.

chapter 14

Dante stepped out of the Union Club on Cockspur Street. A damp fog had rolled into the city. He had seen it coming and had walked, so the horses would not be left standing in the mist.

He debated whether to go home. He wondered if Fleur would still be awake. Probably not. She made very sure that they would not be alone together again while the household slept. She even avoided him during the days now.

She probably realized that it did not take the silence of a sleeping house to tempt him. His desire was not waning, but instead gaining a keen edge. Three nights ago in the garden, he certainly had proven that. Whenever he saw her, whenever they spoke, he contemplated seducing her.

He headed in the direction of Mayfair anyway. He tried to block the fantasy that she waited for him so that the garden's intimacy could be repeated. And expanded and prolonged.

Memories of Fleur's naked body and breathless passion completely distracted him. The image of her at her window later, still connected to him by thoughts if not by flesh, dulled his senses.

The blow caught him totally unprepared.

It smacked into his shoulders with a force that sent him sprawling. A kick to his side made him flip onto his back. He instinctively crossed his arms over his head. Another blow aimed there, but he caught it on his forearms.

The stick crashed against his bone. Snarling, he grabbed for the weapon and held on despite the pain in his arm.

A flurry of kicks punished him. "Think to fight, do ya? Not so fancy now, is he? Give it to 'im good, for making us wait all this time in the cold."

A passing carriage pulled to a stop in the street. The coachman yelled something and another voice joined the alarm. Through the mind-fogging pain, Dante heard boots running toward him and others running away. He fell back on the pavement, still clutching the thick stick.

"Hell, it *is* you," he heard St. John say. "Thank God curiosity got the better of me and I followed you out of the club to learn what transpired in your conversation with Cavanaugh. Say something, Duclairc, so I know you are not dead."

"I am only half dead, and regretting the part that lives," he muttered.

"That will pass." Firm arms braced under his shoulders. Two men lifted him to his feet. "My coach is right here. Easy now."

"That hurts more than the blow." Dante tried to move his arm away from St. John's pressing fingers.

"I need to see if anything is broken."

Dante sat on a chair in St. John's library, stripped to the waist, as St. John conducted his examination. Diane St. John stood behind him, pressing a compress to his shoulders. A riot of pain screamed out from both their ministrations.

St. John ordered him to move his arm and fingers in various ways. He then did some excruciating probing around his ribs. "You will survive, although I do not think that was the intention."

"The intention was theft. Where did you learn to be a leech?"

"It was useful on ships in my younger days."

St. John appeared indifferent to both the damage and the pain he was causing. Diane, however, looked very solemn.

"This blow from the back could have killed you," she said, removing her compress and replacing it with another. She loosely draped a blanket over his shoulders. "A few inches higher and it would have gotten your head."

She stepped around and examined his arm. Their return to the house had pulled her from her bed, and her chestnut hair hung down her undressing gown in lengthy waves.

"I think that we should send for Fleur," she said.

"There is no need. I will bring Duclairc home to her shortly," St. John said.

"I will not need an escort. Also, I would prefer that Fleur is not told about this."

Diane pointed to his side and the swelling on his arm. "Once she sees that, she will expect an explanation."

Except she wouldn't see this, Dante thought. St. John's

wife was currently seeing him more naked than Fleur ever had or would.

"I will give a story that does not worry her," he said. "They were just thieves looking for a few pounds."

She raised one eyebrow as she glanced at St. John. "I will leave you to my husband, then. He is far better handling such as this than I am."

She departed.

"Did she mean you are better at handling wounds from a fight, or handling such as me?"

St. John lifted a brown bottle from a nearby table. "The wounds. Although I would never allow my wife to rub this liniment on such as you. Arms up."

Grimacing, Dante lifted his arms. St. John rubbed some liquid from the bottle over his torso. It produced a warmth that burned at first and then penetrated to his muscles.

St. John moved behind him and sloshed some on his shoulders too. "I saw you speaking with Cavanaugh again. Have you learned anything from your inquiries?"

"Absolutely nothing."

"Perhaps there is nothing to learn."

"I think there is. He knows Siddel, you have seen them together. Yet he avoids any mention of the man and changes the subject whenever Siddel's name is raised."

"That is not very artful. If the avoidance had been less absolute, it would not be suspicious, but complete silence makes one curious."

"Exactly."

St. John replaced the stopper in the bottle. "That will help some, but not much. Tomorrow is going to be hell. Now, tell me how this happened tonight."

"They were lying in wait for someone to come by. Whether it was me or just someone who appeared a good mark, I cannot say."

"Let us assume it was you. Let us assume that the goal was not a few pounds but a good beating, and perhaps worse."

"Let us not."

"Duclairc, if you are someone's target you need to take care."

Dante put on his shirt with slow, painful movements.

St. John helped him with his coats. "Could Farthingstone have arranged this? If you are gone, she is again unmarried and vulnerable. With his efforts in Chancery delayed, he may have sought another solution."

"They may have only been thieves, St. John. Or in the employ of someone who wanted revenge for something."

"Or someone who wants you to stop asking questions."

"Or someone from my past who would like to see me thrashed. Husbands can harbor resentments a very long time, I expect."

St. John laughed. "That we can. I will have the coachman take you home now. Since it isn't clear why this happened, and if the goal was your purse, your pain, or your death, I ask that you watch your back in the future."

"I am relieved to see that the bruise on your shoulders is healing nicely, sir."

Hornby made the observation as Dante put on a shirt. His valet had taken great interest in the progress of the swelling and discoloration over the last week, mostly because it gave him a chance to keep inviting the explanation that never came.

"Then you will be happy to know that my arm also no longer pains me, Hornby."

While the valet laid out a choice of cravats, Dante took a little box from his dressing-table drawer and slipped it into the pocket of the frock coat hanging in front of his wardrobe. He intended to give the jewelry inside the box to Fleur this morning, so she would have it when she dressed for Lady Rossmore's ball tonight.

"Do you know if my wife has gone downstairs, Hornby?"

His valet's cherubic, pale face remained impassive beneath his thin dark hair. "I believe that she did, sir. Some time ago. She rises quite early."

Hornby was the sort of person who spoke volumes with the most subtle inflection of his voice. His last sentence, uttered as a mere observation, had contained the barest nuance of dismay.

Dante had inherited Hornby eight years ago from a friend whose budding fortune had sunk with a ship in the Sargasso Sea. Hornby was an unusually loyal valet, willing to economize when bad wagers came due, happy to ignore the excesses of his master's life. Time had bred familiarity, and in some ways Dante knew Hornby better than he knew anyone else.

The timbre of Hornby's voice had not been a slip. The valet knew something that he shouldn't repeat. If his employer insisted on dragging it out of him, however, he could be coerced to put discretion aside.

"Since she does not keep late hours, it is not surprising that she rises early. It may be unfashionable, but my wife is not a slave to society's expectations."

"So Williams has explained to me."

"I hope that the two of you have not been discussing her habits. I won't have it."

"Williams was only trying to settle me in. Alert me to the household customs, so I would not be concerned. There was no tattling intended, I am sure."

Tattling? Hornby must be bursting to be indiscreet if he dangled that word.

"She has customs that concern you?"

Hornby feigned discomfort with the pointed question. He handed Dante the hair brushes and tilted the toilet mirror just so. "Since you demand it of me—She walks out alone quite a bit."

"On my instructions, that practice has stopped. I told Williams either to send for the carriage or have an escort accompany her."

"Yes. Well. So he explained." Hornby allowed himself a little sigh.

"And?" Dante obligingly prodded.

"Since you demand it of me—it appears that the lady countermanded your order, and even implied Williams would be released if he interfered or confided in you."

"Are you saying that my wife disobeyed me and black-mailed Williams into cooperating?"

"He is distraught and does not know how to perform when his loyalties are divided in such a way. No servant would, of course."

Hornby conveyed relief that, as a valet, his own loyalties would never be pulled in two directions.

"Since he does not know quite what to do, he has tried to please you both," Hornby continued, while he concentrated on folding towels. "She goes out alone. However, Williams has someone follow her."

Dante's arms froze with the brushes poised over his crown. "The butler is having my wife followed?"

"To see that she comes to no harm, and to have an answer should you ask where she has gone." He busied himself wiping around the washbowl. "Also, to make sure someone knows where she is, so that the episode from last spring is not repeated."

Dante put down the brushes and turned his attention on Hornby's very bland, very innocent face. "To what episode do you refer?"

"Since you demand it of me—last spring she would disappear and not return until after dark. It went on two days. Williams grew concerned and the third day he followed her. It transpired that she had been . . . visiting a brothel."

"That is preposterous, and I will release Williams myself for spreading such tales. Fleur Monley did not go to male brothels. I doubt she even knows they exist."

"Not a *male* brothel. Good heavens, no. One with women. A short while later she contributed substantial funds to a charity dedicated to saving soiled doves. She often conducts a few investigations, to make sure the charity can make a difference."

Dante imagined Fleur paying morning calls on brothels to ascertain if the women wanted saving. There would be hell to pay if Farthingstone ever learned of this.

Hornby held up his coats and Dante slipped them on.

"It was just such an investigation that led to her arrest in the Rookery the previous winter, which is why Williams knew at once why she was at that brothel."

This casual revelation hit Dante as he buttoned his

waistcoat. He sighed. The day was not starting well. "When was this?"

"February a year ago. You remember, surely. There was that trouble. She was there, looking into the conditions of several widows and their children, and got swept up by the police along with the rabble. Fortunately, it did not become public, but—"

But several people knew, including everyone in this house. Except him.

The servants had not spoken of it, not even when St. John had them interrogated. They had only admitted to Fleur's secretiveness and communicated vague concerns.

Dante checked his cravat. "No doubt you are aware of the accusations that her stepfather is making. I am sure you know it is essential that none of the servants ever speaks of these episodes to anyone, lest it all be misunderstood."

"Of course, sir. However, perhaps it is well that you know, since we all do."

Dante left his chamber and entered Fleur's through its door on the corridor. He heard her maid humming in the dressing room, already making preparations for the long ritual of dressing for a ball. Considering the day she faced, this had been a peculiar morning for Fleur to go out.

He had not seen much of Fleur since that night in the garden. He could not decide if she avoided him because she thought he had insulted and misused her that night or because her own reactions had frightened her.

He fingered the little box in his pocket. He had intended to give it to her personally, but now the gesture seemed somewhat pointless.

He could coax passion out of her, but she really desired no such intimacy with him. She did not think of him as a husband and felt free to ignore his most benign instructions.

He removed the box from his pocket, placed it on her bed pillow, and left.

He went down to seek out Williams. He found the butler in his pantry, counting plate. Williams dropped two spoons when he saw the master of the house at the threshold.

"If you had sent for me, sir—"

"I am told that you have been having my wife followed when she walks out alone."

"You had said . . . then she said . . . well, I did not know what else to do."

"Where has she been going?"

"Most times she only walks in the park. Christopher—that is the footman I send—stays out of sight, but he makes sure she is not interfered with."

"Most times, you say. Other times, where does she go?"

"She has paid calls on a house in Piccadilly, and also on Lady Mardenford here in Mayfair. She has on occasion visited St. Martin's. A bit out of the way, but perhaps she wants a good walk first. That is where she went today."

"She has returned?"

"When Christopher sees that she is going there, he comes home. He can hardly lurk in the portico, and we assume she is safe enough in a church."

"Send for the carriage, Williams. And she is not to be followed in the future. I will not have her subjected to such undignified subterfuge."

chapter 15

"Allow me to explain things to you, *again*," Mr. Siddel said. "Finding the last investor is the hardest, because the most likely men have already been solicited. I urge patience, madame."

"And I am saying that I know people who would be likely as well."

"This is not a proposal that ladies should be confiding in drawing rooms. I trust you have not been doing so."

"Of course not. I am not stupid, Mr. Siddel."

For all their *sotto voce* efforts, their argument seemed to ring off the church walls. Only one other parishioner had entered since Fleur arrived, however, taking a pew far from them. Up near the altar a canon prepared for the next day's service.

"I must say that I find your behavior since returning from France troubling," Mr. Siddel said. "The frequency of your letters, your insistence on this meeting, your shrill demands to know the investors' names—I find myself regretting my participation in the whole matter."

Fleur gritted her teeth to avoid getting very shrill indeed. "And I find your delays in responding to my letters and your prevarication equally troubling, sir."

"Are you questioning my honesty? Since you have no cause to do so, I must wonder about your judgment in other areas as well."

"You keep using the language of my stepfather's rumors today, Mr. Siddel. Is that supposed to put me off?"

"I merely make an observation. There is no logical reason for my prevaricating in this affair. I gain nothing until it is completed. Considering the long-term benefits once the land is sold, you should find some forbearance in the short term. Is this all Duclairc's doing? Did you confide in him and he is pressing you to in turn press me?"

A loud "ssshh" from the canon riveted her attention to the altar. Their voices had risen loud enough to invite the scold.

"Mr. Siddel, my husband has no knowledge of any of this. If my demands have appeared excessive, it is because I fear we will lose the advantage. I would be grateful if you kept me better informed. For example, do you have any prospects regarding the final investor?"

"Actually, I do. I am so confident that he will agree that I will be meeting with all the others today, to introduce them to one another. I had arranged an earlier appointment, in the interests of maintaining secrecy, but your insistence on seeing me required that I change the time." His tone implied that should the investors be angry, or should the meeting now become known, it would be her fault.

She rose and stepped into the aisle. "Then I should not

keep you. I trust that you will let me know the results of your conversation."

Mr. Siddel slid out of the pew. "I will inform you of progress when it occurs. If that does not please you, perhaps you desire to obtain another adviser, who will accommodate you better. If so, you are at liberty to do so."

Of course she had no such liberty. As she sank back onto the bench, she admitted as much. Beginning over would be folly if the goal was so close.

Mr. Siddel knew that and could proceed as he chose. There was nothing she could do about it.

Or so he thought.

She listened to his steps clicking on the floor to the front portal. She waited for the thud of the door closing behind him, and slowly counted out two minutes of time.

She got up and followed.

Dante peered out the closed landau at the facade of St.-Martin's-in-the-Fields.

If Fleur liked to walk alone, this was as good a destination as any, and better than most. At least she wasn't visiting brothels again.

He knew he was reacting more strongly to this continued habit than was warranted, but that did not blunt his annoyance. He had only requested this change for her own safety and reputation, and he did not care for the implications of her disobedience.

When he confronted her about this, she would probably remind him that they were not really married, as she had when he told her to delay the school.

She probably had not obeyed him about that either.

His hand was on the carriage door, to go and get her, when the church portal opened. A man walked through the portico and down the steps and aimed south toward the Strand.

It was Hugh Siddel.

Dante felt his jaw tightening. His memory suddenly saw Fleur's dismay that Siddel had been one of the men who saw her in that cottage bed, and Siddel's own anger at the discovery.

A savage fury roared through him. Of all the men for Fleur to deceive him about, this was the worst.

The least infuriating explanation, and it turned his thoughts hot all the same, was that Siddel was involved in that land sale and possibly trying to defraud her the way Hampton had feared.

Other, far worse explanations had him almost reaching for the pistol hung on the carriage wall.

He forced some rationality. There was no proof they had a friendship, let alone a liaison. Fleur may have left the church long ago.

As if fate was determined to taunt him, the door of the church opened again. Fleur stepped out, encased in a simple hooded cloak. It was the kind of wrap women wore when they did not want to be recognized.

She paused beside one of the portico's columns and peered around it surreptitiously. Then she walked down to the street. Staying close to the buildings and in their deep, morning shadows, she aimed in the same direction as Hugh Siddel.

A furtive quality in her pace and bearing pricked Dante's curiosity.

He jumped out of the carriage, climbed up beside

Luke, and took the reins. "I am in the mood to handle the ribbons myself this morning, Luke."

"As you prefer." Luke crossed his arms over his chest and sulked under the insult.

From his perch, Dante could see Fleur up ahead and in the distance Hugh Siddel turning east, on to the Strand. For some reason, Fleur was following the man.

Dante remembered a love affair from long ago. When the excitement dimmed, his lover had sensed his attention waning. She had followed him one day when he took his leave early, and had discovered him visiting another house and another woman. Society dined on the resulting scene for weeks.

He fought to keep speculation about Fleur and Siddel out of his mind, with no success. The heat of rage gave way to a calmer, more perilous ice.

He gave the signal for the horses to move, but held them in.

"Do you think one of the horses is lame, sir?" Luke asked. "We are going very slow."

"I choose to go slowly. If it embarrasses you to have me up here, get inside."

"No reason for *me* to be embarrassed, sir."

Dante followed Fleur to the Strand. Up ahead, Hugh Siddel entered a shop. Fleur abruptly stopped to peruse a flower stall. As Dante reined in the horses more, he noticed something else. A hundred feet ahead of his horses' noses, a well-dressed man also paused.

"Luke, see that man there with the high hat, the one standing idly on the corner up ahead on the left?"

"I see 'im."

"Watch him for me. If he turns down another street,

let me know. If he looks back and notices us, let me know that too."

Luke gave him a curious look. "Are we following him? Is that why you are going so slow?"

"Not him, Luke. But I think that he is following someone too, and I want to know if I am correct."

"Too? If you aren't following him, who *are* you following?"

"A pretty lady."

Luke pulled down the rim of his hat and folded his arms again. He exhaled a disapproving sigh.

Dante almost boxed Luke's ears. Considering that the pretty lady whom he followed was his own wife, who had just had a secret assignation with a man he hated, he really wasn't in the mood for that sigh.

Fleur had just convinced herself to take a peek in the tobacco shop when the door opened and Mr. Siddel came out. He paused to check his pocket watch. Tucking the watch away, he strode on with more purpose than previously.

He stayed on the Strand, which meant the passing bodies helped obscure Fleur's presence. Even so, she tried to stay a good distance behind because, should he look back, he would probably recognize her hooded cloak.

After a rigorous walk, he angled toward the buildings and his head disappeared into one of them. It was The Cigar Divan, a popular coffeehouse.

That seemed a very public place to hold a secret meeting, but in some ways ideal. A group of men smoking, drinking coffee, and reading papers would not invite speculation.

She debated what to do. The investors were in there with Mr. Siddel, and she wanted to know if she recognized any of them. Then, should there be more delays, she would have the chance to conclude matters on her own.

Unfortunately, women did not frequent such establishments. She could not merely enter the front door unobtrusively and take a quick look. If she tried that, the reaction of the patrons would announce her arrival.

Turning at the next corner, she sought the alley behind the row of buildings. The front door may be forbidden, but perhaps the back door could be nudged open.

Following the smells of coffee and cigar smoke, she found the back of the establishment. The door stood ajar, to allow the spring breeze in. She peeked around its edge and into the back room of the coffeehouse.

Mostly it held sacks of beans and boxes of tea. A metal washbasin, murky from the dried leaves and coffee remnants of dirty cups, stood in the far corner. Two cauldrons of water boiled on hooks set in the small hearth.

The door to the coffeehouse's public room faced her. Slipping in, she aimed for it. She eased it open and peered out.

A frock coat blocked most of her view. A man stood inches from her nose, his back to her. Just past his right shoulder, however, she could see part of Mr. Siddel's face. He was sitting on a divan near the wall and talking to someone.

The man shifted his weight enough for her to see Mr. Siddel completely. She opened the door more, rose on her toes, and angled her head to try and catch a glimpse of his companions.

One came into view. A young man with blond hair and a long face.

Watching the door's edge carefully, to make sure it did not touch the frock coat, she tried to make enough room to get her head through for a moment so she would be able to—

"See here, what are you doing?"

The voice made her swirl around. Another man had entered through the back door, carrying a sack of sugar.

"Stealing tea, are you?"

"I am not stealing—"

"Some went missing last week, and now you are back for more, I can see."

"You are mistaken." She tried to walk past him but he blocked her path.

The other door opened, and the man whose back she had just been facing came in. "What's this?"

"Found this woman in here, Mr. Reiss, making sure you were busy, getting ready to steal. She probably already has a box of tea under that cloak."

"My good man, I have no tea under my cloak and had no intention of stealing anything."

"Oh? Then what did you intend? No reason for anyone to be here, let alone a woman," Mr. Reiss said.

"I thought that I saw someone enter. Someone I haven't seen in many years. I wanted to know if I was correct."

"Did you, now? Who might this person be?"

Head muddled from the worst kind of excitement, she could not think of a good "who."

"Go for the constable, Henry," Mr. Reiss said.

The constable! "My brother. It was my brother, who

has been gone many years. We thought him lost at sea. Imagine my shock when I saw a man who resembles him walk by and then turn into this establishment. Well, I had to know, didn't I?"

Henry was halfway to believing her, but Mr. Reiss would have none of it. "Long-lost brother, eh? Conveniently seen entering this place on a day when you are wearing a cloak that is mighty handy for hiding goods. The constable, Henry. I'll keep an eye on her until you get back."

"Do not be hasty, gentlemen," a new voice said. "I think that you should believe the lady, Reiss."

Fleur knew that voice. Although it inspired incredible relief, it also made her stomach sink. Explaining this adventure to a constable would be easier than doing so to Dante. A constable might even believe her lie.

Taking a deep breath, she faced the back door. Dante stood just inside the threshold.

"Mr. Duclairc, sir. You know this woman?" Mr. Reiss asked.

"I have made her acquaintance. Imagine my surprise to overhear these accusations while I was taking a cut through this alley."

"The evidence is rather strong, sir."

"She has given an explanation, however. Furthermore, it is very obvious that she is not a thief, just from the look of her."

"Thieves come in all sizes and types. The appearance of some quality only makes it easier to escape notice, and there are those who have figured that out."

"I do not think she is one of them. I am sure that the

lady has no goods hiding under her cloak. Why don't you satisfy these two men on that count, madame."

Making her prove she was not a thief was hardly a chivalrous act, but then, right now Dante did not look very courteous. She could not ignore that the darkness had not only risen, it dominated his spirit and gave him a dangerous presence.

Feeling her face burn, she parted the edges of her cloak. Mr. Reiss, who had looked ready to give Dante an argument, raised his eyebrows when he saw the quality of the dress hidden by the serviceable wrap.

"Allow me to escort the lady from the premises. Also, permit me to compensate you for trade that you lost during this distraction." Dante placed a guinea on a shelf stacked with tea boxes.

Mr. Reiss eyed the coin and sniffed. "See you do not come back, madame. Even if you think you see your long-dead cousin enter next time."

Fleur strode past him and out into the alley. As she headed back to the street, she heard steps behind her and looked back. Dante was striding to catch up, and another man was entering The Cigar Divan's back room.

The expression in Dante's eyes made her walk faster. He caught up anyway.

"What are you doing here, Dante?"

"Paying off coffee sellers so they do not lay down information that you are a thief."

"For which I am grateful. However, by my question I meant how did you happen to be available to save me."

"I was passing in the carriage and saw you just as you turned down this alley. A fortunate coincidence." He caught her arm and stopped her before she reached the sanctuary of the street. "What are *you* doing here, Fleur? Besides hoping for a reunion with a brother lost at sea."

He had heard her lie. He must have stood outside the door listening before saving her.

"Perhaps you are doing one of your investigations prior to contributing to a charity. What would this one be? The Society to Prevent the Overimbibing of Coffee?"

"Such establishments have always seemed very convivial to me, and I thought that I would take a look."

"So you walked for blocks on end until you came to this one. Do not treat me like a fool, Fleur, nor expect me to assume that you are one either."

Blocks on end? He had not merely chanced to see her. He had been following her through the city.

"What are you up to, Fleur? Not solitary walks for exercise, it appears."

She was grateful he had just helped her out of a difficult spot, but she resented this interrogation. Worse, his masculine energy filled the air. His anger embodied the same tension that his sensuality did. She did not like the way that confused her reactions. It was very discomforting to find a man vexing and exciting at the same time.

"I am living my life, Dante, just as you continue to live yours."

Her reminder of their agreement did not appease him. Quite the opposite. "I asked you to make some small changes in that life, for your protection. Such as not walking alone."

"No, you presumed to demand that I make those changes. I complied on most."

"Not on the ones that you found inconvenient, it seems."

"Or unreasonable."

"My demands have been anything but unreasonable. As married women go, you have extraordinary freedom to continue living your life as it was, by day as well as night."

The insertion of the last reference, and his tone as he said it, made her cautious. "Yes, I have. *As we agreed.* We are not really married in the normal sense. Do not expect me to submit to every whim you have as if we were."

A very different man was suddenly looking at her. She felt like a mouse caught in a big cat's calculating gaze. "There are several parts of this marriage that I will be renegotiating, Fleur. Regarding your submission, however, I remind you of my warning in the cottage. If challenged, the choice of weapons is mine."

He took her arm and firmly guided her back to the street.

He opened the carriage door.

Considering his last words, she did not want to forsake the street for the privacy of that carriage.

"I would rather walk, Dante."

He smiled slowly. It was *not* a reassuring smile at all. "Are you afraid to ride with me?"

"If it means sharing your dismal humor, yes."

"Get in the carriage, Fleur. You face a long day of preparation and a tiring night. I will continue on foot. We will talk about the reasons for my bad humor tomorrow."

chapter 16

Fleur examined her reflection in the long mirror. A stranger peered back at her.

No, not a stranger. An old friend, not seen in ten years. The girl she had once been greeted her.

She stepped closer so the low lighting could not obscure the details that said she was no longer a girl. The eyes were less innocent than they had been then, and the face less soft in its form. Her body showed curves the girl had not possessed, although not a pound had been gained. She was a woman now.

She wanted to believe that the years looked good on her. She needed to think that tonight. For a decade she had been free of all this fretting about her appearance. Suddenly, however, it mattered again, and she was unpracticed in controlling the way it created dissatisfactions with little flaws. Inside her body, wings of nerves beat and fluttered. She had not even been this unsettled the day she attended her first ball.

Tonight would be a second coming out, only more

important than the one when she was a girl. Back then it was her future marriage at stake—which meant nothing was at stake, since she planned never to wed.

"The carriage is waiting, madame," her maid said as she held up a cream satin mantle.

Fleur took it around her shoulders. The gesture brought her right hand to the mirror. Light crackled back and forth between the glass and the large sapphire shimmering on her finger.

It was a beautiful ring. It looked perfect with her cerulean gown and the hired diamonds that bedecked her neck.

The ring had been waiting in her chamber when she returned today, sitting on her pillow in a little box. No note had accompanied it.

She had not been able to thank Dante for it yet. He had stayed away until early evening and immediately begun his own preparations upon returning.

He had done that to avoid her. Tomorrow, she did not doubt, he would take up the matter of her blatant disobedience. That pending conversation was one more reason for the nauseous worry that plagued her tonight.

Fleur forced herself to move. She walked down to where Dante waited for her.

The sight of him made her pause on the stairs. He was almost unbearably handsome in his evening clothes, a dark, strong column of impeccable tailoring and grooming. The hint of boyishness that usually softened his countenance was absent tonight. The dark ridge was still bared, giving him a hard maturity that made his face and presence very . . . exciting.

She felt an utter fraud suddenly. She would enter the

ball on the arm of this man and everyone present would know the marriage was a farce. The best interpretation she could hope for was that she was an addled fool who had bought a husband she could not hold on to.

In his first glance at her she saw the annoyance about her excursion this morning. However, that anger dimmed as he came toward her. "You are incredibly beautiful, Fleur. I do not think I have ever been this awed."

It was such a kind thing to say that she wanted to weep. She had been lying to him and he knew it, but he still sought to put her at ease.

She held up her hand that wore the ring. "Thank you for this. It is magnificent."

"It was my mother's. I sent to Laclere Park for it. I left it there so that I would not be tempted to sell it when I got in too deep."

"I am honored to wear it tonight."

"It is not a loan. It was given to me to give to my wife, and that is who you are."

Not really.

A hard glint in his eyes almost dared her to say it. She had the good sense not to.

He offered his arm. She slid hers into place. He patted her hand in reassurance. "Once you are there, it will be as if you never missed a season."

It was not as if she had never missed a season, but her fears eased once she was at the ball. It helped that Charlotte took her in hand immediately.

"Go see your friends, Dante, while I take Fleur around," she ordered. "Come back for the third waltz."

Dante bowed in obedience and walked away.

"Now, come with me. I have it all arranged," Charlotte said, guiding her through the shimmering gowns and jewels.

Charlotte brought her to Diane St. John, who epitomized restrained elegance in her dark silver gown. The neckline skimmed her shoulders perfectly; a half inch more or less would have ruined the whole design. The sleeves, while full, did not overwhelm her thin arms. One stunning diamond hung at her throat, and Fleur guessed it was not hired. Her abundant chestnut hair was piled in a style that was not fashionable but very alluring.

Diane stood back and examined Fleur's ensemble. "Perfect. You both did well."

"Diane visits Paris several times a year, so if she says we did well that is a high compliment," Charlotte said. "Where is Sophia? She is part of our troop tonight."

"Coming up behind you," Diane said.

Fleur found herself being introduced to the dark-haired Duchess of Everdon and her somewhat foreign-looking husband, Adrian Burchard. She did not need any prompting from Charlotte on the history of these two. The last decade had removed her from society's balls but it had not removed her from the world's gossip. She knew the story of the duchess in her own right, and of the bastard son of an earl whom she had married.

"My husband has mentioned you," she said to Adrian. "I believe you are friends."

"Good friends, madame. He, St. John, and Hampton form a private circle, along with Laclere, of which I am fortunate to be a part. We have had some unusual experiences together."

"Is Mr. McLean a part of this circle?"

Charlotte and the duchess giggled. Adrian pretended they had not. "Like most men, your husband has several circles. My brother Colin enjoys that of Mr. McLean, not I."

"I certainly hope not," the duchess muttered.

"Mr. Burchard, you must excuse us now," Charlotte said. "We have things to discuss."

He backed away. "If you ladies are plotting strategies, I will wisely make myself scarce."

The duchess took Fleur's hands. "Before there is any plotting, I want to welcome you to our own circle. I would have called on you by now, but I was in Devon until this week. I offer my best wishes for your happiness in your marriage."

Fleur was touched by the quick acceptance. The duchess was a short woman, and about thirty years old. She was not a great beauty, but her clear green eyes conveyed sincerity and frankness far in excess of what one expected in a duchess on first meeting.

"Thank you, your grace. You are too generous to me."

"Finding new friends is a joy, not generosity. And, please, you must call me Sophia."

Now, that *was* generous.

"Did the boys come up with you?" Diane asked.

"Of course. It made for quite an entourage, what with nurses and whatnot. However, Burchard commanded they both come. He has not seen the baby in a month."

"Ladies, we will all assemble in two days to discuss women things, but right now we have work to do," Charlotte interrupted. "You all know the things Fleur's stepfather is saying. Tonight we prove him false. I want Fleur to meet every lady here who can influence opinion. I want her dancing with peers and admirals." She turned to Fleur. "We will position ourselves so that you always have a friend nearby."

"I will go first," the duchess said. "Come, we will start easily. I see Adrian's aunt Dorothy. She probably remembers you from your first season, so will not be a total stranger."

They were as good as their word. Fleur was never alone. When a dance partner brought her to the side of the room, one of them joined her in a snap.

She relaxed as the night wore on. She knew many of the people here, even if she had not spoken to most of them in years. There were precious few allusions to her marriage, and almost none that was unkind.

She rarely saw Dante. Sometimes as she danced she caught a glimpse of him dancing with someone else. When the third waltz began, he was there to lead her into the dancers. The room spun around until they became the center of a whirlwind. The dance evoked memories of the last time they had waltzed, in the garden. His expression did too, but continued to be tinged with the anger of the afternoon.

By the time of the banquet, Fleur was feeling reassured that she had acquitted herself well. Attending a ball and doing nothing outrageous was an easy achievement if you were completely sensible and normal.

Daniel St. John offered his escort to the supper. She guessed that the troop had arranged that.

As she chatted with him, she looked down her table at the other couples. A stunning woman with blond hair and smoky eyes caught her attention. The woman was wearing a gown of dark violet, similar in color to the one

Fleur had just had made by Madame Tissot, and it was the gown that first attracted her interest.

The lady moved slightly, turning to her companion. The shift made her more visible. Fleur vaguely noted that this was probably one of the most beautiful women at the ball.

Then her gaze locked on two details of the woman's ensemble.

Small details. Glittering ones. A pair of amethyst earrings dangled from her lobes, catching the light, matching the gown to perfection.

Fleur's breath caught. Her heart thudded while she stared at those earrings. She had seen them before. She had carried them in her reticule to a gaol.

She tore her gaze away and looked down at her plate. The noise of the room turned into a buzz. She ceased to hear what St. John was saying.

She looked at the earrings again. She could not stop herself. "That lovely woman down there, in the violet. Do you know who she is?" Her question interrupted St. John in the middle of a sentence.

He glanced down. Was it her imagination that he hesitated?

"That is the Baroness Dalry. Scottish title."

"She is extremely beautiful."

"Yes."

He knew. She could tell. St. John knew the baroness had been Dante's lover.

She felt chilled suddenly. Cold and warm all at once. A pain lodged in her chest that would not go away. She had to work at breathing to get some air in.

Dante had resumed his affair with the baroness, and

had given her the earrings again. St. John knew about that too. Maybe Charlotte and Sophia and Diane did as well. Maybe everyone did.

She breathed deeply. She had known this day would come. Eventually it would be one specific woman, and she would learn who it was. She sought refuge in the indifference and acceptance that she had promised, but both deserted her.

She wanted to die. She felt as though she might.

"You appear unwell," St. John said with concern. "I fear the night has been too much for you."

"Yes, unwell." She barely got the words out. The pain in her chest had turned excruciating. It wanted to burst out of her, and the effort to keep it in had her light-headed.

She pushed to her feet. "Please, excuse me. I will . . ."

St. John's hand was under her arm at once. Half escorting and half supporting, he sped her out of the banquet room.

The pain grew until it filled her throat too. She felt tears flowing even though she was not crying.

Somehow the duchess was beside them. St. John handed her into Sophia's yellow satin sleeves.

Fleur did not hear what the duchess whispered to her. An image had entered her head and she could not make it go away.

She kept seeing Dante holding the face of the baroness and gazing into her eyes, then gently kissing her twice, once on the forehead and then on the lips.

Her heart broke. The duchess pushed her into the withdrawing room just as the flood started.

.   .   .

She laid on the chaise longue sniffling like a fool, feeling so stupid she wanted the building to bury her. She could not stop the tears, no matter how much she scolded herself. Her throat burned from her efforts to keep some composure. Women came and went, pretending to ignore her but getting an eyeful all the same.

The troops had deployed around her, forming a barrier with their skirts that offered a modicum of privacy. Charlotte and Sophia stared down any lady who looked too long.

"I cannot believe that none of us carries a vinaigrette," Charlotte said.

"She is not faint," Diane said.

Fleur wished she *were* faint. Better if she had keeled over in the corridor and dropped to the ground. She prayed for oblivion to claim her now. Anything to stop seeing these images of Dante with the baroness.

"We need to know what caused this," Diane said. "If someone insulted her, or spoke of her stepfather's accusations in her presence—"

"St. John said it began right after she asked him about the Baroness Dalry," Sophia said softly.

The three women fell silent. Fleur knew they were pitying her. That made her feel even worse.

"It was the earrings," Charlotte said. "I will *kill* my brother. He should have told her not to wear them. He knows Fleur saw them."

"Well, I will leave you to kill him, while I take Fleur home," Sophia said. "Before you kill him, inform him that she has left. Diane, would you find Adrian and let him know that I wish to depart."

Charlotte made to follow Diane. "Sophia, I hope that

you will never receive Lady Dalry again. There was deliberate cruelty on her part tonight."

"Or total ignorance. She may not have known that Fleur would recognize the earrings."

"Possibly. One person did know, however, and when I am done with him—"

"Please do not," Fleur managed to say. "I have made enough of a shambles of the night. Do not accuse Dante of anything, or blame him. It isn't his fault at all."

Charlotte patted her face. "You let Sophia take you home now. I will visit in the morning and speak to Dante then. Tonight he is completely safe from me."

"You black-hearted scoundrel."

Charlotte hissed the insult as soon as she pulled Dante out of the ballroom and backed him into a private, dark corner.

"You thoughtless, conceited, cruel man. How *could* you? You knew what this night meant. How could you be so stupid when—"

"That is enough, Charl." He was in no mood to have insults hurled at him.

His humor had not improved since putting Fleur in the carriage this morning. If anything, the hours had darkened it more. He had barely maintained civility at this ball, because his head swam with hard questions and infuriating answers.

At some point he had recognized this primitive anger for what it was. He was jealous. Of Siddel, and whatever secret relationship the man enjoyed with Fleur. Speculations on what that relationship might be had occupied most of the day.

Fleur's furtive following of Siddel encouraged a conclusion that made his head split—that Colin Burchard had gotten it backward, and *she* was a spurned lover who kept grasping for the man she had lost and who refused other men because of her love. Only his conviction that Siddel would have grabbed Fleur's fortune if offered it kept him even partly sane.

Now, to finish off a day that had started badly and then gotten worse, he was suddenly the object of curiosity and sympathy. From what he could tell from the buzzing gossip, Fleur had just created a disaster. When Charl had found him he had been trying to figure out how to limit the damage.

"It is *not* enough, and there is plenty more," Charl snapped. "Do you know what has happened?"

"I overheard the story, so I have a good idea of how it will be remembered tomorrow. My wife abruptly lost control of her emotions at the banquet, had to be carried away, wept hysterically in the withdrawing room, and eventually had to be spirited from the ball by the Duchess of Everdon before anyone else could hear her ravings. And, to hear of it, there was absolutely no reason for this display except her unstable constitution."

"Oh, heavens, that is all much exaggerated. By tomorrow the gossiping fools will be saying that she tried to drink poison."

"Yes. Farthingstone should be delighted."

Charlotte stepped closer, hands on her hips. "It was not for no reason, you wretched excuse for a husband. She saw the earrings."

"What do you mean?"

"The amethyst earrings that I had her bring you in gaol. She saw them on the baroness."

"Are you saying that Fleur caused a scene because she was jealous?"

"She did not cause a scene. She behaved magnificently, considering that she was devastated. The worst part is that she blames herself and not you."

Of course she didn't blame him. *She didn't dare.* If he had resumed his affair with the baroness, she could not object.

Except that the baroness was not his lover, which made the entire drama ridiculously ironic. Almost as ironic as the fact that *he* had caught *her* secretly meeting with a man this morning.

He would laugh except that a scathing fury filled his head.

Charlotte noticed. "You are angry with her."

"Damn right."

"Perhaps you think that she should be sophisticated about this. She has been out of society for some time, however, and it may take her a while to reaccustom herself to the casual infidelities expected of husbands."

He was tempted to explain the whole impossible predicament to Charl and exonerate himself. She was not the woman he needed to have it out with, however.

"If you want to insult me further, you will have to call tomorrow. I will leave now and attend to my wife."

chapter 17

Fleur lay in the dark, as miserable as she ever remembered being. The images of Dante and the baroness had been joined by others. She kept seeing how she had made a fool of herself tonight.

She thought of Charlotte confronting Dante in the morning. She would have to rise very early herself and go to Charlotte and beg her to say nothing to Dante about the reason for tonight's behavior. Better if everyone concluded she was unstable and strange than anyone learned the truth, especially Dante.

Because she was awake, she heard the rapping that began on the door. It was loud and sharp enough, however, that it would have probably woken her even if she were asleep.

She sat up in bed and reached for her pink robe. The sound was not on the corridor door but on the little one that separated her chambers from Dante's.

She tiptoed through the dark to her dressing room. The raps sounded with a staccato demand.

The knocks stopped as she stood there, holding her breath. It appeared he had given up.

"Open the door, Fleur, unless you want me doing this in the corridor where all the servants will learn of it." His voice came low and tight, as if he knew she was standing on the other side of the wall and could hear him.

She turned the little key. The handle moved and the door swung toward her.

Dante stood there, with one arm raised and resting on the jamb. He had removed his coats, collar, and cravat, and his white shirt glowed in the light thrown from a brace of candles on the washstand.

There was absolutely nothing of the carefree, good-humored wastrel in his face or body.

"You are recovered?"

She nodded. "I am very tired, however."

"I am sure you are. However, I need to impose on your time for a while." He stepped into her dressing room. The light from the candles illuminated enough of his expression to show that he was angry.

He reached around the door and extracted the key. "I have grown to hate this door. I erred in insisting you lock it. It was one of several mistakes I have made with you." He threw the key back to his chamber and it clattered into the washbowl. "I do not ever want it locked again."

She did not know what to do or say. They just stood there in the dressing room, facing each other through the shadows.

"That robe does not look at all attractive without the moonlight in a garden. I told you to buy some prettier things."

"It seemed unnecessary, since I am asleep when you return home."

"You have taken great care to make sure of that. However, despite your efforts, here we are." He gestured to the wardrobes. "You wore something else that night in Durham. Where is it?"

"I do not think—"

"Put it on, Fleur."

She went to a wardrobe and removed the nightdress and boudoir robe.

He was beside her suddenly, a dark, male presence in the night. His hands began to unbutton the blue dots on the robe.

She pictured him doing that with the baroness and wanted to weep again. "I do not need your help."

"I choose to help. Do not object, Fleur. This is not the night to remind me of what you think we should not share."

He barely touched her as he peeled the robe away. His fingertips hardly grazed her skin as he untied the bed dress and slid it down. He might have deliberately caressed her naked body, however. Undressing her proclaimed a right just as intimate.

She reached for the bed gown, but his hand closed on her wrist, stopping her. She froze like that, arm outstretched, with him much too close.

She did not look at him, but she felt him looking at her. Very little light entered the dressing room, but enough did for him to see her nakedness.

"Let me put on my bed gown, Dante."

He pulled off her cap so her hair fell.

"Dante—"

"Not yet. It gives me pleasure to look at you."

She closed her eyes and suffered it. Despite her humiliation, a slow excitement beat like a pulse. That rhythm was in the air, coming from him, being carried into her, stimulating her body.

"I should insist you stay like this," he said. "I should make you come into the light and look at you for hours. I have damn few rights in this marriage, but this is one I did not bargain away."

"You are being cruel."

"Are you in pain? Am I hurting you?"

"I am embarrassed."

He released her wrist but cupped her chin instead. "You are not only embarrassed. You are also aroused. Do you think that I cannot tell?"

He released her. "Come to my chamber now."

She trembled as she scrambled to get into the silk ensemble.

She had not been in his chamber since it became his domain. Nothing of her old sitting room remained, and she felt a stranger as she examined the carved bed with its dark-green drapes and the tables littered with his personal things.

He lounged on a chair, as confident in his physical presence as ever. She chose to stand, far away. She crossed her arms and pretended to study the redecorating.

"Charl and her friends took good care of you tonight. They have my gratitude."

"I know I behaved badly. I know it will only give Gregory's lies validation. If you intend to tell me what a mess I made of things, you do not have to. I have been castigating myself for the last hour."

"I did not seek you out to scold. I want to know what made you lose your composure."

"I was overtired."

"Charl said it was something else. She said you were distraught because you concluded I am having an affair with the Baroness Dalry."

She was so humiliated she could only stare at the floor. She wished Charlotte had been good to her word and waited until tomorrow to upbraid Dante.

"Was she correct? Did seeing those earrings distress you this much?"

She could not admit she had been so stupid, so pointlessly jealous.

"Well, Fleur, we have created a little hell for ourselves, haven't we? You promised never to be jealous, but then break down when you suspect you have seen my lover. I promised never to take you, but spend my time thinking about little else."

He was thinking of it now. It was in his eyes and body. It still affected the air. She told herself she was safe with him, but she did not entirely believe it right now.

"I should have guessed that somewhere in that ballroom there would be one of your lovers—from the past, surely, and possibly your current one. I just did not think about it, and so I was surprised. I will know better in the future. You are understandably angry, but this will never happen again."

"I am not angry because you were jealous."

"I have no right. I know that."

"No, you have no right. All the same, you became jealous on very little evidence. I, on the other hand, actually saw you meeting with a man this morning. At least my jealousy is based on something of substance."

Dear Lord, he had followed her longer this morning than she thought. If he knew about that meeting, he had been at the church.

She strolled around the room and debated her response. She tried not to look like she was pacing, but he was making her very nervous. The aura was pouring off him without restraint, filling the chamber, washing over her without mercy. His calm tone did not hide his mood, and his gaze revealed a mind making calculations that she dared not guess.

"I will not lie," she began. "You are correct. I met with Mr. Siddel this morning. Surely you know that it was not—that we are not—that would be impossible."

"So you claim."

"Are you doubting me? Good heavens, are you wondering if I lied about that? You cannot believe that I would so callously play you false when I proposed this marriage."

"I do not know what I believe anymore, since very little of this marriage has met my expectations and since you have not been honest in other ways."

"I am being honest now. Mr. Siddel and I do not have that kind of alliance. We are not even friends. We met on a matter of business."

"What business?"

"I cannot tell you."

"You mean that you will not tell me. Are you going to throw our agreement at me if I insist? As I said, this is not the night for that."

She felt trapped. She desperately sought words that would appease him.

"Is Siddel an adviser to you in the use of your inheritance?"

"Yes, you could say that."

"Then you are to find another one. You are to have nothing more to do with the man. No communication, no meetings. If you require a counselor, retain Hampton. If you want advice on business affairs, St. John will gladly help you, and when Vergil comes back he will be as good an adviser as you can find. Hugh Siddel, however, cannot be trusted. I'll be damned before I tolerate your meetings with him."

He had no idea what he was asking. *Demanding.*

Any thoughts she had of arguing disappeared when Dante rose from the chair and strolled toward her. She eased away to keep some distance.

It did not work. In no time she was standing against the wall and he was in front of her.

"You do not care for my instructions about Siddel, do you?"

"No."

"Do you have affection for this man?"

"It is not that, I have told you. However, these matters are supposed to be mine alone."

"Ah, yes. Because of our settlement."

The way he said it, the sparks in his eyes and the dangerous smile that slowly formed, had her sinking into the wall.

"If you are finished, I will get some sleep now, Dante."

He rested his hand high against the wall, propping his casual stance, but it also seemed a gesture to block her path to the small door. "Not yet. There are several other things I want to say to you tonight, Fleur."

"Then say them." She wished he were not so close. When he sat in the chair and she strolled the room she could avoid looking at him, but she couldn't now with him hovering like this.

"She is not my lover. I returned the jewels because they belong to her, and I had no need of her generous gesture after we married. They are hers to wear when she chooses, however."

She resented the way her heart rose with joy at his announcement. She hated how the night's sadness simply fell away. Her reaction only proved how enslaved her emotions were.

The humiliation did not disappear, however. This reassurance mortified her. "Then I handed Gregory a victory and I don't even have an excuse. This has truly been a disastrous night."

His fingertips feathered some strands of hair back from her face. "I disagree. I learned that you are jealous of all these lovers I am permitted in this marriage. I am glad to know it. That changes everything."

His vague touch had her senses alert and alive. Her body could feel the warmth of his even with twelve inches between them. "I do not see how it changes anything."

"We both gave up rights when we spoke in that sponging-house yard. You gave up the right to jealousy, but you are still jealous. I gave up the right to want you, but I still do. It could have worked anyway, except for one problem. You want me too. If you didn't, my interest would fade. If you didn't, you would not be jealous."

"So it is my fault."

"It is mine, for assuming I could want to protect a woman and not also want to possess her." He watched his finger draw along the line of her jaw. "This arrangement is impossible now that we know the truth of what exists between us, Fleur. It cannot go on. I am not inclined to live my life like this."

Heaviness returned to her heart. He wanted to be free of this false marriage. He wanted to be free of her.

"We can arrange never to see each other. Even sharing this house, we can do that. After Gregory has retreated, you can move elsewhere. Unless . . . unless you want to cooperate with him, and then procure an annulment. If you are truly unhappy, I will not fight that solution."

She dreaded the implications of that annulment, but if Dante wanted one she would not ask him to change his mind. He was right, and this marriage had not been what they expected.

"Those are all solutions, Fleur, but not the one I want. We are married, and I think it is time to act as if we are."

"Not—"

"Not really married. That is what you were going to say, isn't it? Not really a husband. The agreement led you to think of me that way. That locked door did too. I don't much care for this belief you have that we are not really married. It is time to admit that we are."

He rested his fingertips on her cheek. "It is also time to admit how much we want each other."

"That will only lead to unhappiness."

He kissed her, lingering, letting the power of that kiss do its worst, forcing her heart to accept what her body wanted.

"Did that make you unhappy, Fleur? When I held you in the garden, were you unhappy?"

She stared at the gap in his shirt where it lay open at his neck. A jumble of reactions confused her. Pleasure and gratitude clashed with the memory of a fear so visceral it could turn her to stone.

"It will eventually. I cannot give you what you want."

He did not respond. She snuck a glance up. His expression stunned her. A man who had never been refused by a woman was studying her, judging her strengths and assessing her weakness.

He lifted her into his arms. Another kiss, a ravishment, demonstrated his hunger and called her own forth. The heat of his passion almost made the roots of the fear wither and die, but she knew it survived in her. Even as she responded, while her body flushed and her breasts got full and sensitive, she knew that even Dante Duclairc could never conquer what lived in her.

He embraced her, pressing kisses to her shoulder and neck as his hands caressed her through the silk. "The door stays unlocked, Fleur, and we will share a bed."

"No. You promised—"

"I am not going to force you, but I never promised that I would not try to overcome whatever it is that makes you deny me."

"It cannot be overcome."

"I'll be damned before I accept that."

He kissed her furiously, giving expression to the angry determination of his declaration. With one hand sprawled possessively across her bottom, he arched her body against his and caressed up with the other until he cupped her breast.

Wonderful sensations streaked down her body, and the pulsing warmth grew. The excitement he so masterfully created almost overwhelmed her. For a brief while, as he stroked her nipple through the thin silk, she pretended they were behind that Durham hedge and this pleasure would be limited and benign.

He stopped kissing her, but his fingers still made titillating patterns on her breast. She opened her eyes and saw him watching how she reacted.

The sensual severity of his expression frightened her. The realities of the night assaulted her. They were not behind a hedge. They were in his chamber, and he would not stop this time.

The hated fear rose with a relentless wave. He must have seen it, because he kissed her again, as if the force of his passion could stop the tide.

It almost did. A blaze passed from him to her, burning away her sense of everything but intimacy and pleasure.

His embracing arm pulled her closer until she lined his body completely. He moved her toward the bed. "You will sleep here with me tonight. I want you in my arms."

Not only in his arms. She could not lie to herself about that. With each step the fear grew, threatening to deaden her.

She wanted desperately to believe he could win this battle for her. The poignant memory of sleeping with him in Newcastle made her throat thicken with tears. But if she got in this bed, it would not be like that. It would be horrible and humiliating. Even if he stopped it would be dreadful, and if he didn't—a little whirlwind of panic spiraled up her body, into her head. Images of blood and soundless screams flashed through her mind.

Already her nature was having its way, killing the pleasure and the joy, making her so miserable she thought she could never be happy again.

She pressed her hands against his chest. "Please, do not," she whispered, trying to hide how terrified she had become.

"I said I will not force you. There is no reason to be afraid."

There was every reason to be afraid. This was not Dante the kind friend, offering chaste intimacy. It was Dante the man, a prince of sensuality, wanting her more than was safe.

She pushed harder, until he released her. "I do not want this."

"Yes, Fleur, you do."

She turned and ran to the door. "Something in me does not, Dante, and even you cannot defeat it."

chapter 18

Dante was already in the breakfast room the next morning when she went down. She wondered if that meant he had slept as poorly as she had.

For the next half hour she sipped coffee while he read his paper and mail. The room seemed filled with last night's events. The silence became a continuation of them.

She caught him looking at her once. His gaze communicated no contrition. No backing down. He had made a decision about this marriage, and her flight last night had not changed his mind.

He had taken the key, so she could not lock the door now. She expected that some night he would walk through those dressing rooms to try and seduce her.

That was hopeless. She wished it was not, but it was.

Williams announced that Dante's sister had come to call. Charlotte entered the breakfast room, full of apologies for the early hour.

"If you have come to upbraid me further, there is no

need," Dante said. "I have explained to Fleur that the baroness is not my current lover."

The bold announcement left Charl chagrined. "Oh."

"Yes. Oh," Dante repeated pointedly. He rose. "Since you ladies will want to discuss the ball in tedious detail, I will retreat." He did so before Charlotte could say another word.

Charlotte took Fleur's hand. "I hope there was no row when he got home. He appeared angry when he left the ball, and I feared there might be one."

"He was understandably displeased, especially since he says she is not his current lover." Fleur had not missed the wording of his statement. It left open the real possibility that some other woman *was* his current lover.

"Your misunderstanding was excusable. Any woman would have reached the same conclusion."

Not any woman. Not one who trusted her husband to be faithful, the way Charlotte had trusted Mardenford and the way, Fleur suspected, Diane trusted St. John.

Not a woman who joined her husband in passion instead of demanding he find it elsewhere.

Not a woman who accepted the intimacy he wanted instead of running from the room.

"It is good to see you in good spirits, because I think Dante will want to make a short journey with you soon. If he had not left so abruptly, I would have given him the news forthwith."

"A journey to where?"

"Sussex." Charl plucked a letter out of her reticule and waved it. "It came this morning from Laclere Park. Vergil and Bianca have returned from Naples."

Fleur's stomach jumped, then landed with a sickening plop. "How wonderful."

"Penelope decided to stay in Naples. Vergil reassures me that she is back in good health and that he will explain everything when he sees us."

"Does he indicate that he knows about our marriage?" Fleur asked feebly.

"He says nothing specifically, although I expect that the servants have told him. Dante will probably want to go down soon, unless that will inconvenience any plans that you have."

Fleur wished she had a diary full of important plans that could not be inconvenienced by a visit to Sussex. Weeks of them.

The last day had tilted her world in ways she did not understand yet. If she had to face Laclere, that world might turn upside down.

The rambling neo-medieval manor house came into view, then grew in size as the carriage rolled up its approaching lane. Two boys played out front, throwing pebbles up against the house, seeing how high they could make the missiles land.

The sound of the coach distracted them. The younger one, who looked to be about four, jumped up and down, waving his arms.

"Someone is excited by your visit," Fleur said.

"That is Edmund," Dante said. "The elder is Milton. The little one adores me, although I don't understand why."

"Perhaps he knows you are not the type to scold him for throwing stones at the house."

Both boys crowded the coach door as soon as they stopped. Dante had trouble getting out. Edmund tugged on his coat, squealing an endless sentence about big ships and a new pony and his hateful tutor and some secret spot near the lake where he had seen a little snake yesterday.

Dante took the child's face in his hands and bent to calm him. "We will see the pony soon, and this afternoon we will go looking for more snakes. Right now, however, there is a lady who cannot descend from the carriage. Make room, and welcome her like the young gentleman you are."

Milton offered his hand to help her down. Unlike Edmund, who was fair-haired, Milton had the dark hair and blue eyes of his father, the viscount. "Welcome, Auntie. We are not supposed to know that Uncle married yet, but I overheard the butler giving Papa the news."

"*Married?*" Edmund looked up at Dante in horror. "Tell Milton he is wrong."

Dante placed his hand on the child's shoulder and gave a gentle squeeze. "Remember, like a gentleman, Edmund."

Face folding into an expression of heartbreak, Edmund made a little bow. "We are joyed to meet you."

Fleur bent down to the distraught little man. "And I am joyed to meet you, Edmund." She gave him a conspiratorial wink. "Mr. Duclairc made me promise not to interfere with important manly affairs like ponies and snakes, so I doubt you will find me much bother."

His relief bloomed and his smile returned. "Oh, *well*, then, *welcome*."

"Yes, welcome," a very adult voice said.

Fleur looked up into the piercing blue eyes of the Viscount Laclere.

His wife, Bianca, stood beside him, wearing a big smile. As two girls skipped down the steps to join their brothers and the greetings flew, Bianca embraced Fleur. "The news was a wonderful surprise. We are so pleased that Dante has found happiness."

Fleur played her role as best she could. She was grateful for the confusion of children and baggage, however. Laclere and Dante managed a few quiet words together. Since both laughed, it did not appear that the visit would be *too* uncomfortable.

"Come," Bianca said. "I will take you to your chamber. I was going to put you together, but Vergil scolded that you should each have your own."

Fleur glanced over to where Laclere was lifting Edmund down from where he had climbed up next to Luke.

Bianca did not know the truth, it appeared. Laclere, however, had reached his own conclusions.

Two horses cavorted on the field. Milton rode the new pony. Dante rode a gelding, with Edmund on the saddle in front of him.

Fleur watched from the terrace of the house. Even from a distance she could see the fun all three boys were having.

"My wife will permit the child on a horse with no one but Dante, me, or herself. Of the three of us, I worry least when he is with my brother."

Fleur startled and turned. Laclere stood a few feet away, watching the joyful play as well.

She glanced around anxiously, but Bianca was not present. The two of them were alone.

"They appear to love him very much," she said.

"He is the perfect uncle, willing to plot with them against us. Every boy should have an uncle like him." He stepped forward, until he stood beside her. "He loves them too, and can still take pleasure in their games. If ever a man had the temperament to be a father, it is Dante."

She swallowed hard and kept her gaze on the horses. Dante had arranged a little race and was in the process of letting Milton and the pony win.

"He is my brother, Fleur. My *brother.*"

She closed her eyes at his tone. He was not making any allusions to her past with Laclere himself or to any unseemliness in this marriage on that count. He was dismayed that she had not considered their old friendship before luring Dante into the marriage and that she had not spared Dante out of respect for that friendship.

"I am correct, am I not? That you offered him a marriage such as you once offered me?"

"I was very honest. I did not play him false. He knew what the arrangement would be when he made his choice."

"He was up to his nose in debt and you threw him a line. It does not sound like much of a choice to me."

"He had other choices, didn't he? He could have relied on friends. He could have turned to you once more. He preferred not to. He knew what he gained and what he lost in this marriage."

"He has no idea what he lost, because it is something he never had, and therefore he could not comprehend its value." He gestured to his sons and brother. "However, he is of an age when he will begin to think about it soon. No children. No intimacy with a woman he loves and wants to hold forever. He is condemned to live the rest of his life as he has so far, with passing passions and no center to his life. A young blood forever."

She had to look away from those horses. She focused on some blades of grass just below the terrace. She wanted to tell Laclere he was wrong, that Dante did not care about such things. Only she wondered if he did, and if he had already begun to resent that he had given them up.

"I have been dreading your return," she said. "I knew you would disapprove and blame me for using him badly."

Laclere's hand covered hers on the stone railing of the terrace. "I do not blame you. I apologize if it sounds that way. I am only concerned for his happiness, and yours."

She welcomed his touch. Until Dante, it had been the only masculine one she could bear. Chaste and caring, it had always been an expression of deep friendship and trust.

She had thought she could have the same friendship with Dante. Only Dante affected her as Laclere never had. As no man had. Now that was leading them to misery.

"Did you explain it all to him, Fleur? I expect it would help if he understood the reasons."

She finally looked at him. His harshly handsome face showed acceptance and concern, not anger. He was Dante's elder by only two years, but he had always been the big brother of the family, even when the firstborn was alive and held the title. Responsibilities had seasoned him at a very young age, and if Bianca had not entered his life and turned it upside down, he may have grown old before his time.

"Of course I explained. He understands it is my nature to be thus, and that it is not my choice."

"I meant, have you explained why it is your nature?"

"There is no why to it, Laclere. I was born this way."

He cocked his head and studied her as if she had said something curious.

"Yes, I expect it is not something you would want to contemplate much," he said. "Let us go and find Bianca. She is very anxious to get the details of this elopement from you. She finds it very romantic."

"Then she does not know the whole story, I assume."

"No, Fleur. Only three of us will ever know that."

Dante knew that sooner or later he and Vergil would have to have a man-to-man. That was what he called the often furious private conversations that they periodically held. Normally Vergil would be at wits end over Dante's debts and bad behavior. Dante had come to view those meetings as the cost of being the viscount's brother, and the price of the allowance that kept him in acceptable style.

This man-to-man, however, was going to be different.

Therefore, he chose to avoid it.

He had other business in the county, and in the afternoon he took a horse from the stable and set out through the park. His ride brought him to a hill that bordered the estate and looked down on a large neighboring house.

He rode toward it through fields that looked well farmed, and noticed a couple of cottages that had been built since the last time he saw this property.

The butler took his card, then returned to lead him to

the library. A blond-haired man in his mid-thirties was buttoning his frock coat as they entered.

"Duclairc," he said. "This is a pleasant surprise."

Dante greeted Nigel Kenwood. Kenwood was Bianca's cousin and the second baronet of Woodleigh, the title that Bianca's grandfather had been granted by the Crown.

"My congratulations on your marriage. My sincere hopes that you overcome Farthingstone's challenge to it," Kenwood said. He sat in a handsome chair near a pianoforte. Kenwood could play the instrument very well. Dante expected that music gave him great comfort while he lived in obscurity, land poor in ways that prevented other luxuries.

"Despite your exile from town, you heard about that," Dante said.

"One hears everything if one wants to."

"It is some people's ability to do so that I hoped to discuss with you today."

Kenwood made a display of checking how the closure of his frock coat lined up on his chest. He had always been an elegant man, much enamored of fashion.

"I should have guessed this was not a social call, Duclairc."

"Hardly that."

"Hell, it was years ago. Laclere receives me. You should let it all be buried too."

"At the moment I cannot. I need to know something."

With a deep sigh of resignation, Kenwood lazily flipped his hand. "Go ahead, then."

"That little blackmailing scheme you had ten years ago. Were there others involved who escaped detection?"

"I had *no* blackmailing scheme. If others, whom I thought were friends, used me—"

"You blackmailed Bianca, so do not plead innocence with me."

Kenwood turned sullen and silent.

"Were there others involved?"

"How the hell would I know? I didn't even realize I was involved. What transpired with Bianca—fine, I accept your condemnation. However, I knew nothing about the others. Laclere understands how it was."

"Did you ever sense that there were others involved besides the ones we learned of, however?"

"I suspected that Nancy had other lovers. It is possible that one of them knew what she was doing."

"Was Hugh Siddel one of those lovers?"

"Siddel? Possibly. I wouldn't know."

Dante felt as if he were chipping away at granite. Kenwood had been in the dark about most of that business. It had been unlikely he could shed much light on it now.

"She did know him, however," Kenwood added. "He drifted around the edges of her circle. He even called at her house. That is how I met him. I arrived early one evening, and he was there."

Well, that was something.

Kenwood's lids lowered and his gaze turned contemplative. He rose and strolled around the library, eventually ending up at the pianoforte. Frowning down at the keys, he casually began poking them, creating the slow opening bars of a Beethoven sonata.

"There is something else. I never thought of it before, never considered a connection."

"What is that?"

"Siddel pointed me on the path I took, in a way. It was the night Bianca first performed. He was in the corridor when Laclere came to bring her home. He insinuated they were lovers. Well, the need to both save her from ruin and save her inheritance for myself became of paramount importance. It was very obvious he was right, once he pointed it out. The potential scandal over that became my wedge, so to speak."

Dante pictured Siddel dangling the bait in front of Kenwood, and then a certain ruthless woman making sure it was swallowed.

"That is all useful to know. I appreciate your willingness to speak of it."

The melody stopped. "Do you have cause to think all of that is going to come to light now? I have tried to make what amends I can to Bianca and Laclere, but—"

"I have no reason to think the past will be unburied. You do not have to flee the realm."

"In the event I should, you will warn me, I hope."

"I will see that you are warned."

Dante took his leave and began the ride back to Laclere Park. He sorted through what he had just learned. It wasn't much, but Kenwood's memories added a few more threads to the knot that tied Siddel to recent events, and to old ones.

"Why don't we have our port in my study, Dante?"

Dante almost laughed as he walked beside his brother down to the viscount's study. A man-to-man almost always started with that suggestion. Vergil vainly hoped that the privacy of the study would prevent the servants and family from hearing their arguments.

Little had changed in the study since his last visit to it. Dante noticed a new watercolor on the wall and an extra little wagon among the toys lining the window's deep sill.

"Did one of your sons make this?" he asked, testing the wheels by giving it a little push.

"Milton," Vergil said as he handed over a glass of port.

"His interests take after yours, then. Machines and such."

"Yes. His temperament, however, is closer to our father's and brother's. The water runs very deeply."

"Perhaps he will become a famous poet." He raised his glass. "To your return. Bianca appears as lovely as ever."

"Performing infuses her with life. I could not refuse her this opportunity, even though it meant neglecting my duties here and in the government. She was magnificent, Dante. The years only clarify her voice. It has been some time since I wept when she sang, but I confess that I did in Naples."

Vergil's love for his wife had always awed Dante. The frank way he admitted it, and his willingness to defy society because of it, had always been astonishing. Dante had never understood the deep emotion Vergil clearly experienced, but seeing his solid, self-possessed brother laid low by any sentiment was impressive in itself.

Today his reaction to Vergil's naked admiration was different than in the past, however. He realized that he better comprehended why Vergil believed his wife was worth any cost.

"Penelope must have enjoyed Naples a great deal, if she has chosen not to come home," he said.

Vergil sat in the chair behind his desk and set his glass on the desk's top. "I do not know the whole story with her. She received three letters from the earl while we were there. She abruptly made her decision after she got the last one."

"The man must know by now that she will not return to him."

"Who knows what he thinks. I suspect that Pen realized that in Naples she does not have to live under his shadow. She made friends there, and no one cares that she separated from her husband before giving him his heir." He watched the port swirl as he turned his glass. "As to her decision to remain there, if it relates to the earl, I expect Hampton will know soon. She sent a letter back with me for him."

"He will never tell us what she wrote."

"No, unfortunately. His professional discretion is welcome in my own affairs, but an irritation when he holds secrets I would like to learn. Your marriage, for example. I received two letters from him written after it transpired, but not once amidst all those business details did he even allude to the surprise waiting for me."

"I decided to wait until your return to inform you of the happy event." Dante sat in the chair on the other side of the desk. He turned it sideways against the front and let his legs sprawl.

How often over the years had they sat thus, Vergil in the position of family head on one side, while he made it clear by his pose and demeanor that, no matter where he sat, he was not a petitioner?

"Hampton advised me not to marry her," he said, to

make it easier. "I told him I would explain to you it was just my being reckless again."

"Why would he advise that?"

"The terms of the settlement are not typical."

"Since she had you in a bad place, I expect she could demand any terms she wanted."

"You could say that."

He looked at Vergil, who looked right back.

"I assume that Hampton does not know all the terms," Vergil said.

"No."

Vergil got up and strolled over to the window with its toys. He looked out into the night. "When Fleur offered me a white marriage, the family finances were in dire condition. I confess that I was tempted to solve the problem with her money."

It was an admission that Vergil could understand a man grabbing such a prize. It was not the reaction that Dante had expected. "It must have disappointed you to learn she demanded it be white. You had courted her a long time."

Vergil turned, surprised. "You misunderstand. I always knew. The whole time. The ruse of our courtship was not only hers. I agreed to it. In fact, I arranged it. So, when she suggested marriage, I knew what kind she meant."

"You knew from the beginning? She told you this before you were close? That is hard to believe."

"I learned almost by accident. One day, when I called on her, she confided in me. So I learned the truth, and the reasons. The episode resulted in a friendship and in the mutually beneficial lie that there was more between us."

"Reasons? What reasons?" He was not sure what angered him more—that there were reasons he had not discovered, or that Fleur had confided it all to Vergil but not to him.

Vergil read his mood with a glance. "She did not tell me the reasons. I surmised them. I wonder now if she is even aware of them herself."

"She told you enough that you had grounds to do your surmising, however. What damn reasons did you damn surmise?" His voice cracked through the room.

Well, hell, it wouldn't be a true man-to-man if one of them didn't yell.

"In my entire life, I have never been as tempted to betray a confidence as I am now, Dante. I have debated all day whether I should do so. However, this is between the two of you, and I should not be in the middle."

He reached down and with one finger rolled his son's wagon back into place beside a carriage he had made when he was a boy. "You might ask her, however, about the day I found her in her parents' garden, weeping. The day when she told me my courtship was in vain."

chapter 19

The knock on her bedroom door interrupted Fleur's dressing. She sent the girl assigned to assist her to fetch the morning tea, then turned to check her finished hair in the mirror of the dressing table.

No tea arrived. Nor did the girl return. Instead, a frock coat and high boots appeared in the mirror's reflection.

She glanced over her shoulder. Dante leaned casually against the wall behind her, watching her primp.

He appeared handsome as sin, as usual. She wished that he didn't. Living with him might be easier if there were some glaring flaw on which she could concentrate whenever she saw him. Perhaps then her heart would not begin a little jig and her skin would not feel so flushed.

She fussed pointlessly with the hairpins and scent bottles on the table. "You rose early today. Do you have something special planned with the children?"

"I told them I am not available today. I rose early to have some time alone with you."

She glanced quickly at his reflection again. His expression reminded her of how he looked the night of the ball. Too composed. Too serious. Too hard, as if the edges of his mood had affected those of his countenance.

"We will go for a walk," he said.

Not an invitation, but a command. No doubt that was part of his plan to be *really* married.

It was the other parts that worried her. "I will join you as soon as the girl returns and I finish dressing."

"I sent her away. I will help you."

"You are inclined to assert your rights this morning, I can see."

"Demanding your company and watching you dress are the least of them, so you should have no objection. Besides, it will not be the first time I did this."

Not the first time that he had dressed or undressed a woman, that was certain. Not even the first time with her.

She began to untie the ribbons that held her powdering gown together. Suddenly he was behind her. She watched in the mirror as his hands came around and gently pushed hers aside. His masculine fingers drew the ends of the ribbons so that the ties came undone, one by one. His hands were so close to her breasts that she imagined their caress even though he did not touch her.

He slid the robe off her shoulders until it pooled around her hips on the chair, leaving her in her petticoats and stays and chemise.

He did not move. She dared not either. She could not see his face, only his torso and hips behind her. She could feel the warmth of his body, however, and the gentle firmness of his hands on her shoulders, where they came to rest.

Excitement and anticipation lured her. Memories of

the numbing dread, however, made the moment threatening too.

He moved away. "Let us get you into your dress, so we can enjoy the day."

In the reflection she saw him lift the garment. Her heart flipped with relief, but she also experienced a visceral disappointment.

They walked side by side, not speaking. Their silence was heavy with words waiting to be said. Fleur did not doubt there was a purpose to this outing.

He brought her to the lake in the park. They ambled along the wooded path that surrounded it until they reached a clearing where the family often held parties and picnics. The site provoked old memories, and Fleur couldn't help smiling.

Dante saw. "What amuses you?"

"I am thinking how this visit should be awkward, but is not," she explained. "After all, your brother once courted me, and I once saw you kissing Bianca not far from here."

He laughed quietly. "I had forgotten that you were one of the witnesses to that. I assure you I did not initiate that kiss. She grabbed me."

"Do you think she was trying to make Laclere jealous?"

"I hope so, since she succeeded magnificently."

He did not follow the path through the clearing but aimed to a little rise with a stand of oak trees.

As he did in Durham, and then in her garden, he removed his frock coat and spread it for her to sit on the ground.

"You will have to excuse me for being cautious, Dante, but every time I sit on your coat, I end up in your arms."

"I only want to talk to you this time. In the house the children will find me and interrupt us, unless we hold this conversation in your bedchamber. Would you prefer that?"

He did not intend it as a threat, but his manner indicated that would not be wise. His sensuality had been rippling all morning, like a power that he barely contained. It had been thus since the night of the ball, and her spirit kept waiting, waiting—the waiting itself would be delicious, if she did not know the hell she would experience if the waiting should ever end.

She settled herself down on the coat and Dante sat beside her. He rested an arm on one bent knee and looked to the lake.

"My brother spoke with me," he said.

"Did he say that you were a fool to make this match?"

"No, not that I would have cared if he had. He spoke of the marriage you offered him."

"I think that Laclere should mind his own affairs. He is your brother and my dear friend, but sometimes his arrogance can be annoying and—"

"He also alluded to the reasons you demand a white marriage."

"I told him there are no reasons, except the simplest one."

"What is that?"

She felt her face burn. She hated Laclere for provoking Dante to ask such cruel questions.

She began to rise. "I do not want this conversation and will not be subjected to it."

He grasped her arm before she could stand. Gently but firmly, he forced her to sit again. "What is this simple reason?"

Her whole face tightened. Her teeth clenched. She wanted to hit him. No, she really wanted to hit his brother, who went around meddling in other lives as if he had the right.

"I was born deficient. Lacking. There, are you happy, Dante? I have said it outright. I am unnatural. Incomplete. Less than a full woman. I am inadequate. *Cold.*"

She was close to tears by the time she finished. Only indignation and resentment held her composure together.

She tried to jerk her arm free.

"Darling, you are not—"

"Release me so I can walk my worthless self back to the house where the totally fulfilled wife of my friend the viscount can show off her children and remind me with every look she gives her husband of what I will never have."

"Fleur—"

"*Let me go.*"

"Fleur, you may have thought all of that about yourself once, but you cannot now. We both know you are not cold. There is no deficiency in your nature. There is a difference between being lacking and being afraid, and you are the latter."

"Whatever I am, it is not what you want."

"That is where you are wrong."

She felt the tears coming, burning their way up her throat. She turned her head away, so he would not see them.

He pulled her to him until she rested in the sanctuary

of his arms. His embrace soothed her as nothing else ever had, and very few of the brimming tears actually fell. A million might have, however. The mood between the two of them was as heavy as if she had poured out her heart.

He pressed a kiss to her head. "Tell me about the time my brother found you in your parents' garden. The day when you told him you would never marry."

"Please, Dante, let us be done with this."

"Tell me, Fleur."

She sighed. "I had gone to the garden to read a letter I had received. Laclere called, and my mother left him in the garden while she went to find me. She did not know I was there, of course. I think she wanted to speak with me before I met with him, to give me instructions on how to handle this suitor. She often did that. So he was alone, and while strolling the garden he found me in the arbor and we had a chance for some private words."

"You used the opportunity to confide that you would not marry and that his addresses were in vain?"

"Yes. I admired him and did not want to treat him unfairly."

"Did you tell him why you would not marry?"

"Of course not. I was not in the habit of explaining it to acquaintances."

"Yet he knew it was not a girl's whim. He knew you were very serious. When you later offered marriage, he knew what kind you meant."

Seething resentment scorched through her again. It was furious and dark and very frightened. The sensation of panic in her head was similar to when the dread took hold.

She pulled out of his embrace. "I do not want to talk about this anymore."

"I do."

"Then talk to your brother. He seems to know everything about everyone. Get your explanations from him."

"I want to talk to you, not him. You are my wife."

"Not really."

She said it deliberately. She noted with satisfaction the flash of anger in his eyes. Good. Now maybe he would leave her alone instead of picking away at this scab that never healed.

He looked right in her eyes. Determination glowed in the lucid depths that examined her. "He said you were crying when he found you in the garden."

"Was I? I don't remember. Perhaps my father had scolded me that day for not giving an important suitor enough encouragement. He often did that."

"If he often did so, it would not reduce you to tears."

She shrugged, and turned her attention from him to the lake. She contemplated the little ripples the breeze made on the water and allowed her thoughts to wander away from him.

"What was in the letter you were reading that day? Who was it from?"

Heavens, the man was relentless. *Enough*.

"Perhaps it was a letter from an old love, whom I lost and have never forsaken. Maybe I refuse other men because of him."

She threw out the spiteful lie, trusting it would silence him.

It did. Dante went icily still.

She looked over and saw fury flickering in his eyes. He

had considered the possibility of that explanation before, she realized. He was prepared to believe it.

She knew two things in that instant. She knew that she wanted so badly for this conversation to end that it maddened her.

She also knew that if the only way to end it meant losing Dante completely, she could not do it.

"I am sorry. I do not know why I said that. It was a cruel thing to throw at you, and it is not true."

"Tell me what was in the letter, Fleur."

Why did she cringe from speaking of it? Why did her heart become so heavy and her throat so tight? "It was written by the mother of one of my girlhood friends, who had married the year before. The letter informed me that my friend had passed away."

He plucked at some grass, watching his fingers while he wore a thoughtful frown. "You must have told my brother what the letter contained."

"I do not remember telling him."

"If he surmised as much as he did, you must have." His hand moved to cover hers. "Did your friend die in childbirth?"

"Yes. How did you know?"

"You were distraught over that letter, and the next thing you did was tell Vergil you will never marry. He saw a connection."

"Then he saw wrong. This did not start that day with that letter. I have always been like this."

"Maybe only for as long as you remember. I think he was right, Fleur. We both know that you are not cold. Not deficient, as you put it. You are by nature very passionate. It is not intimacy you avoid. It is having children."

She rose to her knees in shock. "Now you are insulting me."

"There is no insult."

"There is, and you are vile to——I love children. I would give anything to have them. It breaks my heart that I never will. How dare——"

"I do not think it is motherhood that you fear or deny. I think it is the danger women face in giving birth, darling. Making love can put you in that danger, as it did your friend, and so you will not accept the intimacy."

It was a startling suggestion. She began to object again, but her fury and its words died on her lips as she considered what he said.

He rose to his knees too. He took her face in both his hands and looked down at her. "Do you remember what you said to me that night in Durham? That out by the hedge you could lie to yourself, because you believed in your heart that I would not make love to you there, while a farmer was nearby."

She *had* believed that. But later, in the house, she had known differently.

"Even if you are correct, it makes no difference, Dante."

"It does if you understand that you are not unnatural."

"It is still unnatural. Other women have a normal life, even knowing of the danger. They do not think of death but of the life they carry. They are joyful. Catherine, my neighbor——I worried for her, but she never did for herself. And then——"

He pulled her into his arms and stroked her hair as he held her. "How many friends have you lost this way?"

"The same as most women, I expect." She nestled in his arms and rested her head on his shoulder. She tried to remember if there had been others. Her mother's friend, Mrs. Benedict, had died lying in, now that she thought about it. Her mother never said so, but Mrs. Benedict was big with child and then gone.

Three then. Not so many.

Too many.

An image came to her suddenly, either from her past or her imagination, she did not know which. A picture of blood and of a woman screaming soundlessly. It was the same horrible thing she saw when the panic gripped her, and now it flickered through her mind and made her shudder. Only this time she was watching it, and there were others around the woman, holding her down as she screamed and screamed.

"I think I saw it once, Dante. When I was a girl." She tried to remember when it had been, and where. "Not at my home. It was in the country. Maybe I passed a cottage and heard something and looked in. I think I saw it through a window. I still see it when—when I get afraid. Not clearly, just pieces."

He kissed her temple. "Do not force yourself to remember."

He sat again, and rested against the tree. When he reached out his hand, she took it, and he pulled her back into his arms.

It was wonderful snuggling there with him. White clouds moved across the sky above the lake. They reminded her of the clouds in Durham and the game she and Dante had played. The breeze was cool, but his warmth saturated her.

She let herself go limp against him, more spent than tired. She felt very close to him, as close as when they were in the cottage.

She was glad that he had made her talk about this if it meant that intimacy could return. He said he could not live in their false marriage, but maybe they could remain friends now.

"Laclere said if you knew the reason it may help," she said. "I cannot see how it would."

"He was right. I am glad that I understand."

"Understanding does not change me."

"Perhaps not, but it makes very clear which intimacies you cannot permit and which you can."

And which you can?

"There are ways to make love that do not result in pregnancy, Fleur." His voice flowed to her ear quietly. "You would need to trust the man in order to avoid the fear, I expect. You would need to believe that he would not take those things that you cannot give."

She stayed very still, listening to his heartbeat, luxuriating in the warmth of their embrace. But she sensed a change in him. He had released that special vitality. It entered her and made the waiting return.

He turned her in his arms, cradling her shoulders so he could see her face.

"How much do you trust *me*, pretty flower?"

"I am not sure it is possible for me to trust any man the way you mean."

He kissed her. Not a kiss between friends. She suspected that whatever else this day wrought, his kisses would never pretend to be chaste again.

The long connection moved her deeply. Her heart

wrenched with the awareness of what it could not have, but also filled with the sweetest longing. She almost regretted that he understood and accepted what was wrong with her. That was how confused and aroused his kiss could make her—her body wanted him enough that it betrayed her own defenses.

"It may be that you cannot trust any man enough, Fleur. However, I will have to find out now."

She half-expected him to try and find out then and there. She half-wanted him to. The likelihood that she would fail the test saddened her, however. When that happened, he would never hold her like this again. He would stop kissing her in a way that shook her soul.

Did he sense her hesitation? See her concern in her eyes? Suddenly his embrace was gone and he was helping her to rise.

He dipped his head to kiss her again. "Later."

Taking her hand, he led her back to the house.

"A letter came today from Adrian Burchard," Vergil said as he and Dante sat in the music room that night, politely listening to Vergil's oldest child, Rose, play the pianoforte. "It was the usual welcome back to the country. However, it included a message for you."

Dante had not been paying much attention to Rose, except to notice that with her blond hair, blue eyes, and heart-shaped face, she resembled her mother, who turned the pages for her.

His attention had been on the other females in the room. In a far corner Fleur sat with Vergil's younger daughter, Edith. Fleur patiently plaited the little girl's dark hair, taking her time, prolonging contact with the child.

"What was the message?"

"He asked that you call on him when you return to town. He has some information for you. That was all he wrote."

Fleur finished the plaits and pinned them into a circlet that made Edith look too old. The child grinned impishly at her cohort, as if they had done something naughty.

Edith gave Fleur a big hug and then skipped over to her father to show off her grown-up hair.

Dante watched Fleur's attention follow the girl. He saw her bittersweet expression as Edith climbed onto her father's lap and began beguiling his attention away from her sister's performance.

Fleur's gaze shifted and she caught him watching her. The conversation from the morning suddenly echoed silently in the air between them. Especially the last part.

He went over and sat with her. "Your expression is enigmatic. Both welcoming and cautious. You probably do not know how alluring that can be to a man."

Her face flushed adorably. Her nervousness was palpable, charming, and provocative as hell.

"I will not be coming to your chamber tonight, if that is why you are so unsettled."

"Not unsettled . . . More confused and . . . Well, *somewhat* unsettled, but—"

"I will be borrowing a horse from the stable and riding back to town early tomorrow, to call on Adrian Burchard. You can come home in the carriage later. So you are safe for another day."

She laughed lightly, and looked so beautiful that she almost was not safe tonight after all.

"Are you thinking that you should deny me, Fleur? Is that the debate I see taking place behind those lovely eyes?"

Her lids lowered, and it appeared that she reflected deeply for a moment. She gave the subtlest shake of her head. "I have realized how vulnerable I will be, however. In ways that have nothing to do with trusting your restraint."

"You fear it will be as in the past?"

"Yes, that too."

"Then we will discover for certain what can and can't be. I think it is time to know, don't you?"

"Yes, Dante. I think it is time to know that."

chapter 20

It was time to know.

Fleur chanted that to herself the next day as she supervised the packing of her trunk.

"We will be coming up to town next week," Bianca said. She sat on the bed, watching the preparations. "I count on your accompanying me to the theater as soon as possible."

Fleur appreciated the invitation. It had not been the first such overture, and Fleur wished she had used this visit with Bianca better. If she had not been so absorbed in herself, they might have become good friends. Then perhaps Fleur could have asked her about things.

Such as those other ways to make love that Dante mentioned.

She had no idea what he meant. Her imagination utterly failed her when she tried to puzzle it out. Perhaps she should put him off until she found out. . . .

No, it was time.

"Laclere is very pleased with your marriage. He confided to me that he sees a change in Dante and thinks no woman would have suited him better."

"Did he really say that?"

"Just last night. You look surprised."

"I thought that he considered the quickness of it unwise."

"He may have at first, but a letter from Charlotte yesterday gave him a right understanding. She explained the matter with your stepfather. Vergil had no idea, and neither Dante nor you had said anything about that."

"I suppose it seemed a world away." That was not the only reason. She had not explained about Gregory because it would sound calculating and selfish—that she had married Dante to save her own skin.

"It was very noble of Dante, of course, but also hardly a great sacrifice. Not because of your fortune, but because of his affection for you."

Bianca's frankness only unsettled Fleur more. Somehow she saw to the closing of her trunk and Bianca called for the footmen to carry it down.

Alone in the chamber, Bianca gave her a very direct look. "So, everyone is agreed that this marriage is good for Dante, that it will ensure both his solvency and his happiness. Is it also good for you?"

The bold question took Fleur by surprise. Bianca was not a woman who dissembled much, and that could be disconcerting in a world where most people dissembled all the time. It left Fleur with either responding honestly or not answering at all.

"There have been many surprises in my alliance with him. In many ways, this marriage has not been what I anticipated it would be. As to whether it will prove good for me, I think there is a chance that it will."

"I am happy to hear that, and hope if there is that chance, you will grab it. I believe a woman should decide what she wants and fight for it, not allow herself to be merely buffeted by the winds of life."

As Fleur took her leave of the household and rode through the Sussex countryside, she thought about Bianca's advice. She did not know if the winds about to blow through her life would bring good or ill, but it was time to decide what she wanted.

It was also time to know if she could experience passion with a man without turning to stone.

It would only be possible with Dante. No other man had stirred her at all, let alone enough to contemplate such a risky experiment. If he had not entered her life again, she would have never suspected that she had been wrong about herself all these years.

However, in thinking all night about what was to come "later," she had thought about other things too. As she lay in her bed, so saturated with anticipation that she wished "later" did not mean in London, her thoughts had turned to what being really married to Dante would mean.

Pleasure, to be sure. He had already shown her that.

Friendship, she hoped. Friendship unfettered by the confusion that had interfered with it recently.

But also, maybe, unhappiness. He had warned as much in Durham.

He would not be faithful. She accepted that he could not give her that, just as he accepted what she could not give him. He himself did not believe he had it in him to be constant.

However, if his affairs had wounded her while they were not really married, when his visits to other beds were not betrayals of her, how would she live with them after "later"?

She could not deny Dante because of it. She would not give up the chance to know what they could share. But she did not lie to herself. Knowing the passion would leave her exposed to horrible heartbreak.

As the carriage entered London's environs and aimed to the city, all thoughts of potential unhappiness fell away. Most other thoughts did too. An image invaded her mind and stayed there, banishing all emotions except excitement and longing.

It was the memory of Dante on their wedding day, looking in her eyes as he held her face in his wonderful hands. The rest of the way home she experienced again the perfect, sweet unity she had known that day when he kissed her, once on the forehead, and once on the lips.

A woman should decide what she wants and fight for it.

She experienced an instant of total honesty as she glimpsed her future in all its possibilities. She knew which one she wanted with a security that all the arguments in the world could not have achieved.

It astonished her how easy it was to make her decision. She did not know if she had the courage to fight for it, however.

Especially since the person whom she would be fighting was herself.

.   .   .

An empty house wears its abandon in invisible ways. One senses the silence as one walks past. It exudes loneliness onto the street.

That was what Fleur thought as the carriage stopped in front of her home. For a moment she felt it had been closed forever.

It startled her, therefore, when the door opened and Dante came out to the coach.

"Your meeting with Mr. Burchard was successful?" she asked as he handed her down.

"It was interesting. I will tell you about it later."

Luke removed her trunk, and Dante helped him carry it into the house. "The day is fair, Luke. Take the afternoon for yourself after you have done with the horses. We will not need a carriage today."

Delighted by this unexpected gift, Luke hurried out to get on with his duties.

Fleur stood in the reception hall and listened to . . . nothing. "Are they all gone?"

"Yes."

"I do not think I have ever been alone here before."

Arm along her waist, he strolled with her toward the stairs. "You are not alone now. Think of it as another cottage, where you find yourself with no one but me for company."

"Who will cook for us, and dress us?"

"We will do for ourselves, as we did there."

"I did nothing there. You did it all."

"Then I will here as well." He handed her up the stairs. "I want no one else here today. No sounds, no service, no interruptions. We will read together, or hold conversations, or just sit together, with no duties or demands.

There will be no world outside these walls, and the only world inside them will be the two of us together."

He parted from her on the first floor and went into the library. She continued on to her chambers.

Essential comforts had been provided. Water had been left in the dressing room so she could refresh herself. Scones and jam and punch waited in her sitting room. Knowing Dante, he had instructed the cook to leave enough prepared food in the kitchen so they would not starve.

Alone. The lovely silence derived from more than the lack of sound. The absence of people brought an exquisite peace to the house. She could feel Dante's presence distinctly, even far away, because absolutely nothing else intruded.

Conversation and companionship. Confidences and friendship. She had no idea how Dante had seduced other women, but he knew her very well.

She drank a little of the punch and looked at her *secrétaire*. Inside it were all the pieces of her Grand Project. It astonished her to realize that today, right now, she did not care about it at all. Dante occupied her mind, and the most poignant emotion swelled her heart.

She allowed her hope and longing to have its way. She was beyond fighting either. She would not know how to contain what owned her even if she wanted to. The hope gave her strength too. She would need that.

Looking in her mirror, she removed her bonnet. She gazed in her own eyes and admitted the sad truth. She was not a girl, not a child. She was a woman who had allowed an unknown fear to waste the best years of her life.

She was also a woman who was hopelessly in love with

a man, and who wanted all of that man that she could have.

Gathering her courage, praying that she had enough, she went down to the library.

She found him sitting on the divan, waiting for her.

She walked over and stood in front of him. "I do not think it was wise to empty the house of servants, Dante."

"Whatever you require, I will see to it. What do you need?"

"I would like to remove this dress, and I have no maid to assist me." She turned her back to him.

She expected him to say something clever and to help her at once. Instead, a stillness formed behind her, and he did not move. She kept her pose long enough that she began to feel foolish.

She glanced over her shoulder.

His gaze met hers. "You are sure, Fleur?"

She loved him so much right then. It had always been like this, however. He had always protected her, even when it went against his own interests and desires.

"I am very sure that I want to remove this dress, Dante."

His hands went to work on its closure, but his gaze did not leave her face. The sensation of the cloth parting and his hands touching caused the restrained anticipation of the last day to deluge her. The look in his eyes captivated her. She had come down determined to be bold and confident, but already she was in his power.

"Will you be requiring assistance in donning another dress, Fleur?"

She could not find her voice. She merely shook her head.

He plucked at the knot where the lacing to her stays ended. "Then I should attend to this as well."

Holding her steady with one hand on her hip, he unlaced with the other. "You surprise me, darling."

"I have been working on my courage all day, and thought I should not risk its deserting me. Am I being too forward?"

"Not at all. I had planned a slow seduction, but only because I expected to need one."

She faced front and closed her eyes to savor the sensations already titillating her. "You have been seducing me for weeks, Dante. We both know it has been slow enough."

The stays gaped. She had to grasp her garments to her breast to keep them from falling to the ground.

He rose behind her. Holding her shoulders, he pressed a kiss to the side of her neck. A sparkling shiver danced through her.

She stepped away, out of his reach. "Thank you. I can manage the rest."

Heart pounding, she hurried back to her chamber.

Somehow, she held on to her resolve. Even though she shook as she peeled off the rest of her garments. Even when she slid the pink silk bed gown over her nakedness. Even when she heard the movements on the other side of the wall that said Dante was in his chambers.

She stood still, listening, deciding what to do. Initiating this so quickly had used up a lot of her bravery.

She summoned more.

She needed him to believe that she knew what she wanted. She also needed to prove it to herself.

She turned the latch and opened the door to his dressing room.

She intruded while Dante was removing his shirt. He turned in surprise.

She entered and closed the door behind her. She rested her back against the door.

"You intend to stay while I undress?"

"Should I not?"

He shrugged. "As you wish." He continued with the shirt.

He shed his upper garments. Naked from the waist up, he sat on a chair to remove his boots.

His body fascinated her. She had seen sculptures and paintings, but never a real male form without clothes. How beautiful he was, leanly framed but tight with muscles. She had thought it would be embarrassing to see him unclothed. Instead, nothing could be more natural, and she was not embarrassed at all. Aroused, but not embarrassed. She recognized the physical purr inside her for what it was now.

He looked at her, and she could tell that he knew what she was thinking and experiencing. He stood and faced her, as comfortable with his physical presence as ever, in control of this disrobing even if he was the one who stripped.

"Do you intend to continue watching?"

"Shouldn't I? Do you want me to leave?"

"I do not want you to leave, although I cannot remember ever being watched so obviously."

"I thought that since you have seen me, it was only fair for me to see you."

"I am not seeing you now."

No, he was not. She had stacked the deck, to buy herself some courage. Nor had she planned to just stand and watch him. She had intended to speak with him when she opened that door. Seeing his body had become a delicious distraction.

He had challenged her, and she was determined not to play the shy virgin today. She stepped away from the door. "Do you want to see me? Will that make it more fair?"

"Yes."

She walked over to him. That brought her very close to his chest and shoulders and skin and hardness and . . .

He did not touch her. He looked down, as if waiting for something.

"Aren't you going to assist me, Dante? I thought it was one of your rights."

"You said that you can manage it yourself, and you are certainly acting as if you can."

"You would prefer I did it myself?"

"Sometimes."

This time.

Removing that gown was more difficult than she expected, because of the way he watched. She wondered if he had found her gaze so disconcerting a few minutes ago. She could not deny, however, that she enjoyed the wicked thrill of sliding the silk down her arms and lowering it to the floor. She liked the way his expression tightened with the subtle signs of how she affected him.

Her initial awkwardness passed, replaced by a sense of power and pride. His gaze made her magnificent and noble and strong. Standing naked in the afternoon light in front of Dante, she became a goddess.

He reached for her hand and drew her toward him, into his arms. The embrace astounded her. The warmth of his body, touching hers skin on skin all over, pressing her breasts, surrounding her completely—the new sensations piled up, threatening to bury her sense of everything else.

Somehow she held on to her mind. She had come through that door with a goal, and he needed to know what it was.

"I need to say something to you, Dante."

He nuzzled her neck. "Tell me later."

"It must be now. You see, I have changed my mind about this."

His embrace loosened until he was only holding her waist. His lids lowered. "You have not been acting like a woman who has changed her mind."

"You do not understand. I am not saying that I want you to stop. In fact, I do not want you to think that you have to stop at all. Ever."

"You are correct. I do not understand."

"If I believe you will not do anything to impregnate me, I am sure that the fear will not come. That is how much I trust you. There is no need to test that. It is always there for us."

His expression turned serious, and perplexed. "Are you saying that you would like to test something else instead?"

"Yes. I think that even if you do not promise restraint, the fear still will not come."

She had assumed he would have more enthusiasm for her decision than he now revealed. He looked deeply in her eyes, as if searching to see if her heart supported her words.

"I do not want this dread to own my life anymore. In naming it, maybe I have defeated it." She laid her cheek on his chest, so that the taut warmth of his skin touched hers. "I want us to be fully married, Dante. I want to have a family. I want these things so much that I believe my desire for them can conquer any fear." She looked up at him. "I want you too. Completely. That alone would be enough for me to make this decision."

He laid his hand on her face. "If you are wrong . . ."

"If I am wrong, we will know very soon."

"I do not want to frighten you or hurt you."

"I will not let you. I will not try to brave it out. I am incapable of controlling this if it takes hold. You must promise me, however, that you will not make the choice for me. I will only know if I am free if I believe your intentions have changed."

A small, charming smile broke. "I think I can promise that if you demand it."

"I do demand it."

"Then know now that I will take you if I can, Fleur. Believe it."

His kiss displayed his resolve. It also revealed the passion of a man who had been listening to too much talk, even if he welcomed what he had heard.

The kiss awoke all of the anticipation her body had buried during the long weeks of wanting him. Her skin was wickedly alert as he caressed parts of her that had never felt his touch directly before. Her back and hips and thighs responded to his warm palms and fingers. New sensations startled her again and again.

He kissed her deeply, in a way he never had before. She could not ignore the subtle difference. It came from his aura more than his action. A primitive part of her could tell that he had not lied. The man who kissed her, who dominated her with his body and embrace, who handled her so possessively that the claim of rights could not be ignored—this man intended to have her if he could.

She understood that without thinking it. Her soul knew.

The fear knew.

It shot out one of its strangling tendrils. She recognized it for what it was. Images of crying faces invaded her head. Her body wanted to recoil defensively, to end the assault.

She would not let it.

She embraced Dante desperately and focused her physical awareness on the delicious feel of his skin and muscles, on the tension in his body and the hardness under her hands. She let her consciousness dwell on his reality.

She summoned more than pleasure to her little battle, however. She let her love for him free. In the warmth and glow of its promise of fulfillment, the fear abruptly withered and shrank and ceased to threaten her.

The victory left her euphoric. Liberated. She had thought she could not control this dread, but she could. With Dante she could. Acknowledging her love gave her a weapon the fear could not face.

Dante knew what had happened. She could tell that he

did. He stopped kissing her but his caresses continued, following her curves and feeling her nakedness, tantalizing her. He looked down with eyes that recognized what had just occurred in the last few moments.

A hard challenge entered the lucid depths gazing at her. His caress moved down her body. Daring the fear by making his intentions explicit, his hand smoothed up her bottom, then slowly descended. His fingers skimmed down her cleft and followed the line to where it met moisture and softness and a maddening pulsation.

The touch on that spot shocked her. Wonderfully. Gloriously. Her whole body reacted, but not with fear. She stretched up, seeking his kiss hungrily, needing a way to release the stunning, deep, sensual throb.

The war was won, and they both knew it. She announced her victory by kissing him as intimately as he did her. With her tongue she expressed her pride and excitement.

Heady with liberation, proud of her boldness, she kissed down his neck and his chest, tasting him, enthralled by unfettered pleasure.

The full force of his sensual vitality broke free, encompassing her more completely than his arms. She welcomed the way it dazzled her, controlled her, taught her.

He lifted her in his arms and carried her into his chamber. He laid her on the bed and finished undressing while he looked at her.

"You are very beautiful, Fleur."

She did not doubt him. Right now, lying on this bed in the filtered light, euphoric from fighting for her right to love and feel, she was sure that she was the most beautiful woman who had ever lived.

The most beautiful man in the world now stood by the bed, his full magnificence revealed, so stunning that her heart did not know whether to race or simply stop. He was a fitting consort for the goddess she had become. His body fascinating her so much she could not look at him enough.

He came to her.

"This is a remarkably singular occurrence, Miss Monley. Finding you, of all women, in my bed."

He had said that in the cottage, but his tone was different this time. He was not teasing.

Only she was no longer Fleur Monley, the saint, the angel. She was a queen, a warrioress, a handmaiden of Venus, a—

"You are very proud of yourself, aren't you?" He kissed her nose, which hardly befitted her new power.

"Bursting with pride."

"As you should be." He watched his hand caress down her neck and around her breasts. "All the same, you must let me know if I frighten you."

"I am not going to stop you, Dante."

"You can still let me know your pleasure, Fleur. If I do something you do not want, you can tell me that."

"There is nothing I do not want. I have been denied this too long. I have no intention of missing one thing because of cowardice."

"You do not understand what I am talking about, darling." He kissed her lightly on her cheek. "You will soon, so remember what I said. I do not want any silent sacrifices. You have a whole life to try everything."

She stretched her fingers through the hair on his head. "I would not be cautious if I were you, Dante. I am probably braver now than I will ever be again." She pressed him down so she could kiss him.

He did not allow her to control the kiss long. With a masterful embrace he took over and bestowed dozens of nuanced pleasures on her lips and neck and ear. He made her want him with kisses alone until the waiting possessed her again, and built and built.

Her body craved the return of his caress. He was slow in giving it to her, so that when his hand trailed down her chest she almost begged him to touch her.

He teased as he had in the garden. The same wanton pleasure enslaved her. His circling fingertips had her gritting her teeth. She was helpless to the hunger he demanded.

His head dipped and his tongue began the same slow patterns on her other breast. The desire deepened, went lower. It filled her hips and made her vulva cry. She lost awareness of everything but the sensations and the pleasure and the frantic desire.

His fingers gently touched one nipple. His tongue flicked at the other. An arrow of shivering pleasure shot down her body.

Then another, and another. It felt so good that she wanted it to go on forever. Her body demanded, ached, for relief even as it begged for more.

She could not contain the chaotic need. She heard the sounds of her delirium but did not care.

His head moved and he kissed her again. His hand moved and she rebelled at the pleasure's end with a muffled cry. He broke the furious kiss and looked down her body. His caress slid lower, to her stomach and thighs.

Her desire moved lower too. The waiting became very

focused, very intense. Her legs parted to encourage the caress she desperately wanted. The newly freed primitive part of her comprehended this passion in ways her mind did not.

He caressed closely until her hips were rising toward his touch, begging for more. She saw the expression of hard command when he finally responded to her body's demands and her audible cries. He looked back at her face with the first touch and then watched as his slow strokes created a pleasure so intense that she lost all control.

She did not care that she had forsaken sanity and dignity and begged for something she did not understand. She did not care that he controlled her madness with his hands and eyes.

He kissed her lips, then her breast, then her stomach. He kissed lower, leaving her arms bereft as his body moved down.

"I am glad that you are so brave today," he said softly. "Because I have been wanting to do this for weeks."

She watched, confused. Her body understood, however. With each kiss closer, her vulva shivered.

His kisses went lower yet. His body moved more. Her mind finally comprehended. The notion shocked her. His hand lured her. Prepared her. She closed her eyes just as he moved his body between her thighs and gently lifted her hips.

His tongue replaced his fingers, and her brief spike of sanity shattered. She submitted to the excruciating combination of pleasure and devastating desire. It just got better and better and worse and worse as he drove her to the edge of a terrible, wonderful experience.

An unbearable peak beckoned. She reached for it

because there was no place else to go. Her passion leapt, touched a glorious spot of pure pleasure, and showered through her essence.

He was with her suddenly, back in her arms, lying between her legs as he had in Durham. No garments interfered this time. She grasped him, intensely aware of his weight and warmth.

Her vulva still pulsed, still possessed that craving need. The sensation of him entering brought incredible relief. He pressed deeper and the fullness astonished her emotions.

Pain wanted to intrude on her daze. Her passion absorbed it, ignored it, conquered it. He thrust and they were fully joined and he filled her completely. The intimacy of holding him, of feeling him a part of her, moved her more than the highest pleasure she had just learned. She closed her eyes and savored the complete bond.

His passion guided the rest. She sensed a restraint on his desire, and knew when it fell away. His power controlled them both then, creating a whirlwind of tumultuous, fevered kisses and thrusts that awed her. She could only accept and absorb and feel. Nothing at all existed for her but love and intimacy and the reality of him in her body and arms.

The end left her dazed and astonished by her own emotions. Holding him in the stillness afterward, it was as if her heart and soul had been left without any protection. She held him to her, so alert to his scent and breaths and skin that it seemed new senses had been born in her. Special ones, which existed only for knowing this man.

She wanted him to stay on her forever, bound like this, but eventually he moved. Even after he withdrew and shifted his weight off her, she still pulsed as if they were connected.

"Did I hurt you?"

"No." She did not know if he had. It did not matter.

"Did I shock you?"

"No . . . well, a little." She turned on her side to face him. "Was that everything?"

"No."

She smiled. "Stupid question. Of course it wasn't. After all, you forgot to show me that sensitive spot behind my knee."

"That I did."

"And the trick with the base of my spine—no doubt you are saving that for another day too."

He laughed quietly. "I promise to do better next time, when I am not so impatient."

She drew a little pattern on his chest. "And the discovery about how a woman's body can be more sensitive after . . ."

"It is not too late for that." His caress moved down her body. "Part your legs wide, then do not move."

She obeyed. His first touch shocked her whole body. His finger stroked low, caressing flesh unbelievably sensitive from their lovemaking. The pleasure was almost unbearable.

Abandon claimed her with a violent break in her control. Almost instantly she tottered on the highest point of arousal, begging for more, shuddering with desperate expectation. It was more intense and dangerous than the last time. The pleasure was unearthly, excruciating, shattering.

Her body released her. She cried as a powerful climax

quaked through her. She floated in a bliss of perfect sensation, with the echo of a cry filling her head.

Awareness of the bed and chamber returned to her slowly. It was some time before she rose above the sensual stupor, however.

Dante was waiting for her when she did. She opened her eyes to find him watching her. It seemed that the room still rang with her scream.

"I think it is a good thing that I sent the servants away," he said.

"Oh, yes." She also thought it had been wise to delay "later" until after they left Laclere Park.

chapter 21

It is just as you said it would be, Dante. No world exists outside these walls, and only the two of us exist inside them." Fleur nestled closer. "When will they return?"

Her words pulled him out of the cloud of contentment in which he had been floating while he held her closely.

"I handed out enough coin to keep them busy at theaters and taverns most of the night."

He turned on his side and propped his head on his hand. Her beauty awed him. Her courage did. He had not been able to lure her from the fear with pleasure. It had taken her own will, her own choice, to do that. It humbled him that she had donned such bravery in order to share passion with him.

She had been determined, magnificent, glorious.

I want to have a family.

Her soft, pale skin felt more luxurious than the most precious cloth. He caressed her shoulder and arm slowly and her lids lowered as they shared the touch.

I want you.

He had never in his life heard such flattering words. They had been spoken by others, but not in this way, or for this reason. He wanted her too, also in ways he had never desired before.

That is how much I trust you. There is no need to test that.

He would never forget those astonishing words.

I want us to be fully married.

He glanced over to his writing desk and thought about the letter in its drawer. It was from Farthingstone and had been waiting for him when he returned this morning. The man wanted to negotiate, and Dante suspected the direction those negotiations would take.

He gave his wife a kiss, to put thoughts of Farthingstone and his maneuvers out of his mind.

It was not to be. Fleur turned to him, looking so lovely with her hair half down and her nakedness draped with the sheet.

"What did Mr. Burchard want? You said you would tell me later."

The meeting seemed a lifetime ago, not mere hours. Dante had to force his memory back to it. Anticipation of Fleur's return meant he only partly listened to Adrian's information, and he had not deliberated its meaning at all.

"Burchard undertook some inquiries on my behalf."

"You asked him to do this?"

"No. He has some experience in such things and used his own initiative as my friend."

"Much as St. John and Mr. Hampton used their initiatives and made inquiries about me, you mean. You have very dedicated friends. Although one might also say they are a little presumptuous."

"One might say so."

"What sort of inquiries did Mr. Burchard make? More regarding me?"

"He inquired about Farthingstone. He learned little that could not be discovered by anyone. That Farthingstone received a legacy as a young man, which included that property in Durham that neighbors yours. He lives simply considering his income and is well regarded."

"We already know that."

"The rest was more interesting, however. Farthingstone was not always so sober and upstanding. He had a wilder youth, and as a young man looked to be one who would come to no good. Burchard's aunt remembers him from back then and related how a miraculous transformation occurred rather suddenly when Farthingstone was nearing thirty years old. The change was so complete that his past has been all but forgotten."

"I would prefer he still gambled and drank and ruined himself than that he presented himself as so respectable while he tried to imprison me and then destroy my reputation. The world is too quick to judge for good or ill in these things. I daresay your friend McLean is more honorable than Gregory, but McLean is notorious and Gregory is admired."

There it was, the world as seen through Fleur Monley's eyes. He was glad that she tried to perceive the essentials, even if sometimes she saw more than was there. When she looked at Dante Duclairc, her optimism blinded her.

"If that was all he could tell you, it wasn't very interesting at all. Was there more?"

"That was most of it." Dante was not sure he wanted to broach the rest. Not now, at least. He did not want it intruding on this day and this bed.

"I am curious now, so you must tell me all."

He caressed her shoulder again and turned his gaze away from her face so he would not see her reaction. He was not sure what he avoided witnessing. "He also discovered that there is a connection between Farthingstone and Siddel. A distant one, and it probably means nothing."

She did not respond for a while. He might have said nothing at all.

"Did you ask him to make inquiries regarding Mr. Siddel, Dante?"

"I asked him if he had cause to think they are friends."

"They are not."

"Fleur, your stepfather learned you were in that cottage. Siddel is a man who could have told him. If he did, it meant that Siddel knew he was in the county that night. It may even have been Siddel whom you overheard speaking in the next chamber the night before."

She tilted her head and looked up at him. She did not appear angry, but thoughtful. Very thoughtful. "What connection did Mr. Burchard discover?"

"Farthingstone has no apparent friendship with Siddel. He did, however, have one with Siddel's uncle. They shared bad behavior together."

"Much like you and McLean?"

"Much like that. Siddel's own comfort depends upon a legacy of his own, from this uncle."

"Or from his business affairs. I expect his success in those has enhanced his fortune considerably."

"It is not at all clear that he is so successful in business. Burchard could find little evidence of any grand financial schemes, despite Siddel's reputation for them."

"No doubt he keeps them secret."

"Burchard has the means to discover secrets when he wants to. He undertook inquiries for the government when he was younger, and there are men willing to share information with him that they would not give to others."

He could see her weighing that, although her expression did not change.

The night of the ball, he had demanded that she not use Siddel for an adviser any longer. She had not welcomed that command, and he had not been convinced she would obey it. She may not have.

She looked right in his eyes. "You do not like him at all, do you?"

"As I told you, I do not think he can be trusted."

"It is more than that. You get very hard when you speak of him. Even now, your mood has darkened."

"Perhaps that is because I wonder if your relationship with him continues."

Her fingers touched his face and drifted over his cheek and jaw. "What is this man to you?"

He stopped her hand and took it in his own. He gazed down at the delicate fingers and ran his thumb along the back of her palm.

She waited for him to answer, but she would accept it if he did not. If he kissed her, the question itself would be forgotten.

"Some years ago, there were some people blackmailing prominent men. They were stopped by my brother. I think that Hugh Siddel was one of the blackmailers but escaped detection."

Her expression fell in surprise. "That is a serious accusation to make, Dante."

"I will not make it publicly unless I have proof. It is doubtful I ever will."

"If you don't have proof, how—"

"He knows things he should not, Fleur. Things he could not know unless he was involved." He hesitated, and told himself no good could come from explaining it. Yet the impulse to go on was greater than the one to spare himself the pain of forming the words.

She said nothing. No prodding or insistence. She just watched him. Her expression was so thoughtful. Her eyes held worry and concern, but no expectations.

"I inadvertently helped them, Fleur. A woman among them used my desire for her to gain access to some documents. Those papers were then used to blackmail two men. Both of those men killed themselves."

He had never told anyone this. Never even said it aloud. It sounded even more damnable than he expected. His chest felt heavy, as if the air in his lungs had thickened.

Fleur caressed his face again, more deliberately. "The crime was not yours, but theirs. No man could have foreseen what would happen. You should not blame your—"

"One of the men who killed themselves was my eldest brother."

A flicker of shock flashed in her eyes. Then she looked at him with the warmest sympathy he had ever seen.

She understood. He did not have to say more. Her honest, clear eyes seemed to see into his mind and even his heart and perceive the guilt he carried. He could tell she knew that no excuses or absolution could make a difference.

And yet, somehow, just her gaze changed things. That accepting silence eased the weight of this old memory.

Finally sharing it with this friend brought some peace to the corner of his soul where he kept this disgrace hidden.

She shifted closer and embraced him, laying her soft cheek against his chest, holding him more than he held her.

"We have let the outside world intrude, after all," she said quietly. She sounded a little sad.

Not the outside world. Their world. The one in which they lived, full of the people and events that affected their lives and this marriage. He knew what she meant, however.

He gently tugged on the sheet. It slowly slid down her body as the soft folds receded. He caressed her, his hand following the same path as the sheet's edge over softness and curves. He pulled her closer, to his heart.

"I know a way to make the world go away, Fleur. I know a place where it cannot find us."

"Yes," she whispered. "Take me there, Dante."

The next afternoon, Dante waited in the study for a visitor to arrive. He had spent little time in this chamber, and this was the first time he would conduct official business here. Or anywhere.

He had always avoided the serious financial dealings that he associated with studies. As a young man he had found them boring and bothersome, the kinds of matters best left to old men and dutiful sorts like his brother.

He studied the Piranesi engravings lining one wall and the Canaletto painting showing the Grand Canal of Venice on another. If meetings like this became a habit, he would keep the engravings but the Canaletto would have to go. He did not care for the artist's *veduti* of Italy. They were so dully acceptable. No risk at all.

The door opened and Williams brought the expected card. Farthingstone was precisely punctual.

"It was generous of you to receive me," Farthingstone said when he arrived. "May I say at the outset that I hope you and I can settle amiably the entire problem that besets us, and in a way that ensures the welfare of Hyacinth's daughter."

They sat in two chairs. Farthingstone took in the room and smiled when he noticed the painting. "Ah, the Canaletto. I remember when Mr. Monley purchased it. I favor his art. That is an excellent example, if I may say so."

Dante studied this dull man who favored dull Canaletto and tried to picture him chasing naked girls through a summer garden, as Burchard's aunt had described one scandalous rumor of a long-ago bacchanal.

"You had important matters to discuss, you said," Dante prompted.

Farthingstone's expression grew very serious. "I regret to say that I suspect you do not know the full extent of Fleur's condition. What I have to say may come as a shock to you."

"Consider me prepared for the worst."

Farthingstone had the decency to flush and feign hesitation before he gave the bad news. "I have discovered that prior to your alliance with her, her behavior was even more odd than I knew. Among other things, she visited brothels and went about town so unprotected that she even was arrested during a disturbance."

He treated Dante to the details of both events, while

Dante speculated on which of the servants had been coaxed to reveal this.

"It sounds as if both episodes were long ago."

"Even a brief lapse does not bode well, sir, not at all. However, there are more recent happenings of a more serious nature." Farthingstone tilted his head and looked up dolefully. "She was caught stealing. Tea, no less. She hardly needs to, which makes it all the worse. For all we know, she goes about the city on those solitary walks of hers, acting the thief for reasons only her sad condition explains."

"I know of the incident. She stole nothing. It was a misunderstanding."

"Indeed? Then her explanation for being in the back room of The Cigar Divan should stand? Better she admit to theft, sir. The alternative is even worse—her belief that she saw her long-lost brother enter. Especially since she never had a brother." Farthingstone shook his head sadly. "I fear that part of the time she lives in a world of her mind's own making. Normal proprieties and judgment do not exist for her because of it."

"Farthingstone, I have no evidence that my wife lives in any world other than ours. I have witnessed nothing that indicates she is anything other than completely rational."

Farthingstone's lidded gaze implied he found his host stupid at best. "I think that you do not fully comprehend her mind, sir. You force me to a matter that I had hoped to avoid."

"If you feel forced, do not blame me. This conversation was not at my request."

"Hear me out. It is in your interests to do so." He managed to appear shocked, stern, and sad all at once. "I regret to say that I have reason to believe that she has formed an alliance with a man besides yourself." He peered over, waiting for the reaction.

Dante let the silence stretch past the point of drama. At least now he knew who had arranged to have that man follow Fleur.

"You appear remarkably indifferent, sir," Farthingstone said disdainfully. "If you do not care about her welfare, I at least expected you to have an interest in your own reputation."

"I care a great deal about both. I am merely wondering what you expect of me and why you have come here to lay out all this information for my consumption."

"As things stand, you are responsible for her. I did not approve of this marriage. I can still go forward on the question of whether she had the presence of mind to make such a contract. I believe that if I do so with what I have just told you, in addition to what I knew before, I will succeed."

"I doubt that."

"With this new evidence, I am very confident. It is Fleur's well-being that concerns me, however. If I were convinced that she was in good hands, that her husband understood the need for her to be controlled and her fortune to be preserved, I might be willing to stand down and avoid the lengthy legal battle that looms. After all, she cannot move in any way without your approval. You must sign any contracts or deeds. The law gives you total authority, no matter what independence she may be under the illusion she still has."

Dante kept his expression bland, but Farthingstone had finally said something interesting.

Farthingstone knew about the private agreement regarding the disposition of Fleur's inheritance.

Which meant Fleur had told someone. Dante guessed who that someone was. Her adviser would need to be assured that she still had control over her fortune; otherwise, any advice would be meaningless.

She had told Siddel, and now Farthingstone knew.

"Sir, surely you understand the implications of what I am saying? I know that you have little interest in financial matters or business, but—"

"I understand the implications for me. I am wondering what you think they are for you."

The door opened, Farthingstone rushed in. "Her frequent sales of property must be stopped. Land is still the best investment. She has spoken for some time about selling the land in Durham. I think that would be unwise."

"Is her welfare your only concern on that matter?"

Farthingstone reacted with insult. Halfway to high dudgeon, he thought better of it. Somewhat sheepishly, he shook his head. "You are sharp, sir. Very sharp. I always said that you were underesteemed. You force a confession from me."

"Do not feel any obligation to explain anything to me."

"No, no, it may be for the best. I must confess that I have an ulterior interest. It is not only the rashness of selling that land that I deplore. I also do not care for the use to which a part of it will be put."

"The school."

"My land adjoins hers. This will not be a school for sons of gentlemen. She is not planning another Eton, is she? It will be full of the rabble of the world, ill-mannered boys who lack discipline or intelligence. Not only is it a fool's errand, but it is one that will significantly affect my enjoyment of my own property."

Dante liked Farthingstone even less than before. He also wanted to laugh. If Farthingstone was being honest, if all of his machinations had been for this reason, it meant that Fleur had gotten married because her neighbor did not want a boys' school ruining his view while he rode his horse through his farms.

"I trust that no sale has occurred yet. That no deeds have been signed," Farthingstone ventured.

"No, not yet."

Farthingstone could not entirely hide his relief. "I am willing to make it worth your while to keep her from selling that land and building that school," he said. "Shall we say, oh, two hundred a year to ensure that the land remains as farms. I calculate that the proceeds of a sale, if put in the funds, would give that amount. Accommodate me on this, and you can have the money and still hold the rents."

It was an outright bribe, but an interesting one. Two hundred pounds a year would not support a school, but if Fleur sold those farms and put the money in trust, it appeared that was all the income would be.

Farthingstone's bulbous nose reddened as he awaited an answer. That rosy glow announced the man's excitement as no physical agitation could.

"I will need some time to consider this," Dante said.

"There is no time for long consideration, sir. She is having the designs for that building drawn even as we speak." He cocked his head curiously and assumed a very smug expression. "Or didn't you know that?"

Dante suddenly knew why he disliked business affairs. It was not the affairs themselves that he found tedious and unpleasant, but the sorts of men so often drawn to them. Men like Gregory Farthingstone.

"Your offer is a handsome one. I will let you know my decision," he said, rising.

"Soon, I hope. As I said, I would rather not present what I know to a court, since that is so public. It would embarrass both her and you. I expect we all want to avoid that."

A bribe, and now a threat.

"I will decide soon, I assure you."

Farthingstone took his leave, and Dante sat at the desk. Someday Fleur would lay out contracts for him to sign regarding the school on this surface. He had thought it would be a year at least before she did so, but it appeared not.

It was time to learn how thoroughly his wife had disobeyed him while they were not really married. He also needed to know what she was really up to with that property.

chapter 22

Fleur sat at her *secrétaire* laboring over a letter. Dante's revelations about Mr. Siddel had weighed on her mind since hearing them. She could not deny that the evidence was mounting against him. That did not speak well of her judgment in allowing Siddel a role in the Grand Project.

It was time to demand an accounting, and if he did not give one it was time to release Mr. Siddel of his obligations to her.

Dante's unexpected arrival startled her. Her head snapped around at the sound of his bootstep.

She set down her pen and, as she turned toward him, closed the *secrétaire*.

She tried to do it casually, so she would not appear furtive. It did not work. She saw his gaze take in the action.

He stood over her, with an expression both serious and alert. With one hand he opened the *secrétaire* again. "You do not need to stop because I am here, my dear."

The lowered lid revealed her recently received mail and sheets of papers. It also displayed the letter she had just been writing. He did not really look at any of it, but she worried that he saw the salutation to Mr. Siddel penned at the new letter's top.

He caressed her face much as he did when they made love, with thoughtful concentration. She sensed something besides desire in him as he looked at her.

"What is it, Dante?"

"I am wondering if you are truly willing to be completely married, Fleur."

"I would think after yesterday it is obvious that I am."

"I am not only talking about sex. Nor did you, in the dressing room. There is more to marriage than sharing a bed."

His gaze made her uncomfortable. Her open *secrétaire* did too. Her heart jumped when he gestured to the papers. "You are very busy with something that you do not want me to know about."

She shifted the papers around, pretending to dismiss them as insignificant. It gave her the chance to slip the letter to Mr. Siddel below some others. "I engage in the usual correspondence of a woman. It would be of no interest to you."

"I would find the usual correspondence very dull. However, there is a part of your life that I would find very interesting, I think. Not only for practical reasons, or those relating to my responsibilities as your husband, but because it is something very important to you. I cannot know you fully unless I know it."

He was accusing her of withholding herself from him. Of giving him her body but not the deeper parts. She could not say he was wrong. The last two days she had felt guilty whenever she considered the Grand Project. Being really married had turned it into the Grand Deception.

His hand moved to the desk's surface. With alarming precision, he slid the letter to Mr. Siddel out until it was visible.

"I told you not to communicate with him further, Fleur."

She closed her eyes, mortified. Disobeying him before had not seemed so terrible, since they were not really married and she had reserved rights to her own life in their arrangement. All that had changed now, and the letter was a betrayal.

She had known it was. It had been impossible to write because of how acutely she felt she denied Dante in doing it. After half an hour, only two lines had been penned because of how guilty she had felt.

"You told me once that you have a purpose in life, Fleur. One that made you feel alive and young and that could not be denied. I would like to learn more about it, as your husband and lover, because it is important to you. If Siddel is involved in it, I want to know how."

"Are you demanding to know?"

"Yes. However, it is my hope that you would like to share this with me. If you were willing to trust me with your fear, I would like to believe that you can trust me with this."

She looked up at him. She had promised not to tell him, but she had made bigger promises since then. With her body and with her heart. She had made promises even Dante did not know of, in choosing the kind of marriage she wanted. That was why it had been so hard to write this letter. She did not want to deceive this husband. She did not want to compromise what this marriage could be.

She rose and walked over to a coffer in the corner. "I intended to tell you, when it was all arranged. I would have had to. There was no way you would have signed the documents without hearing it all."

"Did you fear that I would not keep my promise?"

"I think that you always keep them. It is why I extracted one from you. However, if you learned of it before it was all arranged, I expected you to worry that my plans were unwise and try to stop me." She opened the coffer. "Not only unwise. A little addled. The sort of thing that a woman who was not entirely sound of mind would dream up."

"There is nothing addled about a school, Fleur. I told you to delay it, but I never said it should not be built."

She lifted some long rolls of paper from the coffer. "It is not only about a school, Dante."

He followed her into her bedchamber. She dumped the rolls on the bed. Choosing the largest, she opened it fully.

It showed plans for a large building of four levels. Chambers had been denoted for various uses. The architect's address, on the bottom, was in Piccadilly. That must have been where the footman followed Fleur.

"The school," he said. It was much bigger than he expected.

"It is only preliminary. There are changes to be made, and much work to be done."

"You had this made recently, didn't you? Even though I told you to delay it."

"I wanted to see how the building would look. I also needed to estimate the costs."

"You also had no intention of delaying anything." He was not truly angry, but he was also not in the mood for even mild dissembling.

"No. I had no intention of delaying."

She had intended to go forward and arrange the sale of whatever land she needed to finance this school. She was going to present him with documents to sign that he thought should not be signed for her own protection. In gaol, Hampton had predicted just such a development and laid out the conflict between honor and responsibilities that could result.

"I could not delay," she said. "The rest of the project was going to happen soon or not at all. Once it became known, the school would have been a mere addendum. The school was only my private reason for the rest."

"The rest?"

"It is all here." She unrolled a smaller sheet. It bore a map of County Durham.

He bent over it. "What are these little squares with numbers, along these lines?"

"Parcels of land. The numbers refer to a key I have created that indicates the ownership. See, here is my property, and I am number one. Up there is Gregory's, and he is number two, and so forth."

He noticed the number one in some tiny parcels, in some cases at a distance from her large property. "You have been purchasing some of this land, haven't you?"

"That is how I used the money from the lands I sold."

She had sold land and bought other land. It would not be notable, except that her plan was to sell the Durham lands too. Why bother, unless she thought it would be easier to make one big sale instead of many when the time came?

"The first thing you must know is that I realize my plan is risky," she said. "I expected some resistance from you. That was why I wanted to wait until every piece was in place, which I thought would be very quickly done."

He lifted the map to examine it more closely. Those little parcels flanked lines on the map. Two long, sinuous lines moved from the center, joined, then snaked to the coast to form a long "Y." The point of jointure was right on Fleur's lands.

"What is risky about it? You are selling land to endow a school. It sounds quite simple."

"It is not the proceeds from the land alone that will endow the school. There would not be enough. It costs a lot of money to support all those boys."

He saw another line, much like the "Y," stretching from Darlington to the town of Stockton.

"I will be using the proceeds from the land sale to make another investment. That is the risky part."

He only half-heard her. His concentration on the map sharpened. Suddenly he realized what he was looking at.

Those lines were not there to help Fleur keep track of bits of land she had bought. Nor were those lines roads. The turnpikes had other markings.

"What is this risky investment?" he demanded, already guessing the answer.

She stepped close and ran her finger along the "Y." "That is going to be a railroad, Dante."

.   .   .

A railroad.

His wife, the saintly Fleur Monley who had put herself on the shelf and devoted herself to helping the downtrodden, planned to build a railroad.

He looked at her. Her expression was a combination of pride and worry.

"It is more than risky, Fleur. It is almost untried."

"Not completely so."

"Did Siddel lure you into this?"

"It is all my idea. Look." She peered over his arm and pointed. "There is coal here in central Durham. Everyone has known that for a century. Only it is difficult to transport it to the coast, and the land is not suited for canals. With a railroad, however, it can be moved and those coal fields can be opened."

"You have the coal going to Hartlepool, not to Newcastle."

"The surveyor said it would be easier that way, and also it will not have to cross lands owned by members of the Grand Alliance. I do not think they would allow it."

He let the map fall back on the bed. He stared at it, more stunned than he wanted to admit.

She had devised this on her own. She had seen the possibilities and had paid for surveying the route of this railroad.

Not only so she could endow her school. He guessed that more had driven her than that. Not greed either. *Purpose.* Accomplishment. The satisfaction of doing it first and doing it well. *It is all my idea.*

"I hope that you don't disapprove. Many people do not favor the railroads and think they are blights. They will not go away, however, and—"

"How long have you been at this?"

"Two years. I had thought about it, and when the land came to me after my mother died, I began planning. It was a game at first, just to see if the idea had merit."

"On your own? No help at all?"

"I had some advice at the beginning."

"Siddel?"

"Not Mr. Siddel. Mr. Guerney of the Friends answered some questions for me. He is Mrs. Fry's brother, and—"

"Quaker Guerney? The financier? He is your secret adviser? He is behind this?"

"He gave me some advice, early on. He is not behind it. One railroad is enough for him. He was able to tell me the sorts of profits that could be made, however."

Huge profits, when it worked. Huge losses when it didn't. Dante did not know the details, but he knew that the Stockton-to-Darlington line that Guerney had invested in had cost over a hundred thousand pounds. And Fleur's "Y" was much, much longer.

"You were correct, Fleur. When you brought this to me, I would have demanded a lot of explanation. I will not be able to sign anything unless I get it."

She sat on the bed and gazed forlornly at her map. "I will explain it all, Dante, but I think it is unlikely now that I will be asking for your signature. I made one very big mistake."

"Siddel."

"Yes."

"How did he become involved?"

"I knew of his reputation in forming investment partnerships. So when he came to me, offering to purchase any land I may want to sell—he had heard of my recent dispositions—I made use of the renewal of our acquaintance to eventually propose the plan. Now I wonder if he already knew of others who had similar plans and wanted to purchase my land for that reason to begin with."

"I think it more likely that he first spoke to you on Farthingstone's behalf. Whether Farthingstone has his own plans for a railroad or just doesn't want a school there, I cannot say."

She began rolling up the drawings. "I have been wondering if he approached me for Gregory too and has been stalling me at Gregory's request. I wish I knew for certain if he and Gregory have an association."

"I am sure that they do, Fleur. I just met with Farthingstone. He knows about our arrangement. He knows that you believe you can make plans like this without my approval and that I have agreed to give my signature."

She did not move. Did not look at him.

"You would have had to let Siddel know that, after we married. Otherwise his efforts on this railroad were a waste of time."

"We had separate lives, Dante. You did not have to end your old one because of our marriage." She looked up at him. "I am sorry anyway. It was hard to keep this from you, even if it was my right to, and even though secrecy was vital. I wanted very much to share it with you, as my friend, because it was so important to me."

He understood, more than he wanted. She wanted to share it with him, but instead she had shared it with Hugh Siddel. Siddel's involvement with this project, and Fleur's involvement with Siddel, dated long before those days in that cottage.

It angered him anyway.

The jealousy was not rational, not fair. He knew that. He controlled it. For now. It gave him one more reason to dislike Siddel, however.

"I want you to remove Siddel from this project, Fleur. Can you do that?"

"He has put me in an impossible dilemma. When I asked him to find the investors, I emphasized the need for secrecy. However, I never expected him to keep secrets from me. He refuses to tell me the investors' names, even though he claims to be close to finding enough. I have begun worrying that he is stalling me while he works with others to pursue an alternate route. If so, I will lose the advantage and there will be nothing I can do about it."

Dante ran his fingers over the northern strip of the map. "It he is stalling, it is possible that he is merely preventing any railroad from being built. For Gregory or someone else. New pits will produce coal that competes with that in the north. If the port of Hartlepool grows because of coal shipments, it will compete with Newcastle. If one connects the western coal fields to the coast, there are powerful men who will not be pleased."

"Do you think Siddel told them?"

"I know that he has a relationship with a man who is employed by a family in the Grand Alliance. However, whatever he has done, it does not matter. Siddel is out of this now. Do you understand that?"

"Yes. I think that one way or another, he betrayed me. Which means I have failed. I do not think that I can go forward on the school. I can afford to build it but not to create the endowment that will ensure its thriving."

Her voice was firm but her expression very sad. She appeared bereft as she announced the death of her dream.

"We will find a way to build the school, Fleur. You will fulfill your great purpose. If a different way must be found, we will find one."

She looked up with a trembling smile. It was not clear that she believed him, but the warmth in her eyes said that she appreciated his resolve.

"I must write my letter to Mr. Siddel."

She walked toward her sitting room, and he aimed for his own chambers. He also had a letter to write.

"Dante," she said, stopping him. "When I told you about the school being my purpose, after we met with Mr. Hampton, you said you understood."

And he did.

"You said that you could comprehend what it meant to live without one and then to find it."

He could.

"Perhaps one day you will tell me about your purpose, Dante. I would like to hear about it, and share it with you."

He watched her disappear into the sitting room.

You, my love. The purpose that I found is you.

chapter 23

Hugh Siddel stared in shock at the letter he held. It contained only one sentence, penned in Fleur's neat hand. With no ceremony or explanation, she released him from their agreement regarding his role in the railroad project.

His fingers closed on the paper until they made a fist. That bastard Duclairc had forced her to write this. The stupid woman had confided in him after all, and he was using this opportunity to exact a little revenge for that game of cards.

Forcing some calm, he calculated what this meant. There was no way for Cavanaugh to learn this letter had come. If Fleur was giving up on her project, Cavanaugh would remain ignorant of that too. Those payments Cavanaugh made to ensure the project was delayed could continue a long while.

He smiled to himself. Actually, Fleur's decision concluded matters very neatly. Stalling had gotten difficult. He had worried how long he could continue putting her off. If Duclairc had discovered their association and forbidden her to continue it, he could not have chosen a better moment to interfere.

Then again, perhaps Duclairc was still ignorant. Another whim had captured her attention, perhaps. Some other project. Maybe her social diary was filling so completely with parties and diversions that charitable endeavors now bored her.

Contented that the letter afforded the opportunity to dangle Cavanaugh indefinitely, Siddel left his chambers to go out. He met his butler on the stairs, coming up with a salver in his hand.

Siddel read the card. "In broad daylight? Astonishing. Where did you put him?"

"He is in the morning room, sir."

Siddel detoured to the morning room, where a very agitated Gregory Farthingstone paced the floor.

"I am surprised to see you here, Farthingstone. Did you just walk in the front door, where the world could see you?"

"This could not wait for the dawn, sir. I face such ruin that it may not matter what the world sees in any case." Farthingstone's face had gone very red. He paused in his pacing and breathed deeply to compose himself.

"Sit, my friend, and calm yourself."

Farthingstone obeyed. Rest only brought an expression of extreme desolation. Overcome, he did not speak, but merely held out a piece of paper.

Siddel took it. It was a letter from Dante Duclairc. Brief like Fleur's, it also contained but one sentence: *My wife will have her school, even if I have to cut and carry the stone myself.*

"He is mad," Farthingstone muttered. "They both lack the sense of newborns. She found a man just as impractical as she is. A fitting match, and I am destroyed because of it."

"Why did he write this?"

"I met with him. I laid out my evidence, and it is very strong, sir, very strong. New facts have come to my attention, you see. I believed I had a right understanding with Duclairc regarding the scandal that would result if we went to court. I offered him a handsome sum to leave that property as farms."

"That was your solution? To bribe the man?"

"I can do without your scorn. It was hell on my pride to approach him as a gentleman."

"With the fortune he has now, I doubt the amount you could offer would sway him."

"You do not need to remind me how little is at my disposal for negotiations. Nor should I have to remind you how those negotiations will benefit you as well. A man in your position may even decide that half a loaf is better than none and aid me out of my predicament."

Siddel let that suggestion pass. The thing about loaves was, if you gave away half, you went hungry.

Farthingstone dully accepted that the overture would have no symphony. "Duclairc would have been better off with two hundred than if she sold. The man is an imbecile if he did not comprehend that. I thought he did, but—" He gestured to the letter and his face reddened again. "It is very vexing to have one's future at the whim of such fools, I tell you."

Siddel looked at Duclairc's letter again. He comprehended its implications more than Farthingstone ever could.

Duclairc knew everything. Even the parts Farthingstone did not. Worse, Fleur was not giving up. She planned to pursue her Grand Project as well as build that school, and her worthless husband had agreed to permit it.

If she succeeded, not only the payments from Cavanaugh would stop. All of the income that supported him and his pleasures would cease. His uncle's legacy would become worthless.

He handed the letter back to Farthingstone. "You cannot allow this to happen, of course."

"Damnation, I know that. However, I am at a loss as to discern how to stop it. Duclairc's barrister has drowned Chancery in petitions and my own man cannot make headway quickly enough. It could be months before my standing is even accepted, and by then . . ." He shook his head and closed his eyes. "I learned that she is having the school designed already. She intends to move soon."

"Not soon enough, if you move more quickly." Those designs must have been commissioned when she thought most of the investors were collected. Starting over would take some time. Still, it did not look good.

Farthingstone exhaled his misery and his body shrank in on itself. "Duclairc will probably get his brother to buy the rest of the land so she has the funds to build. Or his friend St. John. Or his friend Burchard. Land is always desired. Once the funds are in hand, she will start on the school."

"You must stop them from selling. You definitely must stop them from building. It is that simple."

"Easy for you to demand. There is no damn way to damn stop them, I tell you."

"Of course there is."

Farthingstone went still. He stared at the floorboards.

Siddel strolled over to the window and gazed out. He pictured Fleur in that hooded cloak the first time they met in the church, her blue eyes sparkling with excitement while she explained her insane scheme. She had looked so much like the girl he had loved that—

Well, no good would come from such sentiment now. She was not a girl anymore but a married woman who was determined to take actions that would inconvenience him most severely.

"Tell me, Farthingstone, I am curious. What happens to that Durham property if the current owner passes away without children?"

The answer was slow in coming. "It is bequeathed to a charity devoted to the reform of prisons."

Siddel turned to him. "I have always thought that prison reform is a worthy cause, deserving of support. Haven't you?"

Farthingstone looked away. He said nothing. The flush in his face drained, leaving him very pale.

Fleur collected all the letters and papers relating to the Grand Project. She removed them from her desk and placed them in the coffer along with the drawings for the school.

As she closed the coffer lid, she admitted that she would miss the thrill of planning for her railroad. It had been exciting. Even the secrecy had appealed to her. She had been foolish to think that she could bring it off, however. Such elaborate plans can founder on one wrong step, and she had taken a big one. His name was Hugh Siddel.

Eventually she would build her school. No Grand Project would derive from doing so. No great endowment would ensure its survival. She would find a way to support it, however. Dante would help her.

Dante. She regretted that she did not have the Grand Project to distract her tonight. She had attended the theater with Laclere and Bianca, but Dante had not joined them. He had gone elsewhere, and she was trying hard not to speculate where that elsewhere might be.

A new kind of jealousy wanted to take root in her heart. She fought to prevent that. She suspected how desolating it would be.

She had decided not to think about the life he led when he left this house, but only about the one they shared when he was here. When she had chosen the kind of marriage she wanted, she had known she would probably not have it exactly the way she hoped.

The night was still young, but she prepared for bed. She would continue this habit, she decided. She would not lie to herself, nor would she picture him with other women, but she would make sure she never knew if he did not return of a night.

She got into bed, but sleep did not come peacefully. Her dozing was fitful, full of images of Dante, and her heart heavy with a fear of heartbreak.

Suddenly she was very awake. Instantly alert. She turned her head and saw candles in the room, over near the door to her dressing room.

"Dante?"

He came to her. "I thought you were asleep."

"Not yet."

He put the brace of candles on a table and sat on the bed. "Did you enjoy the theater?"

"Very much. Your brother's box was busy, with everyone visiting to welcome them home. I wish you had come."

She instantly regretted saying that. She scooted around and sat beside him on the bed's edge. "I am sorry. I know that even being really married does not mean that we spend every evening together. I am out of practice being sophisticated, that is all."

He untied his cravat and pulled it off. "Do not be sorry. I do not want you to become sophisticated. I know all too well that it also means becoming indifferent."

He shed his collar and waistcoat in silence. She could sense his mind working.

He paused a good while before turning to his shirt and other garments.

"You have not asked me about my evening, Fleur."

She did not know what to say.

"I know why you did not ask. You have been practicing that part of being sophisticated for some time now, haven't you?"

Yes. And not mastering the skill at all.

"I went to my clubs. It was fairly boring. The cards do not interest me as they used to."

"Did you win?"

"Yes, but it still grew dull after a while. I found myself thinking that your company would be much more interesting."

"I am glad that you did."

"McLean thinks my sobriety is your fault. He says that marriage games have ruined me for all others."

"I would like to believe that, Dante. However, you have been a man on the town for many years and I think that you know more games than I can imagine. I am at a disadvantage."

"There is no competition taking place. You are at no disadvantage."

That was not true. The saintly Fleur Monley had little to offer a man with his worldly experiences. Even the goddess Fleur Duclairc was at a disadvantage.

He turned to her and began unbuttoning the top of her bed gown. "Are you trying to say that you want to learn other games, Fleur?"

"I am so ignorant of what they could be that I do not know if I want to learn them."

"I have already shown you one."

She knew what he meant. "These other ways seem to ensure the woman's pleasure, not the man's."

"I get great pleasure in making you scream for me." He slid her gown off so that she sat naked beside him. "However, to be precise, I only showed you half of one."

He kissed her, embracing her against his skin, still sitting side by side as politely as if the bed were a garden bench.

Her mind worked on what he had just said. A very shocking notion of what the other half could be presented itself.

He sensed her astonishment. As he kissed her, she felt his small smile form.

Turning her in his arms, he laid her on her back across his lap, with her head and shoulders on one side of his thighs and her hips on the other, and her body sprawled, arched and vulnerable. She could not even embrace him like this, and her arms fell limply on either side of her head.

His gaze slowly moved over all of her. His trailing hand followed the same path. Both made her body very sensitive, all over. The most delicious anticipation purred through her.

His light caress titillated mercilessly. Anticipation of more purposeful touches had her half mad. His fingers kept glossing close to her nipples and thighs, but never actually touched the places she really wanted. It aroused her anyway, slowly, relentlessly, incredibly.

"There is no competition, Fleur." His lids lowered and his hand brushed against her nipple, making her gasp and arch. "It is very good with you."

His palm gently circled over her breast, teasing the tight tip. Laying here like this, watching him watch her arousal, unable to embrace him or hide her growing madness, was incredibly erotic.

His phallus pressed against her right breast and she bent her arm so she could touch him. His gaze moved to her face while his hand continued its breathtaking patterns. She touched him lightly, as he touched her, so the erotic torture would be mutual.

He raised her shoulders and she expected him to kiss her. Instead, he gently flipped her, so her face and breasts pressed the sheet and her hips crossed his lap. A long, firm caress from her neck down her back commanded she stay like that. Blind now, she could only feel.

"You are so lovely, Fleur. By day or night." His hand smoothed over her bottom. She could not contain how arousing it was to lay in this submissive position. A wicked, dangerous element colored her climbing desire, even though his caress was gentle.

His hand moved down to the flesh of her inner thighs. Her excitement immediately centered near his hand, and her muddled mind started a silent begging.

"I have never seen anything more beautiful than you in your passion, darling."

The slow caresses on her back, her bottom, her thighs pushed her past control. She heard the notes of wonder and pleading on her own gasping breaths. The waiting became wonderful and unbearable.

His other hand lifted her shoulder. "Kneel."

She did not understand. He showed her. Hands on one side of his thighs and knees on the other, she propped herself. He reached below to caress her breasts, and the sensation was so intense her whole body shuddered. Her hips squirmed impatiently as his other hand ventured closer, closer.

"Part your knees more."

She did, half insane with furious need.

The touch made her cry out. She heard the sound on the edges of her awareness. The way he touched her nipples only intensified the sensation. He kept creating more hunger even as he partly relieved it.

He moved the caress to her back and bottom again. His fingers trailed along her cleft to touch her from the rear. Her body arched into it, hips rising and shoulders lowering, demanding more, anxious for relief and completion.

The movement made her arm press his phallus. In her stupor she turned her head and kissed it.

He instantly went completely still.

A wicked sense of power tinged her abandon. She kissed again, right on the tip. "No?"

His fingers twisted into the hair on her head. "Yes." His voice sounded a little savage.

She rearranged herself a little and kissed again. A different arousal and madness owned her now. She flicked her tongue, very pleased with her own boldness. It was not nearly as scandalous in the doing as in the thinking. She used her mouth more aggressively.

The fingers in her hair tensed and lifted her head up. He claimed her in a furious, ravishing kiss that left her mind and lips numb.

He laid her down and bent her knees high to her chest and entered her deeply, so deeply that she felt him touch her womb. Rising on his arms, he withdrew entirely and entered again, slowly and completely. Her vulva throbbed with the fullness of him and with expectation when he left.

His face remained hard with control and determined passion. The slow, commanding thrusts continued, demanding that her passion rise with his. Her own body was grateful to accept and submit and follow once more.

The end was hardly gentle, but she did not care. Her own passion welcomed his wild intensity and ruthless domination. She loved feeling and seeing his completion. She reveled in the hard, deep thrusts that bound them together in a beautiful madness.

Most of all, however, she loved the way he slept beside her afterward, in an embrace that kept them heart to heart.

"Has my wife gone down yet, Hornby?"

"It is not for me to notice such things, sir."

"Certainly. However, has she?"

"Since you demand it of me, Mrs. Duclairc left her chambers a while ago."

Dante turned to leave his as well.

"However, I do not think that you will find her below, sir, if that is the reason for your question." Hornby walked over to the open window and inhaled deeply. "Such a lovely morning this is. It is mornings such as this that beckon one to a long turn amidst grass and flowers."

Dante could not muster any annoyance at this indication that Fleur still walked out alone in the mornings. After last night, he would be incapable of anger over anything that she wanted to do.

"I think that I will take a turn in the park, Hornby. Is there any spot in particular that is singularly pleasant in the mornings?"

"I have heard the footman Christopher say that strolling around the reservoir is quite lovely this time of day."

Dante left the house and walked the few blocks to Stanhope Gate and entered Hyde Park. At this hour no carriages rolled down the lanes and only a few people strolled. Women dotted the green, accompanied by maids or friends. Several older men walked by briskly, taking deliberate exercise. Most of the noise came from the songs of birds.

He strolled slowly, enjoying the quiet and the odd experience of visiting this park merely to enjoy its beauty. He rarely came here except for the reasons most people did, to see and be seen. The park merely served as a stage for the social dramas of the fashionable hour.

He decided that he liked it just as much now. He

understood why Fleur walked here most mornings. He looked forward to sharing it with her today.

He approached the reservoir and surveyed the landscape, looking for Fleur. He could see no woman at all, just a man walking away toward the Grosvenor Gate beyond it. He stopped and looked all around.

He turned and swept his gaze over the rest of the park, looking for a figure in a hooded cloak. All of the women he could see were decked out more fashionably.

He must have missed her. She had probably been leaving through one gate as he entered through another.

Deciding to take a turn around the reservoir anyway, he ambled toward it.

He strolled around, looking more to the ground than the park or water, thinking about last night and the last days. His mind turned to Fleur's school and her Grand Project and the likelihood that either would come to fruition.

He laughed to himself. Farthingstone claimed she was addled. Far from it, although there were many men who would think any woman who dared dream up such a scheme was totally mad.

She was hardly mad. Audacious and smart, but not mad. He was still accommodating himself to just what he had in her.

He passed a section of the reservoir where some reeds had taken root. Out of the corner of his eye he saw their vertical lines and the way the water pooled around them.

Something else caught his eye and pulled him out of his thoughts. He turned and looked at the water. A five count passed before he accepted what he was seeing.

A yell roared through him, both soundless and deafening. Too horrified to think, he laid down on the reservoir wall and reached toward the dark shadows floating just below the surface, fluttering in languid folds.

He grabbed one edge and his heart stopped. He knew what it was. Just knew. Pulling hand over hand, he dragged up the cloth and could feel how a weight held it down in the water. He pulled harder and a body bobbed at the surface.

The roar in his head became a howl. A vicious, savage, terrified yell. He grabbed her body and hauled her up. The sodden cloak fought him. He got her face above water and dragged her to the reservoir's edge and up on the ground.

Half-blind, his gaze shot around. Small dots moved in the distance, too far away to respond to a call for help. He yelled one anyway as he turned Fleur on her side and began forcing the water out of her.

Time slowed. His blood raced. She looked dead. He turned her stomach-down anyway and pressed her back. Water left her mouth in a steady stream.

Then he saw the blood.

It oozed through her hair, mixing with her damp locks, adding to the wetness. He bent closely even as he continued pressing her back and saw the wound on the back of her head.

For an instant, primitive fury cracked through him. The next moment it was gone, replaced by an icy-cold resolve.

He would kill whoever had done this, even if she lived. If she died, he would kill the man *slowly*.

A sound broke through his horror. The smallest cough shook Fleur's body. He turned her on her side again and coaxed another out of her. Water spewed out of her mouth as a convulsion racked her.

He laid his palm against her face and felt some warmth beneath the chill. "Come back, darling. Look at me."

Her lashes fluttered. Her body flexed. Her lids rose. Her eyes appeared sightless for a few dreadful heartbeats, then focused on him.

"Dante."

"Do not speak. Do not move." He released the cloak so it fell away from her body. He stripped off his frock coat and tucked it around her. He wanted to weep with relief. Only caring for her kept him composed. The total realization of what he had almost lost began penetrating his shock, terrifying him.

A curricle approached on the closest path. Kneeling, he lifted Fleur in his arms. As he stood, his body reacted to the weight, but he ignored it. He could have carried her a mile if he had to.

He bore her around the reservoir, shouting for the carriage to stop.

"You should calm yourself before you go to her," Laclere said. They paced together in Fleur's sitting room while a physician attended her in the bedroom. "She should not see you like this."

"Like what?"

"With murder in your eyes."

Dante strolled over to the mantel and examined the porcelain figures it held.

His brother was wrong. He did not need to calm himself. He had never been calmer in his life.

"It will not be murder. Burchard will return soon and tell me where to find him."

"Calling out a man like Farthingstone is as good as murder. You do not even know for certain that he—"

"I do not need lectures from you, today of all days. I *know* he arranged this. If it were your wife lying in there, you would not be so damnably dispassionate. If you are here to dissuade me, get out."

Vergil sat in the chair near Fleur's *secrétaire*. "My apologies. Of course you must deal with the man as you choose." He paused. "I am not dispassionate, Dante. I have been where you are, when the woman I loved was endangered. I may have challenged a man in the name of a different person and a different honor, but my heart was not so pure."

Dante folded his arms and looked at the cold hearth. Vergil was speaking of that duel, fought to protect the honor of their dead older brother. It was a topic they had never discussed. Vergil had demanded to stand to that man, but now admitted more had motivated him than his right of precedence or fear that Dante would fail.

It was a generous confession, in ways Vergil probably did not know. It dimmed Dante's anger at his brother's attempts to mollify him.

"Farthingstone had a man following her," he said, to reassure his brother. "He knew that she walked in the park in the mornings. I saw the man once, and Farthingstone told me enough of her movements to indicate this man had trailed her for some time."

"Do you know why he had her followed?"

"To accumulate evidence that her mind was not right and her judgment impaired." He shook his head. "Better for her if he had succeeded in killing me instead. When I think how close . . . a few more minutes—"

"Do not think of that. She is safe and that is the important thing." Vergil got up and came over to the mantel. "However, what is this about succeeding in killing you?"

Before Dante could answer, the door to the corridor opened and Adrian Burchard entered.

"Where is the bastard?" Dante asked.

"Not in London. His manservant said he went down to his house in Essex."

"It appears that you will have to wait to confront him," Vergil said.

"I want to know when he returns to London. I want to make sure he is nowhere near Fleur until I can deal with him."

"I know a good man who will watch the Essex house if you want," Adrian said. "As soon as Farthingstone sets foot off that property, he will let us know."

"Do you know another one who will watch Siddel?"

"It can be arranged."

"Siddel? What has he to do with this?" Vergil demanded. "And what was that business about someone trying to kill you? When did this happen, and why wasn't I told of it?"

"Ask St. John," Dante said. The physician had just opened the door to Fleur's bedroom and beckoned.

Vergil headed for the corridor with an expression that said St. John was in for a severe interrogation.

"I am not ill, Dante."

"You have had a shock and you will rest."

Fleur sank back on the pillows and suffered his attention as he tucked the bedclothes around her.

She did not have the heart to argue with him. He had saved her life, after all. Concern had veiled his expression since he entered the bedchamber and banished Charlotte and the physician and taken over her care himself.

He had also kindly not mentioned that he would not have had to save her if she had taken an escort when she walked in the park.

Mostly, however, she did not argue because the experience had left her docile and frightened. The specter of death kept breathing on her neck, as if refusing to leave unsatisfied.

"I will rest if you say I must, but I do not think I will sleep. Could you ask Charlotte to come back?"

"I will stay with you if you don't want to be alone, Fleur."

"I would rather not be. Not yet."

He pulled a chair near the bed and sat in it, propping his boot on the bed's edge. "I think that we will pass the time in a little game, since you are indisposed and cannot be seduced."

She laughed. Her heart glowed at this evidence that he remembered those hours in the cottage as well as she did.

"What kind of game?"

"Not that kind. That will have to wait until you have recovered. This is a simple one. I will ask you questions, and you will answer them."

"If I play this game, do you promise to play the other kind when I am recovered?"

"Certainly."

"Another new one? I still have a lot of catching up to do."

"Darling, I am trying to be good even though you look adorable in that bed. Even the bandage becomes you. You could help a little and not tempt me by offering anything I want."

"My apologies. Ask your first question."

"Could you recognize the man who passed you as you took a turn around the reservoir?"

"Not with certainty. I was not watching him. I was walking, he approached, we passed, and then . . ." And then she remembered nothing at all until she opened her eyes and saw Dante looking down at her with eyes wild with worry.

She felt the bandage wrapping her head. "I suppose he hit me with something."

The humor had left Dante's eyes. Talk of the attack had turned them into sparking, cold crystals.

"Are there more questions?"

"Is there any reason why Farthingstone would want to keep you from building that school?"

"I doubt he approves of educating boys of lower condition."

"That is not enough reason to try and kill you."

"We do not know Gregory was behind this, Dante."

"I can think of no one else. He wants to stop you from building it, Fleur. Very much. I think that everything he has done, all of it, was to prevent that. He came and offered to pay me to stop you."

"He tried to bribe you? That is very insulting."

His expression showed he had not missed the insult

that Gregory assumed he would choose money over loyalty to his own wife. "I think it is not a coincidence that this happened to you right after I refused."

"There is nothing special about that piece of land, Dante. It is just a cottage and a garden and some fields. It isn't even the best land there. The soil has too much clay, which is one reason I was going to use it for the school to begin with."

"Could there be something underground? Coal or minerals? Something that he hopes to own someday?"

"If there had been, he could have profited while he was married to my mother. He controlled the farms then. He could not sell them, but he could exploit them."

Dante thought it all over. "His tenacity regarding you has been odd, Fleur. There is a reason for it. A good reason. This attack on you speaks of a man getting desperate."

"I cannot imagine what the reason is. If you had agreed to accept his payment, the property would not become his. It would have stayed as it is now and as it has been for years."

"Then he must want it to stay as it is. We need to know why, and the answer is in Durham."

chapter 24

Fleur rarely visited her Durham property. Her arrival with Dante, so soon after her last visit, sent the couple who cared for it into high agitation. Mr. Hill set off at once to the village, to hire women to bring back before it got dark. Mrs. Hill bustled around the house, lighting fires and removing covers from furniture.

She interrupted her work to help Fleur settle into her chamber. As she shook out dresses, she gossiped about the tenants and local happenings.

"The Johnson family has left their place, of course," she concluded. "But they are happy with their new cottage, and grateful that the fields are still theirs to work."

The Johnson family had been living in Aunt Peg's cottage while the plans for the school unfolded.

"They were unhappy at first, even with the offer of the other cottage, since it is not so convenient to the fields, but now that they have made the change they are content."

"There was no need for them to be inconvenienced. I do not need that property yet."

"There must have been some confusion, then. Your stepfather wrote on your behalf and said that you did. The Johnsons knew how he still watches matters here for you."

Of course they assumed so. They thought of the land as his to control because for years they had paid the rents to him while her mother owned the property.

"Has he moved any other families?"

"Not that I can think of. He has always kept an eye on things for you, however. The tenants understand how it is."

"Where did the Johnson family move?"

"A new cottage, right on the edge of Mr. Farthingstone's land. Not too far from the fields."

Not so far to cause Mr. Johnson to complain to her because he lost a season's plantings or had to walk miles to reach the fields.

She left Mrs. Hill to complete the unpacking and went outside. Standing in front of the house, she looked west. One could see the old cottage from here. It was a gray speck against the overcast sky, sitting atop a low rise in the land, close enough that Peg could see her sister's home.

She went back upstairs in search of Dante. He was in his chamber, washing. He had taken the ribbons most of the way from London because his skill with four-in-hand far surpassed Luke's and he had no interest in a leisurely journey.

"I believe you were correct, Dante. The answer may be here in Durham. Or at least, the answer to something may be here."

She told him what had transpired with the cottage.

"Since that is where you intend to build the school, it

may be connected to our mystery in some way." He had removed his coats and now put them back on. "It will be a while before dusk. Let us visit this cottage. I have grown very curious about that property."

He took her hand as they walked. The day was not breezy and bright as it had been the last time they strolled together along this lane. Gray clouds threatened rain and blocked the setting sun, and the air held the pending dampness. Fleur felt as lighthearted as she had that day, however. Even her brush with death had not dimmed the glow that her love gave the world.

The cottage slowly grew in size with each step.

"How long was this cottage vacant?" Dante asked, looking toward it.

"While Aunt Ophelia was alive. She hoped that her sister would be found at first, but even after the body was discovered, she did not put a tenant there."

Dante paced on another few yards. "When did your aunt Peg disappear?"

"Years ago, Dante. I was just a girl. Aunt Peg and I used to play together back then. I would visit her and we would play with our dolls."

"How old were you when she went missing?"

She had to calculate that by working back through the milestones of her life. "I think that I was eight or nine. My mother and I had come to visit as we did most summers. I remember going to play with Aunt Peg, and then the great confusion when she went missing. It was a very sad time, and I do not remember those days much. However, Aunt Ophelia died eleven years ago, and that was soon after Aunt Peg's body was found and she had been missing at least ten years then."

It made her uncomfortable to speak of this. The damp penetrated her more, and the heavy clouds appeared darker.

So did Dante's expression. A frown marked his brow and he observed the cottage they approached with thoughtful speculation.

"The woman who cared for your aunt. What became of her?"

"She left. She took a position elsewhere. Hill probably knows where. I wish that you would not dwell on this, Dante. It is as unpleasant as our conversation by the lake at Laclere Park."

In some ways it was more unpleasant. His questions evoked memories of those days after Aunt Peg disappeared. Sensations crept into her of loss and shock and walking through a house heavy with dread. Another reaction nibbled at her as well. Guilt. If she had been playing with Aunt Peg that day, she could not have wandered off and gotten lost.

The cottage was close enough now to see its shutters and stones and the little garden that the Johnsons had planted. She remembered running along this lane, carrying her doll, to go play with Aunt Peg in the sitting room while the caretaker read a book in the corner.

She had not realized at the time how odd it was to have such a playmate. Aunt Peg had been gone for years before she understood why this grown woman enjoyed a child's games. At the time she had simply thought that Aunt Peg was kinder than most adults, and much more fun too.

They approached the cottage from the side. Dante went up and peered in the window. "It is too dark inside to see, and this window too dirty in any case."

She held back. That window . . .

"Has the walk been too much for you, Fleur? You are looking pale."

"I am fine." Only she really wasn't. A very unpleasant sensation churned in her stomach. She kept looking at the window. She knew the chamber inside very well. She could see Aunt Peg sitting on the floor, dancing her doll across the rug toward her.

It was a happy memory, but she was not feeling happy at all. She was feeling very sick. The notion of looking in that window with Dante made her cringe.

She searched her memory, trying to make things fit right.

Dante came back to her. "What is it, Fleur? You do not look fine at all."

"I am thinking that perhaps Aunt Ophelia had tenants here after all. I must have forgotten that. We came less often once Aunt Peg was gone. Yes, that would explain it."

"Explain what?"

"The window, Dante. Do you remember how I said that I thought I once saw a woman in agony while giving birth? I see her face and body through a window. That window."

"Then I am sorry that I brought you here."

"Do not be. It explains part of the fear." She shrugged. The uneasy sensation had retreated. "I think that I would like to go in. I loved Aunt Peg in ways I could never love most adults then. She was a playmate every summer. I feel bad that I do not think of her much anymore, and have not for years."

They walked around the house. Dante opened the door and she stepped over the threshold.

And froze.

"Dante, look."

He stepped in behind her.

Little light entered except from the door, but it was obvious that the cottage had no floor. All of the boards had been removed and neatly stacked along one wall. The packed earth underneath had been completely exposed.

Dante kicked the ground with his heel. "Dry, and hard as rock. Difficult to dig with a shovel."

"Do you think that is the intention?"

"I can think of no other reason for removing the floor."

"Dig for what?"

He did not answer at first. He paced around the walls, studying the ground. "Something valuable enough to not want others to find it when they began digging to build a school."

His expression appeared very hard in the dim light. He crossed his arms and stared at the dirt. She sensed anger in him, but not directed at her.

"Then Gregory has arranged for this," she said.

The low rumble of distant thunder rolled in the door. "A storm is coming. I will come back tomorrow and see if I am right."

"Right? What do you think is here, Dante?"

He shrugged. "Who knows. Perhaps Farthingstone learned there is a great treasure hiding." The thunder rumbled again. "Come along. We need to get back before the rain comes."

The storm was moving fast. Lightning sliced the distant sky. It was not the rain that Dante wanted to beat, however. It was the dusk.

In a corner of the cottage, almost hidden by the floor-boards and the shadows, he had seen two oil lamps.

He helped Fleur down the threshold to the cottage. As they walked back to the lane, he heard a sound besides thunder float on the heavy air.

He turned. Two horses rode cross country, barely visible in the graying world. At the same time that he saw the riders, they noticed him. One gestured and the horses broke into a gallop.

Fleur's eyes widened when she saw the horses.

He began pulling her back to the cottage. "No doubt they are only travelers aiming for the mail road, trying to outrun the storm," he said. "All the same, let us go back in here and see if they pass."

He did not believe they would. They had actually been aiming toward this cottage. But he and Fleur could not outrun them and he would have a better chance of protecting Fleur if she was not out in the open.

Not much of one, if that shorter rider was who he thought. Very little chance at all if what he suspected about this cottage was correct.

Cursing himself for not anticipating this, blood already coursing with the sickening excitement of the hunted, he threw the bolt over the door as soon as he had Fleur inside. He checked to see that the kitchen was secure as well. He went to all the windows on the first level and closed their shutters, shrouding the cottage in darkness.

Returning to Fleur, he examined their sanctuary. The stone walls and thick door would make it hard to get in, but this was hardly an impregnable fort.

"The rider on the left . . . I could barely see him, but I

thought it was Gregory," Fleur said. "I thought he was in Essex."

He heard the tremor in her voice. He pulled her into his arms. "So his servant said. Even if it is Farthingstone, there is no reason to be afraid."

"Do you think he is coming to do the digging?"

"He may have only been riding and not recognized us. He may be coming to see who is trespassing. He still watches these farms for you."

She felt in the dark for his face. "You do not believe that. You would not have bolted the doors if you did."

"I am only being cautious in the way of husbands, Fleur." He kissed her. "Do not worry. I think that I can thrash him if I have to."

She laughed. He held her closer while he listened hard for the sounds of approaching horses.

They arrived with the storm. Fat droplets began pounding the windows as hooves pounded up the lane. The heavens broke as a hand worked the latch and met the resistance of the bolt.

A man cursed. Dante recognized the voice.

So did Fleur. "It appears he did not go to Essex," she whispered.

"See here, open this door and show yourself," Farthingstone ordered. "We know you are in there, by Zeus, since the damn door is bolted."

"There seems little point in pretending we are not here," Fleur said quietly.

Dante did not agree. Farthingstone knew a couple had entered this cottage, but he had not recognized who they were. There was a chance that the rain would discourage him and his companion and they would leave and come back later.

In any event, he was not going to make this easy for them.

Mumbles sounded on the other side of the door, then silence fell. Dante felt Fleur's heart racing and the tension tightening her body. He held her and listened for the sounds of horses leaving.

A crack blasted the silence as a huge weight fell against the door. A metal point poked through a plank, then disappeared.

They had come tonight to dig after all. The had a pickax with them.

The pick fell again. The plank splintered.

Fleur cringed closer. "Dante . . ."

"He will be chagrined when he goes through such trouble only to learn it is the owner of this land inside this cottage."

She tucked her head against his neck. "You do not have to pretend for me. I know that we may be in a very dangerous spot."

The pick landed again. A hole appeared in the door. The shadow of a face peered in. "Cannot see a thing with it all closed up," Farthingstone said.

"Stand aside," another voice replied. A voice that Dante did not recognize.

The pick made short work of the door, enlarging the hole. An arm reached through and lifted the bolt. The door swung in.

Two men ducked in from the pouring rain. "Who is there? Who are you?" Farthingstone demanded, peering into the corner where Dante held Fleur.

"Just me, Farthingstone," Dante said. "What are you doing, destroying property like this? I got caught by the storm and took refuge here to wait it out. I did not expect a trespasser to come by and break down the door."

The other man fetched one of the oil lamps and lit it. A yellow glow spread, showing Farthingstone peering gape-mouthed from beneath a sodden hat.

When he saw Fleur his eyes widened in shock, as if he had seen a ghost. He shot his companion a horrified, furious glance.

"You have an explanation for this intrusion, I trust," Dante said, making the most of Farthingstone's astonishment at seeing Fleur alive.

The other man lit another lamp. That gave enough light for Dante to examine this stranger. He had dark hair and narrow, unpleasant eyes.

Not entirely a stranger. He had seen him before, following Fleur from St. Martin's down the Strand. If he was surprised by Fleur's living body, he at least did not show it.

"I thought *you* were the trespassers," Farthingstone said, fumbling through the words as he tried to collect himself. "Closing the shutters, bolting the door—why did you do that?"

"I was thinking that the rainstorm and this cottage afforded a splendid opportunity to make love to my wife, and the shutters and bolt would assure her of privacy. I see that I erred."

Farthingstone's face reddened. He appeared just as chagrined and confused as Dante had hoped.

"I would invite you gentlemen to stay and keep dry, but I am sure that you want to be on your way."

"Yes, well, perhaps we will be off—"

"He knows." The statement came from the other side of the chamber, where the other man stood near the stacked floorboards. "No reason to barricade himself and his lady in here otherwise. Not to dally for pleasure, I don't think."

Farthingstone pivoted in alarm. His gaze darted to his companion, then back to Dante. No longer chagrined, he examined the embracing couple suspiciously.

"Who might you be?" Dante asked.

"This is Mr. Smith, an acquaintance of mine," Farthingstone said.

"He knows," Smith repeated. "This one is not stupid, and he is playing you for a fool with his talk and manner. He saw these boards here, and the lamps. I think he knows what is happening here, and maybe why."

Farthingstone almost burst from agitation at these allusions to the cottage. "I would prefer if you did not speak of—"

"I think he knows about matters in London too. If so, I don't like that I've been seen with you." He had been holding the pick, but now he let it drop. Reaching under his coat, he withdrew a pistol.

Farthingstone almost jumped out of his skin. "Good God, man, what—"

Smith quieted him with a scowl. He paced over and looked out the door. "Getting dark, and no one will be about in this rain anyway. We best be taking them back with us, while we consider how to deal with this complication."

Dante eyed that pistol, trying to judge whether he

could lunge for the man before it fired. As if expecting such a move, Smith had pointed it more at Fleur than him.

"We are no complication, so there is no need to deal with us. We do not even know what you are talking about, nor do we care," Dante said.

Smith chuckled and gestured to Farthingstone. "He may not know how to judge a man, but you could say my life depends on it. I want to think a bit before I let you out of my sight. You ride with him. The lady comes with me. That way I know you will behave."

chapter 25

Let us get you out of those wet clothes so you can wrap yourself in this and get warm." Dante stripped a blanket off the narrow bed and handed it to her.

The ride to Farthingstone's house in the pouring rain had drenched everyone to the bone. Fleur's ensemble hung in sodden folds and water still dripped off the brim of her bonnet.

The fire Dante had started in the tiny attic chamber helped some, but getting the wet garments off would help more.

Fleur looked at the blanket skeptically. "What if one of them comes up here?"

Dante bolted the door. "Now we are locked in, but they are also locked out."

"They could use an ax again."

"It was left at the cottage. Get dry, Fleur. I don't want you catching a chill."

She removed her bonnet and threw it in a corner. She turned her back so he could help unfasten her dress.

"Not quite like the last time," she said sadly as his fingers worked at the closure. "That man. He was the one who hurt me, isn't he? He did it for Gregory. The look on Gregory's face when he saw me . . ."

"We do not know that for certain." He tried his best to lie, because he did not want her frightened. He wanted to spare her as much of that as he could.

He should have seen Farthingstone's tenacity for what it was, the desperate stubbornness of a cornered man. He should have comprehended weeks ago what that spot of land meant to him.

If he was right, he and Fleur were in danger for their lives. Right now, down in a lower chamber, Smith was probably explaining that to Farthingstone. How long would it take to convince him how it had to be? How much longer to devise a plan that might escape detection? Dante calculated that they had the night for certain, and maybe a day at best.

The dress fell. Fleur stripped off the rest of her clothes and wrapped herself in the blanket. While Dante undressed, she laid her garments over furniture, then did the same with his as he discarded them.

Finally the chairs, washstand, chest, and wall hooks were covered with their clothing. Wrapped in their blankets, they sat in front of the hearth.

"This would be very cozy," Fleur said. "If not for—"

"We will not be disturbed tonight."

"You sound very confident."

"I am."

She seemed to accept that. The fear dimmed from her eyes. "You do not really think that Gregory intended to dig for buried treasure in that cottage, do you?"

"Who knows what he may be seeking."

"Dante, I said that you do not have to pretend for me. I know that there is only one thing to explain what he has done. His attempt to imprison me or put me away. His legal maneuvers to have my independence revoked. Finally, the attempt on my life. There is something in that cottage he does not want found, because it will endanger him if it is. He fears exposure of a crime."

"Yes, that is likely."

"It would have to be a serious one, for him to go this far. I think there is a body in that cottage."

"It could be something else."

"I think it is that, or something just as dangerous."

Dante was not sure that he wanted her knowing this much. He was very sure that he did not want her knowing the rest.

"Why there, Dante? He could have buried a body anywhere on his land."

"If something happened at or near that cottage, it would be easier to deal with it there than to carry a body somewhere else. The floorboards would hide the grave, and the place was vacant."

A tiny shiver shook through her. She pulled the blanket closer. "Are you very sure that we have the night?"

"I think we have far more than the night. Hill will wonder what has become of us once the rain stops. He will start a search when we do not return."

"The rain does not look to ever stop."

"We will wake up to find the sun, darling."

She clasped her knees with her arms and pressed her chin to them. She looked very young, huddled in that blanket and gazing at the fire. "I do not think Gregory could hurt us on his own. Even if he once did such a thing, I do not think he could now. It is one thing to pay someone to do it when you are not even in town, and another . . ."

Dante wanted to believe Farthingstone no longer had it in him. The problem was that once a man took that step, he probably found it easy to step again. Especially if he saw himself hanging if he did not.

And if he could not do it himself, Smith could.

"They are probably smart enough to know that their best chance is to run, Fleur. They will realize that too many people know we are here and will be looking for us."

It appeared to help. The arms circling her knees relaxed and fell away. She resettled herself and allowed the blanket to fall loosely, as if she no longer needed its comfort.

He got up and went to the small window. "We will close out the rain and share this fire and tomorrow I will deal with Gregory and Smith. You are not to worry, Fleur."

As he opened the window to pull the shutters, he noticed a dark shadow moving below, heading to the stables. From the size, he guessed it was Smith, going for a horse.

Going to dig, Dante guessed. He doubted Smith intended to unearth old bones either. More likely he intended to make two more graves.

He turned and watched Fleur, with her hair a tangle and nothing but a blanket wrapping her nakedness. The fire cast a gentle glow on her. She looked so beautiful. An emotion swelled in him that was so poignant, so exquisite, he could not move.

She was more precious to him than anything he had ever had or known. The very thought of life without her was so blank, so frightening, that his mind shrank from such contemplation. He had been nothing before she stumbled into his life. Taking care of her had become his first welcomed responsibility. She was his purpose for living.

He had not done his duty by her very well. He had not fathomed how dishonorable Farthingstone could be. She had, however. She had known in her heart all along that Farthingstone was constructing a lie for his own ends. They should have been looking for his reason all along, not merely working to thwart the man.

He pushed a heavy chest to the door, not caring that its scrapes on the floor would be heard below. He positioned it to block entry even if an ax cut through the door itself. It would not stop someone, but it would delay them.

He went over to Fleur and sat facing her, so he could see her face and her eyes and all the parts of her that would be beautiful forever.

The fear left her gaze as she looked at him, and the most generous warmth took its place.

He took her face in his hands, painfully alert to the softness of her skin. He kissed her forehead and her lips, and each instant contained a lifetime of perfection.

Not caring where they were, indifferent to time and place, he pulled the blanket away and lifted her. He moved her legs until they circled his hips and she sat on his thighs. His own blanket fell away with their embrace.

She glanced down at her position. "The new game that you promised me?"

"A new closeness, so that I can see you in this lovely light. There have never been games with you. Not since the first time I touched you."

She looked down and gently caressed his arousal, making his teeth clench. "I do not know whether to be jealous or happy, Dante. The latter, I suppose. I do not like to think of your sharing things with other women that you do not with me, but I like that it is different with me in some way."

He watched his own fingers gloss over the curve of her breast. "It is very different, in all ways. Even the pleasure is different. Nor do I share anything at all with other women, Fleur. Not even games. Not since those days in the cottage at Laclere Park. Even when we both believed we could never have this, I have wanted no one else. I have loved you too much."

Her caress stopped. The way she looked at him stunned his soul.

"I do not think I could have been loved by a better man, Dante. Nor could I love one better than I love you."

He wrapped her in a caressing embrace, tasting her skin, feeling her heartbeat. It was very different this time. He could not control how it affected all of him—his senses, his pleasure, his body, and his heart. He felt her awareness of him just as he was filling himself with her.

He lifted her hips and joined. The most profound contentment slid through him, warm and serene. He wanted to hold her like this forever, connected and expectant, seeing her face as the tremors of pleasure enlivened her.

They touched slowly, watching each other, letting the passion build gradually so it would last. Her kisses, warm and velvety, slowly covered his neck and chest. Her soft fingers stroked his arms and back, his shoulders and torso, while his own circled her nipples.

He felt her arousal rise with his in perfect union. Abandon claimed her at the same moment that need maddened him. Their kisses turned fevered and their caresses grasping as they pulled each other toward a ferocious peak of carnality.

They jumped together, clinging to each other. He did not lose her, even in that physical climax. She was completely there, totally his, shuddering with him as the intensity split the world with its power. Her pulse and her love and her essence filled him, and replaced his own.

The morning did not bring the sun.

When Fleur awoke in the bundle of blankets in which she and Dante slept on the floor, the patter of rain could still be heard on the roof.

His arm circled her, and even in his sleep his strong fingers held her. She closed her mind to the rain and the chamber and drank in his embrace and warmth.

As long as they stayed here, just like this, he was safe. If he never woke, he would never do something noble and brave and dangerous. If they remained in this blissful cocoon, the world would go away.

He stirred. She stayed very still, hoping that he would sleep on. Then she could hold on to the beauty of lying in the arms of a man she totally loved.

Who loved her too. Hearing that had been wonderful. Seeing it in his eyes had been breathtaking. Feeling it in their lovemaking again, knowing it for what it was, giving it a name, had left her completely at its mercy.

It would echo forever, speaking to her heart. Even after they were both gone, she did not doubt that the love would be a part of her.

Dante shifted. He rose up on his arm and gently kissed her shoulder.

"It is still raining," she said. "Let us keep the shutters closed and pretend it is still night."

He laid her on her back and kissed her on the lips. It was a long, sweet, regretful kiss. "I must dress, and so should you. When this is over we will find a bed and stay in it for a week."

He rose and went to the window. He opened the shutters to reveal a sky still heavy with rain. Gray light streamed in.

So did the sound of a horse galloping away.

Dante leaned out the window. He stayed like that, his naked torso half out the small opening. As she dressed, Fleur could see him taking in the surroundings.

"No way down, and too far to jump," he said. He looked at the blankets thoughtfully. "We are too high up to let you climb down those. It would still be a dangerous drop."

"Whose horse was that?"

"An express post rider, I think."

"Gregory has received an express post?"

"Or he has sent one."

He pulled on his clothes and fished for his pocket watch. "It is ten o'clock. Later than I expected."

Later than he expected them to be left alone, was what he meant.

"Perhaps no one is here but us."

"I doubt that, darling. Someone is below."

"If we yelled, perhaps a servant would come and we could explain we are being held—"

"I saw no servants when we arrived, and have heard none in these attic chambers. Farthingstone must have sent them away when he knew Smith would be coming. He would not want it known he associates with the man."

She looked out the window. It faced the back of the house and looked toward the stables. If only there was a way for Dante to climb out—

A movement below in some bushes caught her attention. She squinted through the rain.

The bushes moved again. A bit of brown and a glimpse of straw showed, then disappeared.

"There is someone here besides Gregory and Mr. Smith, Dante. In the bushes by the path to the stables." She waited, and the thatch of straw rose and dipped again. "I think . . . I think it may be Luke."

Dante stuck his head besides hers. The straw crown rose and eyes appeared, sneaking a peek at the house. "Get me something to throw, so I can get his attention when he looks this way."

She glanced around the chamber while she tried to contain the excited hope that began shrieking through her. Her gaze lit on an old wooden candlestick wearing years of crusted wax.

"Will this do?" She handed it to him.

Dante angled his shoulder and arm and head out the window and hurled.

He stayed like that, waiting. Fleur saw his finger go to his lips and then a broad gesture.

Angling to peer out and down, she saw Luke slip from the bushes and come to stand beneath their window.

Dante made gestures that Luke understood better than Fleur did. His soaked straw hair moved along the back of the house surreptitiously as he peeked into windows.

He came back more quickly. "None in these chambers

back here that I can see." He spoke just loudly enough to be barely heard. "What are you doing up there, sir? When you did not return I thought it odd, but Hill said you most likely got caught by the storm and found shelter, but I—"

"Whatever you thought, we are grateful you are here. Mrs. Duclairc is with me, and Farthingstone is up to no good. Go and get help, Luke. It has to be someone who can stand up to Farthingstone and who listens to what you say with interest."

"I don't know people in these parts, and they don't know me. Who will—"

"Find the justice of the peace or another man of position. Use my brother's name. Go now."

Luke did not wait for another command. He dashed through the rain to his bushes, then aimed away from the house.

Fleur threw her arms around Dante as soon as all of him was back in the chamber. "Thank God for Luke. If we had waited for Hill to sit out the storm . . ."

He held her, grateful that she had found reason not to be fearful. He wanted her to stay that way and not be too conscious of time passing. He led her over to the bed and pulled her down to sit beside him on it. "We have some time until Luke returns. Tell me all about your school and your railroad, from the day you first conceived the mad scheme."

She nestled against him and told her story. He asked for details to lengthen the tale, so that hours passed before it was done.

"It is an impressive plan that you conceived and followed, Fleur. I do not think any man could have done better."

"Do you really think so? Do you think it could have worked if I had not been betrayed by Mr. Siddel?"

"I think so, yes."

"It makes me very proud that you say that, Dante. Your good opinion is worth more than actually succeeding with the plan itself."

He thought that a very flattering thing for her to say, but also a little odd. Since he was hardly famous for financial judgment, his opinion on such things wasn't worth much at all. Her conviction touched him, like all of her trust had. It was one more example of the unwarranted optimism she had about him.

He pulled her closer and kissed her, to let her know he was grateful that she had been addled enough to think Dante Duclairc was worthy of her trust and love.

A sound interrupted their embrace. Boot steps sounded outside their chamber. They both looked toward the door.

A key turned in the lock.

chapter 26

The voice demanding entry between wheezes and coughs was Farthingstone's.

"I've some food here, Duclairc. Don't you want it?"

"If I can convince him to take me down below, do not object," Dante whispered to Fleur. "Once we leave, block the door with whatever you can move."

She did not like the plan, but she helped move the chest away from the door, then scurried to the farthest corner.

Dante threw the bolt. He opened the door on a very flushed and breathless Gregory Farthingstone.

Who carried a pistol.

His other hand, which had been holding his chest, pointed down to a tray of ham and bread on the floor. "Pick it up and bring it in. Only a bit of ham. None to do for me right now."

Dante lifted the tray and placed it on the bed. "Of course not. You could not host a man such as Smith with servants about. Nor would he want you to. Of course, I doubt his name is Smith, don't you?"

Farthingstone got redder. He continued catching his breath and pretended to examine the chamber to hide his physical discomfort.

"He is not coming back," Dante said. "If he has not returned by now, he will not."

Farthingstone scowled. "He will be here soon."

"He rightly concluded that his odds were better if he ran. He will disappear into the world from which he emerged." Dante stepped toward Farthingstone. "I am sure that there is a way out for you as well. Let us go below and think it through."

Farthingstone backed up and pointed the pistol more directly. "Stand back, sir. I am not without allies even if he has run."

"Since you are the one with a pistol, you are safe from me. Allow me to come down so my wife can have some privacy without my disturbance. She is weak from this ordeal as well as an accident she suffered last week, and these close quarters have become a burden to her delicate sensibilities."

Fleur managed to appear faint on cue.

"A few minutes, Farthingstone, at least," Dante whispered. "So she can have privacy for personal matters."

Farthingstone flushed a deep red, from embarrassment this time. He eyed Dante skeptically. "You stay a good distance from me or I will shoot. I am well versed in firearms, and I will not miss."

"Certainly. I am not a man famous for courage, nor do I welcome a demise that is any earlier than necessary."

Descending the stairs left Farthingstone as breathless

as mounting them had. He sank into a chair in the drawing room and gestured Dante into another some twenty feet away.

"You appear most unwell, Farthingstone. Perhaps you should have a physician see to you."

"It will pass. It always does."

Dante let the time tick by. Despite his distress, Farthingstone kept a surprisingly steady hand on that pistol.

"A man who brings food to the condemned is not a man likely to play the executioner," Dante finally said. "If I am correct, and Smith has run, what are you going to do?"

"He will be here soon."

"He was willing to attack me and Fleur in return for money, but the outcome of this is not secure and your silence if you are caught not guaranteed."

"He never caused *you* harm. I have been cursing myself that I did not deal with matters that way, I assure you."

Dante was inclined to believe him. That meant someone else had set those men on him outside the Union Club. Or it had just been an attempt at theft after all.

"What do you intend to do with us?"

"You will learn soon enough."

"Are you expecting one of your allies? Is that why you told Smith to send you an express rider? I saw the rider from the window above. It was generous of Smith to accommodate you before he disappeared. A criminal's loyalty does not amount to much, but that was something."

Farthingstone's expression fell.

Dante leaned forward and rested his forearms on his knees. "If you sent for Siddel, I do not think he will come either. That is your ally, is it not? He is the man whom you think can do what you lack the stomach or heart to complete."

"I do not know what you refer to. I barely know Sid—"

"He owes you nothing in this and would not risk his neck for you. Unless what you have been paying him is so high that he cannot live without it."

Farthingstone's eyes widened. "You do not know—"

"I know that he may be a blackmailer. I think that he has been blackmailing you."

"What do you mean, you know he is a blackmailer? If anyone knew such a thing, he could not do it. Unless—" His eyes bulged in astonishment. "Has he bled you too?"

"Not me. Others whom I knew. It was a clever scheme, unearthed ten years ago. The people responsible were stopped, or so it was thought. Siddel knows what they did. I think he was one of them. As for you, I think that he kept you for himself and did not share with them. When he escaped detection, you kept paying."

Farthingstone's disquiet was visible, and it now had nothing to do with climbing stairs. His eyes misted. He appeared on the edge of his composure.

"It has been hell, sir. Hell, I tell you. To be at another's mercy . . ."

"What did he have on you? The secret buried in that cottage?"

Farthingstone glanced over sharply and suspiciously. "It was *not my fault.*"

"How did he learn of it?"

"His uncle. My *friend.* He told him while on his deathbed. That is the legacy he left for his nephew, and the only one of value. The means to bleed *me* of *my* legacy."

"How much did you pay?"

"All of it." He gestured furiously around the drawing room. "The rents from this estate. Every pound, for thirteen years now."

That was not good news. If Siddel was receiving that much while the secret remained buried, he had good cause to want it to remain undetected.

He might come after all. And he could do what Farthingstone needed done. Dante did not doubt that Siddel had it in him to kill in cold blood.

"It is a hell of a thing," Farthingstone said dolefully. "If I do not solve this dilemma, I will swing. If I do, I will go on bleeding."

And the man bleeding him was his only hope of not swinging.

The day still was gray, and the drawing room grayer. Farthingstone's body slumped and his fleshy face sagged too. His eyes glazed in contemplation of his situation.

Dante watched the barrel of the pistol, waiting for it to move so he could lunge.

The time passed. Farthingstone appeared quite dazed. Still the pistol did not waver.

"If he does not come, I have seen that he will go down with me," Farthingstone said into the silence. "He will be very sorry that he left me on this precipice." He patted his chest again, but not because of any exertions this time.

Dante let Farthingstone drift back into his daze. With any luck, the man might fall asleep or drop his guard. He had probably been up the whole night, and the hours were taking their toll.

A half hour later, a sound intruded on their mournful silence, half-drowned by the relentless patter of rain.

Distant and vague, it reminded Dante of nothing he had
ever heard before.

It grew louder bit by bit, sounding off the hills and
ground outside, finally defeating the rhythm of the rain.
It began sounding like the noise of a festival.

Farthingstone finally noticed. It pulled him out of his
thoughts. He cocked his head and his brow creased in
perplexity.

Keeping one eye on Dante, he went to a window and
opened it to the rain. The noise poured in, not far away at
all now.

Farthingstone squinted. His body straightened in
alarm. He slammed the window shut. "Gypsies! What in
the name of Zeus—"

Dante went over to the window. The scene outside
amazed him as much as it did Farthingstone.

"Not gypsies, Farthingstone. Gypsies do not arrive on
a coach and four."

The coach rolled up the lane at a good speed. Luke held the
reins. Beside him sat a substantial woman of middle years
with a pinched face and straw hair, wrapped in a simple
woolen shawl that also shielded her head. Her resemblance
to the young man beside her was unmistakable.

Other women peered out the coach windows. Four
more sat on its roof, clinging to the wood. Two more took
the place of footmen.

They all carried pots that they pounded and beat with
spoons and ladles, making a noise that rang through the
countryside.

Luke's mother climbed down as soon as the coach

stopped. She spoke to a young matron, who ran to the back of the house.

Farthingstone just stared out the window, speechless and confused.

The young woman came back and nodded. From his place where he still held the horses, Luke called for Dante.

Alarmed, Farthingstone backed away from the window and aimed the pistol right at Dante's chest. "Do not respond. They will go and——"

"They know I am still here, Farthingstone. That woman just called for Fleur at our chamber window and knows she is above."

Farthingstone's face flushed again. The red just kept coming. He looked frantically to the window.

A woman's voice called from the drive. "My son says you've Miss Monley in there. We don't leave until she comes out and them that knows what to do with the likes of you arrive." Pots clanged in cacophony to punctuate the announcement.

"Good God," Farthingstone mumbled. "It is not to be borne! To have such rabble trespassing——"

"I sent Luke for help. He must have gone to his collier village up north."

"Colliers! What have they to do with me?"

"Fleur's charity kept the children of those women from starving when their men withheld labor last year. I expect they would kill for her." Dante gazed out the window. "They certainly look prepared to if necessary."

Luke's mother called again. "All the farmers we passed saw us coming. No way to hide we were here. There's them back at the village that know we came, and why. Our men will learn of it once they leave the pits."

The other women began calling for Miss Monley too. The pots and pans sounded louder.

"Tell them to stop that hideous noise," Farthingstone groaned, moving farther back into the room.

"It sounds like the harps of angels to me."

"I will shoot them all. I will—"

"You will have to shoot me first, and by the time you reload they will have you on the ground."

"Good God. This is an outrage! To be besieged in my own home by a horde of mad women! I will—I will—!"

Dante surveyed the little troop. Luke's mother had placed herself front and center of a phalanx of colliers' wives. Proud and brave, she faced the house with her hands on her wide hips, full of the determined strength that hard living bred in such women. She did not look like someone a sane man would want to cross.

"Good God." The mumble came lower this time, and with a much different tone. A heavy thud punctuated the last word.

Dante turned. The pistol had fallen to the floor. Farthingstone's face had turned unnaturally pale. Holding his chest, he stared at the rug with unseeing eyes.

He looked up at Dante with an expression of horrible comprehension. His legs folded.

His body fell.

"Get them all warm. Find them food," Fleur instructed Hill as the women climbed off the coach and filed into the house. "Build up the fire in the drawing room and—"

"Don't need such a fine fire," Luke's mother said as she passed. "The kitchen will do for us."

"Make yourselves comfortable, wherever that is," Dante said. He stood beside Fleur at the door, welcoming their unusual party.

The ride from Gregory's house had been quite an event. Fleur imagined how odd it would have appeared to anyone who saw them, with women hanging off the coach and those pans clanging, now with excitement and heady victory.

Jubilation when Dante freed her from the attic chamber had crashed into shock when she saw Gregory's body. It still lay in that house, covered with a blanket, awaiting removal.

Luke sat at the reins as the women disembarked their ship. Fleur squeezed past them and went over to him. He was bent down and angled, peering back at the coach with a deep frown.

"You have my gratitude, Luke," she said.

"Please don't blame my mother and the others that the coach is badly scratched. I had a few scrapes with cottages in the village. The lanes are narrow and not fit for a coach like this, and my handling of the horses—"

"Luke, you may have saved our lives. I do not think that a few scratches on the coach signify much, do you?"

He blushed. "I didn't know where to go here. Then I figured if I took the mail road north, even in the rain I would get there in an hour or so. I knew there would be those who would believe me and know what to do."

"Your plan was unusual, but effective. You brought an army back."

"Was my mum's idea. She said it would be a sin to allow ill to befall you after you had helped them."

"She has my gratitude as well. All of these women do."

Dante came out to join them as the last cotton skirt entered the house. "Luke, tomorrow morning hitch two of the horses to Hill's wagon and he and I will go get Mr. Farthingstone."

Luke flicked the reins and headed the coach back to the stables. Fleur used the moment of privacy to embrace Dante.

"I almost fainted from worry up in that chamber. I kept listening for sounds, of Mr. Smith returning or Gregory hurting you or your doing something reckless. I could not move, I was listening and praying so hard. I kept hoping I would hear a coach coming, bringing help—"

His kiss quieted her outpouring. "One did come, and all is well now."

She laughed. "The county will be talking about it for weeks."

"We will give out a story to satisfy curiosity. There is no reason for the true one to be known. He is gone and nothing will be served by letting the truth be told."

The image of Gregory sprawled on the drawing-room floor flashed in front of her. She had only caught a glimpse before Dante spread the blanket, but there had been an expression of utter astonishment on Gregory's face.

She snuggled deeper against his body and within his circling embrace. She closed her eyes and savored everything about him, even the scent of his damp wool coat. She allowed his warmth to conquer every chill and fear and saturate her mind until all sad images left it.

"Did he explain it to you? Did he say who it was?" she asked.

"He said it was not his fault, that was all. You were

correct, I think. He did not have it in him to kill. What-ever happened at that cottage, it was not at his initiative."

"Except that he had it in him to pay Mr. Smith to try and kill me."

"Yes. For that alone, I am glad he is dead." He lifted her chin and kissed her lips again. Slowly. Sweetly. "When I go back to that house in the morning, I may not return with the wagon. There is something I must tend to there first."

"What?"

"A small matter." He turned with her surrounded by his arm. "Now, let us find a chamber where we can be alone. I want to hold you in my arms and forget about Farthingstone until morning."

chapter 27

Loving a good woman provokes change in even the least angelic of men.

Dante was contemplating that astonishing truth the next day when he heard the horse outside Farthingstone's house. He closed the steward's account book, which he had been perusing in the library, and placed Farthingstone's pistol on top of it on the table beside the divan where he sat. Next to the pistol he laid the letter that he had found in Farthingstone's coat.

The silent house echoed with boot steps, first hurried, then very slow. Pauses indicated that the chambers were being checked.

The library door opened. A dark head stuck in.

"Farthingstone?"

"He is not here, Siddel."

The head snapped around. The door swung wide. Siddel's glance darted around to ensure they were alone.

"Where is he?"

"He expired. Fate was kind to him."

Siddel exhaled with great relief. "Kind to you as well, I am happy to see."

"You worried for my safety?"

Siddel took a chair and made a display of calming himself. "He sent me an express post of the most alarming nature, rambling about your threat to him. I feared he would do something very rash."

"I did not think you had enough acquaintance with each other to inspire such a letter."

"I advised him on occasion. I do not know why he would write to me, but having perceived his state of mind I could hardly—"

"You did not ride all this way to save me and my wife, Siddel. Quite the opposite."

Siddel straightened with indignation. "That is a damnable thing to say. Of course I—"

"You could not risk his going in the dock if that body in the cottage was discovered. He would speak of you, and of the money he has been paying you all these years for your silence. You would hang right after he did."

Siddel's face went very blank. He revealed no consternation at learning the story was out. His gaze slid from Dante to the account book and the pistol and the folded paper.

"He left an explanation," Dante said, pointing to the paper. "I think it was just written, probably yesterday morning. I suspect that if you had not come, he would have taken his own life and seen that you followed him to hell."

Siddel's gaze locked on the paper. "There is no proof."

"The confession of a dying man is considered very strong evidence. He also admitted most of it to me. Not the part about your encouraging him to kill my wife, of course. That is only in the letter."

Siddel laughed. "Your swearing evidence is the least of my concerns."

"For all my sins, I am not known as a liar. The court will believe me, since I gain nothing either way."

Siddel thought that over, then lowered his lids. "I assume that if you do gain something, it will make a difference."

Dante did not reply.

"What do you want?"

"I want to know what happened ten years ago."

Siddel settled deeper into his chair, the image of a man back in control of matters. "Actually, it was thirteen. My uncle was dying. I was his heir, and I was eager to see his illness conclude. Imagine my annoyance when he called me to his deathbed and told me there was almost nothing left. The man had inherited a handsome fortune but had squandered it."

"That must have been disappointing."

"Hellish. However, he made a deathbed confession to me. He told me a story of an event from years ago. From when he and Farthingstone were partners in sin."

"He told you about the cottage. Who is buried there?"

"Since you know that someone is—my uncle often visited Farthingstone when they were much younger. There would be scandalous debauches in this house. In addition, they formed a casual liaison with a woman in the area who would enter their games. She lived in that cottage, where she cared for the simpleton sister of the woman who owned the neighboring estate.

"They would go over to enjoy the favors of this woman

late at night when the idiot was asleep. Only one day they got very drunk earlier than normal and they decided to pay a visit in the evening. The woman put her charge upstairs, and things were well under way when this half-wit comes down, looking for her doll."

"Hardly worth killing for. No one would have comprehended if she told, assuming she even understood what she saw."

"Oh, it wasn't that. My uncle was very drunk. The simpleton struck him as rather pretty. He had his way with her."

Dante found Siddel's telling of this story sickening. The man was completely dispassionate as he described the sordid crime.

"How did she die?"

Siddel shrugged. "She was confused and docile with Uncle, but when he was done and Farthingstone was about to take his turn, she went mad. Screaming, fighting. My uncle sought to silence her. He succeeded rather too well."

That was what Fleur had seen through that window when she ran to play with her friend that evening. The blood had not been that of childbirth, but a virgin's blood on a woman's thighs, and maybe other blood too. Her aunt Peg had then disappeared.

Shock had confused the episodes in her mind quickly and obscured the meaning of it all. If she had spoken of it immediately, things may have been different. But her child's guilt would not allow that, and the shock had done its work to protect her.

"Years later bones were found and everyone accepted

that they were that woman's remains. No doubt Farthingstone had encouraged that assumption," Dante said.

"He was relieved to. And that is what happened thirteen years ago," Siddel said. "I inherited a legacy."

"Your means to blackmail, you mean."

"It was in the caretaker's and Farthingstone's interest
to keep silent, of course. The crime was theirs too. Farthingstone knew that. When I told him what my uncle
had revealed, he actually offered the money."

"When it appeared that Fleur was going to have that
cottage torn down and foundations dug for a school, it
was in your interest to make sure it did not happen. The
payments from Farthingstone would stop if he was exposed. As would those from Cavanaugh, if that railroad
partnership ever succeeded."

Siddel's face fell. "Cavanaugh? I have no idea what—"

"I know all about my wife's Grand Project. Cavanaugh's
patrons would not want it to be successful," Dante said.
"Your situation is not good, Siddel. I hope that you have
been laying aside some money, because both of your in-
comes have abruptly ceased. Once this letter is given to the
magistrate, your position becomes dire."

Siddel smiled. It gave his face an unpleasant countenance, because the smile itself was half a sneer. "I do not
think so. As I was riding here, it occurred to me that you
will probably want to continue Farthingstone's payments. You will definitely not want that letter to land me
in the dock."

"There is nothing you have that I would pay for."

"I think there is. Your dead brother's good name, for
example. Your own honor, for another."

Dante studied the man's slyly contented expression. Blotches of white heat began breaking in him. He fought to control it.

For Fleur's sake, he had decided not to broach this part of it, much as he wanted to. His responsibility for her outweighed any to the dead.

"You do not appear surprised," Siddel said, with admiration.

"No."

"You are smarter than I thought."

"You should get on your horse and run. I hear that Russia is pleasant in the summer, even if the winters are hell."

"Russia? My, you are clever. You have seen it all. It was my indiscreet slip about the duel that alerted you, wasn't it? I thought that I saw something in your eyes besides insult."

"Yes."

"I do not favor living abroad. Nor, I suspect, is Nancy half as lovely as she was when you and I and so many others queued up for her. I do not think she will be very useful at all in getting young men to do things that unearth their family secrets."

This reference to the woman who waited in Russia made the heat spread. Siddel's taunt about young men had been direct and vicious.

The fury wanted to consume him. The icy cold that would freeze out good sense already loomed on its edges.

"If I choose not to run, what can you do? Give Farthingstone's letter in evidence against me? See me on trial? Who knows what I will confess to then. Or perhaps you will tell Laclere about my other doings and get him to call me out." Siddel began laughing. "I can see it. Laclere and I meeting, and the world assuming that he did so to protect *your* honor. I will let it be known how your wife has secretly met with me."

The heat burned away all rationality, furiously demanding that he deal with this man once and for all.

"Or maybe I will give out the story of that attack on you and say Laclere concluded I was responsible."

"If you know about it, you were."

"Your questions to Cavanaugh were making him concerned. You were becoming a nuisance. However, the world will only know that your brother is fighting a duel because you are too much a coward to do so." He grinned. "Nothing new there."

Cold blasted over the fire, killing it and its fury, replacing it with a dangerous calm.

He would enjoy killing this man. He had been preparing to do so for a decade.

Siddel's expectant expression was one of a man who assumed he would survive. "Farthingstone's letter must be mine if I win," he said.

Dante tucked the letter inside his coat. He picked up the pistol. "Of course. Let us find you a weapon."

Siddel reached under his coat. "As it happens, I have one right here."

"Then let us go outside."

Side by side, pistols in hand, they walked out to the reception hall. Ice crystallized inside Dante as they moved. The satisfaction he would soon know made him euphoric. Not only Siddel would die. Memories and resentments would too. An old guilt would be expiated.

Siddel opened the door.

The sun was streaking through the clouds and the rain had turned the earth redolent with lovely smells. As if carried by the fresh breeze, an image came to Dante, breaking through the ice with its warmth.

It was a picture of Fleur proposing at the sponging house, trusting against all evidence that he would protect her and honor his word to her. It was Fleur in his arms, opening with a love that made life worth living, that gave it purpose. It was Fleur carrying their child, needing his strength as her worst fears loomed.

Siddel had paused, and Dante realized he had as well.

"We have visitors," Siddel said.

That pulled Dante back from his thoughts. He discovered that both fire and ice had left him. So had the justice of this duel. If he did this, it would be for all the wrong reasons.

He looked down the lane. Two riders, a quarter mile away, approached at a good pace.

"Witnesses would be useful," Siddel said. "Whoever they are, they will do."

Dante stepped outside the house. He gestured to Siddel's horse. "Take it and run. I will see that you are not followed."

"I am not riding anywhere."

"Then you will hang. I will not play your executioner, much as I want to."

"It will all come out. Do not think it won't."

"Then let it come out. I am not going to kill you. It will change nothing if I do."

"You are a coward."

"If we meet you are a dead man. Now, go."

Siddel's swagger left him. He looked frantically at the riders, then at his horse. "I must demand that letter first."

Dante watched the riders get nearer. "Leave while you can or—"

The crack silenced him. An impact on his left shoulder made him stagger. Fiery pain sliced through his chest.

Astonished, he swerved to see Siddel toss aside his smoking pistol and stride toward him with murder in his eyes. Siddel's gaze was fixed on Dante's own pistol.

Dante raised his gun and fired.

Dante stared at Siddel's body. His own legs held him up, but he had no sense of why, since he could barely feel them there. On the edge of his consciousness he vaguely heard horses approaching at a hard gallop.

"Damnation," a familiar voice roared.

A horse stopped nearby and suddenly Vergil was beside him, taking his weight in his arms.

"Morning, Verg."

"Hell. Don't talk." Vergil lowered him to sit on the ground. "When Burchard's man reported Siddel had left London on the northern road, St. John and I decided to follow, but I never thought Siddel had murder on his mind."

Dante did not much care what had brought Vergil here. He did not care about anything at all, actually. The pain was getting worse, and fog had entered his head.

St. John joined them, stepping over Siddel's body to kneel down and examine the wound. "It was so close the ball went through, but we need to stanch the bleeding."

He began pulling Dante's coat off. "I asked you to watch your back, Duclairc."

Before St. John succeeded in stripping off the coat, Dante pulled out Farthingstone's letter and handed it to his brother.

The fog closed in and turned black.

chapter 28

Dante appears in good health," Diane St. John said. "Your care of him made for a quick recovery."

"I do not think my care made a great difference, but I enjoyed the duty," Fleur said.

She had relished every minute of caring for him. Sitting with him, changing his bandages, sharing his relief when it became clear that the wound would not leave his shoulder or arm infirm—a mellow intimacy had developed between them the last two weeks. It astonished her how the love just kept getting richer. Deeper.

She had resented the frequent intrusions of his friends and family, because they robbed her of a few moments of bliss. Laclere in particular had been a trial because he visited for at least an hour every day, and she was banished from the sick room while the brothers talked.

She suspected that today's unexpected onslaught of visitors indicated that the idyll of privacy was over for good.

Diane sat with Fleur in the drawing room, enjoying

the sweet breezes of the early June afternoon. Diane had called with her husband, who now conversed with Dante in the library.

Not only the St. Johns had visited today. Three other women completed their circle in the drawing room. Charlotte had arrived first, then Bianca and Laclere, and finally the Duchess of Everdon and her husband. The men had gone off together, and other men, whom Fleur did not know, had been brought directly to the library upon arrival.

Fleur was trying not to worry about the business being conducted in that other chamber.

"I expect that they are settling matters," she said to her friends. "Clarifying what happened up north, and explaining how Dante was shot."

"Why do you think that?" Bianca asked.

"Mr. Hampton wore his solicitor's face, for one thing. Then that last man who came appeared very official and sober. Dante told me that he would have to explain how it was and even stand trial. The deaths of two men cannot be ignored."

"You should not worry," Charlotte said. "There were witnesses, and the wound in my brother's shoulder is evidence that he defended himself. The trial will only be a formality."

"It is taking a long time for all of them to settle that. They have been in there an hour."

"I am certain that whatever is transpiring in that library is only good news for you," the duchess said.

Williams appeared at the door of the drawing room. He came over and bent low to Fleur's ear. "Madame, your presence is requested in the library."

Fleur swallowed hard. She did not doubt that Dante would be completely exonerated. The question was whether they could manage that without telling the whole story of Gregory and that cottage and Mr. Siddel's blackmail and the Grand Project and—

She rose. To her surprise, the duchess and Bianca did as well.

"We will accompany you," the duchess said. "I once faced a whole phalanx of men in a library, and it is not something a woman should have to endure without a few troops of her own by her side."

"I hardly go to meet the enemy," Fleur said as they walked to the library. All the same, she was grateful for the troops.

"All of those frock coats can be intimidating if there are no dresses present. When men are together alone, they have a tendency to start acting as if women are children, even if as individuals they know better. Don't you agree, Bianca?"

"It is an ongoing battle that we fight, Sophia. Fortunately, it can be a pleasurable one."

The two ladies giggled. Fleur let herself enjoy a few precious memories of the various engagements and pleasures her own marriage had produced.

The library doors swung and they entered. Adrian Burchard did not appear surprised to see his wife, but Laclere raised an eyebrow at Bianca.

Which she blithely ignored.

The duchess had been right. Facing a library full of frock coats was daunting. They all turned their attention on her. All except Dante. He sat in a chair off to one side, reading some document.

Mr. Hampton addressed her. "Madame, we need you to read these paperss and give your signature if you agree they are in order."

She glanced to Dante. He had taken care of all of it. She would not have to answer questions and dissemble on the details. She had only to sign a statement accepting the events as laid out on paper.

Relieved, she walked to the desk. "Of course."

She dipped a pen and began to sign.

"I advise you to read it very carefully, to make sure you accept its contents," Mr. Hampton interrupted.

Swallowing a little sigh, she put the pen down. She was very sure that Dante had produced a story that she would find acceptable. All the same, she scanned the top sheet of paper.

The first paragraph stunned her.

It was not a statement regarding those events in Durham.

It was a partnership agreement regarding a proposed railroad in Durham.

Ten of the men in the library, including Laclere, Burchard, and St. John, were named as primary partners. So was she, with most of her shares to create a trust to endow her school. Additional shares would be sold to others later.

She looked at Dante, sitting off to the side, flipping through the pages of his copy.

He had done this. He had made it happen.

"Burchard and I will present the bill to Parliament that gains approval for it to go forward," Laclere said.

She sat down in a chair and read the whole wonderful text. It laid out the risks as well as the benefits. When she got to that part, where the partners pledged their fortunes to debts incurred, she looked up at Bianca and the duchess.

It was their fortunes as well that their husbands pledged. They had accompanied her in here to announce that they approved.

"Mr. Tenet will be managing partner as the project goes forward," Mr. Hampton explained, gesturing to an official, sober-looking man. "He has experience in such affairs."

Mr. Tenet bowed. "I am honored to meet you, madame. May I say that the preparations that you put in place regarding the land and the surveying will enhance our success and our speed of construction."

"Yes, well done," St. John said.

They knew. Dante had told them it had been her idea. She accepted the nods and smiles of approval. Only the ones of the Duchess of Everdon and the Viscountess Laclere lacked a tinge of amazement.

"Speaking of land, these deeds will also have to be signed by both you and Mr. Duclairc," Mr. Hampton said, tapping another stack of papers. "Please now state before these witnesses that your husband in no way co-erces you to sell these properties deeded in your name."

She gladly stated it. With a shaking hand, she signed everything.

Dante remained on the periphery, his expression very bland, allowing her to complete the ritual on her own.

When the last signature was completed, he rose and came over to sign as well.

She stood beside him, so excited that she could barely contain herself. She wanted to be rid of all these people so that she could embrace him the way she desperately wanted to do.

The duchess came to her rescue. "Gentlemen, let us join the ladies in the drawing room. Mr. Duclairc instructed that some appropriate refreshments be brought up for a little celebration."

The frock coats filed out, congratulating one another. At the door Laclere looked back. He gave her a smile full of the familiarity of their years of friendship.

The look he then gave Dante was of a different sort. Not one of approval, but of admiration.

She threw her arms around Dante as soon as the door closed on them. "Thank you." She did not know whether to laugh or cry, so she just held him tightly and pressed herself against his strong chest and let the heady joy overwhelm her.

He encompassed her with his arms. "I said you would have your school, Fleur. It wouldn't do for it to lack the endowment you had planned."

"They believe in the Grand Project, don't they? Laclere and the others did not only do it to be kind, did they? I would not want—"

"None of the men in this chamber was ruled by sentiment. I explained your plan to my brother and showed him your map. He was sufficiently impressed that he brought it to St. John, who made some inquiries to confirm your judgments. After that, finding the others was easy. They count themselves fortunate to be a part of it."

"So planning this is what was occupying you while you lay abed."

"This, and counting the days until I could make love to you again."

She looked up into his eyes. They contained the most exciting warmth. She could gaze in them forever and be a contented woman. There had always been honesty and truth in those lucid depths, ever since those first days in the cottage. Her heart had understood from the first that this was a man whom it would be an honor to love.

"I am so grateful that you accepted my proposal in the sponging house, Dante. I lied to myself and said it was a fair trade, my money for your protection. I really knew it was not."

"It sounded very fair to me."

She shook her head. "I do not think that I really did it to escape Gregory either. I did not want to lose you. I already loved you, only I could not call it that, not even in my heart, because I could not have that kind of love."

"It is just as well you did not call it love. Admitting you married me for that would have landed you in Bedlam for certain."

"If this is madness, let me never be sane." She slid her hand behind his neck and pressed him down so she could kiss him. "I am so glad that we are completely married and I can completely love you."

They shared a long kiss, full of the excitement of the day's surprise and the anticipation of the private pleasures waiting when their guests left. Dante's aura saturated her, but there was no danger in it any longer, because love flooded with it.

Her eyes dampened with the best kind of tears. She wished there were no guests in the drawing room and they could stay like this for hours, holding each other, enjoying the triumph of the day and their love, not separate in any way at all.

Dante took her face in his two hands. "I want you to know something. I was always glad that we married, Fleur. If you had never been able to give yourself to me, I would have still cherished you and the love I have for you. I would have never regretted becoming your husband."

Cherished. Yes, that was the word for how she loved him. That was the word for the sweet unity she experienced in his affection and friendship and passion.

He gazed down with those mesmerizing, wonderful eyes. No one else in the world existed but the two of them.

Holding her face gently in his two palms, be kissed her twice, once on the forehead and then on the lips.

ABOUT
THE AUTHOR

MADELINE HUNTER's first novel was published in 2000. Since then she has seen thirteen historical romances and one novella published, and her books have been translated into five languages. She is a four-time RITA finalist and won the long historical RITA in 2003. Twelve of her books have been on the *USA Today* bestseller list, and she has also had titles on the *New York Times* extended list. Madeline has a Ph.D. in art history, which she teaches at an eastern university. She currently lives in Pennsylvania with her husband and two sons.

Read on for a sneak peek at

LESSONS

of

DESIRE

by

Madeline Hunter

On sale October 2007

MADELINE HUNTER

LESSONS *of* DESIRE

BANTAM BOOKS

Hero. Seducer.
Heartbreaker.
He's the one lover no
woman can resist....

LESSONS OF DESIRE

On sale October 2007

CHAPTER ONE

Phaedra rose from her writing table in response to Signora Cirillo's call. If the woman wanted more money so soon—

A wonderful sight awaited her when she opened the door to her apartment. Signora Cirillo was not alone. Lord Elliot stood beside her.

Phaedra kept her composure even though she wanted to shout for joy. If he was here, it meant only one thing.

"Lord Elliot, please enter. *Grazie,* signora."

Signora Cirillo raised her eyebrows over her dark cat eyes at this dismissal. Phaedra shooed her away.

"You bring good news I hope, Lord Elliot," Phaedra said when they were alone.

"Your house arrest is over, Miss Blair. We have Captain Cornell of the Euryalus to thank. He spoke with Sansoni on our behalf."

"Thank God for the British navy." She ran to the window and threw open the shutters. The guard outside was gone. "I must take a turn along the bay this evening. I cannot believe—" She skipped back to Lord Elliot and embraced him. "I am so grateful to you."

He smiled kindly when she released him. He seemed to understand her excitement and forgive her exuberance. If his gaze had warmed just a little from her impulsive embrace, well, he was a man after all.

He appeared quite magnificent right now in his perfectly tailored brown frock coat and high boots. His smile did much to soften the severity of the Rothwell face. Unlike his older brothers, Lord Elliot was reputed to smile often, and it appeared that was true.

He looked around her sitting room. His gaze lit upon her writing desk. "I have interrupted your letter, I fear."

"An interruption I most welcomed. I was writing to Alexia, and pouring out my story of woe, on the chance I could at least throw my letter down to you when you returned here."

"Why not complete the letter at once, and let her know all is well? I will take it to Cornell. He sails in two days for England, and will post it to London when he docks."

"What a splendid idea, if you will not think me rude to jot a few more lines."

"Not at all, Miss Blair. Not at all."

She sat down and quickly added a paragraph telling Alexia that all had been resolved happily, thanks to Alexia's new brother-in-law, Lord Elliot. She folded, addressed, and sealed the paper, and stood with it in her hand. Lord Elliot walked over and gently plucked it from her fingers. He tucked it into his frock coat, to bring to Captain Cornell.

He resumed his perusal of the sitting room and its views. "You came to the door yourself, Miss Blair. Where is your abigail?"

"I have no abigail, Lord Elliot. No servants. Not even in London."

"Is that due to another philosophical belief?"

"Rather it is a practical decision. An uncle left me a modest income, and I would rather spend it in other ways."

"How sensible. However, your lack of a servant is inconvenient."

"Not at all." She turned on her toes and the drapes of her black gauze garment and long hair fanned out. "A dress like this does not require a maid to truss me and my hair requires only a brush."

"I was not speaking of your dressing. I need to speak with you about this development, and with no maid in this apartment . . ."

He worried for her reputation should she be with a man alone. How charming.

"Lord Elliot, it is impossible for you to compromise me because I am above such stupid social rules. Besides, this is a business meeting of sorts, is it not? Our privacy is not only allowed in such situations, but also necessary." She doubted he would accept her reasoning, logical though it was. Men like him never did.

To her amazement, he capitulated immediately. "You are correct. Therefore we shall proceed. Will you not sit? This could take some time."

He appeared very serious all of a sudden. Serious and stern and . . . hard. His gesture toward the divan carried more command than his polite request implied. The temptation to remain standing nipped at her. She sat, but only because he had just procured her freedom.

He settled into a chair that faced her. He gave her a good look, as if sizing her up. He might have never seen her before and now tried to interpret the peculiar image she presented.

She could not shake the sense that, in a manner of

speaking, she had never seen him before either. There was none of his quiet amusement now, just a long, examining, invasive gaze that made her uneasy. A very feminine response rumbled deeply in her essence.

That was the damndest thing about handsome men. Their beauty left one at a disadvantage when they directed attention at you. This man was very handsome. He was also very masculine in most ways, and subtly so in the worst ones. Right now he seemed to be deliberately trying to unsettle her. He did not do it for carnal reasons, she was sure. Yet his aura projected that lure too, and her blood reacted to it.

Protecting, possessing, conquering— They were all facets of the same primitive instinct, weren't they? A man could not follow one inclination without arousing the others in himself, and a woman was easily vanquished if she did not take care. She wondered which ancient part of the male character motivated him now.

"Alexia did ask me to look in on you, Miss Blair. That was no lie. However, I had other reasons to seek you out and they must now be addressed."

"Since we only met once, at Alexia's wedding, and very briefly, I cannot imagine what your reasons might be."

"I think that you can."

Now he was annoying her. "I assure you I cannot."

His tone indicated that he found her annoying in turn. "Miss Blair, it has come to my attention that you are now a partner in Merris Langton's publishing house. That you inherited your father's interest in the business."

"That information has not been given out, Lord Elliot. With men assuming a woman cannot succeed in business, and with many believing it unnatural for a woman to even try, I chose to keep that quiet so prejudice would not affect the business itself."

"Do you intend to be active in it?"

"I will have a hand in choosing the titles published, but I expect Mr. Langton will continue to oversee the practical matters." Not that this was any of Lord Elliot's concern. "I would like to know who informed you of this. If my solicitor has been indiscreet—"

"Your solicitor is blameless." His attention left her for a spell, and his eyes assumed a brooding darkness. She had seen that in the past, ever so fleetingly. It hinted at the brilliant mind inside this elegant man about town, and the intellectual absorption that had led him to pen a celebrated historical tome before he turned twenty-three.

"Miss Blair, I regret that I bring you some bad news. Merris Langton passed away from his illness after you left London. He was buried a few days before I sailed myself."

She had feared Mr. Langton would not recover, but hearing of his death was surprising anyway. "That is bad news indeed, Lord Elliot. I thank you for informing me. I did not know him well, but a man's passing is always sad. I had counted on him helping me maintain that publishing house, but it appears I will be left to do it on my own."

"Is it all yours now?"

"My father founded the press and subsidized it all along. His share was his to bequeath, but Mr. Langton's became my father's if Mr. Langton died. So, yes, I do believe it is all mine now."

His distraction disappeared. The sternness returned. Coldly. "Prior to Langton's illness, he approached my brother. He spoke of your father's memoirs being published. He offered to omit several paragraphs in the manuscript that touched on my family, if a significant sum was paid to him."

"He did? That is terrible! I am shocked by this betrayal of my father's principles, and sincerely apologize for my partner."

She rose and began pacing, agitated by this dreadful revelation. Lord Elliot politely stood too, but she ignored him while she tried to take in the implications of Mr. Langton's foolish scheme. This might be all it took to bring that shaky press down.

She knew too well its precarious finances, and as a partner she was responsible for the unpaid debts. She had counted on her father's memoirs to pull them through, but if Mr. Langton had compromised the integrity of that publication, the world might dismiss the book entirely.

"This is all Harriette Wilson's fault," she said, her dismay edging into anger. "She set a disgraceful precedent in asking her lovers to pay to have their names removed from her book. I wrote and told her so, mind you. Harriette, I wrote, it is unethical to take money to expunge memoirs. It is just a pretty form of blackmail. She only thought of her empty purse, of course. Well, that is the result of the dependent life she chose and the foolish extravagance that she practiced." She strode more purposefully. "Mr. Langton no doubt approached others too. I cannot believe he would impugn the ethics of our publishing house in this way."

"Miss Blair, please spare me the theatrical outrage. My family was prepared to pay Langton. I sought you out to say that we will now gladly pay you instead."

Theatrical outrage? She paused in her pacing and faced him squarely. "Lord Elliot, I hope that I misunderstand you. Are you suggesting that I would accept this money to edit the memoirs to your liking?"

"It is our hope that you will."

She advanced on him until she was close enough to see the thoughts reflected in his eyes. "Good heavens, you think that I knew Mr. Langton was doing this, don't you? You believe I was an accomplice to it."

He did not respond. He just looked back, visibly skeptical of her astonishment.

Furious about his assumptions, affronted by the insult, she turned away. "Lord Elliot, my father's memoirs are going to be published as soon as I return to England. Every sentence of them. It was his last wish, sent to me directly, and I would never pick and choose which of his words the world should read. I am sincerely grateful for your aid with Mr. Sansoni, but it would be best if we ended this conversation. If I had a servant I would have you shown out. As it is, you will have to find your own way."

To make her dismissal of him complete, she strode to her bedchamber and closed the door.

She had not collected herself before the door to her bedchamber reopened. Lord Elliot calmly followed her in and closed it behind him.

"My visit is not over, and our business is not completed, Miss Blair."

"How dare— This is my *bedchamber,* sir."

He crossed his arms and assumed that irritating masculine pose of command. "Normally that might check me, but you are above stupid social rules, like the one that says I should not intrude here. Remember?"

She did not consider that particular social rule so stupid. It existed for a very good reason. A primitive one. This was her most private space, her sanctuary. She undressed and bathed and slept here. Every object symbolized activities that only a husband or lover should see.

The air began altering while he glanced at the wardrobe where her garments were stored and the dressing table that held her private items. His gaze swept over the bed slowly, then returned to her.

His thoughts were not as masked as he thought. She noted the subtle changes in his expression, the way the hardness he wore rearranged itself ever so slightly. A man could not be near a bed with a woman and not start wondering. It was just a curse of nature that they bore.

It irritated her that she wondered too. The manner in which he had just insulted her should provide the best armor against the intimacy threading through this chamber. The air grew heavy and full of a magnetic excitement that stirred her.

An image blinked in her mind, of Lord Elliot looking down at her, his face mere inches from hers, his dark hair mussed by reasons besides fashion and his desire completely unmasked. She saw his naked shoulders and felt the pressure of his body and the firm hold of his embrace on her skin. She felt . . .

She forced the image from her head, but acknowledgment flashed in his eyes. He knew her mind had wandered there, just as she knew his had.

He unfolded his arms, and she thought he might reach for her. She wondered if he would insult her further now by giving voice to what they were feeling. There were men who misunderstood her life and beliefs and proposed things in ignorance, but Lord Elliot was not stupid. If he attempted to act on the sensual awareness whispering between them, it would be deliberately and cruelly offensive.

He turned his attention from her, diluting the intimacy but not completely vanquishing it. Her pride was spared but her sexuality simmered with discontentment.

"Is the manuscript here?" he asked. "Did you bring it with you?"

"Of course not. Why would I do that?"

He eyed the wardrobe. "Do you swear? If not I will have to search for it."

"I swear, and don't you dare search. You have no right to be here at all."

"Actually, I do, but we will discuss that later."

What was that supposed to mean? "I left it in London, in a very secure place. It contains my father's memoirs, his last words. I would never be careless with it."

"Have you read it?"

"Of course."

"Then you know what he wrote about my family. I want you to tell me about that now. His exact words, as well as you can remember."

He was not requesting to know, but demanding. His dominating high-handedness was making her gratitude for his help dim fast.

"Lord Elliot, your family's name, and that of Easterbrook, is never mentioned in that manuscript."

That surprised him for an instant. His sternness cracked long enough for her to glimpse the amiable, helpful man who had first entered her apartment. It did not last. The brooding distraction took over and the sharp mind assessed what she had said.

"Miss Blair, Merris Langton approached my brother and described a specific accusation against my father. Is there anything in that manuscript that in your opinion could be interpreted as relating to my parents?"

She wished he had not phrased his question quite that way. She debated her answer. "There is one part that might be so interpreted, I suppose."

"Please describe it."

"I would rather not."

"I insist. You will tell me now."

His voice, his stance, and his expression said he would brook no argument. She had never before in her life been so pointedly ordered to do something by a man.

Perhaps it would be best if he and his family were warned, and could prepare for the scandal. The passage they discussed had been one of several in the memoirs to give her pause.

"My father describes a private dinner party several years before my mother died. They entertained a young diplomat just back from the Cape Colony. My father wanted to learn the true conditions there. This young man drank rather freely and turned morose. While in his cups he confided something regarding an event in a British regiment in the Cape."

The mention of the Cape Colony had garnered his attention too well. She inwardly grimaced. She had always hoped that rumor was untrue, but—

"Go on, Miss Blair."

"He said that while he was there, a British officer died. It was reported as from a fever, but in fact he had been shot. He was found dead after going out on patrol. There were suspicions regarding another officer who had accompanied him, but no evidence. Rather than impugn that other officer, a false cause of death was reported."

He masked his reaction very well now. She looked upon a face carved of stone. His silence turned terrible, quaking with the anger leaking out of him.

"Miss Blair, if you associated that man's story with my family, you must know the rumor about my father, and how he is said to have used his influence to have my mother's lover posted to the Cape Colony. A place where that lover died of fever."

She swallowed hard. "I may have heard something to that effect once."

"If you did, many did. Neither Langton nor you had any difficulty adding up the references and drawing a conclusion. If you publish that section, the insinuation will stand that my father paid another officer to kill my mother's lover. The lack of names in your father's memoirs will not spare my father's reputation, and he cannot defend himself from the grave."

"I am not convinced—"

"Damn it, that is exactly what will happen and you know it. I demand that you remove that portion of the memoirs."

"Lord Elliot, I am sympathetic to your distress. Truly, I am. However, my father charged me with seeing his memoirs published and it is my duty to do so. I have thought long and hard about this. If I remove every sentence that might be construed as dangerous or unflattering to this person or that, there will be little left."

He strode to her and looked down hard. "You will not publish this lie."

His determination was palpable. He did not require expressions of anger or verbal threats to emphasize the power he would use against her. It was just there, surrounding her, tinged by the sexual awareness that had never left this chamber, creating a mood that held all the edges of that dark instinct.

"If it is a lie, I will consider omitting it," she said. "If you can obtain proof that man died of fever, or if my parents' guest recants, in this one case I will do it. For Alexia, however, not for you or Easterbrook."

That checked him. "For Alexia? How convenient for you. Now you can retreat without giving me a victory."

He understood her rather too well. She did not care for the evidence of that.

He looked down much more kindly. Their closeness, born of his fury, became inappropriate suddenly. As his anger ebbed that other tension flowed again.

He did not retreat the way he should. The way her raised eyebrows demanded. Instead he lifted a strand of her red hair and looked at it while he gently wove it between his fingers.

"Did your father include the name of either of these men, Miss Blair? The young diplomat at the dinner party or the officer who was suspected?"

He was not touching her as such, but his toying with her hair claimed a familiarity that she should not allow. Their isolation in this bedchamber, even their confrontation, had demolished all protective formalities. The subtle tingling he created on her scalp was delicious, cajoling her to contemplate other physical excitements.

Conquering, possessing, protecting— She did not doubt that he was prepared to be ruthless and toy with more than hair if necessary. Nor was she confident she could defeat the challenge should it come.

"The young diplomat they invited to dinner was named Jonathan Merriweather."

He looked in her eyes, suspicious again. "I know of him. Merriweather is now an assistant to the British envoy here in Naples."

"Is he? How convenient for you. I had no idea."

"Didn't you?" His hand wound in her hair more firmly. The subtle play became controlling. "Did you journey here to speak to him, Miss Blair? Is that why you are in Naples? Do you intend to annotate those memoirs and fill in the names and facts that your father discreetly omitted? The book will sell all the better then and I daresay your press could use the income."

She purposefully took hold of the hair he held and pried off his fingers. Her indignation helped her ignore the sensation of his warm hand beneath hers, and the way his eyes reflected his awareness of her touch.

"I expect my father's memoirs to be popular without annotations, but I thank you for the suggestion. I am not here for that purpose, however."

That was a bald lie, but she felt no compunction about misleading this man. Her own interest in filling in the memoirs' gaps did not bear on his family. Her investigations concerned other portions, the ones that spoke of her mother.

"I am a mere tourist here, Lord Elliot. I have come to visit the excavations and ruins to the south. I need to prepare to leave this city at once and continue my journey as I originally planned. Therefore, I must ask you, once more, to leave."

He did not move immediately. Perhaps he believed that doing so would amount to giving quarter in whatever battle he thought they fought.

"Your tour will have to be delayed a few days more," he said. "I cannot allow you to go just yet."

She laughed. The man's presumptions had become ridiculous. "What you would allow is not of interest to me, sir."

"It is of essential interest to you. I warned that freeing you might entail conditions, and you promised to accommodate them."

She frowned. "You said nothing about conditions when you arrived."

"Your warm embrace distracted me."

She peered up at him distrustfully. "What are these conditions?"

He slowly looked down her flowing locks, which meant he looked down most of her body. She thought she detected a possessive interest, as if he had just received a gift and judged its value.

"Gentile Sansoni would only release you if you entered my custody," he said. "I had to accept total responsibility for you and promise to regulate your behavior."

Hot anger flared in her head. No wonder Lord Elliot was preening with arrogance and command all of a sudden today. "That is intolerable. I have never answered to a man. To do so would make my mother turn in her grave. I refuse to agree to this."

"Would you prefer to take your chances with Sansoni? It can be arranged."

The threat left her speechless.

Lord Elliot did not exactly laugh as he strode to the door, but he did not hide his amusement at her dilemma either.

"We will journey on to Pompeii together, Miss Blair, after I speak with Merriweather. Until then, you are not to leave these chambers without my escort. Oh, and there will be no Marsilios or Pietros visiting you either. I'll be damned if you will provoke more duels while you are under my authority. I swore an oath to control you, and I expect your cooperation and obedience."

Authority? Control? *Obedience?* She was so stunned that he was gone before she found the voice to curse him.